Praise for Sam Ts

Errands & Espionage

"Perfect for fans of Elle Cosimano, this is fun and sexy with intrigue that will keep you guessing."

—Alicia Thompson, *USA Today* bestselling author of *Love in the Time of Serial Killers*

"Gabby Greene is the perfect heroine for anyone who's tired of being underestimated and unappreciated, not only by everyone around them but also by themself. Finlay Donovan fans, welcome to your new insta-buy series! —Mia P. Manansala, award-winning author of *Arsenic and Adobo*

"I loved Gabby! So fun and so relatable. I'm just waiting for a knock on my door with an offer to run off and become a secret agent."

—Sara Desai, author of *To Have and To Heist*

"Gabby Greene is to spying what Finlay Donovan is to contract killing and Stephanie Plum is to bounty hunting. You'll be laughing on one page, and your heart will be beating on the next."

—Kellye Garrett, award-winning author of *Missing White Woman*

"Gabby Greene is like all working moms with too much to do—she has lunches to make, kids to pick up, and some codes she has to steal for the CIA. A delightful romp with an affirming message that women really can do anything. Fans of Finlay Donovan will devour this." —Julia London, *New York Times* bestselling author

Siri, Who Am I?

"Tschida took me on a wild ride in the quick read with endless turns and a happily-ever-after ending fit for a Friday night, feel-good rom-com movie."   —*USA Today*

"A fan of HBO Max's *The Flight Attendant*? Tschida's debut novel...is definitely for you."   —E! Online

"[A] biting satire for the internet age."   —POPSUGAR

"[An] uproarious debut."   —*Bustle*

"A strong debut that's fun and funny, perfect for lovers of modern romantic comedies and light mysteries."
                                    —*Kirkus Reviews*

"Tschida's debut is a millennial *Bridget Jones's Diary* meets *Legally Blonde*."   —*Booklist*

"Keen character work and a unique premise distinguish Tschida's riotously funny, remarkably assured debut...Tschida is a writer to watch."   —*Mystery Scene*

Errands & Espionage

SAM TSCHIDA

FOREVER

New York   Boston

Forever
Hachette Book Group
1290 Avenue of the Americas, New York, NY 10104
read-forever.com
@readforeverpub

First Edition: August 2024

Forever is an imprint of Grand Central Publishing. The Forever name and logo are registered trademarks of Hachette Book Group, Inc.

The publisher is not responsible for websites (or their content) that are not owned by the publisher.

The Hachette Speakers Bureau provides a wide range of authors for speaking events. To find out more, go to hachettespeakersbureau.com or email HachetteSpeakers@hbgusa.com.

Forever books may be purchased in bulk for business, educational, or promotional use. For information, please contact your local bookseller or the Hachette Book Group Special Markets Department at special.markets@hbgusa.com.

Print book interior design by Taylor Navis

Library of Congress Cataloging-in-Publication Data
Names: Tschida, Sam, author.
Title: Errands & espionage / Sam Tschida.
Other titles: Errands and espionage
Description: First edition. | New York : Forever, 2024.
Identifiers: LCCN 2023058723 | ISBN 9781538757215 (trade paperback) |
    ISBN 9781538757222 (e-book)
Subjects: LCGFT: Romance fiction. | Spy fiction. | Novels.
Classification: LCC PS3620.S44 E77 2024 | DDC 813/.6—dc23/eng/20240117
LC record available at https://lccn.loc.gov/2023058723

ISBN: 9781538757215 (trade paperback), 9781538757222 (ebook)

Printed in the United States of America

CW

10 9 8 7 6 5 4 3 2 1

To my niece, Dagny Tschida, who called and requested that I dedicate this book to her, and this book instead of that other book I'm writing about vampires. At first, I hesitated. Should I take orders from a ten-year-old? But why not? I mean, I dedicated my first book to some cute baristas whose names I didn't know. Also, it's only appropriate to dedicate this book to a girl who knows what she wants and asks for it, so, Dagny, this one's for you. Keep that spirit your whole life. You are creative, hardworking, and fierce. You deserve all the dedications and more. As you grow up, don't forget that, which is easier to do than you'd think. Also, I request that you dedicate your first book to me.

Regarding your second request, a children's book about guinea pigs: I'm not going to be able to manage that, but I did include a guinea pig in this novel. Dr. Piggie has a non-squeaking but important role.

PROLOGUE

Friday, 8:00 p.m., Pasadena, California

This had not been the day to get shot.

As a female special agent, Darcy knew how to fight—that's the only way she got where she was—and she knew how to take a hit. A gunshot to the upper left quadrant was one hell of a smackdown, but it wasn't enough to stop her.

She just wasn't dressed for it. Darcy would give anything for some tactical pants with a gusseted crotch and pockets for a high-beam flashlight and at least two knives.

Darcy was dressed for her undercover gig as a damn executive assistant, not a gun fight. The Betabrand yoga pants that looked like office clothes weren't bad—thank you, Facebook ads, for that suggestion—but it had been Hawaiian shirt day at the office, and she had caved to the peer pressure. Hiding in the shadows would only do so much good. Her hot pink shirt was plastered with smiling pineapples. The dancing hula girl awarded to her for being the best-dressed employee sat on her desk next to the stapler. To top it off, the stupid shirt had been too tight to hide a gun, so Darcy had to leave Sister Mary Clarence, her P220 .45 caliber, at home. Sister Mary wasn't government issue, but she shot true.

Darcy loved winning, but not enough to die for the honor of being best-dressed employee at eStocks Enterprises.

If she had to guess, she'd say the perp shot her with a nine mil—small caliber, traveled at over a thousand feet per second, burned like hell. If the shooter had balls, they would have used a .45. Sister Mary Clarence would have smote them and sent them straight to hell. Not only that, but whoever it was, they couldn't aim for shit. Darcy only took headshots.

She ran down the street as fast as she could with her hands pressed to the wound to stanch the bleeding.

A construction site near the office beckoned her in, its loose Tyvek sheeting blowing in an open doorway. Tomorrow morning, a couple of guys would be shooting the shit, drinking cheap coffee, and catcalling girls right here. Someone had whistled at her yesterday. What that told her: 1) her ass looked fine in Betabrand, and 2) there was not enough cover from the street even for momentary shelter—find higher ground.

On the third floor, she threw herself against a pillar and peered across the expanse, lit only with ambient light from the neighboring businesses. She dialed her boss.

Alice Strong picked up on the first ring, "Agent?"

"I've been compromised."

"By the target or his affiliates?"

"Someone else. I haven't made an ID."

"We have your location. Help is on the way."

"Affirmative. I'm sending what I have now."

"Hang in there, Agent. The team will be there in approximately four minutes."

Darcy clicked off the phone. She'd been so careful. She'd followed procedure. Hell, she'd worn a Hawaiian shirt just to blend in. How she'd been compromised was beyond her.

As promised, she prepared an encrypted file. When she hit SEND, she left a bloody smear on the screen. Waiting for a file to load while bleeding out could literally take a lifetime.

At seventy-eight percent uploaded, a gun sounded, and the phone blew clean out of her hand and skittered across the concrete floor.

Instinctively, Darcy squared off. Her attacker wore a mask. There was nothing to give away their identity—black clothes and a medium-sized athletic build. "I bet you were aiming for my head," she said.

In chess and hand-to-hand combat, it's best to make the first move, so Darcy grabbed a stray pipe and swung it with everything she had. It connected with the attacker's knee with a dull thud, and they staggered. Before Darcy could gather her strength to swing again, the person punched right where the bullet was lodged.

Even before she recovered enough to move, she knew there was only one option left: escape. Ignoring the pain, she turned and ran as fast as possible, which wasn't fast. Her attacker followed with disturbingly slow and deliberate footfalls.

Her heart pounding and the stain blossoming on her dumb shirt, she ran blindly until she hit the edge, literally. "Fuck!" There was nothing but air where a floor-to-ceiling window was set to be installed.

The attacker walked slowly into the office with a confidence born of having the upper hand.

"So how'd you find me?" Darcy said. If she stalled long enough, maybe backup would arrive. It'd been two minutes already.

"It wasn't hard with that shirt."

"But the earrings are perfect with it, right?" She'd ordered over-sized pineapples in shades to go with the shirt for $5.99 on Amazon. They'd actually arrived on time. Lucky her.

Below, a black SUV squealed to a halt, and a team of agents spilled out. Darcy screamed, "Up here!"

"Nice try, Darcy."

As the shooter pulled out an embarrassingly small gun, they took off their mask.

"You!" Darcy shouted.

Another bullet hit her, and she tumbled backwards through the open window, the closing image on her life nothing but the soft glow of the LA sky at night.

CHAPTER 1

Thursday, 7:13 a.m., 113 Avocado Avenue

A Nerf bullet sailed across the kitchen and nailed Gabby Greene square in the back of the head.

She twirled around and aimed her spatula at her eight-year-old devil child. "Lucas Daniel Taylor, there are no guns at the breakfast table!"

How did that even need to be a rule?

"She started it!" Lucas pointed at Kyle, a fourteen-year-old replica of her mother, except with purple streaks in her brown hair and a sparkle in her eye that hadn't yet dimmed.

"Just put the gun down and eat your pancakes. Okay?" How hard could that be? The shirt he'd just put on was already sticky with syrup.

A glance at the microwave clock—fifteen minutes until the bus arrived. Gabby ladled out another batch of the pancakes. There was something so comforting about a pancake—perfectly round and tan as a buckskin pony. Wanting kids as an adult was a lot like wanting a pony as a child—you couldn't know how much work they'd be until you got them home.

As she watched for bubbles in the pancake, Lucas yelled, "I

can't find my socks." It wasn't his fault. Finding and wearing socks wasn't part of his skill set yet.

"I got it." But did she? Were there even matching socks in the house? It was amazing how quickly you could go from "Do matching socks matter?" to a full-blown existential crisis. As long as she could delay it until after the bus picked up the kids.

She turned up her audiobook, almost loud enough to drown out the kids' arguing. Sloane Ellis was revolutionizing divorce and single parenting, at least according to everyone on daytime TV. Supposedly, she made divorce just as fun as Marie Kondo made organizing sock drawers.

Gabby handed Lucas two mismatched socks, one knee-high and rainbow striped, the other a white tube sock—the best she could come up with. Where all the socks went was currently the biggest mystery in her life. Her number one suspect: Mr. Bubbles, her bichon.

Kyle looked up from her phone and noticed Lucas slipping on the rainbow sock. "That's *my* sock!" She reached for him. Lucas feinted to the left and stuck out his tongue.

"It's mine now. Mom gave it to me!" Lucas pulled the trigger, and a second Nerf bullet hit Kyle.

One hand on her hip and the other with a spatula, Gabby let them have it. She leveled her gaze at Lucas. "Lucas! No shooting your sister. No shooting at all! Give. Me. The. Gun." Then, in her sternest mom voice, she barked, "And, Kylie, get ready for school and forget about your sock."

"Don't call me Kylie!"

"Oh, sorry, sweetie," she apologized to the kid engaged in hand-to-hand combat over breakfast. Her daughter had gone from Kylie to Kyle last year. Gabby didn't ask questions. If she wanted to drop an "i," that was fine. "Kylie is so cutesy," she had said. "What were you thinking, Mom?"

She should have gotten ponies.

The smell of burnt pancake hit her nose. Why had she made pancakes on a school morning?

Another glance at the clock: three minutes left.

If they missed the bus again . . . For a fraction of a second, she shut her eyes and imagined getting on the bus herself. It could take her away for once, just a quick trip, maybe to Las Vegas. She could see the Thunder from Down Under and let it all go for a weekend. Linda from down the street went away all the time. Gabby couldn't decide whether to judge her and act superior or be jealous. She chose judgment because she didn't have time or means to go to Vegas. But deep down she knew it wasn't just the caffeine burning a hole through the lining of her stomach. It was jealousy.

"Kyle, Lucas, grab your bags. It's time to go!"

Just as the clock ran out, they made it out the door, Gabby following behind, her arms full of confiscated items: a Nerf gun, an umbrella that Lucas liked to use as a sword, and a bag of Laffy Taffy that would wreck Kyle's braces.

No please or thank you. Her kids had no respect. None. It was her own damn fault. She hadn't demanded it, hadn't felt she deserved it, the same reason she'd accepted shit from Phil for all those years. And he had been the one to leave. *Him.* After she had done everything except make the money. On the night he'd told her, she'd been washing her face and trying out some new cream that promised to erase the bags under her eyes. Phil had stood behind her. "Gabs, I'm leaving."

"Where?" She'd glanced at her phone. It had been ten o'clock. She'd asked, "Are we out of ice cream?" because that's all that she could imagine. Turns out they were out of a lot more than Cherry Garcia, which she would never eat again, thank you very much.

"No. I'm *leaving* leaving."

She had stopped rubbing the cream into her face and stared at his reflection in the mirror. He had been talking to the back of her head. Coward.

"Don't worry, you can have the house. I'll get an apartment closer to the office."

It's not like she had enjoyed Phil recently, but she hadn't worried about that. Their marriage had been about the kids, at least for her. She thought it had been for him too.

He said there wasn't anyone else, he had just "outgrown her," but she knew better. Men never left a wife unless they'd already lined up the next one. That man couldn't even feed himself.

A marriage that crumbled without her noticing, kids that didn't know how to wash a dish to save their lives. What was she supposed to do about it now? Kyle was half-grown. Lucas had a Y chromosome that didn't bode well. If she knew how to load the Nerf gun, she would let a bullet fly—Lucas didn't need to know she broke the rules—but guns weren't her department. What was her department?

Kyle texted: S and I need a ride to horseback riding after school.

She had kids and then rented them ponies. What was her life?

CHAPTER 2

Thursday, 8:10 a.m., 113 Avocado Avenue

Alone at last, Gabby walked into the house to the waiting disaster. Spilled syrup, stray Nerf bullets, piles of paper from backpacks, and a never-ending mountain of dishes. Why did she bother? Housework was the background noise that no one cared about or even saw. A good wife and mother was basically a servant, completing all the tasks without drawing any attention. Gabby was so good at it that she'd achieved the highest degree of skill: invisibility. She was invisible when she was married to Phil, and she still hadn't materialized.

Those thoughts weren't helpful, though. They sure wouldn't get the dishes done.

It had been four months since Phil moved out. She should probably get a job, but it had been fourteen years since she'd worked outside the house, not since Kyle was born. And she had been a travel agent. Her skills: buying plane tickets and booking hotels. She might as well have worked at Blockbuster. People booked their own travel these days.

She hit PLAY on her audiobook. Sloane Ellis would help her help herself.

The agency had been nice, a little place in a high-end strip mall in Pasadena next to a Verizon where she used to flirt with a hot phone guy. He'd given her a secret discount on her phone bill once. Those had been the days—grabbing a coffee or lunch with co-workers and planning tours of Irish castles. That's how she'd met Phil. He'd planned a vacation for two to Mexico. At the end, he'd asked her to go with him. In retrospect, that was creepy. At the time, she'd really wanted a beach vacation, and Phil had had all of his hair. It had felt like something that would happen in a movie.

Sloane Ellis cut through her feelings like a knife. "Divorce is a new beginning. A rebirth."

Was it? What was she going to be reborn as? She had an English degree (almost), two kids, and experience buying airline tickets. Her targeted ads were for online therapy, an endless list of vitamins to alleviate PMS, and vibrators. Who knew her better, Sloane Ellis or the algorithm? Of course, it wasn't up to the algorithm to see her potential. She rinsed a plate and slid it into the dishwasher.

"Stop with the negative self-talk. You might have a prehistoric résumé, stretch marks, and a house you can't afford, but you can change it all."

Could she? She scraped a plate of sticky burnt pancake into the trash.

"*You* are ready for an adventure."

She ran the garbage disposal. The sound of grinding metal assaulted her ears, and she fished a spoon out of the drain.

"Not just a weekend away, you are ready for the adventure of a lifetime: self-discovery. A rewarding career, romance, parenting, and above all, self-determination. A life of your own."

Gabby caught a glimpse of her reflection in the window above the kitchen sink and tried to imagine herself as someone else. Her frizzy hair tamed into a sleek style, her skin lasered extensively. What would a freshly lasered Gabby do?

"The first task on your adventure is—"

The sound of the doorbell cut off Sloane's comforting yet commanding voice. The dog sprang to action, a low rumble in his throat starting as he ran toward the suspected intruder. Gabby tried to block him with her body while she cracked the door. Mr. Bubbles, a persistent devil, ran between her legs like he was a one-hundred-and-fifty-pound rottweiler instead of a ten-pound fluff ball wearing a bow tie.

"Mr. Jonathon Bubbles!" Jonathon was for Lucas's preschool teacher, whom Lucas idolized because he did balloon tricks and also had a penis. Gabby once had had a short-term relationship with a guy who made balloons, so she couldn't blame Lucas. She grabbed the dog's collar while he pawed at the air. "Sorry."

The mailman asked her to sign for a package and hurried away with a muttered curse. Another legal document from Phil. Damn divorce papers, like they were even in English. She tossed it into the corner without opening it. Then she held Mr. Bubbles high in the air and stared into his unrepentant face. *"Mr. Bubbles, you are such an asshole!"*

She stopped herself. She was taking out her feelings for Phil on poor Bubbles.

He panted, exhausted from his effort defending his home, and wagged his tail.

Her heart melted, and she smiled at the little asshole. Why did she have such bad taste in men, even dogs?

She grabbed a broom and hit PLAY on the audiobook. "The first task on your next adventure is to assess yourself coldly and objectively. Your physical self, your emotional self, and your potential. Let's start with physical."

That was easy, she was twenty-five pounds overweight in a pair of black yoga pants. She took a swig of coffee.

Sloane started in, "Sorry, but you can't have yoga pants. They are lying to you."

Gabby choked on her coffee. Had Sloane bugged her house?

"I'm serious. Stop laughing. Your first task is to stand in front of a full-length mirror completely naked. See yourself for who you are and stop lying. Pause the audio, find your workbook, and press play when you've stripped down physically and emotionally."

Shelly across the street had recommended this book to her. Had Shelly stood naked in front of a mirror and cataloged her faults?

It seemed dumb, but if she was really going to try to change her life, she needed to actually try. So far Sloane was the only one with any ideas.

Gabby expelled a breath, grabbed the workbook, and walked upstairs. In her bedroom, she pulled off her sweatshirt and yoga pants. She was still wearing a nursing bra. Lucas was eight. That joke about "easy access" had stopped being funny five years ago. Had Phil ever laughed?

The workbook was a basic drawing of a woman, like the one pathologists used for autopsies, at least TV pathologists. Sloane wanted her to autopsy her old self, catalog her self-esteem's cause of death. It wasn't a single, crushing blow, it was a combination of so many little things.

Gabby was game. She was gonna change her life even if she had to count every bright white stretch mark.

"Don't lie to yourself. Know your advantages and disadvantages. No blame or guilt. Only then can you make a plan."

She was fully naked and wondering if she should draw a double chin on her sketch—everyone had a double chin from certain angles—when the doorbell rang again.

The mailman must have forgotten a package, hopefully something other than legal documents.

She threw on her robe and hustled.

It wasn't the mailman. From the landing, she could see two women dressed in black. They looked serious. Not Mormons. Mormon missionaries were always eighteen-year-old boys in button-down shirts and skinny ties their moms had probably bought. Too polished for lawn care people.

Tupperware? Someone on the neighborhood LISTSERV had been hyping Tupperware sales like it was 1977, and Gabby had gone down a rabbit hole. Tupperware came in a lot of colors these days and was part of a strategy for saving the planet by reducing single-use plastic. "Be part of a movement that creates change every day," the website proclaimed. She had clicked on the link that read, "Embrace your inner entrepreneur," but then the kids got off the bus, and she hadn't finished filling out the online form.

If she was going to buy Tupperware, she was going to sell it to herself. Thank you very much for the pep talk, Sloane Ellis! These ladies would have to find some other housewife to sell silicone muffin tins to.

She opened the door resolved to say no politely but firmly so that they wouldn't ask twice. This time, Mr. Bubbles cowered behind her. Just like Phil, he had a problem with strong women.

"I'm so sorry, but I don't need any Tupper—" she started to tell the women whose outfits were giving TV cop vibes. They were clearly newbies to door-to-door sales. If they wanted to sell stack-able storage containers for yesterday's spaghetti, they should try to look more approachable.

The short-haired woman waved a badge in Gabby's face. "Ma'am, we're with the CIA. Can we come in?"

CHAPTER 3

Thursday, 10:20 a.m., Greene household

What was the CIA doing at her house? Her mind reeled with visions of drug cartels, secret codes, and Claire Danes pursuing the truth at any cost in outfits remarkably similar to the women on her doorstep. She had zero clue, less than zero, what the CIA was doing at her house. Had she called Ted Cruz too many times? Everyone she knew did that. He had been her whipping boy throughout the whole divorce.

"Is this about Ted Cruz?"

The short-haired agent flashed a look of confusion.

Duh. Ted Cruz would be a Secret Service issue. Any woman with a buzz cut didn't have time for Ted Cruz's bullshit. She had Clint Eastwood energy.

It was something else...All those cheap products she'd been ordering from suspicious websites for almost nothing. Gabby stood back to let the CIA agents enter. "I know I shouldn't have ordered that face mask." It was too good to be true—$3.99, made of gold, and shipped from Russia. It was probably made out of plutonium or cocaine. "I have to stop clicking on my Facebook ads."

Standing in her entryway next to a pile of kid shoes and

backpacks, the agent with Clint Eastwood's stare said, "My name is Agent Alice Strong, and this is Agent Valentina Monroe."

Agent Monroe didn't just look like Sofía Vergara, she had a name to match. Gabby loved *Modern Family*.

Gabby swallowed a lump in her throat and looked directly at Agent Strong. "What is this about?"

Agent Strong glanced around the entryway that led into a comfy living room. "Where can we talk, ma'am?"

Gabby walked toward the kitchen. "If you don't mind a mess." She was starting to shake.

Agent Strong stared pointedly at the coffeepot, and Gabby responded, "I'll get us some coffee."

She was about to be interrogated by the CIA in her kitchen wearing nothing but a robe with "MOM" emblazoned across the right breast. They hadn't even asked a single question yet, and she was sweating like she was forty-five minutes into a spin class. A coffee wouldn't help, but she shoved the pot under the basket of grounds and flicked the red button to ON.

They stared back.

"Cream and sugar?" she asked.

"No thank you."

The women looked out of place at the table. Agent Strong peered down her nose at Kyle's biology homework. Agent Monroe sat in front of a large plastic place mat featuring a cheerful map of the United States complete with cartoon Mount Rushmore in the center and a smiling alligator over Florida. "You're probably used to more detailed maps," Gabby quipped.

"Please take a seat, ma'am." They were telling her to sit down in her own kitchen. It hit her, maybe they were here because someone else was in trouble.

"Is it Phil?" Was he some kind of white-collar criminal and she'd never known it? Last time she'd seen him, she'd barely recognized him in skinny jeans, a tight shirt with a flipped-up collar, and a fake tan with a radioactive glow. The divorce was wearing him.

"Relax, ma'am, and take a seat."

Gabby moved a lunch box off the chair. In the chaos, Kyle had forgotten the leftover ramen she had begged to take. School lunch was fine for Kyle. Lucas not so much. Between all of his allergies and his gluten intolerance, she needed to take a Xanax to let anyone else feed him. The woman who looked like an honest-to-God Bond girl started pushing papers in front of her. "Please sign here."

Gabby tried to stop shaking, but her signature came out like her grandmother's, overly careful but still squiggly. "I got syrup on the paper. Does it matter?" The pages were definitely going to stick together.

Bond Girl blew out a breath, clearly exasperated. "Initial here and add your date of birth, please."

Gabby didn't have enough time or focus to read any of the documents. She caught glimpses of words: Nondisclosure, National Security, Secrets, Severe Penalties, Punishment, Jail Time.

She looked at their belts for handcuffs and guns. Who was going to take Kyle to horseback riding tonight if they arrested her?

Alice Strong looked like her name, all hard angles with a severe face, the kind of woman who didn't ever need help opening jars, the kind of woman who probably didn't even need to open jars because she only ate takeout at her desk.

Gabby looked between them. "I'm sure whatever I did was an accident. I'm very prone to accidents." They stared back, and she kept going. "Give me a simple task, and I'm bound to turn it into a national security problem."

As she laughed nervously at her own joke, the women exchanged a look, and Gabby said, "See. I can't stop putting my foot in my mouth." All they needed to do was feed her a few details, and she'd confess to anything.

Gabby started straightening up, making piles of paper that should be recycled, just for something to do with her hands.

Loud and slow, Agent Strong explained, "You're not in any trouble."

"Yet," Valentina said sharply.

Agent Strong cautioned the other agent with a look. In a dead-serious tone of voice, she said, "We're here to offer you a job." She didn't appear to be kidding.

Gabby dropped the paper she'd been straightening down on the table. When she saw it was the schematic of all of her flaws, including the distance between her boobs and her navel (4.5 inches), she snatched it back.

"What?" She couldn't have heard them right.

"The CIA needs your help."

Hadn't they noticed her double chin? "You're kidding."

Alice Strong looked at Gabby, the same way Gabby looked at the kids when she was at the end of her rope. "Kidding? This is no laughing matter. We need you."

Gabby had seen movies where the CIA approached genius college students who knew tae kwon do and had brains like supercomputers. Gabby had just burned pancakes. She was eight credits shy of having an English degree she would never get.

The CIA had interrupted her while she was inspecting a mole on her inner thigh and trying to remember the signs of cancer:

irregular edges, color variations, growth. Maybe the CIA needed a mom who could solve problems with a ramped-up anxiety level and mastery of WebMD.

"I do need a job," she said. "I got divorced recently, and you know how that goes." She looked up to see two blank faces. Alice and Valentina looked like they had no idea what she was talking about. "I was thinking of something at a department store over the holidays, but I guess, if the CIA wants me."

Agent Monroe looked like she was trying hard not to roll her eyes.

Agent Strong said, "This is serious, Ms. Greene."

"But really, I don't understand. Why on earth do you need *my help*?" She fingered the corner of Kyle's biology homework. Kyle had gotten a B minus.

Valentina slid a photograph across the table toward Gabby. "This was Agent Darcy Dagger. We need a replacement for her."

Gabby didn't have a sister, but that's what she would have looked like. They had the same wide-spaced hazel eyes and heart-shaped face. If Gabby had red hair and a better haircut, they could be twins. Although this woman had what Gabby's grandma would call "a schnoz."

Gabby could barely focus as Alice went on about facial recognition software. "Facial recognition measures the shape of the face, the distance between features, the similarity of the features themselves, as well as a person's expressions," Alice explained. "We did a thorough search of social media profiles to come up with a facial match to Agent Darcy Dagger. Except for the nose, you and Agent Dagger are nearly identical." Agent Strong scanned Gabby's face. "You both have that weird little divot in your chin."

This was surreal.

"The nose isn't as significant of a difference as it appears. It's one of the easiest features to disguise. A simple prosthetic will do the trick. A different face shape or smile is much more difficult to hide."

"You want me to replace Agent Dagger?" Gabby's world was spinning. She glanced at the clock. Normally she'd be heading to the grocery store or throwing something in the Instant Pot so she could focus on the kids in the evening. Instead the CIA was asking her to replace an agent who did who knows what. In her photo Agent Darcy Dagger looked straight into the camera with a confidence Gabby had never known. Her look said, "I'm ready to save the world, one mission at a time."

Gabby could make a beer can chicken.

"You're kidding, right? This is a joke." If they were still married, she would have suspected Phil. If Alice and Valentina were men, she would expect them to pull off Velcro pants and start singing "Happy Birthday." Or maybe Ashton Kutcher had started filming *Punk'd* again. Anything was more likely than the CIA recruiting her.

"What did Agent Dagger even do? Was it hard?"

Agent Strong took a sip of coffee from Gabby's "World's Greatest Mom" mug. "Darcy was working undercover to take down a Russian shell company masking itself as an American investment business."

Shell company—Gabby wasn't sure if she could use that term in a sentence.

"The company is laundering blood money."

"When you say 'blood money,' you mean someone died?"

"Yes."

Gabby blinked. The more they talked, the less sense they made.

Agent Strong continued. "They are laundering blood money through the business and sending it back to Russia."

Gabby tried to put it all together, but it sounded like the two-sentence description of a movie Phil would love. She usually fell asleep or scrolled through social media until she ended up watching a girl slightly older than Kyle give a detailed makeup tutorial. Then she would ping-pong between being upset at the expectations Kyle would have to face and wondering if she should order new mascara.

If she was going to consider working for the CIA—how had that thought even crossed her mind?—she needed to make sure someone was around to help with the kids. Lucas couldn't make his own after-school snacks yet, and Kyle needed a ride to horse-back riding. Bonding with an animal was supposed to help with her self-esteem. Gabby picked up her phone to dial her mom. "Let me just check and see if my mom can come to town and watch the kids after school."

Valentina reached across the table and grabbed her phone. "Ms. Greene, you don't understand. You cannot call anyone."

"What if I can't find someone to watch the kids?"

Valentina looked her dead in the eye. "Ms. Greene, this is a matter of national security. You absolutely cannot tell anyone anything."

"But—" These women obviously didn't understand how difficult it was to find childcare.

Agent Strong leaned forward with her elbows on the table, getting uncomfortably close to Gabby. "If you breathe a word of this, you will be charged with multiple counts of unauthorized disclosure of secrets related to the national defense. I will not hesitate to bring you in."

"Oh." She dropped her hands to the breakfast table.

"Can I have an extra day to think?" She didn't want Kyle and Lucas to grow up without a mom because she joined the CIA on a whim over coffee.

"Yes, but we have to get an agent back in the field as soon as possible."

Gabby nodded dumbly.

"Lives are at stake, Ms. Greene. We have to move fast."

Before they left, Gabby thought to ask, "What happened to Darcy?"

With no affect, Agent Strong stated, "She was taken out."

"Taken where?" Gabby asked.

Alice stared back, not even bothering to answer the question.

Gabby turned over "taken out" in her mind. Could that mean what she thought it meant?

She looked down at the picture of Darcy Dagger. Valentina's words echoed in her mind: "This was Agent Darcy Dagger."

Was...

Past tense. Darcy Dagger was dead. Gabby was staring at the face of a woman who had been killed. She hadn't died in a car accident or of cancer. She'd been "taken out" while serving her country. Gabby's stomach dropped to the floor next to all the vegetables Lucas had been trying to sneak to the dog.

As tempting as it was, she had to say no. This was not one of those jobs where she could try to massage her résumé to look like a reasonable candidate. Cooking, cleaning, and chauffeuring kids could not be built up into spy credentials. Not to mention, she couldn't even keep on top of the laundry. How was she going to be an undercover operative? Gabby had two children. She needed to be there to pick them up from school; she needed to be there to watch them grow up. Agents Strong and Monroe could take a chance on her, but Gabby didn't take chances. She played it safe. It was part of being a good mom.

With her kids in mind, she said, "I'm so sorry, but I have to say no."

Agent Strong didn't react, so Gabby kept talking. "Thanks so much for the offer. I would love to, but it's just not going to work." She sounded like she was turning down a dinner party invitation.

Agent Monroe looked relieved, but Agent Strong narrowed her gaze and moved a step closer. "Are you interested in the salary?"

She lit up inside. Money—she needed that. "How much is it?"

The corner of Agent Strong's lips quirked up. Like it was nothing, she said, "A full year's salary, eighty thousand dollars. Plus benefits. We will pay for the full year, regardless of how long the mission takes."

The number punched a hole a mile wide in her resolve, but Gabby tried not to let it show on her face. She said, "Okay, I'll take that into consideration," which made it sound like she would make a methodical list of pros and cons. In reality, she would probably hyperventilate a little and think, "Holy shit! What do I do?" over and over for an hour before she had to pick her kids up.

Gabby walked them to the door, Mr. Bubbles trotting beside them in his ridiculous bow tie and freshly styled hair, highlighting just how different her world was from theirs.

"Thanks again," Gabby said, always an accommodating hostess.

Agent Strong simply said, "You have until the end of the day to decide."

CHAPTER 4

Thursday afternoon, Greene household

Gabby looked at the clock. It was one thirty, and she had to be at school in an hour to pick up Kyle and Lucas. Between cataloging all of her faults in a self-help workbook and getting a job offer from the CIA, she hadn't managed to go grocery shopping, clean the house, or pull up her old résumé.

If she told anyone what had happened, they wouldn't believe her. No one. Hell, she barely believed herself. But when she looked at the kitchen table, there were three coffee cups. Agent Strong's "World's Greatest Mom" cup was empty. Gabby imagined that she ran on coffee.

Get it together, Gabby. If she was even going to consider this, she had to chill—have coffee with CIA agents and then seamlessly pick up the kids, breezing past all of the other moms in the parent pickup line like she was just that cool.

Gabby threw on a fresh pair of yoga pants and hoodie. She was fully invested in her athleisure, emphasis on the leisure, look. She had an unused gym membership and brand-new running shoes to go with the lifestyle. There were so many benefits: 1) she liked the way the pants lied to her (sorry, Sloane); 2) it was a uniform; and 3) she could run away from bad guys, which now seemed like a possibility. Athleisure was a solid trend.

With her uniform on, her frizzy brown hair under a hat, and her phone fully charged, she was ready to get the kids. On her way out of the house, she remembered the package the mailman had brought. Another fucking court order from Phil, which made almost no sense. They'd finalized the divorce four months ago, or at least she'd thought. With a deep breath, she picked the damn thing up. She'd open it up while Kyle was riding a horse. Whatever it was, it was definitely going to take a minute to process, and she was late.

"Be a good boy, Mr. Bubbles." She patted him on the head. If he didn't freak the horses out, she'd bring him.

Forty-five minutes later, she was outside a horse barn, the smell of manure and hay oddly comforting, real and uncomplicated, unlike her life. Kyle and Sienna hopped out and ran for their lesson while she and Lucas parked under a tree nearby. Lucas immediately started begging for her phone. "Can I play a video game, Mom?" A horse whinnied in the background.

"Sure." Gabby handed her phone over. She needed him to keep busy for a minute while she dealt with the paperwork. With a deep breath, she peeled open the envelope with all of its ominous "you have been served" language on the outside.

Inside there was a half-inch stack of indecipherable legal documents, stamped and official. Gabby wasn't an idiot, but figuring out what any of this legal garbage meant required a JD or a $200-an-hour lawyer, which she could not afford at the moment. Phil could.

First the CIA, now court documents—Mercury was in retrograde for sure. She didn't know what that meant, but it was nice to be able to blame the universe for something.

She scanned the headings, some of which had become vaguely familiar over the whole process. There was a "request for order" and a "notice of hearing." In other words, Phil was trying to make her do something. Last time he'd been by, he'd taken the guinea pig, Dr. Piggie, to make his place homier for the kids. It was pathetic, living in a hotel down the street with a hijacked guinea pig.

Next to her, Lucas squealed, "I won. Can I play another round?"

"Sure, honey." She gave him a hug because she needed the moral support. He pushed her arm away.

What was it going to be about this time? She'd have to drive through LA traffic and sit in a courthouse with a ton of sad, lonely people. So many of the women there had problems way worse than hers, like abusive partners, kids they didn't have access to, no money. Every time she got there, she counted herself lucky. Kyle and Lucas were healthy, and she had them. She couldn't afford her house, but she knew she could figure it out. Her main problem: an ex who couldn't leave well enough alone.

One of the documents brought it all into focus. Phil had filed something called a seek work order. He wanted the court to force her to get a job because he was sick of paying spousal support. What a fucking asshole. Didn't he realize that her résumé was dead? She'd been raising the kids for fourteen years, during which time he didn't want her to work because he preferred her to take care of the kids and the house and said, "You can't make enough money to make a difference. You'll just push us into a higher tax bracket."

That had always hit her like a sickly sweet cocktail. It was nice being taken care of, the sweet part of the cocktail. But the implication that she had no value curdled the sweetness into something that made her stomach twist. Phil had never thought of her as someone who had something to contribute to society in general or to their family. He had never seen her, if there was anything to see.

He'd stood in her way all of those years, and now he was making Judge Padilla tell her to go get a job because he didn't want to pay child and spousal support. As if she were eating bonbons and living the good life all day. As if divorce had been a winning Powerball ticket.

Little did Phil know.

"We're done!" Kyle and Sienna wandered over, all smiles for once and smelling like horses and exertion. If she had her feet under her, you'd be damn sure she'd be out in the work force not taking any spousal support from Phil. What was she supposed to do, though?

The instructor followed them. "Both girls are doing great. Kyle is about ready to try jumping."

"Oh." Gabby plastered on a smile, but she couldn't help herself. "Are you sure? That sounds dangerous."

"Mom! I've been working all year. I'm ready."

Gabby didn't respond immediately. She was trying to give Kyle a chance to calm down before she said, "NO WAY IN HELL," but Kyle was off and running.

"I'm not you, Mom! I take risks."

Through gritted teeth Gabby said, "We'll talk about this later." Kyle didn't understand. Gabby didn't take risks because she was a mom. Make a nest for the kids and make sure none of the babies fall out—that was literally her mission. She jammed the documents into her purse, stalked back to the minivan, and threw the purse in the passenger seat.

"Mrs. Greene!" She'd thrown the purse a little too forcefully and hit Sienna.

"Sorry, Sienna." She smiled while Sienna composed herself. "I didn't mean to throw that at you." The person she wanted to throw it at was Phil, who wasn't here.

Lucas yelled, "Can we get a pizza?"

Gabby had never heard a better idea. She was in no state to make dinner. Between the CIA and divorce woes, she didn't even want to put together a bagged salad. It was a screw-top wine kind of night.

At home, Gabby sat in a chair with Mr. Bubbles and a glass of wine. Her credit card info was saved with the pizza place, so she clicked on a gluten-free pizza with nut-free vegan cheese for the kids, and because she was sick of putting herself last, she tacked on an order for an Athenian pizza with extra Greek olives and real cheese for herself. She'd have a second glass of wine too. "It's family movie night," she called out, aka Mom ain't got nothing left.

I'm not you, Mom! I take risks—the accusation gnawed at her peace. Someone in this family had to make sure that Kyle didn't get bucked off a horse and Lucas had his EpiPen. It sure as hell hadn't been Phil. She wasn't boring, was she?

"Kyle, Sienna's mom doesn't pick up you kids in the red convertible, does she?" She couldn't have Kyle riding around in someone's midlife crisis while she was at work.

"I hope so!" Kyle yelled.

Lucas ran across the room with a fork, and a vision of an ER visit materialized. "Lucas, carry your fork with the tines down! You could literally poke your eye out like that."

"OMG, MOM! Calm down!" Kyle flashed a look of shock.

Had she become too uptight and conservative? Someone had to watch out for forks to the eye, right? But the truth of Kyle's accusation seeped in along with the alcohol. The last few years had done something to her—she was scared. In college, she'd delivered pizzas on a moped, and she hadn't always worn her helmet. She bought furniture on Craigslist and ate suspiciously undercooked food without thinking twice. Kyle and Lucas probably weren't as likely to die while walking across the living room with a fork as she sometimes believed.

Kyle sat down on the ottoman next to her, and the late afternoon sunlight caught the purple streaks in her hair, some fading to pink. "I have to interview someone about a job for my Achieve class tomorrow." Achieve was one of those classes where kids learned to set goals and "achieve!" It was the same rhetoric Sloane Ellis used but aimed at middle schoolers.

"You can talk to me, sweetie. I could talk about being a mom. I have some pretty good stories about being a travel agent too." This might be a great moment for bonding.

Kyle gave her a smug teenage look. "Mom, I mean a *real* job."

"It would actually be very progressive of you to identify housework as work despite the fact that society places little to no value on it."

Kyle sighed. "Um, no thanks."

"I'm actually thinking of taking a new job. It would start really soon. Tomorrow." Agent Strong was waiting for her call at that very moment. "If I take it, I won't be home after school like I've always been."

Kyle shrugged like it wasn't the most important decision of Gabby's life, like she didn't care whether Gabby was there or not. Still focused on her assignment, Kyle said, "Um, I'm going to call Dad and ask about his job. Can you order some of those cheesy garlic breads with the dipping sauce?"

Kyle walked out of the room without a second glance. Gabby called, "I would appreciate a please and thank you!"

"Thanks for getting the cheese bread, Mom." Kyle trilled a hollow thank-you that made Gabby question all of her parenting decisions.

Her kids didn't respect her. She was boring. Her ex was dragging her through the mud after fourteen years of marriage. She was done. She didn't need to take that kind of disrespect anymore. Two goddamn CIA agents had come to the house and asked her, Gabby Greene, to be a field operative. She picked up her phone and dialed.

Agent Strong picked up on the first ring. "Ms. Greene?"

"Hello, yes, Agent Strong?"

"Speaking."

"I...I think I'm in."

CHAPTER 5

Friday, 7:20 a.m., Greene household

The kids got on the bus at 7:27 a.m., give or take ten minutes. Valentina was picking her up at seven forty-five sharp, which gave her eighteen minutes to transform into a CIA agent. She shoved lunch boxes into their hands. "Kyle, remember that Sienna's mom is picking you up from horseback riding today."

"Why?" Kyle flashed her a bored teenage look. "What are you doing?"

"Remember that job I mentioned last night?"

Kyle looked skeptical. "You were serious about that?"

"Yep. Starting today I'm a . . ." She realized that she had no clue what she was supposed to tell people.

Luckily Kyle wasn't worried. "Gotta go. Love you, Mom!"

As soon as the bus folded in its stop sign, Gabby ran for her room. It was go time. When she'd resurrected pants from her travel agency days, she'd proved Sloane Ellis right—her yoga pants had been lying to her. Her best black pants from 2010 would not be returning from the dead. This left her with a choice: 1) yoga pants or 2) a wrap dress she had worn to Becky Buckholz's baby shower last year. With no time to spare, she went for her Becky wrap—a dress meant she didn't have to pick a shirt.

In the end, she was waiting for Valentina in her foyer dressed in the exact outfit she'd worn to Becky's baby shower: a lavender dress with pantyhose, Mary Janes, and a crocheted cardigan. She had pulled her hair into a French twist and secured it with a brown bitey clip. The only accessory she was missing was a pastel gift bag with a breast pump and diapers inside.

Valentina pulled up dressed in all black, in a black Dodge Charger, with her wavy hair freshly blown out and a bold red lip. Gabby was living inside a joke: "A Bond girl and your mom walk into a bar…"

She sat down and pulled the wrap together over her boobs because it kept falling open, and not in a sexy way, more in a "Mom, cover up your boobs!" way. Always cordial, Gabby said, "Thanks so much for picking me up."

"I had to. The building's location is classified."

"Any chance we can run through a Starbucks? I didn't have a chance to make coffee." Finding pantyhose took up all of her time. She had even used clear nail polish to fix a run, like she was her granny. She knew pantyhose were out, but the CIA seemed formal. Would Valerie Plame wear pantyhose? Gabby guessed yes. The only thing she knew for sure was that she could really use a coffee.

"There's coffee at the office."

As Valentina swerved through LA traffic like a NASCAR driver, Gabby clutched the armrest. Valentina headed down the 134 to the 5 toward Echo Park. Last time Gabby had been in this neighborhood, she'd gotten a cupcake at Ms. Em's. So that was one bonus of working for the CIA—cupcakes. Red velvet was her favorite. Instead of heading for the trendy spots, Valentina veered toward Glendale. The Glendale Mall hadn't been cool for a very long time, but there had been one store Gabby loved...

International Rug had been a knockoff Pier 1 chock-full of Mexican sodas, colorful dried noodles, bamboo chairs, and all of the best rugs. Basically, it sold ambiance. Before she could finish walking down memory lane with an imaginary pineapple Jarritos soda, Valentina pulled into the parking lot of the store itself.

Gabby gave her a questioning look. "International Rug?"

"Used to be. When it went out of business, the CIA scooped it up. It's a perfect facility—no windows and lots of space for training. The government has been repurposing as many abandoned big-box stores as possible."

"For real, this is the CIA?" Gabby had bought a papasan chair here, not to mention some vaguely tribal masks that Phil had objected to. She had meant to come back for a hammock when they were going out of business, but Kyle got the flu that week.

"Well...we are a specialized division of the CIA, an off-the-books division. We're officially called the EOD, for the Elite Operatives Department."

Gabby blurted out a shocked laugh. She wasn't going to be a regular CIA agent; she was going to be an *elite* one. Her stomach tightened at the thought.

"Most people on the inside call us International Rug." She looked at Gabby with a flat expression. "It's a joke, an inside one."

"I got that." Gabby smiled back, mostly tickled that she'd found something Valentina wasn't good at. The woman wouldn't make it as a stand-up.

"Is there any merchandise left?" Maybe she got a job *and* there would be a stockpile of lingonberry pancake mix.

Valentina told her to shut up with one stern look.

The businesses nearby were also closed, except for a Thai take-out place that Gabby would definitely be trying and a Total Wine at the end of the block. The only thing keeping those businesses alive must be Instacart and Grubhub. There was no foot traffic in this neighborhood anymore.

The outside of the building hadn't changed. It had always been plain concrete. The cheerful red sign for International Rug still hung on the front, the final "g" dangling at an angle.

"Why didn't they call it International Rugs? That would have made more sense," Gabby wondered aloud.

Matter-of-factly, Valentina said, "It was run by a faction of the Russian mob. Oleg, the guy who started it, wasn't super great at English.

"When the EOD took down his business, we confiscated his assets, including this building."

Gabby's jaw dropped imagining herself pushing a stroller down the aisles with zero clue she was at a mob business. And now she was working here.

Valentina explained, "The higher-ups just decided to go with the abandoned look. It's working so far. No one seems to notice us."

Gabby had once heard that the best spies could be easily overlooked—average height, average weight, plain clothes. Valentina applied a coat of gloss to her lips with one hand on the steering wheel. Gabby had never seen anyone less average than Valentina. That might not be a criterion.

Valentina pulled into a parking garage, at which point things became much more than average. There was a series of biometric screenings to get into the building. Gabby remembered all the movies where someone killed a man and stole his eyeballs or a finger to gain access to a place like this. And now she, Gabby Greene, was working here, a place where her eyeballs might be stolen.

Even she had to admit that the risk of stolen eyeballs seemed pretty low. More of a Hollywood trick than a real strategy. With the soul gone, the eyes were windows to nothing, just balls of jelly. Last year, Gabby saw her grandfather die. In life, he'd been the sweet to her grandma's spicy. When Gabby was a child, he would sneak treats to the kids before dinner when her grandma wasn't watching. With soft brown eyes, crinkled at the edges from smiling, he'd always looked like he was about to tell a quiet joke, the kind you might miss if you weren't listening.

"I'll send you down to security later so that you can get in and out of the building."

The inside of what used to be International Rug looked like a Best Buy these days, a windowless room filled with screens and gadgets. Thankfully, there were still some rugs. Intricately patterned Persian rugs gave the EOD a much-needed pop of color, and Gabby could still detect a hint of eucalyptus in the air.

Agent Strong was waiting for them in what used to be the candle section, looking stern, her hair freshly buzzed.

"Morning, Ms. Greene. I'm glad you made it."

"If you'd told me you were at International Rug, I could have driven myself. I loved this store!"

Agent Strong gave her a perfunctory head nod and said, "I'm glad you like the office," which wasn't what Gabby had said at all. She had much preferred International Rug the import store to International Rug the off-the-books CIA office.

Agent Strong ushered her into the briefing room, which was 180-degrees opposite of her kitchen. No dishes or piles of paper, no kids' backpacks. "The room has been cleared."

"Of what?"

"Bugs. We can never be too careful."

Gabby tried to wrap her head around that and couldn't. Were there counterspies in the EOD?

"Thank you for coming in, Ms. Greene. Time is of the essence in this mission. It is essential that we get you up to speed ASAP."

"I'm still trying to figure out what is happening. What was Darcy doing?" Gabby asked.

"Agent Dagger." Alice emphasized her title in a way that made Gabby's breathing constrict. She would feel more comfortable if they could just call Agent Dagger by her first name. She could replace a Darcy, not an Agent Dagger, though.

"Agent Dagger," Alice continued, "was working undercover as Camille Walker, the personal assistant to the CEO of eStocks Enterprises. That is the role you will be taking over."

Personal assistant—Gabby had that covered at least. She'd been an assistant to so many different men, including Phil. She could do that job in her sleep.

"The CEO, George Kramer, is a puppet for the Russian mob boss Sergei Orlov. Any questions so far?"

She had nothing but questions. Agent Strong might as well have been explaining calculus, but Gabby answered, "Nope. I got it." She would rather do anything than disappoint Alice. Disappointing people was her nightmare.

Alice pulled out pictures of Sergei Orlov and George Kramer and slid them across the desk for Gabby. "We need evidence proving that Kramer is Orlov's puppet."

"What kind of evidence?" Gabby congratulated herself on asking a logical question.

"Agent Dagger managed to send us a string of invoices from shell companies that linked Orlov to dummy services, lots of payments for nothing. The invoices were all labeled 'services rendered' when nothing was actually done."

"He sounds like my ex-husband." Phil cost a lot and didn't offer anything in return.

Alice ignored her. "eStocks' expenses are through the roof, and they never appear to make a profit, even though they make millions in the stock market each year."

Gabby stood up straighter and focused intently on whatever it was that Alice was trying to tell her. The temperature in the room was slightly too cold, and it made Gabby intensely aware that she should have worn pants, that every choice she'd made this morning was wrong, starting with her clothes. How was she supposed to fill the shoes of someone a roomful of EOD agents viewed as a peer? EOD might just be a few initials, but the name sounded ominous—the end of whose day? The bad guys, she hoped.

"Where do I come in?" Gabby asked.

Alice made uncomfortable direct eye contact. "You are going to work as Kramer's assistant. We want you to observe and report back about what is happening in the office. We think Orlov is on his way from Russia for a meeting with Kramer. We need you on the inside to let us know what is going down."

She nodded. That sounded fine. She could do office work and report back to Alice—easy-peasy.

"It's fairly simple. Just pay attention to where the money is going at eStocks and who Kramer is in contact with."

Gabby laughed. "Every time you say stocks I think of bouillon.

The only stock I know about is the little cubes I use to make soup." The minute it came out of her mouth, she wished she hadn't said it. The word "bouillon" landed worse than her dress in this room.

Valentina flashed a look of horror and interrupted. "Agent Strong, we can't send her in. She's not prepared."

Agent Strong looked at Valentina. "What do you propose instead?"

"Send me. I can be Agent Dagger's replacement."

"No, Agent Dagger worked there for nine months, and Kramer just started to trust her. She spent six months doing nothing but making coffee."

Gabby would love a coffee.

"Darcy was one of our best agents, and she died." Valentina gestured to Gabby. "This one doesn't stand a chance."

CHAPTER 6

Friday, 9:00 a.m., EOD headquarters

The EOD conference room smelled like canned air and dry-erase markers. It was empty of clutter, color, noise, and apparently, listening devices. Calculating the risk of death across the empty expanse of table in the cleanest room she'd ever seen struck Gabby as both foreign and oddly familiar. She calculated the risk of death about twenty times a day but normally on the fly. "Is Kyle safe to walk home?" "Is that tree too tall to climb?" "If I take a nap, will the kids burn the house down and me with it?" Gabby fidgeted with one of the buttons on her crocheted sweater. How likely was this job to kill her?

She wanted a job, and being recruited by the EOD was the most Hollywood her life had ever been, but she didn't want to die for it. Valentina, pain in the ass that she was, had a point—Gabby was not trained for this. Following the punch-and-jab motions of her instructor at cardio kickboxing was almost impossible. How was she going to defend herself from an actual attacker?

She sat up straight and looked Agent Strong in the eyes. There was no calculating the odds unless she knew the facts. "What happened to Darcy exactly?"

Agent Strong took a deep breath and exhaled. "Someone compromised Darcy's cover. Not Orlov or Kramer. It was an outside source."

"That means someone knew Darcy was a fake, right?"

Agent Strong shrugged. "Eh."

"Which means the minute I step foot in that office, they'll know I'm even faker."

Valentina sat back and let Gabby's words hang in the air.

Alice tapped her stylus on the table. "This is a low-risk mission, not zero obviously, but we've managed the risks as best we can. We're following a lead on who killed Agent Dagger, and we believe we can contain the threat within the next day or two. We will not set you up for failure."

The answer gave Gabby a queasy feeling. If they couldn't protect Darcy, what chance did she have? "I won't go in if you don't find the person, right?"

"The last thing we want to do is place you in danger."

Agent Strong's answer was too vague for Gabby's comfort. She sure as hell wouldn't let Kyle go to a party if she was only pretty sure it was safe. Russian mobsters were probably a little trickier than middle schoolers, but still. Gabby calculated the pros and cons:

Pros:

- Being a travel agent was no longer an option, as the industry barely existed. At the moment, it was Tupperware, Avon, or the EOD.
- Agent Strong had promised her $80,000 a year.
- This would save her the trouble of updating her résumé.

- Last but not least, it was flattering that the EOD wanted *her*, not Phil, not her best friend Justin who owned a successful business, not the women at parent pickup who looked like they had their lives together. She, Gabby Greene, had something to offer.

Cons:

- Possible death.

"Could I tell my ex that I work for the CIA?" That would be a big pro.

"No." Agent Strong tapped one of her shiny, black loafers.

"Not even like in a secretarial capacity?"

"No. Absolutely not."

Was it worth working for the EOD if she couldn't lord it over people who'd been looking down on her and not taking her seriously?

Valentina ignored the entire exchange and passed Gabby a file. A quick glance showed pictures of everyone at eStocks and Russian mobsters. It was like a school yearbook of bad guys.

"Memorize everything."

Gabby nodded. Names and faces were not a problem.

"And a basic knowledge of RICO would be a good idea. Don't you think, Agent Strong?"

"Who's Rico, the office perv?" You always needed a heads-up on that guy.

"Not a person. RICO is the Racketeer Influenced and Corrupt Organizations Act, the laws we will use to take down Orlov."

Now that they mentioned it, she'd heard of that on TV.

Gabby said, "Not to poke holes in your plan, but how will my boss not notice that I'm an entirely different person. Sure, Darcy and I might look alike, but we're not twins." It was an absurd plan when you thought of it.

Agent Strong smiled. "We are very good at disguises at the EOD. Hollywood would be lucky to have our makeup artists."

There was so much more to it. Height, weight, presence, voice, posture, mannerisms. The way she could identify one of her kids from a block away just by the way they moved. There was no way she moved like Darcy. Darcy was probably a panther. Gabby was a lapdog.

Alice gave Gabby a woman-to-woman look. "Kramer is a man. He's notorious for never seeing the women who work under him."

"I'm sure that's true, but even so . . ."

"We are going to give you a simple script. Darcy has been out of the office for three days. By the time you return in her place, it will have been a full week. Tell a few key people that you are on a heavy dose of steroids. The slight difference in your appearance can be explained by steroidal weight gain and swelling."

Gabby swallowed her reaction to that. Her self-esteem was yo-yoing between "I am the chosen one!" and "Fat Darcy." They were right, though. A few pounds changed a person's face.

Agent Strong was quiet for a moment. She tapped her stylus on the table again and acknowledged Valentina. "Agent Monroe, you raised a valid concern. Ms. Greene is untrained."

Gabby nodded enthusiastically. Better to have this information out in the open. Valentina looked more than happy to move from runner-up to queen of this particular undercover op, and Gabby valued her life more than the crown and the bouquet.

Agent Strong wasn't having it. "This is something we can fix. With a few days of training, we can give you the basic skills to negotiate a simple mission like this. There will be no hand-to-hand combat or sharpshooting, no advanced computer hacking."

Did that mean she would be expected to do basic hacking? She couldn't get into her own computer half the time. All of the household passwords were written in big, bold print on a whiteboard on the kitchen wall. MrBubblesFarts was the household Wi-Fi password. The Apple ID was MrBubblesFartz! She was not a hacker.

"Kramer is expecting her back next Wednesday. This only gives us three days for a crash course in spying."

"What will that include?" Gabby assumed tactical driving, shooting, explosives, Russian language.

Alice said, "Because your mission objective is uncovering evidence of money laundering in an office, we'll teach you what to look for, how to cover your tracks online, and tactics for eavesdropping."

Gossip—she didn't need a course in that. Between her neighborhood and the moms at school, she was ninja level.

"Besides remedial covert procedures, we'll also focus on basic self-defense." Agent Strong paused, as if to think, and added, "While we're at it, I'll have Markus teach you how to shoot. We can't send you out there defenseless."

Self-defense, covering her tracks online, shooting...Gabby inhaled sharply and gripped the arms on her chair. And to think yesterday she'd almost filled out an online form to explore the possibility of selling Tupperware.

CHAPTER 7

Friday afternoon, EOD headquarters

If nothing else, the EOD was efficient. Alice Strong had her headed for the basement to start spy training less than ten minutes after Valentina suggested it. It took Gabby about a week just to turn an idea over in her head before she acted. Then she'd have to start and stop ten times.

"Valentina, take her down to meet Markus. He can take charge of her training."

A shadow crossed Valentina's cover girl visage. It was fleeting but noticeable. Gabby might not have martial arts training but she had EQ, and Valentina just had some sort of feeling related to Markus, and it wasn't good. Regret, loss, unrequited love—or maybe she was just being dramatic. That's what Gabby's mother would say.

Somehow Valentina's beauty was even more pronounced under the shadow of disappointment. Gabby wasn't one of those women who looked better crying. Her chin turned into a lumpy wad, and her eyes almost disappeared. After, it took a day for the swelling to go down.

Valentina made a play to wash her hands of the whole business and make a break for it. She said, "Excellent. If Markus is in charge, can I get back to the field? I'd like to find Agent Dagger's killer myself."

"Stand by. Getting Agent Greene up to speed is our number one priority right now."

Another shadow crossed Valentina's face. Gabby was pretty sure this feeling was related to her and not Markus. There were so many dark clouds for Valentina this morning.

Turned out the man of the hour, Markus, was downstairs in the EOD gadget lab. The lab was state-of-the-art, stainless steel and sterile white. The only bold splashes of color were from the warning signs: CAUTION! STAY 10 FEET BACK! BIOHAZARD!

Gabby's Mary Janes clicked on the concrete floor. Looking at the signs, she had a vision of that time she brought Lucas to the dentist with her. He had been three or four, and she couldn't find a sitter. She'd been having recurring dreams about her teeth falling out that seemed about to come true, so there was no way she was skipping the appointment. He'd pushed the buttons on the hydraulic chair until the hygienist had nicked Gabby's gums with her Captain Hook tool. While she was dribbling blood on a paper bib, the woman behind the desk put Lucas in a room with cartoons. Later she'd heard that dreams about teeth falling out represented losing control. That rang true.

"Do you have kids, Valentina?" Gabby decided to just call her by her first name. Valentina was probably twenty-five and looked good crying. It would be unfair to give her a title on top of that.

"No. Kids don't really work with this lifestyle."

Seemed like.

A guy at a workbench testing a motor of some type said, "I've got kids. Don't know what you're talking about, Val."

Valentina looked flatly back at him. "Go back to your microscope, Gerry. If I had a wife, I'd think kids were no big deal too."

Gabby gave Valentina a look of understanding. Men were idiots. Gerry's wife was probably driving three kids through LA traffic to three different schools while getting her PhD in nuclear physics or running a day care.

When Valentina said, "Hey, Markus," Gabby followed her eyes.

At the sight of Markus, Gabby's ovaries overrode all of her lived experience. Markus Parks was the guy who should have been cast as James Bond—rugged good looks in a sophisticated package. More important, she knew why Regé-Jean Page had quit *Bridgerton*. He had taken a job at the EOD and would be training her to go on a vital mission. This was now her life.

Markus held out his hand, and Gabby nearly swooned.

Valentina said, "Gabby, this is Markus Parks. He'll be training you." Her loud and pointed tone said, "Get yourself together."

In a deep, authoritative voice, he announced, "It'll be my job to look after you during this mission. I'm not going to let one hair get out of place."

She must have been flushed, because he held out a hand to steady her. "Are you okay?"

"I'm fine." She waved off his concern. "This is my baseline, sort of perpetually in need of a V8." She laughed awkwardly. Once she got used to the intense male pheromone levels in the room, she would be fine. Being around someone as attractive as Markus was like visiting Denver. It took a minute to get used to the lack of oxygen.

"Are you going to be in the office with me?" Gabby asked Markus. That would be a relief. Gabby was more than happy to let an armed protector open doors for her and make sure she didn't die.

"No, but I'll be with you every step of the way." He pulled out a small, easily hidden earpiece. "I can talk to you all day long."

Gabby nodded. It would be like when she stayed up all night talking to Jace Baxter in high school, twirling the phone cord around her finger and painting her toenails a shade of pink she thought he might like. Except it was the EOD.

He held up a brooch. "And this will be my eyes." He stooped to attach the brooch to her crocheted sweater. His face only inches from her, his steady breathing brought her own heart rate down. While his scent did its best to bring it right back up. A hint of citrus hit her nose, probably from his body wash, but there was something raw beneath it. Markus's pheromones smelled good.

When he flipped the brooch's hidden camera on and turned a screen her way, Gabby could see his face in high-def. "There's no telling what could happen out in the field. It's important that I can see everything you see."

From the tone of his voice, she could tell he was thinking about Darcy. Had Markus been Darcy's eyes and ears too?

For a moment, she'd forgotten. This job had real consequences. At home all she could do was burn a pancake, forget to send Lucas with a lunch, or worst-case scenario, get a divorce. A mistake here could get her killed. No matter how much Agent Strong tried to reassure her about the safety of the mission—Darcy was dead.

Markus saw the panic in her eyes and turned off the screen and pulled a stool out for her. "It's okay, Gabby. I've got you. I promise nothing bad will happen."

Even though she knew deep down that he was promising something he couldn't guarantee, his reassurance settled her. Markus might be a beefcake, but his eyes were kind and they crinkled with well-worn laugh lines when he smiled.

"How about the cool gadgets?" Gabby loved to distract herself with shopping. Who didn't? "Is there a lipstick that turns into a dart gun or a compact that is really a bomb that will blast through a steel door?"

Valentina, who had zoned out scrolling through her phone up until now huffed loudly. "Gabby, you are not Jane fricking Bond. We just need you to go to the office, make the guy coffee, and keep an eye on things. End of story."

Markus smiled. "Well, I have a few cool things." He pulled out a decoy mobile phone. When Gabby reached for it, he held it just out of reach and tsk-tsked her. "Wait a second. It's a Taser."

"Oh." She pulled back.

He demonstrated how turning the phone on activated the Taser.

"I'll try not to get my phones mixed up," she joked.

"And pepper spray is a self-defense staple. Do you know how to use this?"

"Yes." The canister Markus handed her was a standard bottle of pepper spray. Just a black tube with a red button at the top.

"No need to disguise pepper spray. It's something every woman should carry." He handed it over. "Careful with the lid."

Darcy had died on the job. Pepper spray didn't seem like enough. "Pepper spray is good, but what about a real gun?"

Before Markus could answer her question about a gun, Gabby accidentally hit the button. A stream caught Markus right in the face, and he doubled over.

Valentina grabbed Gabby's arm in a viselike grip and whispered, "Drop the weapon."

The canister clattered to the floor, and Gabby started in with the apologies. "I'm so, so, so sorry! I didn't mean to—" She waited for a response. "Are you okay?"

Markus shook his head. "I'll be fine. Val, let her go."

Valentina shrugged. "Standard procedure when a weapon is fired."

While he tried to catch his breath, she went on. "I think you should rinse with milk. That's what I do when I'm making guacamole and I get jalapeno on my skin."

"I'm fine!" He held his hand up. "No milk, please."

Markus spent the next five to ten minutes getting his eyeballs hosed out with high-pressure water in the eyewash station while she waited in shame. If she had done permanent damage...She rubbed her temples and stole a glance at the eyewash station. Hopefully, it wasn't government-strength pepper spray, like ghost pepper spray. Ghost pepper Cheetos were practically weapons.

After what seemed like an eternity, Markus returned. "Let's hold off on the gun. I'll start going over some self-defense techniques on Monday."

Thank god. That gave her the weekend to collect herself.

He looked at her Becky Buckholz baby shower ensemble and said, "You'll need to wear something you can move in. Do you have yoga pants?"

She smiled genuinely for the first time that day. Boy did she.

CHAPTER 8

Friday, cocktail hour, Justin's house

It was neighborhood cocktail night on Avocado Avenue. Every Friday, a different neighbor hosted. Thank god it wasn't her turn. She'd been too busy with national security concerns to even pick up. Everyone's dirty laundry was on the floor at her house.

"Have fun, kids!" she called out as they ran across the street to the Alvarez house. "Don't make too big of a mess!" Who was she kidding? She didn't care what they did as long as they came out alive.

Justin Casey was her neighborhood BFF and Beverly Hills' go-to party planner. He moonlighted at a drag bar after hours as Betty Danger because, he said, "Deep down I've always wanted to be a housewife." Where Gabby could neither lip-synch nor plan a party, Justin couldn't stop. They balanced each other out.

Tonight, all Gabby wanted to do was chill with her BFF and tell him all about the EOD, but she couldn't unless she wanted to end up "prosecuted to the fullest extent of the law." How did EOD agents do it? Could she even have a therapist?

Like Gabby's, Justin's house was a Spanish-style two-story with a xeriscape yard and fruit trees. Unlike hers, Justin's had imagination. It was all kitschy wallpaper and statues he'd picked up on trips to France or at flea markets in Arizona. Justin bought something everywhere he stopped. If he went in a gas station, he'd walk out with a monogrammed keychain, a charming air freshener, and a coconut water. He'd never spent less than twenty dollars at a stop in his life.

Gabby stepped through the door. "Honey, I'm home!" There were cocktails, and Justin was dressed in a onesie with a pinned-on tail, cat ears, and painted-on whiskers. God help her, but she couldn't remember why. "What's the theme tonight?"

"Broadway." The look on his face said, "Duh."

"Oh right." She smiled. "I love *Cats*."

Justin was always the only one dressed up. He would be in full makeup while everyone else stumbled in wearing wilted button-down shirts, jonesing for a beer after work. For once, that was her.

She wanted to scream, "THE EOD RECRUITED ME." Instead, she stated the obvious. "Justin, no one else is going to dress up," as if it was at the top of her mind.

"Just because they're dull and boring doesn't mean I have to be."

She nodded before dipping a toe into what she actually wanted to say. "It was *a day*! I ended up—" She paused. How was she supposed to describe this situation? With a frustrated sigh, she said, "I just ended up with some extra things to do, and I had to get one of Kyle's friend's moms to pick up the kids."

He put his paw on her forearm. "Gabby, I would love nothing more than to babysit. I've been dying to watch Kyle and Lucas. Those kids need a strong male figure in their lives."

She blurted out a laugh. "You're in a cat costume!"

But he was right. Justin had been there. Since the divorce, and even before, Justin was always there. He'd offered to watch the kids so many times, and she'd never taken him up on it. She'd lost a lot of friends since the divorce—people just stopped calling or made excuses. Some people she hadn't bothered calling because she didn't want to have to rehash the last year of her life before they had coffee. Justin—painted-on whiskers and all—was her rock.

Gabby hugged him.

"Love you too, Gabs." He tilted his chin up and leaned back. "But careful of the makeup."

Phil might not have been, but Justin was there for her for better or worse, till death do us part.

He gestured for her to come outside to the garden. "Now I want to show you where I put Rocky."

"Rocky?"

He smiled coyly. "You'll remember. You met him on our last Starbucks run. I'm starting a collection. I already bought him a friend."

She blurted out a laugh when the memory hit. Because his partner, Hugh, was worried about the credit card bill (someone had to be), Justin left most of his purchases in his SUV. The back seat was filled with fabulous knickknacks no one would ever need: figurines, random lampshades, and always a throw pillow or two. It was an International Rug on wheels. "The key is to sprinkle in the purchases so he never notices." Last time they'd gone for coffee, there'd been a taxidermied raccoon in the back seat.

When Gabby had gasped, he'd put his hand on her forearm. "Don't worry. I bought him from a vegan," as if her first concern were morality.

The raccoon had been stuffed between a Costco-sized container of trail mix and a spangled throw pillow and had looked alive.

"I got him from this really lovely vegan lady who taxidermies roadkill." He had readjusted the review mirror to get a good look at the animal. A smile of satisfaction spread across his face like butter. "Isn't he marvelous? She found him just up the road, hit by a car. It's amazing how wild animals have adapted to live in neighborhoods among us."

Gabby didn't point out that the animal was dead. Also, she was sure Hugh would notice a dead raccoon in the house. Taxidermy wasn't something you could "sprinkle in." But without Justin, Hugh would be bored out of his mind.

"Can we sneak into a corner somewhere? I want to tell you something." She wasn't sure what she'd tell him. Maybe she could talk about her day in pig Latin. I am an ecret-say, py-say.

Before he had a chance to show her the rest of his taxidermy collection, Shelly flagged them down. "Justin, Gabby, over here!"

Gabby groaned. Shelly was the neighbor Gabby never wanted to talk to and the one person she always ran into. Shelly always had an opinion. Tonight was no different.

"Are these shrimp from Costco?" Shelly looked at the shrimp on her plate like she found it wanting. She hadn't even tried to dress up.

"Uh, no. I got them at the market."

"Oh." Shelly looked like that explained it. "You might want to try Costco next time."

Gabby and Justin exchanged a look. Shelly was insufferable. To hammer home her annoyance, she said, "Did you try that book I recommended, sweetie?"

The way she said "sweetie" made Gabby cringe.

"Yes, I did." In retrospect, it wasn't surprising Shelly had been behind an activity that involved cataloging all of Gabby's flaws.

Shelly set her uneaten shrimp down and said, "Neither of you have seen Tarragon, have you?"

Gabby had been hearing about Shelly's missing cat, Tarragon, for weeks. At one point, Shelly had implied that Mr. Bubbles had something to do with it.

Justin shook his head no—in full cat face. When Shelly looked down at her phone, he mouthed to Gabby, "Who is that?" and she loudly whispered back, "Her cat."

"I try to keep him inside, but he always manages to sneak out."

Justin waxed poetic, as if he hadn't just realized that Tarragon existed. "Nothing is meant to be cooped up inside all day long. I'm sure Tarragon is living his best life."

The pros and cons of a dangerous life versus a safe life trapped in a house—it was like they'd tapped into Gabby's thoughts. If only she could sneak away and talk to Justin about it.

As Shelly and Justin got into a heated conversation about how much a house cat should be allowed to explore, Gabby's thoughts turned to the EOD and Markus. She sent a quick text to calm her anxiety: R u OK? It was only polite to check after the pepper spray incident.

He responded almost immediately: At ER.

The look on her face must have been bad, because Justin rubbed her arm in a comforting way. "Sorry, sweetheart. I didn't know you were passionate about cats."

Before she could decide how to respond, Markus answered: JK. I'm fine.

"It's something else." Sharing personal info with Shelly was always risky, but she needed to download. "I started a new job today, and I'm not sure I'm up to the challenge."

Shelly stopped short. "A job? I didn't know you were looking." She seemed offended for not being in the know.

For that matter, so did Justin. His expression was the same as if there'd been a dramatic reveal on *Real Housewives* that he hadn't seen coming. He rejected all plot twists he didn't predict.

"*What* are you doing?" Justin looked ready to talk her down from a stripper pole.

"Just some . . . office work."

"I suppose you had to because of the—" Shelly mouthed, "Divorce," in an exaggerated whisper as if it were a secret, as if Gabby might have forgotten she was divorced.

Gabby nodded. It was easier than explaining that the EOD needed her because she was the only one on Facebook who looked like a dead secret agent.

Shelly started in with the condolences. "I'm sorry, honey. If you need anything, I'm here. I thought about going back to work once, but it's just not worth it." Shelly got so defensive about her choice not to work outside the house that she ended up attacking anyone who made a different choice.

Justin stood and motioned for Gabby to follow. "Can you excuse us for a minute, Shelly? I need Gabby to help with some kitchen duty." He was clearly just helping her out of the conversation. Gabby was grateful, because she could have been there all night.

After they refreshed their cocktails, Justin said, "Back to my taxidermy collection. You are going to die!"

She said, "Great," but she mostly wanted to talk about her job problem. "Justin, I'm just not sure I can do this job."

"Hold that thought, babe." He gestured to the raccoon and another animal next to him. "I picked this lynx up at the flea market yesterday." He scratched under the stuffed cat's chin. "Kitty kitty would have been lonely by himself."

At the sight of the stuffed creature, Gabby started choking

on her drink. In between gasping for air and coughing, she said, "That is not a lynx. That is Tarragon."

"Tarragon?"

"You remember Shelly's cat, the one that's missing?"

"Noooo." He rocked back on his heels and looked at the cat. "That's not a house cat."

"Cross my heart and hope to die, that is Shelly's cat. Maine coon cats look like lynx." Shelly had always bragged about how Tarragon was twenty-five pounds. Mr. Bubbles was only ten. Shelly was off her rocker for blaming him for Tarragon's disappearance in the first place.

For a moment, neither could say anything. Justin crossed himself. He looked to the heavens and said, "God forgive me for my shopping habit. I've gone too far."

Gabby asked, "How much did you pay for him?"

"Five hundred dollars, which was a bargain. You can't find a taxidermied lynx anywhere, especially ones that have died of natural causes."

"You didn't find a lynx!" Because she hadn't lost her senses, she said, "We have to get him out of here before Shelly sees."

Justin picked up the cat and started carrying it under his arm toward the back. "I don't understand how this happened."

"People are always driving too fast down this street. If your taxidermist was finding roadkill in the area..." It stood to reason, even if it was preposterous.

"I'm putting him at your house, Gabs."

Gabby didn't want Shelly's stuffed cat at her house, but this was an emergency. She needed to save Justin. They hustled out the side gate. Gabby held the cocktails. Justin held Tarragon. Halfway across the yard, he paused to reflect. "This is almost the dumbest thing we've ever done." He looked behind her, dead serious, and said, "Don't tell Hugh."

She made a zipping motion across her lips.

"I know I'm the fun one, but I've been a little too fun lately, if you know what I mean."

She did. This was what happened when you tested your limits—you ended up displaying your neighbor's dead cat in the garden and inviting them over for cocktails.

"I got you, Justin. We got each other." They were trying at least.

Out on the empty street at night, the music and the conversation gone, it was just her and Justin. The smell of magnolia blossoms from Justin's tree filled the air. Justin inspected his cat and frowned. "Goddamn it, Shelly."

"How did you not know her cat? She bragged about it constantly." She was always telling everyone how much better her cat was than any other cat—glamorous, hypoallergenic, looked just like a lynx.

"I don't pay attention to cats!" he exclaimed.

He was dressed as a cat. She would have pointed it out except her phone buzzed. It was Markus. I know I said Monday, but need to meet tomorrow. Start training ASAP.

"Damn it." She scowled at her phone. "They want me to come in tomorrow."

Can't I call in sick for a few more days?

Nope. Boss said you're fired unless you show up Monday.

She wanted the weekend to lose ten pounds and get in shape. At the very least, she'd wanted to buy some of those yoga pants that would force her butt into the shape of what she expected a butt to look like. Fabletics assured her that "there are no bad butts," and she was ready to be convinced.

Justin must have sensed her rising stress level. "Tell me about this job, honey."

"It just came up, yesterday. They needed me to start immediately." She sighed. "I'm not sure I can do it, though. I haven't worked outside the house for ages." Look how much she'd fucked it up in just one day. She'd pepper sprayed Markus ten minutes after meeting him.

And she didn't know anything about money laundering. She could barely handle actual laundry. Her shoulders slumped, the voices of all the haters, her own the loudest, echoing in her mind.

"I'm going to text them and say I'm out." She typed a quick note to Markus: I can't do this. I wish I could, but I can't. It's not you, it's me. Xoxo Gabby

Her finger hovered over her text breakup with the EOD. This was the first time "it's not you, it's me" really applied. She would love to be a superspy, but how could she be? Valentina was right. She'd just get herself killed or, worse, someone else. She hit SEND.

Dressed like a cat and holding Tarragon, Justin looked at her with the energy of one of Oprah's hand-selected lifestyle experts, someone who was about to start inspiring change. "Gabby, don't even joke with me. You can do an office job. Make coffee, file, book appointments. How hard can it possibly be?"

If only he knew.

"Throw your shoulders back. Booty in, chest out. Whatever they want you to do, you can do it." His right hand in the air and his other hand on his hip, he did some sort of Fosse dance move. "You can do it backwards in high heels!"

She smiled weakly. Justin could but not her.

"Give me that phone right now."

He took the phone from her: Nvm last text. See you tomorrow!

He picked up his tail, walked over the threshold into her house, and with major attitude, announced, "You're welcome." Not a beat later and in a casual tone, he asked, "Where do you want to keep this cat?"

"I don't want to keep it, Justin. What if Shelly comes over?"

He shrugged and set the cat down. "It'll do for tonight, right? We can figure something else out soon."

She nodded. What was one more thing to gloss over with a half-truth? "No, Shelly, I haven't seen Tarragon." "No, I'm not a spy. I have a normal office job. All I do is make coffee."

Gabby was going to be a pro at lying in no time, at least if she was going to succeed. "It'll be fine," she said, looking at her cluttered dining room, where she was now displaying the neighbor's dead cat and piles of unopened mail, her main support standing nearby dressed as a cat. She said it again, "It's fine, right?"

"Of course it is. Why wouldn't it be fine?" Justin twirled his tail.

So many reasons, none of which she could say.

CHAPTER 9

Early Saturday morning, Greene household

Gabby woke up to a text from Phil, who was supposed to have the kids: Busy today. Tell kids I love them. Normally, she'd be perfectly content to keep the kids on a Saturday, but not today. With a groan of despair, she buried her face in her pillow. Even though she'd behaved like a seventeen-year-old last night, this morning she was going to be thirty-eight like her driver's license said. Thirty-eight-year-old Gabby needed to get her ass to EOD HQ.

For her first day of spy training, Gabby was hungover, without childcare, and unsure whether she had broken up with the EOD via text or not after that second cocktail.

She had three choices:

1. Drive the kids to Phil's anyway—but what if he wasn't there?
2. Bring the kids to work. They could just play with iPads in the corner while she learned how to take down the Russian mob. EOD would know what it was getting that way.

3. See just how serious Justin was about his babysitting offer.

She went with door number three, and praise Leslie Knope and RuPaul (the gods of her universe), Justin was at her front door with two lattes within fifteen minutes. He breezed into the house and handed her a coffee. "Auntie Justin is here to save the day! Lucky girl, you caught me in the Starbucks drive-through."

While Gabby swigged some coffee, Justin went to the medicine cabinet. "Ibuprofen? You look like roadkill, Gabs."

True statement. Her hair was partially plastered to her head like she'd been run over. Tufts of frizz that hadn't been crushed by tires were free to blow in the breeze of passing semis. She was something you would pass and think, "Poor thing, I wonder what that was?"

Gabby gestured to Tarragon, still on the dining room table. "Maybe your taxidermist could do something for me. She seems to be really talented."

Justin flashed her the same annoyed look Kyle used and said, "Kyle, brush your mother's hair. We can't send her to work like this. It's an emergency."

Kyle stood like a deer in the headlights. It had probably never occurred to her that Gabby needed help. Her children were growing up like they were Melissa Joan Hart, except without a gig as Sabrina the Teenage Witch.

Like a NASCAR pit crew member, Justin hit Gabby's cheeks with some blush and handed her a lipstick. "At least you don't look freshly dead now. Go get 'em, tiger!"

Forty-five minutes later, Gabby found off-street parking outside the EOD and pulled her mom-mobile in. Her Dodge Grand

Caravan screamed, "My vagina is exit only!" and the bumper sticker on the back included a stick figure of everyone who had entered the world through said vagina, plus Mr. Bubbles, and Phil. The bumper sticker was worse than a wedding ring, but she hadn't taken the time to scrape it off the van.

That was a problem for Future Gabby. She took a deep breath and walked into HQ looking more confident than she felt, at least she hoped. Markus, who had probably never driven a minivan, was waiting inside the entrance. She and her exit-only vagina were going to be training with someone who looked like he might make it through to the next round on *American Ninja Warrior.* There wasn't a single TV show that Markus wouldn't be great on. He was handsome enough for a soap opera and a shoo-in on any dating show, except that he'd have to pretend to be a marketing executive or a tech guy.

Gabby sputtered, "I'm sorry about the weird text last night. I was—"

He raised one eyebrow. "Gabby, if you wanna break up with me, you have to do it to my face."

She laughed with relief. "Text breakups are the lamest," she said, as if she were wheeling and dealing relationships via text all the time. Last time she dated, smartphones didn't exist. Did anyone break up via text on a flip phone? She hadn't.

On the way to the gym, he explained the day's agenda. "We're going to do some basic hand-to-hand combat and maybe some fighting with improvised weapons. Most fights aren't planned."

True. She and Phil had always gotten into it over appetizers on a "date" or while furniture shopping. They might still be married if not for that Härlanda love seat episode at IKEA.

Markus gave her an up-and-down look, probably searching for some athleticism that wasn't there. "Do you have any experience?"

"I can give a backhanded compliment." She thought deep. "And I've thrown a guy's clothes on the front lawn before. That was more of an early twenties move, though."

"That's not in the manual, but it could come in handy. You might not even need knife throwing."

Knife throwing? Gabby started sweating. She was in over her head.

Because it was Saturday, they had the training gym to themselves. At least there wouldn't be witnesses to her misery. Markus led her through some light stretches. "What kind of workout routine do you have right now?"

"I belong to a gym." Last time she went to a step class at her gym, the instructor gently suggested she move to the back so as not to confuse the other members of the class. Through a fake smile, the instructor had assured her, "But you're doing great!"

"I'm just trying to assess your base level of fitness."

He could already see that she couldn't touch her toes. That should be his first clue.

Markus looked like a professional athlete, but with soft brown eyes and a doofy smile. It was flat-out disarming. After one final stretch, he stood up in a "let's do this" way and motioned for her to join him.

"Because you're not trained in martial arts and we don't have tons of time, I'm going to teach you how to break free if someone has you pinned."

She nodded. That sounded doable.

Markus locked eyes with her. "I'm going to play the assailant. I'll walk you through what's happening in slow motion."

She smiled without processing what he meant. So far, EOD training was a lot like that free one-on-one personal training session she'd had at the gym. Hopefully, this went better than that. She'd vomited in a trash can by a bank of ellipticals and briefly distracted everyone from CNN and *The Bachelor*, depending on which TV they were watching. After that, she had decided not to sign up for the personal training package.

"In a typical situation, your assailant will come up behind you." He stepped behind her and wrapped his arms around her midsection.

No one had held her like that in a while. With his muscled forearms around her, she went all soft inside. Her vision blurred to sepia tone.

"Tell me if I'm being too rough. I know this is your first time."

"I've had two kids, Markus. You know I'm not a virgin." She could have slapped herself for the joke, but there it was.

"Um…" He cleared his throat, and she died inside for letting her mouth run. She had verbal diarrhea.

"Don't worry. I promise not to talk from here on out."

He snickered. "Good luck to both of us with that one. In a hug hold, your best move is to drop out of their grip and run."

She bit the inside of her cheek. "Okay."

"Try to escape my hold. Drop down and roll away."

She let herself fall to the floor through his arms. Instead of catching herself, she just dropped like a sack of flour. "Ouch!"

"Now roll!" he yelled. He dropped to the floor and showed her how to roll. He made it look good.

Gabby got to her hands and knees and crawled at the pace of someone looking for a remote under the coffee table.

"I thought you said you weren't a virgin."

Relief washed over her at his reference to her tasteless joke. Nothing was sweeter than when someone pretended your bad joke was funny. She should be in time-out, and he was being straight-up gallant. She smiled and kept her mouth shut.

"Let's try it again. This time drop to your knees and make it look like you've done this before," Markus said. "I'm going to put you in a sleeper hold. With my arm around your neck, you won't be able to drop out."

Gabby took a deep breath and focused. She needed to get it together!

He gripped her hard and explained. "You have a three-part move. Stomp on my foot, elbow me in the gut, and throw your head back to break my nose. Pantomime it, though."

She did an exaggerated fake stomp.

"Good."

She elbowed him.

"Nice work. Let's go through that one more time a little faster."

Stomp. Elbow. She threw her head back, but this time she connected with bone and Markus dropped his arms and buckled. He grabbed his nose, which was pouring blood.

"Ohmygod! Did I break it?"

He didn't answer because he was running for the men's locker room.

After a few moments, she followed him and knocked softly. "Are you okay, Markus?" She googled "broken nose symptoms and treatment."

Depending on his pain level and whether it was out of joint, she'd have to take him to the ER in her mom-mobile. God help her, but she wanted to peel Phil out of the customized family window decal on the back of the van right now, as if Markus would notice the sticker with his eyes swelled shut. Either way, that stick figure dad needed to go.

"What's your pain level?" she called through the door.

"I'm fine, Gabby."

Her pain level was climbing by the minute.

She texted Justin: Idk if I can do this.

U have been there 10 minutes. CHILL!

It's bad. Once again, she wanted to call and tell him exactly how bad this was. Then he sent a follow-up text filled with insanity. He was thinking of putting the cat on Craigslist to recoup his money but wasn't sure on the price. Kyle wanted to go to the mall with Sienna, and were they out of the lactose-free milk?

You're right. I'll stay.

CHAPTER 10

Saturday, midafternoon, EOD headquarters

Gabby splashed water on her face in the women's locker room and pulled herself together. If she broke Markus's nose, that's what happened. It was over, and she would need to deal with it. Broken noses were part of her new post-divorce, Sloane Ellis–prescribed adventure. Back on the training mats, she found Markus waiting, blood spatters down the front of his shirt. His eye wasn't bruised yet, but it was swollen. It could be worse. He could have asked her to make him lunch and drive him to the mall.

"Is it broken?" She held her breath and waited for bad news.

"No. I'm fine."

She wasn't sure if she believed him, but it was a good story, so she went with it.

"Let's take a break from hand-to-hand tactics."

She exhaled with relief. She hadn't been one of those "gym and recess are my favorite parts of school" kids. Library and quiet reading time had been her thing. It showed.

"Next is target practice."

Target practice . . . She mulled it over. You didn't need to be an athlete to shoot.

"I was considering a knife-throwing lesson, but…" He let his sentence trail off, and a single drop of blood fell in a perfect splat onto the floor between them, punctuating the reason why she would not be allowed near knives.

If he wanted someone to throw knives, he should ask her bestie. Justin was one of those guys whom people would pay to watch chop a carrot. High-speed, precision chopping. There was no vegetable that he couldn't turn into a rosette. Last year, she had cheated at Halloween and invited Justin over for drinks. She'd had a glass of wine and watched him carve award-winning pumpkins. That was her skill—getting other people to do her jobs without realizing they'd signed on for a day of work. She'd always been great at that. It was un-American of her, but there it was.

Markus looked up, as if asking the heavens for counsel. After a deep breath, he said, "I guess we should do firearms training."

Gabby had grown up liberal, silence and nonviolence. Guns were for police and bad guys only. And Gabby was a good girl. She'd always done what she was supposed to do, never questioned, just good girled her way into nothingness.

It was time to make a mark on the world. She could see herself with Valentina and Alice, dressed in sleek black clothes, shoulders thrown back, a pistol on her belt, and an encyclopedic knowledge of the RICO laws. She would be intelligent, informed, and ready to save the world. It was time for a new Gabby.

Time for a gun.

The gun range was a few stories underground and cold, all concrete and ballistics glass, which she knew because Markus told her. It was arranged like a bowling alley with four lanes. Instead of pins, there were paper sheets with human targets. The smell of gunpowder filled her senses and ignited a fire in her belly.

"We're not breathing in lead, are we?" She'd read a lot about lead in children. It couldn't be good for adults either.

"The smell is strong, but there are exhaust fans."

Markus picked up a gun from a table where he'd laid out materials like a preschool teacher setting up for a craft project. Instead of Popsicle sticks, glue, and googly eyes, his materials were guns, ammo, and a few things she didn't recognize.

"Have you ever fired a gun?"

"Only Nerf." And she wasn't very good at those.

"Not even paintball?" He looked shocked.

"No." She hadn't been the kind of kid who played paintball.

Markus gave her a lesson, and she tried to keep track of the rules:

1. Treat all guns like they're loaded, even if you don't think they are.
2. Keep your finger off the trigger.
3. When holding the gun, face it downrange.
4. When you're ready to fire your weapon, squeeze the trigger gently.

Markus was so competent and good at everything. "Why don't they send you into the field?" Gabby asked.

A melancholy smile that hinted at some sort of trauma played across his face. Something had happened to Markus.

Gabby couldn't help but go into full emotional-support mode. "Well, you look exactly like every spy I've ever seen on TV. They oughta get you in the field stat so you can be out there making them look good."

That earned her a quiet chuckle. "If you're ever in charge, give me a field assignment. I'll take it."

Gabby made a sympathetic face. "In the meantime, please accept my condolences on being so hot, Markus."

He rolled his eyes, but she earned a real smile. "Stay focused. We're shooting."

Was Markus too hot or too black? The EOD looked like a country club in Cedar Rapids, Iowa, except for Markus and Valentina. It made a person wonder.

He handed her a black handgun. "This is a Glock nine."

The weight of the gun in her hand sent shivers of excitement up her spine. It was a drug, and she wanted to feel like this all the time—important and dangerous. Markus shouldn't be cooped up in this building. He should be out in the field, using all those muscles and skills. Instead, it was going to be her.

"Use your dominant eye, close the other. Line up the sight closest to you between the goalpost sights at the end of the barrel." Markus demonstrated, and she mimicked him.

"Aim for center mass. Don't overthink it, just get a feel for the gun."

Her heart pounded with the feeling of the cold steel in her hands and the image of herself as a secret agent. The EOD had recruited *her*. She was at spy training learning to shoot a gun. Ready to take out the Russian mob. She pulled the trigger and—

She jerked, and the gun fired high. Shocked, she didn't move her finger but squeezed harder. The "pop-pop-pop" of more shots echoed through the room. It was the sound of bullets hitting metal. Gabby looked up to see steam spraying out of a pipe overhead.

"Damn it, Gabby!" Markus looked at the path of her bullets and shook his head. "I've never seen that happen."

An alarm went off, the kind with flashing lights and noise. Her ear protection was the only thing saving her hearing from a wailing siren in a concrete room.

Gabby deflated like a waving Gumby in front of a tire store. She exhaled hard and sank down against the wall. So much for her Super-Agent Gabby Greene fantasy.

Markus took the gun. "Let's stick to Tasers and pepper spray."

Gabby rubbed her temples. This had been a disaster.

After making a call, probably to report that they hadn't been attacked by anything but her incompetence, he made his way back to her. His initial anger had worn off. When he saw her pathetic self, he softened even more. "Don't beat yourself up, Gabby. Sure, you're not ready for a gun or hand-to-hand combat, but no one coming in off the street is. Yesterday, you were in the carpool lane. Today you're at the gun range. We're asking a lot of you."

"How did I even do that?" She pointed at the ceiling.

Markus shook his head. "You anticipated the recoil and jerked. If you overreact to an imagined force or any problem that is not there—you create a problem that didn't exist to begin with." He gestured to the disaster she'd just created.

In her mind, Phil was the bad guy, but Markus's words hit a nerve. She tended to blow things out of proportion. Every time she was worried about something, safety usually, she went straight for the panic button. That time she refused to go on vacation because of a babysitting concern, Phil had gone without her. He sucked, but she wasn't blameless. When she wouldn't let Lucas play outside for a whole summer because she was sure he had a bee allergy, she'd almost lost her mind indoors. She overreacted all the time.

Every overcorrection had led to today, divorced and unemployed, trapped in a minivan with a happy family sticker on the back window.

The alarms still wailing, Valentina walked in. She took in the scene, rolled her eyes, and blew out a breath. There was so much judgment without a single word. She looked at Gabby. "Come with me."

CHAPTER 11

Saturday, late afternoon, EOD headquarters

Gabby scurried to keep up with Valentina as the agent clicked down the sterile EOD hallway in her stilettos. Another reason to be in awe—high heels at work. Gabby assumed that Valentina was taking her to HR, where she would be forced to sign another pack of "take me to Guantánamo" documents before being escorted from the building. You couldn't just show up to a CIA field office and shoot through the ceiling.

"I've never shot a gun before. I didn't mean to—" She didn't say "shoot the EOD full of holes," because it sounded too bad. Plus she needed to stop apologizing.

Valentina still hadn't said a thing in response, so Gabby vomited more words. "It was an accident. Markus said I was too tense." A little more desperate, she said, "Just tell me what's going to happen. Am I going to be court-martialed?" Not that she knew what that was.

"No, Gabby. I am taking you to a salon."

"Don't tease me."

"I wish I was. You are getting a makeover." Valentina looked sincerely annoyed, and some of the pieces clicked together. In

Valentina's eyes, Gabby was the little sister, getting special treatment for no good reason. All Gabby did was screw up and get rewarded—Daddy handed her a job she wasn't qualified for, one-on-one training with Markus, and now some sort of salon appointment. Valentina wanted Daddy to love her more.

"Valentina, I didn't want this. I would rather give *you* the job. I just want *a* job." That was the truth. She would have liked to be a travel agent again. Booking trips for professionals on their lunch hours had been low stress and nonstop vicarious thrills. Vicarious—that's how she liked her thrills.

Her words did nothing because Valentina was shooting sparks. "This job fell in your lap because of the way you look. I, on the other hand, have been working for this my whole life," she said from her lips that looked like they'd been professionally plumped even though it was probably natural.

Gabby blurted out a laugh. Valentina would not be able to see the irony, but this was the first time Gabby had ever gotten special treatment for her looks, at least if you considered hotness.

"What I don't get is what you want. The EOD is my career, my life. Why do you want to do this? For your country?" Valentina drew her perfectly groomed brows together. "You could work at any store in the mall. You could be an actual executive assistant. Throwing yourself in harm's way for the EOD—I don't understand. Why did you agree to this?"

"I don't think you understand how hard it is to get a job after letting your résumé die for fourteen years, after not being that great of a job candidate in the first place." She looked Valentina straight in the eye. "What was I supposed to put on my résumé— 'If I can handle toddlers, I can handle any fools you throw my way?' 'Can get stains out of all your white shirts!'" She shrugged. "No one wants a mom."

Valentina actually laughed. "Just remember, you are only here because a facial recognition algorithm picked you. You have big eyes and a butt chin. That's it."

"Hey, it's called a cleft chin." But the rest was true. She wasn't here because of merit.

"When you're done with this project, you will go back to being a housewife again."

"I'm not even married." The divorce had been final for months now. "I'm a divorced, unemployed mother." Which is why her résumé sucked.

"Okay, well, that's something you might want to think about."

No kidding. Gabby had become a housewife, but it wasn't who she was on the inside. It was a job, a set of duties that she completed every day. Some of those duties she loved, but the laundry did not define her. Taking care of her kids didn't even define her. Still, that was all that other people saw: housewife. If she died today, it was the label that would go on her tombstone.

If she'd learned anything lately, it was that labels matter. She had spent years bending over backwards to help the world see Phil as a professional, to see her kids as clean and happy, to support Kyle's new exploration of her gender and sexuality. She, on the other hand, had let everything and everyone else define her.

She might not know who the new, divorced Gabby was yet, but she would be damned if she died today and her obituary said "housewife." She wasn't even that good at cooking and cleaning to begin with.

Valentina stopped at a door labeled DISGUISES. "We're here."

What a relief! She imagined a room filled with houndstooth cloaks and monocles. She might not be able to shoot a gun, but she could wear a cape and hide behind a corner.

If only she could snap a pic for Justin. A job where she got to play dress-up professionally—he would die of jealousy. A few weeks ago, she and Justin had been watching *Drag Race*, and RuPaul said, "Everything is drag, baby!" Justin had shouted, "Amen, sister!" The moment stuck out to her because it was true. Everyone performs some role in life. Justin's Betty Danger act was an amped-up version of her own performance of a housewife— more lip-synching and less laundry. Her divorce had left her spiraling, partially because of the loss of the relationship and stability but even more because she didn't have a role to play anymore.

All these years, Gabby had been in drag as a housewife. Time to try on another role, something sexier, something she chose, a role that wasn't dependent on a man for context. Hopefully, it wouldn't be written on her tombstone.

The Disguises department was so much more than a musty closet filled with old clothes. It was an actual salon complete with a team of people she could only assume were "fashion agents." Valentina introduced her. "Gabby Greene, this is your makeover team. Today, we are going to turn you into Darcy Dagger."

Gabby lit up on the inside. This was one of those moments. She could hear Bob Barker yelling, "Gabby Greene, come on down!" This was her Showcase Showdown.

Valentina introduced them all. "Tina is on hair. Dante is wardrobe. Ellen is prosthetics." It was going to be like a regular makeover, except instead of turning her into the best version of herself, they were going to turn her into the spitting image of a dead secret agent. Please let there be some overlap.

Tina ushered her into a salon chair. "Ready for red hair?"

"I've never been brave enough for red hair," she said, and she heard someone guffaw, probably Valentina. Red hair was a risk, maybe not as risky as taking on the Russian mob, but it was still a risk. Questions of identity were always serious risks. Walking into battle or walking into high school with a new hair color—similar.

Gabby had never had so many people fuss over her. This might be for a vital mission, but today she was a princess.

"I've been meaning to ask, what about my voice? Do I have a voice coach too?"

Tina shook her head in the negative. "Neither of you have very distinctive voices. Our plan is to make you look so much like her that people will dismiss any tiny difference in speech."

"I guess I can say I have a cold."

"That's right, girl!" Tina said. "You got this. Plus, it sounds like your boss never talks to you anyway."

Tina mixed up a bright red paste in a Tupperware container, slipped on some disposable plastic gloves, and massaged it through Gabby's hair. It was sad, but this was the most physical contact she'd had with anyone for a long time. Things had fizzled with Phil long before he actually up and left.

"The red is going to bring out your eyes."

Gabby didn't care what Tina did to her. She was floating away to a blissed-out state of relaxation.

While her hair marinated, Dante ran some outfits by her, mostly trim black pants and blazers. "I'm going for sleek and professional, but we can add a pop of color with a blouse or a T-shirt."

Valentina huffed. "She needs to stay alive, Dante, not wear fuchsia."

"Not fuchsia. I was thinking emerald green to go with her new hair." He shook his head. "Don't be jealous, Valentina. You know I would love to dress you up too."

She snorted. "I'm going to get some actual work done. Good luck, you guys."

After the door closed behind Valentina, Dante said, "Don't worry. It's not you. Valentina has been having one of those years."

"Oh. Did something happen?"

"Boy trouble" was all he said.

After Tina washed her hair and massaged a ton of deep conditioner in "to tame the frizz," she cut Gabby's hair off at the chin and gave her bangs as blunt as Zooey Deschanel's. "You're lucky that Darcy had a good hairdo."

Wardrobe presented a few more troubles. "You and Darcy are a similar size, but she spent a lot of time in the gym. We're going to Spanx in your curves for this job."

The way he referred to her extra weight as "curves" sent a warm glow through her whole body. She stopped short of hugging him, but barely.

He handed Gabby a tube of fabric that was clearly meant to hold in her stomach and give the impression of an active gym membership. It was the size of a pre-wrapped slice of American cheese.

"Okay. I'll just slip it on." No problem. Gabby was familiar with Spanx. She'd worn them every now and then back when she cared.

But this pair of Spanx maybe not. "Is this the right size?"

"The smaller the better." With a wink, he added, "At least when it comes to Spanx."

Behind a Chinese screen that Gabby recognized from International Rug's Sales floor, confiscated backstock apparently, she slipped out of her yoga pants and started pulling on the stomach shaper. "It's the size of one of my thighs," she called out from behind the screen. "I don't know if I can get in this thing." She couldn't.

"I know it's small, Gabby, but you can do it. Just slip the other leg in."

It was literally fitting snug around one leg. But she needed to get in this Spanx for God and country and to avenge Darcy's death. She got her second foot in and wiggled it up to her thighs. "I might lose ten pounds just getting into this thing."

No one laughed.

"I can't walk," she called from behind the screen. "I've hog-tied myself." She couldn't walk, only jump.

"Keep pulling, Gabby!" They were talking her through it like she was defusing a bomb.

"I might need hazard pay for this. Does the EOD do that?"

She shut her eyes and focused. This was the simplest job they'd given her. She jumped to help yank it over her midsection. In her determination, she knocked over a stool that fell into the folding screen. It all went down. There she was, standing in front of a team of EOD agents with her muffin top spilling over her Spanx. Naked in her truest form.

Dante's and Tina's mouths hung open in horror for a moment. To their credit, they pulled it together and stepped into the battle. They each grabbed an edge and pulled. It took three of them, but they got her into the Spanx. Tina did her makeup, including a wicked cat eye and a neutral lip. Gabby had never looked better. Her eyes popped. Her skin glowed. She was a different person. They would just need some clothing shears to get it off her.

"Just one more piece."

A woman named Ellen introduced her to her new nose. "Darcy had a substantial nose, so we are using a prosthetic. Just a little glue and then we can use makeup to blend it into your skin."

"Okay."

It tickled putting the nose on, the cool glue on her skin. When it dried, she started sneezing.

Ellen stared at the nose like a math problem. Looking more confident than she sounded, she said, "I'm sure the sneezing will stop when you get used to it." Gabby was pretty sure she was allergic to the fake nose, but she hoped Ellen was right.

When all was said and done, they walked her to a full-length mirror. Gabby Greene was gone. She was looking at the face of Darcy Dagger, international woman of mystery.

CHAPTER 12

Saturday, dinnertime, Greene household

Gabby's makeover had her flying high. Who knew she could pull off bangs? She was a superspy in training, a supermom, and she was done up like the actress in *The Queen's Gambit*. She could do it all. To celebrate, she was going to make Justin and the kids dinner. Tonight, it would just be the four of them and one screen, rather than the usual one-to-one ratio of people to screens.

"I'm home!" she called, louder than normal, ready for the kids and Justin to come running and wrap her in hugs like she'd returned after a month away. Of course, for her, it'd been a journey. For them, it had been one day.

Justin walked around the corner in an apron with a spatula and gasped. Slow and deliberate, he said her name like he was lifting a prayer. "Gabriella Greene! Look at you!"

"You like?" She duck-faced and posed like an Insta model.

"I love!" He walked around her, taking in her new pants and blazer and her hair. "Did you get a makeover at work?"

"My boss gave me a gift certificate to a spa as a...signing

bonus." That didn't make sense, but it's not like she could tell him that the EOD gave her a makeover to look like a dead spy.

He narrowed his eyes, clearly suspicious. "What aren't you telling me, girlfriend? Are you working for someone in Hollywood?"

Gabby laughed, savoring her secret. "I wish. It's just some boring financial place. I just knew I needed to look more professional."

Justin smelled a rat. "All this, over lunch? It looks like you had a whole team of beauty professionals working on you…"

Everything was different—hair, makeup, clothes, shoes. They'd even done her nails, and he was right. It had taken hours, longer than her self-defense training.

"Where are the kids?" she asked, changing the subject like she'd been a spy for years.

"Cleaning their rooms and doing homework." He looked smug.

"Did you drug them or beat them?" As a mother, she had no bargaining power, and she knew it. Kyle and Lucas knew that they could never really truly lose her love—at least that's how the internet psychologists explained why they never listened. Bargaining power was important.

He was still eyeing her new look. "Is there a guy?"

"I wish." A vision of too-hot-to-be-a-spy Markus popped into her head. If he was too hot for international espionage, he was definitely too hot for her, but was she rational? No. Her subconscious was just another child she had to deal with, and it seemed like it might be a horny teenage child.

At least she could make dinner. "Justin, I'm making you dinner to thank you for today." She had some frozen pizzas and a bag of salad in the fridge. She could elevate it with some good wine.

Justin flashed her side-eye. "Too late, Gabs. I already made bouillabaisse and a crusty baguette. I had it at this little café in

Marseille on my last trip." He made a chef's kiss. "You're going to love it."

She would. Justin was always going to Italy and raving about tiny restaurants and art museums. All the statues in his yard arrived after he'd visited the Boboli Gardens a few years ago. Gabby hadn't been anywhere except the Pottery Barn in Orange County and an all-inclusive resort in Mexico once.

"Thank you, Justin." She couldn't ask for a more loving and supportive friend.

"And it was good you were out of the way, because I fixed your house."

"Really?" Every time Justin came over, he made the most incredible food, and reorganized everything "the right way."

"You're going to love it."

She wasn't going to be able to find a thing for a month, but she gave him a big hug. "Thank you." The least she could do was break out the best bottle of wine. She had bought it to celebrate her anniversary with Phil. It had been bottled the year they were married.

As she opened the wine, Kyle walked in. For the first time in a while, the look of teenage boredom was wiped clean off her face. "Mom, your hair!"

Gabby struck a pose. "You like it?"

"It's so . . . not you."

"That's the point." She was now Agent Darcy Dagger.

She gave Kyle a hug, and her daughter molded to her side, which melted Gabby's heart. Her big girl was still her baby.

"How was work, Mom?"

"Boring," she lied. "I've never done so much filing in my life."

Justin shook his head. "Ugh. That sounds like a nightmare." Justin didn't do paper.

Gabby sat down heavily on a kitchen stool. "Let me tell you. I definitely need a glass of wine." If they only knew. None of them would believe she spent the day working on hand-to-hand combat and target practice. They would believe that she couldn't shoot and gave her trainer a black eye, though.

Lucas and Kyle looked at their bouillabaisse with confusion. Gabby hadn't introduced them to the finer things in life. It was good for them, though. Everyone would remember this day for a different reason: Gabby shot a hole in the EOD's ceiling, her kids had to eat some weird octopus soup, and Justin reorganized all of her spices.

After dinner, her mom called. At the sight of the number, Gabby's stomach turned. Before she even said hello, her mom said, "Gabby, it's about your grandma."

"Ohmygod." Gabby's stomach dropped as she prepared to hear that her grandma had passed.

"She's been kicked out of her retirement community." Her mom announced it as if it was as bad as death.

"Did she run out of money? What happened?"

Her mom groaned. "Her boyfriend moved in."

Gabby laughed. "Who cares? Can't Grandma have a little fun?"

"Well, Grandma's 'hot piece,' as she called him, moved in and started using all of the services, the cafeteria, laundry, and he's not paying for any of it. Your grandmother wouldn't make him leave, so the home is kicking them both out."

Gabby smiled hard. She only hoped that she'd be getting kicked out of a retirement community at eighty.

"I was thinking…"

Uh-oh. Gabby heard a request coming on. Her mom was going to ask her to take care of her grandma.

"You're home all the time anyway. If we moved Grandma in with you…"

"Mom! I can't. I just got a job."

"I'll pay you. You know it's bad for older people to live alone. I never liked that she was in a retirement community." Gabby hadn't liked that either, but it made more sense for her grandma to move in with her mother.

"Sweetie," her mom said, "your father and I aren't lonely, and we don't need the money."

Gabby hung up with a promise to think about it. Justin poured another glass of wine. "Are you sure you'd have to watch her? I've met Granny. I'm pretty sure she could watch all y'all."

Justin might be right. Granny was a pistol. She'd defected from Moscow long before Gabby was born. Gabby had picked up a few words as a child, mostly things like *der'mo* (shit), *yebat'* (fuck), and *Ya ub'yu tebya* (I will kill you). Granny had been asking Gabby to help her escape from the old folks' home since moving in, as if it was a prison.

A plan formed in her mind. Sienna's mom could take care of the rides to horseback lessons. Her grandma could be here when Lucas got off the bus. This could be the perfect opportunity to learn how to make her grandma's famous piroshki. Grandma was eighty. If the kids didn't hang out with her now, when would they?

Justin asked, "My only request is that she stops trying to set me up."

Gabby laughed at the memory. Her grandma just couldn't believe he was gay, because he was "too handsome."

Granny was going to either turn the house into a three-ring circus or be the answer to her prayers.

Circus or not, Gabby looked around the dinner table with a

new sense of contentment. She was surrounded by love—Justin, her kids—and for the first time, she had something of her own, something that had nothing to do with the family. The EOD needed her. Valentina had said they were only using her for her looks, but there was a flip side to that. She had the leverage. The EOD needed her to complete this mission. And she was getting a job and training in the deal.

With a secret tucked behind her ear like a flower, Gabby didn't feel just happy or renewed, she felt downright sexy. It was good to be mysterious.

Mr. Bubbles hopped up for a pet and made a big show of sniffing her pants. No one else knew a thing, but he could smell the gunpowder on her.

CHAPTER 13

Sunday morning, EOD headquarters

On Sunday morning, Gabby walked into HQ a little less wide-eyed than the day before. Her attitude wasn't all the way down to "just another day at the office," but at least the EOD wasn't giving her nervous diarrhea, verbal or actual. It was a #blessed, diarrhea-free day. Also a gun-free day. After shooting up the range, she was back to the training gym. She needed to focus on escaping sleeper holds because she couldn't be trusted with a weapon. She was as bad as Lucas with a Nerf gun, except a hundred times worse because the bullets were real.

Gabby wanted a gun, though, so she was going to master self-defense and prove herself worthy.

The bone-jarring clatter of dropped free weights echoed through the gym. Markus was the source of the noise: grunting, lifting, dropping a bar of weights that was probably as heavy as a smart car.

"Morning, Markus. I brought smoothies." She was starting today right, with some protein, fruit, and a powdered 3G boost that the teenager at the Jamba made sound like a healthy alternative to meth. She didn't get any additive for Markus because he didn't need any help.

"Thanks." He wiped his palms on his pants and accepted a spinach pineapple concoction.

"I wasn't sure if you were a spinach or strawberry smoothie kinda guy." That was a personality test. Gabby fell squarely in the fruity flavor camp—drinks were red, salads green.

"I like anything I didn't make."

"So I was thinking," she said, "could we just pretend yesterday never happened?"

Markus sucked down a big gulp of smoothie. "You're in training. You try, you fail. That's how it goes."

Gabby pointed at his right eye, which wasn't full-fledged purple but was definitely bruised.

"This?" He gestured to the eye. "Means you did a good job. You scored a point. Go harder on the real bad guys." He held out his hand for a fist bump. "I'm just relieved you didn't break my nose."

"Although they might let you in the field if you weren't so pretty, right?"

He snorted. "Probably. Alice would just say it gave my face character."

It would. He would probably just end up looking more rugged.

Over on the mats, they went through stretches and a routine similar to a kickboxing class she'd taken once or twice. "Not bad," Markus encouraged. "You're getting it."

"As long as the bad guy holds still for at least a minute while I line up my kick and maybe take a second stab if the first doesn't land."

He shook his head. "You have to start somewhere."

Markus was right. She took a deep breath and tried to focus on her goals (get gun). "Embrace the adventure," Gabby said in the same tone Sloane Ellis used. If nothing else, she was following Sloane's advice.

"Divorce is a new beginning." Markus said the next line in the mantra in the same tone Sloane used.

Gabby stopped short. "Sloane Ellis? Have you been reading her book too?"

With a sad smile, he said, "Anything to get through a breakup, right?"

Gabby couldn't imagine Markus getting divorced. He looked so perfect, practically too hot for the apps. How would he choose among all the women who swiped right on him?

"Valentina and I broke up last year. I'm fine now, but it took a while."

"As in *Valentina*?"

"Yep. Work got in the way." He released a heavy sigh. "Everyone in this place is divorced. High stress, long hours. It wears on relationships."

Gabby was trying to wrap her mind around Markus and Valentina. That explained the weird tension in the room when she was with both of them. Agent Strong gave Gabby a job she hadn't earned and Valentina's ex-husband. Even if Valentina didn't want him anymore, that had to sting.

"Do you have kids?" she asked, although she already knew the answer. Valentina had been adamant that kids were not compatible with the EOD.

"Just about a hundred nieces and nephews."

"I have two kids."

He smiled. "Gabby, I know what you ate for breakfast yesterday. I've been briefed."

"Really?" It made sense, but it didn't. She was barely interesting enough for neighborhood gossip normally, and here she was, a hot topic at the EOD.

"I wouldn't have guessed you have kids. You look good." The way he said "good" wasn't the way a woman would say it. It sounded like she looked *good*, aka damn fine.

Champagne bubbles danced in her insides, and heat crept up her cheeks. A compliment hadn't hit Gabby like that in a long time. "I mean, I'm not too pretty for spying, but thanks."

He threw back his head and let out a laugh.

Gabby said, "I still don't get that. Hot spies are more effective, right?"

"You'd think so, seducing everyone into spilling their secrets." He held up his hands, looking confounded.

"That won't be me. I'm going to make coffee and lay low."

Markus dragged them back to the mission. "Speaking of that, did you memorize the names and faces on those sheets? If you're fully prepared, you can get in and out of this mission quickly."

"Yep." Names and faces were easy for Gabby. She'd fallen asleep looking at Orlov's face the last two nights. What she was really worried about was whether the EOD was prepared. She asked, "Have you figured out who blew Darcy's cover yet?"

Markus shook his head no. "We're still working on it." Without warning, he put her in a sleeper hold, and this time not in slow motion. Gabby was ready. She stomped on his foot lightly, elbowed him, and tossed her head back.

"You got it!" he said.

"I didn't hurt you, did I?" The last thing she wanted was to blacken both his eyes.

"Nope. I'm just fine."

With a big exhale of relief, she said, "That only took me a day longer than it should have."

Markus held up his hand. "Gabby, don't. You are extremely brave. You're walking into a dangerous situation with almost no training. Not many people would take this job. You are going to do great on this mission. I'm sure of it." He was standing with a straight back, looking into her eyes and speaking in the most earnest tone she'd ever heard.

Could this be real? It certainly didn't feel real, except for the parts of the day where she had to line up childcare.

"I don't think anyone has ever believed in me before," she said. It was true. Phil hadn't. Her parents had always seemed skeptical that she could make anything happen. Really, she'd never believed in herself.

Markus looked at her with an intensity that made her slightly uncomfortable. "We're partners on this mission. Until you believe in yourself, I'll believe in you enough for both of us. By the time this is over, you'll see in yourself what I see in you."

Nothing could have stunned her into silence more effectively than that. To dissipate the awkwardness and break the silence, Gabby said, "Let's practice one more time." If there was anything harder than hand-to-hand combat, it was accepting compliments.

This time, she kicked him in the foot and twisted around in his grip without breaking free. It was subpar self-defense.

Markus shrugged. "If all else fails, kick them in the balls."

Before she left for the day, Markus said, "When you wake up in the morning, there will be a car in your driveway. It's the one Darcy drove to eStocks. We want to keep things consistent."

Gabby brightened at the idea of a new car, and Markus said, "Don't get too excited. It's nothing sexy."

"Have you seen my van?" Markus might need a reality check.

"You're going to need this." He handed her an iPhone. "This is Camille Walker's phone. When you get into the office, you're going to be friendly with everyone, but remember, there are no friends in espionage."

In the parking lot, she checked the messages.

There were texts from people in the office: Fran, Carmen, Kramer. Happy hour times and lunch orders, nothing interesting.

In the Notes app, she found something a bit juicier.

> *Fran: Ex got her the job. Hung up on some loser, possibly the ex.*
> *Carmen: Hates Kramer.*
> *Kramer: Enough with the cars already.*

Gabby frowned at Darcy's observations. This wasn't the kind of intel that would get a woman killed. Darcy, it seemed, hadn't seen the danger coming until it was too late. The only advantage Gabby had was that she was already scared out of her mind. She might not know how to take down an assailant, but there was a good chance she'd see him coming.

CHAPTER 14

Monday morning, Greene household

It was Monday morning and Gabby's first day on the job as an undercover spy after three days of training. The EOD made it sound like the easiest thing since sliced bread. It was like the opposite of the Army's "Be all you can be!" tagline. The EOD was like, "Be a spy, anyone can do it!"

Make coffee, eavesdrop, enjoy her new red hair—that's all she had to do. Still, Gabby was about to crawl out of her skin from nerves. It was bad enough starting a new job, but a job where the last woman was killed was on another level entirely. She'd watched a special about how they keep the cows calm and happy on their way into the chute to be slaughtered. With every "you got this, girl" or compliment for her pretty red hair, she couldn't help feeling that everyone was petting her on her way down the cattle chute.

Gabby shoved a water bottle in Lucas's backpack and handed Kyle an overdue library book. "Don't forget to turn this in today, and remember, Sienna's mom is picking you up. I won't be home until dinner so Dad is going to—" She stopped short of saying "babysit." That was not the word to use when a parent watched their own child, but that's how it felt.

"Mom, you told me like twenty times." Kyle made a face like she just bit into something bad as she grabbed a juice glass from the cabinet, ignoring the one she'd used for milk two minutes ago.

How many glasses could one person use? It wasn't the time, but seriously, this was getting to be a problem. If Gabby was going to be a spy, Kyle had to start reusing a water glass here and there.

"It's fine, Mom. Seriously, no big deal." Nothing like an ungrateful teenager to make you feel worthwhile.

"Okay. Just making sure," Gabby said. Asking Phil for help rankled. Why couldn't she just smugly walk past him, successful and radiant, a paragon of virtue and sexiness?

Like Gabby was a fifteen-year-old skateboarder, Kyle said, "Chill, dude."

Dude—the word bounced off Gabby's forehead like a Nerf bullet. "I'm not a dude, Kyle. I am your mother."

"Just go to work, Mom. It's fine. We'll see you tonight." Kyle drank half her glass of juice, setting it on the counter nowhere near the sink. She slung her backpack over her shoulder and called for Lucas.

Elsa was going to be her guiding light. Let it go, Let it go...and she forgot the rest of the lyrics. At one point, Kyle had watched that movie on the daily and had worn an ice blue gown with a cape everywhere. Gabby hadn't thought she'd be able to forget that song if she tried. Now she could barely imagine Kyle that small.

The kids, that's all she'd had for fourteen years. Elsa gowns, snacks, playdates—that was literally the fabric of her life. Everyone was so chill about her going back to work, acting like all she did was trivial stuff that anyone with two thumbs and an IQ of seventy could accomplish. She wanted to hang on to her babies and the duties that defined her, even if she hated half of them.

But Gabby had a fake nose to glue on, so there was no time to be moody about a life transition, even if it was major. Before the bus was out of sight, she ran to the bathroom and pulled out the pouch with the fake nose and silicone glue. The makeup person had told her it was easy. Just clean your face with some astringent. Clean the prosthetic, apply a thin layer of glue, hit it with the hair dryer, and voilà! She'd done it three times at the office, no problem.

Her hands shaking, Gabby wiped her nose with a cotton ball and smeared on the glue. A little extra adhesion couldn't hurt. Just like the time she'd wallpapered the laundry room on her own, and damn if that didn't look fresh and cheerful. She stuck the nose on and hit it with the blow dryer. If only she put this much effort into her hair regularly, she would be a different woman.

Camille Walker's gray sedan waited for her in the garage just as Markus had promised. In a blazer, driving a clean car—no wrappers or broken toys on the floor, no stick figure family on the back window—she was an undercover agent for the EOD. She was Darcy Dagger pretending to be Camille Walker. Really, it was a lot to remember.

She searched Spotify for a pump-up spy music playlist. The 007 theme song blasted through the speakers as she headed toward eStocks. It was a little much, but once she hit the freeway, there was no going back. Messing with her Spotify choices while driving in LA traffic was not a risk she was willing to take. A half hour later, she pulled into the eStocks parking lot and grabbed a ticket from the parking meter, the London Symphony Orchestra blasting "Goldfinger" at volumes that seemed normal at eighty miles per hour.

She tucked her earpiece in.

Before she realized he was there, Markus started laughing. "What is that you're listening to?"

"Uh ... I was trying to get pumped up?"

"Slow your roll, Jane Bond," he said, voice dry as a generic-brand Keebler cracker, because why pay for brand-name?

At least he couldn't see her blushing, because her cheeks were flaming.

"You don't need pumping up, Agent Greene. You got this. All you need to do is walk in, make coffee, take notes, answer the phone. You could do that in your sleep."

Could she, though? She itched around the edge of her nose. "Is this fake nose supposed to be itchy?"

"Just relax. You're gonna be fine."

He was probably right. It was all in her head, nervous fixation. Like when she was in a plane and spent the entire time imagining crashing to the ground in a fiery blaze and double-checking where the life vests were located, as if they would help. Today that was her nose. The plane never crashed, and her nose was fine. As she walked through the parking lot, she murmured, "You can do this, Gabby!"

Markus cleared his throat on the other end.

"I was going to remind you not to talk to me in front of people, but I guess, don't talk to yourself either."

"Gotcha." She'd spent the last couple of years narrating her day to Mr. Bubbles like he was listening. At the moment, she would give anything to be safe at home with her dog, nothing to worry about but some dirty dishes and kid pickups.

eStocks was the kind of place that Gabby would drive by and never think twice about. Glass doors with a tasteful sign announcing its very boring name. Inside, a receptionist sat behind a sleek desk. A small lobby had black leather chairs and artwork that looked like it came from a bin labeled "artwork."

It was the kind of place that would activate Justin's claustrophobia. Last year, they'd had drinks at Shelly's house, and he had started breathing too shallow and sweating. "Justin, are you okay?" she had asked.

"No." He had fanned his face.

She had been ready to call 911, sure he was having a heart attack.

"I just need some air."

Turns out, he had felt "trapped by the décor." Like his spirit was literally being crushed. She understood that it wasn't just the bad art. It was the implied expectation that he fit himself into the box with it.

Justin couldn't be undercover at eStocks. He wasn't hardy enough. Gabby could handle bad wall art and a badly behaved finance bro. Hell, she'd been married to one.

She squared her shoulders, while casually walking past the receptionist desk. Carmen Delgado, twenty-five, one kid, loved clubbing. "Hi, Carmen."

"Camille, you're back!"

She smiled involuntarily. Her disguise had worked.

"That is Carmen Delgado," Markus whispered into her ear. "It was her birthday last weekend."

Gabby already knew. "How does it feel to be twenty-five?" Gabby ribbed.

"Ugh!" Carmen groaned and pointed to a half-empty gallon of Gatorade. With a pouty face, she announced, "I'm too old to drink now."

Gabby laughed and said, "I think you have a few years of carousing left in you." It was so funny when people who had just become adults complained about aging. Her granny could drink Carmen under the table any day.

"Your desk is down the hall and to the left. Bathrooms are on the other side of the lobby." The bathrooms were marked, but it was cute how Markus wasn't leaving any detail to chance. He couldn't have her breaking her cover by wandering into a coat closet like it was the conference room.

The offices were floor-to-ceiling glass. The design aesthetic screamed, "Look at our hands. We're not stealing anything." Gabby knew better.

James, the tech guy, spied her. "You're back. Feeling better?"

"Yep. Thanks for asking."

"That is James, tech support, likes to go—"

Before Markus finished his directions, Gabby said, "How was the golfing this weekend? Did your wife let you get out on the course?"

He laughed. "You know how it goes. I managed a couple holes."

"Great work, Gabby," Markus said. "You're killing it."

Martial arts might not be her strong suit, but Gabby understood people. She knew everyone and their dirty secrets, all freely given. It wasn't like she'd asked for it, but she had the kind of face that people just opened up to. She was harmless.

Camille Walker's desk was perfectly clean and organized except for a dancing hula girl, the kind you put on your dashboard.

She was affixed DIY-style to a piece of cardboard that read BEST DRESSED! Gabby set her in motion.

Markus must have been watching through her brooch camera. Emotionless, he said, "She won that the day she died."

Gabby fixated on the cheery plastic statue, its hips swiveling. Nine days ago, Darcy had been "best dressed" employee at eStocks. Now...Gabby shut her eyes and tried to rein in her anxiety. Robotically, she put her purse in a file drawer and smoothed her hands over the surface. Computer, stapler, pens— it looked mundane, a normal office with normal things, but her nose itched and Markus was in her ear and Darcy's prize from the day she died stared back at her, its plastic gaze fixed and dilated, its dancing slowly coming to a stop.

Darcy had died on this job a little more than a week ago. Gabby had been so busy worrying about everything else that she almost forgot her life was in danger.

Before she could completely freak out, which is where she was headed, a woman clomped over in a pair of clogs that were as noisy as they were good for her posture. It was Fran, a woman who looked like her name. Alongside Fran's biographical data in the files (thirty-five, degree in finance from Sacramento State, one child), there were margin notes, presumably made by Darcy: "Dwight Schrute. Why does she want to hang out?"

"Hi, Fran," Gabby said.

Fran was the human version of the boxed-in décor that made Justin claustrophobic—aggressively out of style in pleated khaki pants and a shirt buttoned all the way up.

Fran flashed a smile that didn't go all the way to her eyes, and Gabby's spidey sense prickled. "Did you have a nice break?" Fran asked, passive aggression at ten out of ten. "I'm glad you're back. I've been doing your job *and* mine while you were gone."

Every office needed a Dwight Schrute.

"Well, I appreciate it. I wasn't feeling well at all."

As they were talking, George Kramer burst into the hallway with all sorts of "I'm busy and important" energy. If Gabby didn't already know he was money laundering for the Russian Mafia, she would have considered him a silver fox with his angular features and graying hair. He was the guy you'd swipe right on and regret it ten years later when the FBI raided your home on the golf course.

Without really looking at Gabby, he said, "I'm going to be on calls all afternoon. Keep the coffee coming."

Fran scrutinized her. "You remember how he likes his coffee?"

"Fran, I haven't been gone that long," Gabby said in a sassy tone. She hurried to the office kitchen. In her ear, Markus explained, "Cream and one raw sugar."

Casually, she opened up a cabinet. Stacks of plain, white dishes stared back at her. Someone cleared their throat behind her.

"Hey, Fran." Gabby smiled. "I didn't see you."

Fran opened the correct cabinet and handed Gabby a mug. "Is this what you were looking for?"

Gabby realized she was holding her breath. That was probably a natural reaction to Fran. The woman was insufferable.

"Thanks, Fran. I appreciate the help," she said. The thank-you was meant to be a polite signal that the conversation was over. Fran didn't take the hint.

"You know, there is something different about you." Fran stood, blocking the door while Gabby waited to pass.

Gabby smiled. "I had my hair done this week."

Fran frowned. "Nope. That's not it."

Gabby fought the impulse to curl up and hide like a small forest creature and straightened her posture. With a laugh, she said, "Maybe you've never seen me rested."

Disarmed, Fran laughed as she let her pass. "I've never seen myself rested."

Markus whistled. "Daaamn, girl. You handled that like a pro."

Fran had been unpleasant, but Gabby wasn't born yesterday. Any given day, parent pickup could be one hundred times worse. "Kyle—that's an interesting name for a girl…" "That's so brave of you to let your kids ride horses. I could never risk their safety like that." "Being a stay-at-home mom must be so relaxing! Do you go to the spa all the time?"

If she could handle that gauntlet, she could handle anything. She flipped her red hair and walked to George Kramer's office like she meant business.

Kramer was sitting at his desk scowling at a bank of screens. Even though she could see him through his glass office walls, she knocked.

At his nod, she pushed the door open just enough for her to squeeze through with a hip while her hands were full. Like when kids trip over their newly grown feet, Gabby didn't quite know the dimensions of her new nose, and it brushed the door. To her horror, the prosthetic nose fell off her face and straight into the bottom of Kramer's boiling hot coffee.

The makeup person's advice on the glue echoed in her ears— "less is more." Why was that always such a hard lesson to learn?

While she stood, paralyzed with fear, Kramer barked out rapid-fire commands. "If you don't stick it out, you're gonna lose big-time. Don't be an idiot." Without even looking up, he reached for his coffee and flicked his fingers at her.

Her reflexes weren't fast enough, and he grabbed the mug. Without looking, he took a swig.

"Mr. . . . Mr. Kramer," Gabby stuttered. After a couple of fast, shallow breaths, she said, a little louder, "I think that coffee needs another stir."

He completely ignored her and continued talking animatedly about money, gesturing with his hands while still holding the cup. "The stock price is at an all-time high. You'd be a fucking idiot to sell now. Id-ee-ot!" He emphasized each syllable with his hand, and coffee sloshed up to the rim.

Thank god she'd used the deepest cup in the kitchen. Still. She had about one minute to get the cup back before he sucked the liquid down to nose level. Then it was game over.

She'd never been in a sport, but this must be like the very end of a football game when the team that was about to win lost the ball. Phil always jumped out of his chair and started screaming. Finally, she felt him. She needed that nose back like the guy in the purple needed the ball back from the guy in green.

Kramer shooed her away. "Go get me one of those donuts, would you?"

She made one last reach for his cup, but he pulled it back. "Donut."

Outside his door, she ran-walked to the kitchen and slammed the door shut. "Markus, can you hear me?"

"Yes. What's the status of the nose?"

"It's in his coffee."

She could hear the effort it took for him to remain calm. "You have the get the nose back, or the entire operation will be compromised. Your cover will be blown."

Her heart racing and all of her senses on high alert, she grabbed the entire coffeepot, a handful of sugars, and the requested donut. Her plan: commandeer the cup for a refill. Like her life depended on it, which it might, she speed walked down the hall to Kramer's office. Without knocking, she pushed through the door, praying that he hadn't already found the nose.

Inside his office, Kramer was still yelling into the phone, drinking coffee, her fake nose in the bottom like a gross boba pearl. Gabby wouldn't even let her kids drink out of plastic cups because of the chemicals.

"Baker, you have to learn to pay attention to details. Put your ear to the ground. Stay ahead of the trends. How do you think I've made my way? Paying attention." He swigged more coffee. "Do you watch the news every morning? More than one channel? You can't trust one source. You have to be smarter than everyone."

Gabby moused toward him. "Mr. Kramer, let me get you a refill."

This time he heard her and held out the coffee cup.

She breathed out a sigh of relief. Crisis averted!

Except he had seen her with her normal nose, not that he had said anything.

Apparently, Mr. Paying Attention had missed that detail. If she had to guess, Kramer was one of those guys who put women in two categories: those too pretty to trust with anything besides his dick and those not worthy of notice.

Lucky for her, at least today, Gabby was squarely in camp number two: not worthy of notice. With her back to Kramer and facing away from the prying eyes of people like Fran, she fished the nose out of the coffee cup with a spoon. Her heart sank when she saw that it had melted into a blob. It looked exactly like the Oobleck she'd made with the kids: a mixture of cornstarch, water, and food coloring. Lucas had fallen asleep on a glob, and she'd had to cut it out of his hair.

She palmed the nose, refilled the coffee cup, and added a sugar. She just needed to keep her cool. At least he wouldn't find a melted prosthetic nose in his coffee.

Defeated, she handed him the cup and he took long sip. "Just how I like it," he said. "That Jan kept getting it wrong." He scowled at the name.

"Fran," Gabby corrected him.

For the first time that day, Gabby felt some solidarity with the woman. Fran might be the worst, but she was playing a losing game sucking up to Kramer. The man couldn't even be bothered to learn her name.

"Sit down," he commanded, and Gabby took a seat in one of the chairs across from his desk.

He looked directly at her. His eyes didn't linger on her face. He didn't do a double take. Nothing. He took no notice of the nose. Instead, he said, "This week, your top priority should be party planning."

"Party?"

Kramer looked over across the desk. "One of our most important clients is flying in. Instead of taking him out to dinner, I want a cocktail party with all of our investors on Saturday." His phone flashed with a notification. His wallpaper was a picture of himself posing with a red sports car.

"You mean *next* Saturday?" That didn't even give her two weeks. "That's hardly any time."

"It's not rocket science. Just get all the investors in one room, add liquor, and there you have it."

If he were throwing a frat party.

"Do you have a venue in mind?" she asked. What kind of party was this supposed to be? How fancy? She had literally zero clue.

He took a giant bite of donut. Talking with his mouth full, he said, "Get Jan or what's-her-face to help you if you must. I want to impress the shit out of these guys. They need to go home thinking eStocks is the biggest game in town."

"Could we possibly throw this at the end of the month?"

"You've been at home resting for a week. Kick it into gear, Camille."

"What about the guest list? Do you have a list of major investors you want me to invite? I'll need to know how many people are coming and who to send invites to."

"Figure it out. This is what I hired you for. I'm not going to do your job for you."

She bit the inside of her cheek. Kramer must have sent the email to Darcy while she was busy being dead.

"Please. I want to get right on it."

With an expelled breath and annoyed look, he hit a few buttons on his keyboard. "I don't know how you don't know this, but there's a list of our high-priority investors. Pick it up from the printer."

She started to thank him, but he'd already swiveled his chair to face his bank of monitors.

On the way out of his office, she picked up a piece of paper as it slid out of the printer, literally hot off the press. She scanned the still-warm piece of paper. One name jumped out at her.

Sergei Orlov. Bingo.

CHAPTER 15

Monday, midmorning, eStocks Enterprises

Gabby hurried down the hall to the bathroom, thankfully empty. Like the spy she was, she checked under the stall doors for feet before she started talking to Markus. Sure she was alone, she said, "Markus, can you hear me?"

"I'm here."

She gripped the counter and leaned in close to the mirror for a blackhead-level inspection, and peeled a line of silicone glue off her nose like it was one of those peel-off masks designed to clean your pores. They were probably just glue too.

"Well, you look great, just not like Darcy."

Gabby jumped back. For just a second, she'd forgotten he could see everything. This was a level of closeness she'd didn't typically engage in with anyone other than her kids. She and Phil hadn't been one of those couples who peed with the door open.

After the shock of sharing her pores with him, it hit her—Markus had said that she looked "great." She went all gooey and smiled into the mirror like he'd just hit on her.

"Can you reapply the nose?" Markus asked, ignoring her dopey smile.

Still stuck on the fact that she looked "great," she didn't answer. Sure, it was the kind of word that a teacher wrote on top of a kid's spelling homework, but it did something to her. He was waking her up, reminding her she was a woman, not just a mom.

"Can you reapply the nose?" Markus repeated.

"Oh, uh . . . no." She pulled a wadded-up silicone ball out of her pocket. "It melted in the coffee."

"Damn. That's done."

She could hear him thinking while she cleaned tiny bits of glue off her nose.

"I'll have them make another prosthetic for you and deliver it before anyone else sees you without the nose."

"Markus, I can't stay in the bathroom all morning." Fran would have a conniption. Kramer would fire her. "We might be okay. Kramer already saw me. He didn't seem to notice."

"Ugh," he groaned. "What about everyone else?"

She didn't have an answer.

"Okay, I'm sending a message to the prosthetics people. We'll see how long it'll take."

Even driving it over would take half an hour, and that was without remaking it. There was no way.

"What about the guest list?" Markus asked.

"Sergei Orlov's on the list." Thinking aloud, Gabby said, "Is he flying in all the way from Russia?" What kind of party did a person fly halfway across the world for?

"This is big, Gabby."

"So what, you're going to catch him red-handed racketeering?" Racketeering—it still sounded like an obscure Olympic event to her, like they would need a special location and racketeering equipment, including kneepads and a helmet.

"It's just like everything else. The real business happens over cocktails. This party is a big break."

She'd never arranged a corporate party before. She hadn't even attended one in recent memory. Early on in her marriage, she would do her hair, put on a cocktail dress, and play the part of a wife. It had been a while.

So many questions: How many mini-quiches? What about the vegans? Were as many adults allergic to nuts as kids? Was this a Costco or a catering situation? If a guy was flying in from Russia, probably catering.

The only parties she'd been to recently were kids' birthday parties. Sheet cakes and pizza in the Sky Zone party room. In fact, she'd thrown so many Sky Zone birthdays that she had a freebie coming up.

Markus jogged her back to the present. "This is our chance for hard proof of money laundering."

How the hell was she going to throw a party for adults? And she only had a week and a half to do it. This is what the Sky Zone party package was for—moments like this when you didn't want to take care of the details on your own.

"Gabby, just take—" Markus fizzed out before he could finish his sentence. She wiggled a finger in her ear.

"Markus, I can't hear you," she said.

It was the bathroom. The reception was so much worse in here than it was at her desk, not that she could talk at her desk privately.

"I said—" Markus said before going out again.

"Markus," she said, wiggling a finger in her ear again. Before she had time to freak out even more, the door to the bathroom opened. Gabby jumped liked she'd just been caught tweezing chin hairs, not that she had any. Instinctively she went to wave at Fran, all "hey, nothing to see here, girl" complete with a big fake smile.

When she pulled her finger out of her ear to wave, she snagged the earpiece. In slow motion, she watched her lifeline to Markus sail through the air toward the sink, skitter around the edge and...

She stepped toward the bowl and stared down the drain.

"Camille?" Fran said.

Frantically, she felt around the sink, even though she could see it wasn't there. The earpiece was gone. Markus was down the drain. She was alone.

"Camille, I've been looking for you."

"What?" Gabby managed to pull her attention from the drain toward Fran. "What do you need?"

"Do you need some help? It seems like you're having a little trouble this morning."

"Um..." Gabby could barely remember anything besides her immediate disaster—she was completely alone on her first day of undercover work. Not that Fran could help her with that.

"I'm fine." She touched her nose. Fran was going to notice, and her cover would be blown.

"You know how Kramer is," Fran said. "He wants the best from everyone all the time."

Gabby nodded. So did the EOD. Wearing a fake nose was as bad as trying to keep her bra stuffed as a preteen, except this time it wasn't just her dignity at stake.

"I'd be happy to help with whatever he needs from you. Just for today."

"Um, just some party stuff." Gabby took a breath and talked herself down. This was not middle school. She just lost a fake nose and earpiece. All was not lost—yet.

"A party?" Fran perked up. "Please say I can help!" Fran looked genuinely thrilled. "What are you thinking for entertainment? We could get that jazz trio, you know the one that plays for open mic night at happy hour across the street. Actually, we could do a whole jazz theme." She looked up at Gabby expectantly.

"That's better than anything I've thought of yet, unless everyone is into Sky Zone." Gabby laughed, but Fran didn't join in.

"Sky Zone? Is that like a private jet thing?"

Fran must be thinking of the Delta Sky Club lounge, and not the trampoline park slash arcade filled with screaming ten-year-olds, a place you wanted to wear socks so you didn't get foot fungus.

"That could work. Maybe we could host it out at that restaurant at the private airport. Private jets would be a great theme. That's what we're all shooting for, right?" Fran wagged a finger at her. "And I thought you weren't on your game today."

What kind of person with a child had never heard of Sky Zone?

Fran started to say something else but stopped and frowned at Gabby.

Gabby's heart dropped to her stomach. She'd been found out. It was all over.

With a startled gasp, Fran covered her mouth.

At least if it all went to hell now, she could just go home. A glance at her watch showed she'd be able to pick up the kids. She could text Sienna's mom and Phil and say she didn't need them. Spying just hadn't worked out, which really wasn't a big surprise.

With a self-satisfied smile, Fran announced, "I know what's different."

Gabby waited for Fran to unmask her like the *Scooby-Doo* gang.

You aren't Camille. You are an imposter from the Elite Operatives Department impersonating Darcy Dagger!

"You've had a nose job," Fran exclaimed. "I don't know why it took me this long to notice."

A high-pitched laugh escaped Gabby like air leaking from a balloon. "You got it, Fran."

Five minutes later, she sat down at her desk and wrung her hands. She had no earpiece and Kramer had just asked her to make an Excel spreadsheet.

Her phone dinged with a text from Markus. R u ok?

No. They asked me to make a spreadsheet.

Lol. But r u safe?

Yes.

What about the prosthetic?

Problem solved. Told Fran I had a nose job.

Really?

I'm fine. More worried about the spreadsheet atm.

Lol. Hang tight.

Gabby googled "how to make an Excel spreadsheet" on her phone. The short instructions weren't enough. She needed a full-on YouTube tutorial, and that was just for starters. She probably needed to go back to college. Because watching a tutorial on how to open a spreadsheet would give away that she didn't know what the hell she was doing, she secreted herself away in a bathroom stall to watch an Australian accountant explain what a spreadsheet was while she took notes on a legal pad balanced on her knee. This was not how she imagined the life of a secret agent.

"There are columns running vertically and rows running horizontally," the expert explained in a loud and clear voice. Gabby couldn't pass statistics in college. It was probably a mental block, but she probably wasn't going to overcome it today.

"Um, are you okay in there?" an amused voice called from another stall.

"Oh, sorry!" Gabby hit PAUSE as fast as if she'd just been caught watching porn at her desk. "I didn't realize anyone else was in here." She breezed out of the stall and tried to act normal, like she watched spreadsheet tutorials on the toilet all the time.

Carmen, who worked the front desk, cut her eyes toward Gabby while reapplying some hot pink lipstick. She didn't have to ask anything because the questions were written all over her face.

Gabby, the queen of dumb explanations, started explaining herself. "I was, ah, just brushing up on some Excel."

"On the toilet?" Carmen couldn't hold her laughter in any longer. "Girl, are you okay?"

Gabby started to answer but all she could come up with was "Ehhhhh," so she added on some truth. "Eh, it's just a rough first day back. I had quite the weekend too." An EOD crash course after fourteen years of SAHM life was a lot.

Carmen leaned back and looked at Gabby like she was seeing her in a new light. "I didn't know you partied like that, girl!"

"If you think partying takes a toll at twenty-five, try thirty-eight. I can barely remember who I am or what I'm doing here." The second true thing she'd said all day.

"I got you," Carmen said. "I can't have you over there taking a spreadshit on your first day back." She laughed at her own stupid wordplay.

Gabby felt her cheeks go red. "I'm *soooo* embarrassed."

"Are you kidding? My whole first six months at this place was a spreadshit. Kramer just didn't notice because he never gets up from his desk."

Fifteen minutes later, Gabby was at Carmen's desk getting a live Excel tutorial while they chugged Gatorade and snacked on Chicago-mix style popcorn, Carmen's recipe for a hangover. "Something crunchy for the munchies and the real medicine."

"Thanks, girl!" Gabby said. "You saved my behind today."

"Hos before bros." Carmen gave her a scrutinizing look and said, "Is it just me or was that spreadsheet tutorial practically a makeover? I gave you an instructional glow up."

"It's either that or the nose job I had last week," Gabby said with a wink in her voice.

Carmen laughed at her own silly assumption. "Your nose looks fab. Good for you."

The advantage of not having an earpiece was that Gabby could almost convince herself she was an actual executive assistant instead of an undercover spy in mortal danger. No big deal. She was just doing some light party planning and having snacks with Carmen.

When the spreadsheet was almost done, Fran bustled over.

Even at walking pace, she looked like she was in a hurry. And why didn't her clothes have a single wrinkle at almost the end of the day? Gabby squashed those feelings. Women spent too much time tearing each other down and not enough time building each other up. Like Carmen said, "Hos before bros." They were all working for a money-laundering finance bro.

All business, Fran said, "Camille, do you know whose blueberry yogurt is in the fridge? There isn't a name on it?"

"Um…"

Before Fran could give her the third degree about the unmarked yogurt, her phone rang with an incoming call from someone named "Waldorf," and she bustled away.

"Is her boyfriend named Waldorf?" Gabby asked. Fran and Waldorf—that just didn't roll off the tongue.

"Either that or she lives at the Waldorf Astoria." Carmen giggled.

At the end of the day, Gabby slumped into the driver's seat of her car, sucked dry from pretending to know what she was doing all day and talking to a whole office of new people. It wasn't the worst first day she'd ever had, though. Waiting tables at Chili's took that prize.

CHAPTER 16

Monday evening, Greene household

Gabby pulled into the garage and parked in front of a steel shelf with boxes of Christmas ornaments, tennis rackets they never used, and her grandmother's dishes. She'd never been so glad to see her old, useless crap. She was home safe. No more pretending and no more wondering what everyone thought of her nose or whether she was talking to a killer—not that anyone at eStocks seemed like a killer. They seemed like standard office people: an annoying brownnoser, a hungover twentysomething, and a couple of guys who golfed.

With a deep, cleansing breath, she tried to wipe eStocks from her mind. Sure, the kids had been all "we don't care about you getting a job, Mom" this morning, but they probably missed her this afternoon. What wouldn't she give to be picked up by someone who brought her a snack and asked how her day was?

"Kids, I'm home!" Gabby called as she came through the garage door and chucked her shoes into a pile with the rest of them. Their backpacks were tossed carelessly in the hallway—meaning no one had touched their homework yet. "Kyle, Lucas, where are you?" she called, eagerly awaiting their smiling faces and hugs.

"I'm a vegetarian, Dad!" came a strident protest from the kitchen. Yikes.

"I'm not making steak or anything," Phil said.

"Chicken. Is. Meat."

"Come on, Kyle. It's not like chickens have personalities."

"You don't have a personality, Dad."

Gabby stepped tentatively into the kitchen and waved. "I'm home!" She smiled like she hadn't heard Kyle suggest Phil had no more personality than a chicken.

At the moment, Phil looked like he could reheat chicken with the look on his face alone.

She smiled and said, "Thanks again for taking care of dinner."

Kyle had been flirting with going vegetarian for a while, her commitment usually related to how recently she'd listened to her favorite vegetarian TikToker or if Gabby was serving meat loaf for dinner. She knew her meat loaf sucked. It's just that she had subscribed to HelloFresh for a while, and the mini–meat loaf with garlic mash recipe was so good. Everyone gobbled it up, and she'd been trying to re-create that night ever since. Why couldn't she make it on her own?

"Dad"—Kyle said his name like he'd committed a crime—"I am a vegetarian. I am fourteen years old. You cannot make me eat chicken." She looked at Gabby for backup. "Right, Mom? You said I should live my truth."

On the one hand, she had left the chicken for Phil to heat up. If they didn't eat it, she was going to be the one stuck coming up with something else. On the other hand, it was nice to watch Phil struggle through dinner. "Um..."

Kyle put her hands on her hips and stared both her parents

down. "The carbon costs of eating meat are going to destroy this planet."

Phil fired back, "If that's your only problem, then let's buy some carbon credits and eat the damn chicken. You can offset anything."

"Only if you're rich."

"What do you want me to do then, offset my dinner and give a homeless guy twenty bucks?"

"That would be better." A little softer, Kyle said, "Dad, can you just bring Dr. Piggie back?"

Fucking Phil. Gabby rubbed her temples. This was too much after spending a day trying to convince money launderers she was Camille Walker. Hell, she had learned to use Excel today. That had required equations and math, neither skills that Markus had advertised.

"What's Lucas doing?" she asked Phil.

"Playing a game, I don't know. Not complaining about dinner at least."

Gabby sighed. That didn't sound promising. Lucas was not the kind of kid you could leave to his own devices for long periods of time. You'd think Phil would know that by now.

With a weight on her chest, she walked toward the living room. "Lukie, where are you??"

An ominously gleeful squeal sounded.

Sure enough, Gabby stepped into the living room to find Lucas and Mr. Bubbles covered in paint. She'd left the house for one day, and her children and bichon had gone feral. All she wanted to do was go undercover and work for the CIA. Was that too much to ask? She laughed, not in glee but in despair. Mr. Bubbles trotted over to her with his tail wagging, leaving a trail of blue paw prints.

Lest he misread her reaction, she firmed her face into a mask of disapproval. "Lucas, I need you to clean this up right now."

"I'm sorry, Mom. I was just doing my homework and..."

She gave him an "I don't want to hear it" look and repeated herself. "Clean this up right now. I want all the paint back in the cabinet immediately. You are going to clean the rug too." Even as she said it, she knew that was impossible. She'd have to rent one of those hundred-pound Rug Doctors from the hardware store, lug it home, and spend a couple of hours shampooing the carpet. What had Phil even been doing?

Back in the kitchen, Phil was taking the chicken out of the oven. During the argument over how many carbon credits were needed to offset one dead chicken, he'd managed to almost blacken it, which she was guessing would cost him more credits.

Shaking his head, he dropped it on the counter unceremoniously and poured himself a glass of wine. "You want one?"

She did, but also, why was he staying? He was the one who decided to leave. He couldn't just drop by and pour himself some wine and act like everything was fine, like they were in it together. They hadn't been in it together for a long time.

"Phil, I asked you to watch the kids tonight, but it was not an invitation for anything more."

"Gabs"—he gave her a palms-up, "I come in peace" gesture— "it's just a glass of wine. I screwed up dinner. Let me make it up to you and order a pizza."

"I've had a long day, Phil." Something about the way he called her "Gabs" like he used to didn't work. She was tired, and cracking up, and she didn't want Phil to be the one to talk her down.

That was Justin's job at the moment. She glanced out the window in the direction of his house.

"Who hasn't had a long day? What do you think I've been doing?" He gestured to the burnt chicken.

The absurdity hit her, and she let out a peal of laughter that made her sound like she was on edge, which she probably was. Cooking dinner for an ungrateful family—first time he had tried her job.

"Oh no, it's your crazy laugh," he said. "What kind of pizza do you want—the Athena with extra olives from Biggio's?"

He couldn't weasel his way back into her life with a handful of olives and an on-point pizza order, but still. At this moment, it counted for something. Divorced or not, Phil knew her better than almost anyone—at least in some ways. Netflix preferences, the ratty T-shirts she wore to bed at night, the fact that she liked an insane amount of Greek olives on her pizza. The familiar routines of married life played across her mind in a montage of comfy nights on the couch as she said, "Sure, I'll have a glass of wine, and if you want to stay for dinner..."

Phil filled her wineglass a little too full. "Just drink the wine, and I'll order a pizza. We can decide if Kyle is going to become a vegetarian tomorrow."

She wandered out to the living room, tossed a blanket over the blue smudges on the couch, and settled herself into the inviting embrace of an overstuffed and much-abused sectional. It may have been vomited on, spilled on, and covered in blue paw prints—but it was her mess. Sort of like the marriage she was currently revisiting.

"Lucas. Kyle! We're getting a pizza," she called. Getting a pizza—it was admitting defeat, calling a truce. "Come pick out a show with me!"

She never allowed TV on school nights.

Lucas plopped down next to her with a "Sorry, Mom."

"Lucas, you know better than to mess around with paints on the carpet." She gave him a stern look. "You are getting to be a big boy."

"I cleaned it up."

Ragged wet paper towels tinged with blue were in a pile on the carpet, evidence that he'd tried to clean. It looked quite a bit worse.

"Thanks, sweetie. That's a good start. Go throw the paper towels away, and we'll start a show."

After they'd booted up an episode of *Nailed It!*, something they could all agree on, Kyle slunk into the room as if she hadn't just fought her dad about a chicken. After enough time had passed and her angst mixed with the regular air in the room (kind of like introducing a goldfish to a tank), Kyle looked up and said, "You should be on this show, Mom."

Gabby laughed. "You're right." She was a walking Pinterest fail. She'd tried to make Kyle a *Frozen* cake when she was little, including a hand-drawn picture of Elsa. At the party, everyone had asked why Shrek was blue.

Kyle said, "Remember when you volunteered in Ms. Mendoza's class, and you were supposed to make Easter bunnies out of cotton balls?"

Gabby chuckled at the memory. Ms. Mendoza had held Gabby's project up as an example of what not to do, not realizing an adult had made it.

Her kids were fine. Pizza was good. Everything was okay, except what had she been thinking with Phil?

Looking far too comfortable, he settled into his favorite

La-Z-Boy. Just like old times, he pulled out his phone and started scrolling. Lucas yelled, "Dad," and Phil didn't look up. Relying on Phil to watch the kids at night was not going to work, at least until he got his own place. His hotel room had one bed and a mini-fridge. Sure, he had a pool, but it just didn't feel stable. There was literally no place for the kids.

Three episodes of *Nailed It!* later, Gabby sent Lucas to brush his teeth. "Kyle, did you get your homework done?" She should have asked a couple of hours ago, but better late than never. Phil, meanwhile, reclined his chair even more.

Gabby cleared her throat. "Thanks for the pizza, Phil, but I think we should wrap this up."

"You sure?" he asked, clearly angling to stay the night. While it had been nice that someone knew her pizza order, she did not need to finish the night faking an orgasm, not that she had ever owed him that courtesy. She should have been honest with him and herself from the beginning.

In her chapter on truth, Sloane had said that a relationship built on fake orgasms is a house of cards, ready to go down. Maybe you thought you were being polite. You were also lying—to him and to yourself.

CHAPTER 17

Monday, past Lucas's bedtime, Greene household

Gabby shut the door on Phil and locked it emphatically. Tonight had been a good reminder. Phil hadn't even asked how her day was. In fact, he hadn't even asked what she was doing. If Justin had been over, he wouldn't have burned the chicken, and they would have chatted about their days over wine. Justin would have already made a voodoo doll of Fran to stick pins in.

Inside, the kitchen was still a disaster. The chicken was burnt to the bottom of the pot, no one had loaded the dishes, the cabinets were all open, and flour was spilled everywhere. Had anyone even used flour? After cleaning up everything, she started in with the kids' lunches. She hadn't been to the store, so she had to improvise. She threw some leftover pizza in a bag with a side of Ritz crackers. Full-time work and taking care of the house was definitely going to be a challenge.

After taking a long hot shower and shaving her legs, Gabby rubbed herself down with some firming lotion. Shelly told her this lotion would make it possible for her to wear shorts again. Gabby glanced up at Tarragon, whom she still had no idea what to do with.

She slipped on her fluffy pink "MOM" robe. Being divorced and slathering on toning cream was better than pretending to be appreciated. She knew that much. She wrapped her wet hair in a towel, slipped some gold under-eye masks on that were supposed to help with bags (spies don't have dark circles), and walked downstairs to make sure everything was shut down properly, a last walk-through to turn off the lights and double-check that the doors were locked.

Bubbles took their nightly patrol seriously, trotting ahead of her and smelling every corner, growling into the shadows. Was it bravery or fear? She wasn't sure, but she liked the company. "Good boy, Mr. Bubbles."

In the living room, the TV was still on a "Would you like to continue watching *Nailed It!*?" message from Netflix across Nicole Byer's face. "Night, Nicole. Night, Jacques," she said with a final click. They'd watch the Halloween episode tomorrow.

Bubbles, a caricature of a dog made out of cotton balls and painted partially blue by an eight-year-old, barked and ran toward the door like he was a one-hundred-and-fifty-pound mastiff. Little man syndrome—he had it bad. She should have named him Napoleon instead of Mr. Jonathon Bubbles. That's what happens when two kids under ten name a dog, though.

"Bubbles, shhh!" she whispered loudly. "Don't wake up the kids."

Bubbles was an overenthusiastic guard dog, especially at night when the lights were out. He alerted her to every gust of wind, every unauthorized toilet flush, and God forbid a car should actually drive by. Working at the EOD had her a little more on edge. No one seemed to suspect she wasn't Camille Walker, regular-old executive assistant, but still...Her hair stood on end, and she felt her parasympathetic nervous system kick into high gear, a sudden flood of adrenaline heightening her senses. Quickly, she ran through the list of everything she knew from the EOD.

Brace yourself, bend your knees, drop to the ground, and roll if someone grabs you from behind. What a joke—she wasn't going to drop and roll to safety. All of the other spies had actual weapons. She peeked out the dining room windows at the front through the blinds. Nothing. Her new job had just kicked up her imagination. Everything was fine on Avocado Avenue, unless you counted Shelly's dead cat in her closet.

"It's fine, Bubbles," she said, more to herself than him, but he continued to growl low in his throat.

Sure enough, there was something. Just outside the front door, a small box was nearly hidden next to her potted yucca. She almost missed it in the shadows. Apparently, Bubbles wasn't completely unreliable.

She tucked the unmarked box under her arm and made her way to the kitchen. There was no name or address for the sender or the recipient, just a box on her doorstep. Had Phil dropped it or was it from the EOD?

Inside, she found a tiny earpiece buried in tissue paper. A note read, "Good job today. I'll be back in your ear tomorrow."

Gabby smiled to herself. Today had been hard, and things had gone wrong, but she'd managed. Markus might not have given her a gold star, but he'd sent her a new earpiece meaning: 1) she didn't get fired, and 2) she didn't have to go it alone tomorrow.

As soon as she took out the recycling, she was going to get some rest, after she took a handful of melatonin, because it was going to take a while to come down from the adrenaline rush of receiving an unmarked package. Talk about a reminder that she needed to chill out.

She slipped on some bright orange Crocs with a few Croc gems and shuffled into the driveway with the recycling.

Just as she tossed the recycling in, a van pulled up, dark gray and brand-new. It looked like one of the fleet of EOD vehicles. Markus—he'd probably turned around after dropping off the box. Who knows why—more specific instructions, just a debriefing about her day. He really needed to text her next time. She was in a robe with a towel wrapped around her wet hair like a turban. Oh well.

She cinched the belt on her robe tighter, and just to look busy, she picked up the second bag of trash. That was probably a dumb impulse—but she committed. She strode over to the van to share a strongly worded admonition that he needed to text before he dropped by next time, a bag of leaky trash in her hand for emphasis.

Her admonition caught in her throat as both doors slid open and three guys dressed in black jumped out and charged her. A scream let loose from her involuntarily. She was a mom. Her kids were in the house.

She could not let these men get past her.

Just like she'd practiced, she bent her knees slightly and braced herself. The only weapon at hand—a bag of kitchen trash. She gripped the plastic red straps on the store-brand kitchen bag.

Kyle and Lucas were sleeping peacefully, and she could not let these assholes touch a hair on their heads. Her mind was focused on that and that alone—keep her kids safe.

"What are you waiting for? Put her in the car."

"You can try," Gabby said, playacting at being the spy she wasn't.

When he stepped closer, she leaned back and swung the trash bag as hard as she could. Since Phil left, she'd gotten pretty good at swinging heavy trash bags into the bin. Right in this moment, it paid off. The bag smashed into her assailant's face. It might not have packed a lot of force, but her thriftiness was what really got him. The generic bag didn't have super-stretch technology, and the contents exploded all over him.

"Ugh!" he screamed, and backed off, horrified at the fish juice and squid pieces that had splattered all over his brand-name spy outfit.

"Take that, asshole!" For a second time, she thanked Justin for making bouillabaisse. It was weapons-grade leftover fish smell.

Another one started laughing. "Housewife's got some moves."

That's right. If they thought they were going to get into that house, they had another thing coming. She had a tube of mascara in her pocket from that time she'd tried to sell Avon and had just ended up buying $200 worth of products. She took the wand out and palmed it like a shiv. It wasn't a gun, but any woman knew that a wand to the eye could take down a full-grown man.

"Come on, sweetie, we just need to talk. Come with us nicely, would you?"

She smiled, but when he got close, she jabbed him in the eye with the mascara wand.

"Fucking bitch! Enough of this. Throw her in the van."

A big guy came up behind her and bear-hugged her. Just like she practiced, she went boneless. She tried dropping out of his grip, but the trash bag guy was there to nab her, and the third one hit her with a syringe.

He tossed her in the van and slammed the doors.

The automatic sliding door cut off her view to the house, where her kids were cuddled up safe in their beds. She was out cold before they were out of the cul-de-sac.

CHAPTER 18

Middle of the fucking night, late Monday or early Tuesday,
unmarked van

Gabby blinked herself awake. Hard plastic bit into her wrists when she reached to swipe her hair out of her face. Her cheek was pressed into the floor of a moving vehicle instead of a pillow, and the sound of tires on asphalt roared dangerously close to her ear. Traveling at freeway speeds to who-knows-where in a dark van throbbing with Russian techno—she had been kidnapped. Through the brain fog, she remembered a van arriving, three guys in masks, and defending herself with a leaky bag of trash. She must have gotten him good. This was the worst-smelling van Gabby had ever been in, which was saying something.

On the bright side, she was alive, and they hadn't ever gone in the house. They'd thrown her in the van and sped away, meaning her kids were still asleep in their beds. If Kyle was awake, she was sneaking down to the kitchen in earbuds, and drinking a half a gallon of juice, as if the person who restocked the fridge didn't notice that the raspberry lemonade disappeared overnight. Gabby didn't know how she was going to do it, but she was going to do her damnedest to get back to her kids. They needed her.

One of the men yelled something. It wasn't English. Russian? It sounded like Granny.

If Gabby died today, Phil would marry some big-boobed bimbo who could cook and clean, a replacement mommy, younger and prettier but just as dumb as she'd been. Then Kyle would end up in therapy with stepmom issues, in addition to whatever else she was struggling with. Gabby didn't understand what Kyle was going through. When she'd gone from Kylie to Kyle, Gabby had asked if she wanted to change her pronouns. Kyle had sneered back and said she just didn't want to be a Kardashian.

One of the guys reached back and squeezed her calf and uttered a guttural, "Hey." Instead of recoiling, she played dead—the same move she had used when Phil wanted late-night sex.

She squeezed her eyes shut against the darkness and fear, but she couldn't block out her self-recrimination. Her abysmal sex life, her failed marriage, her daylong career as a spy. She had nodded and smiled her way into a facsimile of Al and Peggy Bundy's marriage. Agreed to a job she wasn't qualified for because it sounded sexy and blown it on her first damn day. If, and that was a big if, Kyle was feeling weird about being a woman, Gabby could hardly blame her. She sure as hell hadn't made it look good.

A blinker turned on, and the van slowed from highway speeds. She couldn't see out the window, but she could see the lights of oncoming headlights cutting across the roof of the van. They pulled off the freeway, headed somewhere more remote, no doubt. These had to be the guys who had killed Darcy. They were probably going to shake her down for information before they did the same to her.

Waterboarding.

Fingernail pulling.

Electric shock.

She still had a towel on her head and those little gold under-eye patches—getting dolled up for her execution, as it turned out. "Just make coffee and smile," the EOD had said.

That never fucking worked out. It didn't get her anywhere in her marriage, and it didn't get her anywhere as a spy. She was going to have some words for Markus—if she lived.

They turned onto another road, a rougher ride. Her skull bounced against the floor of the van with each rut and pothole. No more lights from oncoming traffic. No chance of rescue.

The music changed to "Sweet Dreams" by the Eurythmics. In a dark van, being driven to her death to one of her favorite songs—this was surreal. One of the Russians started singing along in a heavy accent. She wanted to scream, "You've got the wrong person! I'm just a mom." Did being a spy for one day even count?

If Gabby died today, her kids wouldn't even know that she went down as an undercover EOD agent. If only she could live long enough to let her daughter know that she could do more than make bad casseroles. With Phil as his only influence, Lucas might become a finance bro.

If she made it out of this, she needed some way to defend herself. Maybe she sucked at shooting the first time, but she had fired literally only one shot. Didn't everyone need practice? A bag of leaky trash and an old tube of Avon lash-extension mascara would never cut it.

The van slowed. Gabby was tied and lying down, but from the thin slice of sky, she could see the top of an industrial building. Gray concrete splashed with half-assed graffiti. She'd seen those shows where kidnapping victims guided the authorities to their location by describing a few left and right turns, the sound of a traffic noise, and the honking of cranes that only lived in one patch of grass that happened to be next to the bad guy's lair. All Gabby had was a gray building with some gang tags.

After some rapid-fire Russian, they slid the door open. One of the guys grabbed her upper arm and yanked her up and out of the van. She stumbled out and scrambled to stay upright with her hands tied behind her back.

"Suka," one of them yelled, and another guy laughed.

Gabby knew that word from driving with her grandma—bitch. Russian road rage vocab was all she knew.

With the slam of a heavy metal door, she was inside. A quick scan of the room showed nothing but a warehouse filled with boxes, some kind of illegal import-export business maybe. Her stomach flipped weirdly, and she struggled to move forward. Was this where she was going to meet her end?

They pushed her to a room in the back outfitted with a desk and some chairs, a makeshift office. Behind the desk sat a bear of a man, with tanned, leathery skin, and a pelt of thick dark hair.

In a Russian accent as thick as gravy he said, "Darcy. Good of you to join us."

Darcy?

She gave him her best deer-in-the-headlights impression.

"Don't pretend you're surprised, Agent Dagger." He leaned into "Dagger" hard.

"Ummm…" She thought fast. If he didn't know Darcy was dead, he couldn't be the killer. But then who the hell was he? Her mind tried to click through possibilities, but she couldn't think of one.

"Agent Dagger, you with me? Or should I say, Mom?" He looked at the moniker emblazoned across the front of her pink fluffy robe. Her breasts were two loose cantaloupes under the fabric. She'd like them to be a little higher to face this guy down.

For once she said what she was thinking. "Next time you toss me in a van, could you let me put a bra on first?"

The guy threw back his head and laughed. "I see you haven't lost your sarcasm."

One of her kidnappers poked his head in. "Mr. Smirnov, do you need anything else?"

Mr. Smirnov...was that a code name? Was he staring at a bottle of vodka when he came up with it?

Smirnov glared and said, "Leave me. I'll let you know when I want something."

She took a breath. Act more like Darcy, less like herself. "Really. If you want to talk to me, you can just knock on the door, preferably before ten, because I like to get some sleep. If you throw me in a van while I'm taking out the trash, what do you expect?"

He ignored that one. "So where've you been, Darcy?" He leaned into her name again, making some kind of point. "You've missed every check-in for the last week."

She blinked back, her mind devoid of anything but fear, which was short-circuiting all of her other thoughts.

"You're lucky we didn't take you out. I wouldn't extend this courtesy to many people."

"Thank you," she said. *Take her out*—she squeezed her thighs together. It was amazing she hadn't peed herself yet. Lucas had been a ten-pound baby. Nothing had been the same after that.

So who was this guy?

- Not Darcy's killer
- Not the EOD
- Russian accents. Dirty warehouse filled with boxes.

It hit her like a Nerf bullet straight to the forehead. *Russian. Criminal.* These guys were the Russian Mafia.

Meaning... Darcy had been working for the Russians *and* the EOD. She had been a double fucking agent. No wonder she had gotten herself killed.

FUCK. Gabby wanted to scream all of the obscenities. All of the cells in her body vibrated with fear and anger and righteous indignation. What had the EOD gotten her into? What had *she* gotten herself into? It was one thing to take the place of an EOD agent, entirely another to take the place of a double agent. Darcy, that double-crossing bitch—how was Gabby supposed to get out of this?

"Can I have a chair?" Gabby asked, trying to sound like she wasn't completely freaking out. "And dear god, can I have a drink?" Anything to calm her nerves. She gestured to the bar cart behind Smirnov.

Smirnov laughed and poured her a tumbler of vodka.

Gabby wasn't a heavy drinker, just normal wine-mom stuff, which she didn't think qualified as alcoholism, although it was hard to know. Maybe she had crossed a line since the divorce, but this wasn't the moment to worry. She threw back this vodka like it was water. It blazed a trail straight down her esophagus.

Smirnov gave her a nod of approval. "A lady who knows how to drink. I should have known."

"Don't patronize me, Smirnov." Drinking wasn't a talent. It was a vice.

He refilled her glass. This one she didn't throw back. She wanted to calm her nerves, not get table-dancing, walk-of-shame-from-her-kidnapper's-warehouse loose.

More serious, Smirnov said, "So where've you been?"

Better to stick with the same lie for everyone. She pointed to her nose. "Notice anything different about me?" She flashed him her aquiline profile.

He squinted. "You're telling me you had a nose job and took a week off without telling me?" He laughed like it was the dumbest thing he'd ever heard.

Gabby doubled down. She had no choice. "Um, not a nose job. I had a deviated septum, and it was a whole thing with my sinuses." She made a swirling motion around the front of her face, her best explanation for nasal abnormalities she was inventing on the spot. "It's the first time in my life I feel like I can breathe clearly." She took a loud, deep breath to demonstrate. "At least now that the swelling went down. The first couple of days were no good."

"It's going to be the only day you can breathe clearly," he hissed. "Do you know who I am?" He leaned forward over his desk menacingly.

"Yes, and I'm very sorry. It's just that I had a bad reaction to the anesthesia, and I was out of commission for a few days, which was unexpected. The doctor didn't advise it, but he said I should have been able to get back to work almost immediately. And he is the best surgeon in SoCal. He does work for all the actresses who say they haven't had any work done." She was blathering.

Smirnov had settled back in his chair, mixing himself another drink. He dropped in a couple of olives, which looked delicious, but she didn't want to push it.

He swirled the drink and took a sip, letting her stew in her own lies for a minute.

"Do you like it?" she asked, unsure what to do. All she knew was that she could not be a double agent. She'd been balancing three identities for about two minutes now, and it felt about as doable as carrying a tray of drinks with one hand over her head through a crowded restaurant. Gabby had been fired on her first day from Chili's, sent home with a Quesadilla Explosion Salad for dinner and no job.

He gave her a cold, unflinching look.

She decided to stick with what was working: the truth. "I want out. I'm tired, and it's too much to balance. The EOD is pissed that I missed a week." She gestured to him. "Now you're upset too. At this point, I'm just failing at two jobs."

"Are you out of your mind?"

"I know it sounds crazy, but the EOD didn't really care about my nose job. You know health care in this country, not to mention work-life balance issues."

"You have lost your mind." Apparently, the Russian Mafia didn't care about her job satisfaction. That tracked.

"I'm just telling you I want out."

"No." He leaned back in his chair, tipping it onto the back two legs and staring her down, just how she told her kids not to. ("If you tip your chair back one more time, you will eat on the floor!" She never followed through on that threat.) Smirnov was the Mafia, though—he could live dangerously if he wanted.

"Do you know who I am? I think you should rethink the tone you are taking with me, *Gabriella Greene*."

All the air left her lungs, and her world started to spin. He had used her real name. Fuck. Fuck. Fuuuuuuck. The expletive grew in volume in her mind as the implication hit. "What did you say?"

"It was very clever of you to hide your family from me all this time, Gabriella. Very clever. I always thought I had no leverage with you. What was I going to do—key your stupid car?" He shook his head in silent appreciation. "Darcy Dagger, a woman with nothing to lose—what a clever lie." One corner of his mouth pulled up into a sinister half smile.

Despite her efforts to calm herself, her breathing was erratic. This mobster knew her name, knew she had a family.

"Gabriella Greene is a woman with *everything* to lose," he said, smiling through his threats in a way that made her blood run cold. "Did you forget who I am because you are treating me like a dickless office boss?"

It would be nice if he answered that question instead of asking it over and over again.

A line of sweat trickled down her back. Her kids.

Smirnov slid some photos across the desk toward her.

"Lucas," he said. "Such a cute boy. Sort of naughty, but that's good in boys."

Smirnov would think that. She was at toxic masculinity HQ.

"Kyle." He shook his head. "My niece is doing this too—wearing overalls and going by a boy's name. What is with this generation? If you're born with a dick, enjoy it. If you're born with a pussy—I'm sure that's fine too."

Could mobsters get canceled for transphobia? That would save her some work.

"Philip." He slid a picture of Phil standing at the kitchen counter staring at his phone—probably sexting one of his assistants. "How long have you been married?"

Instead of saying, "You can have that one!" Gabby gasped like she meant it. "Not Phil!" she said in a breathless tone.

"If you don't follow through with our plans, I will kill your family." He took a sip of his drink, taking his time with his threat like he enjoyed watching her sweat. "Don't try to be cute and move them. It won't work. I see everything. Like Santa Claus."

Instead of feeling sad and powerless, Gabby felt something inside her harden. She would not let this man near her family, no matter what she had to do. All business, she asked, "What do you need?"

With annoyance he said, "Just follow our original plan. I need you to get Kramer's codes to transfer the laundered money to me."

"And Sergei Orlov?" she asked for clarification.

"Did you get a lobotomy with that nose job?"

There are no stupid questions, especially when considering the stakes. "I just want to make sure everything is crystal clear."

"Orlov can go fuck himself. He's no concern of mine."

Okay, so Orlov and Smirnov were not working together. She was dealing with rival Russian mobsters, a money-laundering finance bro, and an elite branch of the CIA. Last week, she had thought the bake sale was too much. "*No, I really can't add cookie making to my life, Barb,*" she'd said.

"And don't even think of trying anything. Do your job, clean and simple, and I will give you the cut we agreed on."

A cut—she squashed her impulse to ask how much it was. Horse camp was expensive, and college was coming up. Even state schools cost a lot these days. With a gasp, she stopped herself from free-falling into a life of crime to pay for horse camp. *Get a hold of yourself, Gabby!*

"Like I said, don't fuck with me."

She nodded. "No plans to. Sorry I didn't tell you in advance about the nose surgery."

He blew out a breath in annoyance. "I have someone on the inside watching you."

Someone on the inside...It couldn't be Markus. Valentina?

"Don't forget to check in this time. I'll kill Phil first. I don't want to start with the babies, but I will take out your family, Gabriella."

Why did men always call her Gabriella? They said it like she would inhabit the role and become Sophia Loren before their eyes.

"Mischa, take our guest home. Be nice this time."

"No zip ties?"

"No. She will behave herself."

As she walked out of the office, Smirnov called after her, "The nose looks good, by the way."

CHAPTER 19

Tuesday, crack of dawn, Avocado Avenue

The sun was cresting the horizon by the time the goons dropped Gabby back home on Avocado Avenue, just the faintest hint of pink brightening the horizon, the blossoms on her orange tree fragrant in the cool night air. It looked like the perfect neighborhood, the perfect life, a place where nothing could go wrong, not the kind of place where you get hauled away by Mafia guys in an unmarked van.

The driver hit the button to automatically open the side door, the same as she did for the kids. When he realized she was still zip-tied (he hadn't followed instructions), he walked around, helped her out of the van, and cut the ties off her. "Good luck," he said.

She tightened the belt on her "MOM" robe. "Thanks, you too."

He gave her a fist bump, a strange gesture of truce after a truly weird night.

It was the first time she had really looked at him, partially because he wasn't wearing a ski mask anymore. Why would he? They were both Mafia employees. With some remaining teenage acne and a patchy beard, he was probably in his early twenties, a kid basically. "Do you like your job?" she asked, standing in the driveway shooting the shit with a guy who had just kidnapped her.

"Does it matter?" he said with a shrug.

"I guess not," she said with a matching shrug. Who knew the Mafia could inspire such ambivalence?

Normally, she'd advise a guy his age to follow his dreams, not get trapped in a situation he didn't like. Not into kidnapping and murder? Do something else. But Smirnov would probably just off him. Better to keep her mouth shut.

They both stared out into nothingness for a long minute, the freedom of a sunrise and the false promise of a brand-new day. They were both in deep.

A moment later, he started the van and backed out, leaving her standing in the driveway like nothing had happened. Did he have to start work again, or was kidnapping the night shift? Suddenly, she didn't feel as bad for him. That twenty-year-old kid was going back to an apartment to sleep it off. He'd probably wake up at two in the afternoon and order a pizza. Tomorrow night, he'd be tossing someone else in his van.

Gabby slipped on the blinged-out Croc that she had lost in the scuffle earlier, and shuffled back to the house. Her wine from last night was still on the counter, and the dishwasher was almost fully loaded and ready to be started.

Mr. Bubbles padded down the stairs. He wagged his little tail, and Gabby bent down and gave him a vigorous ear scratching. "Thanks for watching the kids, buddy."

Upstairs, Kyle was sprawled out in a tangle of covers, the stuffies on her bed a reminder that fourteen wasn't all grown up. She was still Gabby's baby. As soon as Gabby had a free day, after she'd somehow wriggled out of her current predicament with the EOD and rival Russian mobsters, she'd schedule a hair day. Helping Kyle maintain bright purple hair was Gabby's way of saying, "I got your back. Be whoever you want." Maybe there was something deeper she should be doing, but it's all she had.

Lucas's face was softened by sleep. He might talk a big game, but he had three nightlights on, and his Nerf gun was at the foot of his bed so he could shoot bad guys. That was kind of concerning on a regular day, but now that there really were bad guys, it was even worse. Her heart squeezed, and she bit the inside of her cheek to stifle tears.

No sitting around and crying. She'd gotten them into this mess, and she needed to get them out of it.

The rumble of a big truck and the sound of a bin being dumped served as reminders that it was trash day. She hurried down the stairs, Bubbles at her heels. Nothing was taking a break for her schedule. Kyle had horseback riding again, and Lucas had rec league soccer. And somebody had a dentist appointment soon. Something had to give. It might be Lucas's teeth.

Valentina's statement that "kids don't really work with this life-style" rang true. She wanted some help, but could she really bring anyone else into this mess? *"Go back to your microscope, Gerry. If I had a wife, I'd think kids were no big deal too,"* Valentina had said. The woman was right.

Because she didn't have a wife, Gabby started the dishwasher and then wheeled the bins to the curb before the truck got to her house.

Shelly waved at her from across the street and called, "Beautiful morning, isn't it?"

Gabby nodded. "It's great."

Gabby's spirits sank as Shelly walked toward her. "You haven't seen Tarragon, have you?"

Shelly's fucking cat, the one that was in her closet. Was there no end to the madness? It's not like she could tell her the truth—he was hit by a car and a vegan taxidermist stuffed him and sold him to Justin at the Pacific Palisades Farmers Market.

So many secrets.

At the crack of dawn without her makeup on, Shelly looked more human, more vulnerable.

"I'm so sorry, Shelly. I don't know where Tarragon is, but I'll keep an eye out for him."

"I love my kids, you know, but Tarragon...he's special. He doesn't ask for anything besides food, and he always seems to know when I need him. He's my little sweetheart." Shelly teared up.

Gabby was about to see Tarragon in ten minutes. "Can I do anything?" slipped out of her mouth before she could stop herself.

"Actually, if you could put up some posters. I really don't have time today. I'm getting my hair done, and I have the bake sale."

Gabby meant "no way in hell" but it came out as "Um, sure."

"You're a lifesaver, Gabs."

Shelly ran inside her front door and hurried back with a stack of posters. "If you could put these up closer to the school, that would be good."

The poster featured a picture of the cat and read, "Our beloved Tarragon, twenty-five pounds, friendly, missing from Avocado Ave. Please call." Below the phone number, the poster announced, "$1,000 reward."

Fucking A.

Gabby hustled back to her house with the posters under her

arm. Inside, she set them right next to the dead cat, which sum-
marized how today was going.

She texted Justin a picture of the situation. Shelly roped me into
putting up posters. Hand over face emoji. Hand over face emoji.
Hand over face emoji.

> WHAT WERE YOU THINKING.

> Maybe you can hang them up since you own
> Tarragon now.

> I gave him to you.

> OMG. Will you watch the kids while I take the dog for a
> walk?

Normally, she would leave them alone for fifteen minutes, but
after last night, that seemed inadvisable.

Ten minutes later, Justin was making coffee in her kitchen and
bossing her kids around. "Lucas, where is that shirt I bought you?
I want to see you wearing it." He shook his head in general disapproval of Gabby. "What is the matter with you? One day of work,
and you look like you've been run over by a truck."

"This office is just hell."

Bubbles picked up his leash and dropped it at Gabby's feet
again, demanding his walk.

Justin took a deeper look at her. "Is this job really stressing you
out that much?" He placed his hand on hers in concern. "Why?"

Maybe she could talk it out with Justin. "Well, the problem is that I sort of have two bosses, and ... well, they don't get

along." Understatement of the year. The EOD would love to arrest Smirnov, and probably her, if they found out what she was doing. "I basically feel like I have two jobs, and I just started yesterday."

Justin waved it off. "That's not your problem. You can't be responsible for whether they get along or not."

In theory that was true, but in practice… "I'm kind of in the middle. How can I satisfy both of them?"

"First off, work on setting your boundaries. Tell people no."

When she laughed off his advice as preposterous, he said, "Just say the word, Gabs. It's easy." He directed her with a big flourish of hands like Mr. Barnes, her old choir director, and mouthed it with her. Together they said, "No."

"Okay, good. Tell people no at least three times today. If you let them run over you on week one, it's only going to get worse later." He raised an eyebrow.

She nodded. Maybe she could stand up for herself more. This might be a good moment in time to work on that skill.

"Now, what do they want from you? Is it reasonable?"

"They're very… gossipy. It almost feels covert."

He laughed. "Oh god, I love a good office intrigue. Are they attractive?"

When she blushed, he put his hand over his heart. "Just let me know how you need me. If I can plan a celebrity wedding in under a month, I can help with this."

He was probably right.

"Are the jobs your bosses want you to do mutually exclusive?"

"Um, actually no." A lightbulb came on. Now that Justin brought it up, the EOD and Smirnov had completely separate tasks for her. In theory, all she had to do was 1) get evidence of money laundering for the EOD, hopefully at the party, and 2) find the codes for Smirnov. No one at the EOD had even mentioned "codes," meaning they probably weren't even aware. There was no reason she couldn't do both. Neither one would be the wiser.

"You're right, Justin. I can handle it." So what if it was the mob and the EOD? She just had a to-do list with two things on it. End of story. She gave Justin a quick hug. "Thanks for talking it through with me."

"Anytime, babe. Here to talk you off a cliff whenever."

"Are you sure you don't mind staying while I walk the dog? Last night turned out a little chaotic, and he missed his nightly." She wasn't going to let a mobster keep Mr. Bubbles from his morning constitutional. She needed to establish boundaries and live her life, and that started with walking the dog.

Justin picked up on her vibe and gave her a snap. "That's right, girl. You walk that dog. Don't let anyone stop you."

She laughed at the situation. Justin had no clue, and he was still being supportive. Now that was a friend.

Bubbles started bouncing on his hind legs with excitement. With Gabby working all day, he needed a walk. "When I get back, I need to catch up on you. I've been all me, me, me the past few days. Do you have any shows soon?"

He shimmied a little. "Actually," he said, "there is something big coming up."

"Oooh!" She yelled, "Kids, listen to Justin. I'll be right back!"

The kids didn't look up. Justin waved her off.

She and Bubbles took a left onto Avocado Avenue and headed for the jogging path at the base of Avocado Mountain. It probably had a different name, but that's what her family called it. The trail was a dirt path sandwiched between some green space on the mountain and their backyards. At this time in the morning, it was all people walking dogs before their nine-to-fives and triathletes, not Gabby's usual people.

"Bubbles, do you have to pee on everything?" Phil had refused to neuter Bubbles when he was a puppy, and that had led to a few bad habits, including pissing on everything and leg humping. Pretty much like a tiny Phil in some primal way.

Gabby looked up to see a woman jogging toward them. It's not like she wanted to be jealous. That was counterproductive to female empowerment, but no one should look that good at six thirty in the morning. It was a law—a law Gabby was following. So yeah, she was still shuffling around in Crocs and the robe she'd been kidnapped in. When was she going to do laundry with her schedule? Never.

As the walking ad for Lululemon got closer, Gabby gasped— Valentina. Talk about work following you home. One day in the office and she got kidnapped by the Mafia and accosted by Valentina, all before the next morning. How was a person supposed to eat breakfast and shower, not to mention sleep?

When she reached Gabby, Valentina dropped to her knees and made a show of tying her shoes.

She didn't have any privacy anymore. This must be how Jennifer Aniston feels.

Mr. Bubbles, like most men, assumed it was all about him, and trotted over to Valentina with a "wassup, girl" attitude.

Valentina laughed. "Hey, little man."

"Don't call him *little*. He takes offense." Gabby's joke came off too biting.

Valentina inspected his tags and corrected herself. "Mr. Bubbles, that's much more manly." She scratched the miscreant's ears.

"Didn't expect to see you here this morning," Gabby said.

"Best to be prepared for anything in this job." Shoelaces tied, Valentina stood and checked her smartwatch. "I've got another two miles to get in before work," she commented to herself.

Mr. Bubbles took Valentina's exposed leg as an invitation and started vigorously humping.

With a swift yank on his leash, Gabby admonished, "Bubbles, stop that!" The dog panted like some sort of sexual pervert and ignored her. "I'm sorry. He should have been neutered a long time ago. I can't even bring him to doggie daycare." Not that she could even if he was neutered. If she couldn't afford help for her actual kids, she certainly couldn't pay for doggie daycare.

Valentina stared back, like she was just waiting for Gabby to shut up. "Just keep him off me. I have enough horny men in my life." She pulled a slip of paper from the phone pocket in her leggings and handed it to Gabby. "Add them to the guest list. They're EOD agents. We'll get them into the party with aliases. If anything goes down, they'll be there."

That sounded simple enough. Kramer was pretty hands-off about party planning. She could probably invite half of Avocado Avenue and he wouldn't notice. But then again, could she trust Valentina?

Valentina took her sunglasses off and wiped them down. A little more hesitant, like Kyle when she was angling for more screen time, Valentina asked, "So everything went okay yesterday? Nothing out of the ordinary?"

Was Valentina the mole? Gabby couldn't possibly know. "Nothing happened at all. Just coffee making and a lot of congratulations on my nose job."

"Poor Darcy." More sadly, she said, "I liked her nose."

Gabby smiled. "I wish I'd gotten to meet her."

Valentina let out a short, cough-like laugh, almost as if she was choking on the absurdity of the idea. "That would have been... weird."

"Why?"

"You two had nothing, I mean nothing, in common, except for your face." Valentina sighed and said, "Shit, I miss that woman."

Oh-kay.

Gabby held up the list. "You could have just sent this over text or email?"

Valentina gave her best annoyed, big-sister glare. "No records of anything. When you're done, destroy the paper."

Sarcastic, Gabby asked, "Should I eat it?"

"That's a classic for a reason." Not dignifying Gabby's sarcasm any further, she tightened her ponytail, readying herself to make an escape. "Don't do anything stupid today," Valentina said, implying that Gabby had been pretty dumb yesterday. "Try to stay focused. Be more careful. For instance, I might stop walking the dog alone in the woods."

Now she told her. Gabby tried not to let out a guttural yell of frustration. Through a bake sale smile, she said, "Thanks for the advice. Speaking of safety. I want a gun." Last night, if she'd had a gun, she might have been able to keep those guys from taking her. Next time, they weren't coming to pick her up for a chat. They were coming to kill, and not her. She could barely even let herself think the thought without losing her breath. He had threatened her babies.

"You don't need a gun."

"You just told me not to walk in the woods alone. I don't feel safe."

Gabby knew she'd made a solid point when Valentina blew out

a breath and stared off into the middle distance. "A gun won't help, if you don't know how to use it." Valentina looked hard at Gabby. "They'll take it and use it on you. Just more weapons for the bad guy." Valentina shook her head, clearly imagining the disaster at the shooting range.

"Teach me."

"Why aren't you asking Markus?"

"I don't know. You're here, and I was thinking about it."

"Gabby, I have enough shit to do."

Gabby put her foot down. This wasn't just about her. It was about her kids. "You need me. Look at yesterday, I ended up alone all day. No backup. I need to be able to protect myself. Enough with the cutesy, drop-out-of-a-bear-hug maneuvers. I'm not going to become an MMA champ in the next week. I could however learn how to shoot."

Valentina relented. "I'll be in touch."

"When?" Gabby asked.

"I don't know. I'm meeting with Markus as soon as I finish this run. We'll talk it over."

Someone at the EOD was watching her. The two people with the most access were Valentina and, she hated to even think it, Markus. If Smirnov was trying to keep tabs on her, those were his two best bets. And really, why was Valentina up at the crack of dawn hand delivering a piece of paper she could have given her anytime in any number of ways?

Who knew if she was really meeting Markus at all? She was probably meeting Smirnov.

Gabby might just be making coffee and doing a few minor tasks, but those tasks meant millions of dollars to Smirnov and a big bust for the EOD.

"How do I get out of here?" Valentina asked. "The shortest way, please."

Gabby smiled and said, "Take a left at the next fork. That'll loop you back to the beginning of the trail, where I assume you started." That was actually the long way. If Valentina took it, she was in for another five miles.

Gabby stumbled through a 5K for cancer six months ago. She finished after the organizers pulled up the cones. Phil had made a big deal of comparing her time to the winner, who apparently had run something like six-minute miles. If Valentina took at least thirty minutes, Gabby would have time to get the kids on the bus and follow Valentina and see who she was really meeting.

And to think she had never been good at story problems! Take that, Mr. Heard.

Gabby watched Valentina run away, her ponytail swinging like a hangman's noose. God, she was getting dark. After she scooped up a bag of poo, she hustled back to the house, managing to hang a couple "Lost Cat" posters on the way.

She was in mortal danger but still helping Shelly look for a cat that Gabby knew was dead.

CHAPTER 20

Tuesday morning, getting ready for work and school (almost like she hadn't just been abducted), Greene household

Gabby kicked her Crocs into a growing pile of shoes by the front door and unclipped Bubbles' leash. Twenty-six minutes left to get ready and follow Valentina to her meeting. A little voice in the back of her head needled her. *Why do you want Valentina to be the mole so bad, Gabby?*

It wasn't about Valentina so much—she didn't think—it was that she didn't want it to be Markus. And not only because he was cute. Markus was her partner.

The way Valentina had said she was meeting Markus—that sneaky little smile that disappeared as quickly as invisible ink—Gabby could just tell something was up. If she knew Valentina was the mole, she could go to the EOD for help with the Smirnov situation.

"Justin, can you get the kids on the bus? I just got a text from my boss," Gabby lied.

Justin was sitting in the exact same spot he had been when she left. His voice laden with sarcasm, he said, "What, does he need his coffee early?" The subtext was "What about me?" which was a valid point. Her BFF was showing up for her, and she was running off.

"I'll make it up to you," she said, briefly pausing and sucking down half her latte in a couple of gulps. "I just really don't want to disappoint him on my second day. I need this job."

"It's fine," he said, semi-convincingly. "I'll get the kids on the bus. My client this week canceled, so I have some time."

"Oh no! The ABBA-themed baby shower?" she called from the downstairs bathroom as she tried to quickly put herself together.

"I guess they wanted something more traditional in the end. I'm pretty sure the mother-in-law got involved." More brightly, he added, "So anyways, I'm free for a few days."

She pushed open the door. "I hope you charged them. Does this shirt look okay?"

He nodded. "Looks great. And yeah, they lost their deposit, plus a rotating mirror ball and a karaoke machine I bought for the occasion."

"Was the baby having a coming-out party?" Gabby asked dryly.

"Oh, stop." He waved his hand at her.

"So you're free this week?" Gabby's wheels were turning. Not that she wanted to take advantage of Justin.

"No comment." He took a sip of his latte. "But your granny's coming, right? I thought you were covered."

"We'll see." Granny wasn't coming anywhere near the house if she didn't find the mole and get EOD protection first. It was a "developing situation," to use news terms.

Justin took the request in stride. "Betty Danger needs more practice with her housewifery. Just let me know what you need this week."

"Are you serious?"

With a long-suffering, been-married-for-fifteen-years sigh, he said, "Yes."

"Justin, you're a lifesaver."

"Since Hugh won't agree to children, I might as well drive yours around a little." He held up his hand in the universal sign of "stop before you get ahead of yourself."

"All I need. Thank you."

Kyle and Lucas were both sitting at the kitchen table with blank morning stares. Gabby pulled their lunches out of the fridge and set clean water bottles on the counter. "Lunches are packed."

"Uh-huh," Kyle said, never looking up from her phone. Gabby normally would have said something, but the minute Kyle put it down, the bickering would start. Justin didn't need that. Who did?

"Betty's gonna pick you up," Justin announced. "I have a thing tonight, so I'll just get in costume early."

"Yes," Lucas said like it was a total score, and Kyle looked pleased as punch. Betty Danger really tended to overdo things, but in a good way. There would be gourmet after-school snacks for sure, plus a rotating mirror ball and a karaoke machine, if Gabby had to guess.

Gabby finished changing into her office clothes in less than five minutes and glanced at her watch. She had four minutes until Valentina was done, assuming Valentina ran about the same pace as the winner of that charity 5K. Running was so dumb, especially now that Gabby knew you could just buy some Spanx and take off ten pounds that way.

Before stepping out the door, Gabby slipped on a pair of oversized sunglasses and tucked her red hair under a baseball hat. She pulled Darcy's car, which was thankfully nondescript, in a spot a block from the trailhead, just close enough for a view of Valentina's

Dodge Charger. Clearly, Valentina wasn't playing it low-key this morning. Gabby had already gotten a notice from the LISTSERV with a picture of Valentina's car and the comment "Who bought the Charger?"

Valentina might be a spy, but she had no clue how nosy the people on Avocado Avenue were.

For the first time in her entire life, Gabby's math was perfect. Valentina popped out of the trail, looking sweaty, out of breath, and annoyed. At her car, she took a swig of water and stretched her quads briefly before peeling out of the parking lot.

Gabby followed as far behind Valentina as she dared. Once they were on the highway, she dropped a couple of car lengths behind. In her head, she heard Markus admonishing, "Slow your roll, Jane Bond."

Fifteen minutes later, Valentina pulled into a Starbucks. Gabby looked for some on-street parking with a view of the store, but it was California. After circling the block twice, she almost gave up until someone finally left. It was criminal the way people just sat in their cars, scrolling Insta, taking up space. Rationalizing that no one was looking for her anyway, she pulled into the lot.

While she waited for Valentina to make a move, she dialed her mom. Might as well get that convo out of the way on her stakeout. As she was chatting, she glanced in the rearview mirror and actually startled herself. Her look said "kidnapped last night."

"Hi, Mom. I'm sort of in a rush this morning, but did you get my text?"

"The one where you are backing out of helping your grandmother?"

"Yes, that's the one." She didn't have time to beat around the bush with passive-aggressive comments. She swiped on some lipstick to help with her corpse-like pallor. Smirnov might as well have killed her last night from the way she looked. "I have a major...roach problem. Today isn't a good day."

"Roaches? Oh no, have you been letting the dishes pile up?"

Gabby could scream. Why had she called her mom on a stake-out? Worst decision ever.

"If the roach problem is too bad for your grandmother, is it safe for the kids?"

"I just don't want to add anything more until I get this handled, Mom."

Her mom made a judgmental noise in the back of her throat.

When Gabby was mid lipstick application and only halfway through the convo with her mom, Markus walked out of Starbucks. "Oh fuck!" Gabby muttered and slunk low in her seat to stay out of view. It would have been too simple to catch Valentina in a lie, mole identified and her biggest problem solved before the day started. Real life didn't produce answers that quickly.

Because this car was the devil, the phone call suddenly changed to go through the car's speakers at top volume. "Fine," her mom said, probably loud enough for everyone at Starbucks to hear. "But you know I have that cruise, and Granny has already been evicted."

"I just can't, Mom," Gabby whispered. She tried to change the output from the car back to the phone, but somehow dropped the phone under her seat.

"What?" her mom yelled louder. "Are you talking through the car again? I can't hear you."

"I'm driving. I have to." She was going to die.

She sat up just enough to watch Valentina and Markus in the

side mirror. Markus slid his sunglasses down and strode toward a picnic table probably ten feet behind her car. His walk was unhurried but purposeful—the speed of seduction. She was a grown-up woman with kids. Markus was her colleague, not to mention a candidate for the mole. She needed to get. It. Together.

Valentina and Markus were dressed all in black, looking European and drinking iced lattes. Gabby looked freshly kidnapped and was talking to her mom on speakerphone at top volume. What in the hell was she doing with her life?

"What is this job anyway? How are the kids handling the change? The divorce and now a new job?" Her mom's disapproval was coming through loud and clear.

As if she wasn't worried enough about the kids without sideways comments.

Back at the spy table, Valentina gestured with her hands, looking frustrated. Probably upset about being stuck on a trail all morning. Markus touched her forearm, making Gabby bristle. What was the matter with her? Markus was her handler, not her boyfriend. Not to mention, possibly a mole.

Gabby had never thought she'd be horny as a middle-aged woman, but here she was. It was television's fault. Sitcom moms were never horny, only the dads. Romance novels mostly featured twenty-year-olds. Hollywood actresses could be sexual only if they looked twenty-five. It was all a lie. Her sexuality had not conveniently expired at the age of thirty, leaving her to tend to everyone else's needs without conflict.

With a resigned shake of her head, Valentina seemed to give up on whatever point she was making. Finally, Valentina waved, ending the convo with Markus.

"I have to go, Mom."

"What is going on with you?" her mom said. "Are you dating again? You know the kids aren't ready for that."

Now, to get the phone from under the seat. While trying to stay low, she backed up the seat as far as it would go. While reaching under it, she somehow pressed the windshield wiper lever up. It activated the cleaning mechanism. From her spot crouched on the floor, Gabby watched the windshield wiper fluid miss the windshield entirely and arc over the roof of the car.

"What the fuck?" Markus yelled. It must have been a direct hit. She slunk even lower as the wipers on her car squeaked over a completely dry windshield.

"Where did that come from?"

Her mom repeated, "You didn't answer. Are you dating?"

"I gotta go, Mom." She hit END CALL on the console and took a shaky breath.

Because the car truly was the devil, it switched to the last thing she'd listened to on Spotify. The unmistakable opening chords of the James Bond theme song blared: "Dum di-di dum dum!"

"Gabby?" Markus called as he walked over to her car. "Is that you?"

He appeared at the window. "Markus!" she exclaimed. "What are you doing here?"

"Um…" He looked down at her, still partly slunk down in her seat, which was backed up as far as possible. "What are you doing?"

She laughed. "I'm having a moment." That was the truth. "I was going to get a coffee on my way to work, but I dropped my phone under the seat and my mom called. This little area here"—she gestured to the front seat—"this is the Bermuda Triangle, amirite? Amelia Earhart is probably under the seat with my phone."

He laughed, seemingly satisfied with her explanation. "Let's get you a coffee and get you off to work then. You're going to have to hurry."

He shook his head. "Today should be better. You did great yesterday, even with all of the obstacles."

"Really? You think so?" The pain of the last hour was forgotten with one compliment.

"Yeah. You lost your earpiece and still kept it together all day."

"Thanks," she said. "Oh, and I ran into Valentina this morning."

He nodded. "So I heard."

So she wasn't hiding anything…

While they were in line grabbing a latte, Markus checked his phone. When he swiped up, probably meaning to check the time or his email or something, a show started playing—a bunch of hot young people, poolside, speaking Russian.

A warning sign flashed in her mind. "Do you speak Russian?"

A little flustered, he said, "I'm trying to become more fluent, and I've gotten into some Russian reality TV. This one's about psychics, *Novaya Bitva Ekstrasensov*. I watch Russian *Cops* too. It's more fun than DuoLingo."

"Do all of the agents speak Russian?"

He shook his head.

Something about this didn't sit right. How close were his ties with Russia? Was he the mole? Wikipedia said that you had to be Russian or have significant ties to Russia to join the Russian Mafia. Some sources said you had to have been in a Russian prison for three years.

After she grabbed a four-shot latte, she asked, "Markus, do you think I'm in danger at all?" while watching his expression carefully.

"What makes you say that?" he asked.

"Someone got to Darcy, right?" He didn't answer, because they both knew the answer. She said, "I want to take more precautions. I don't want to be a sitting duck."

"You're as safe as any EOD agent is, at least that I know of." He was looking deep into her eyes. "You're not holding back anything, are you? Did something happen while we were out of touch yesterday?"

She shook her head. "Everything was fine."

"Tell me the minute you get a bad feeling about anything. Promise me. That's how you stay safe. Communication. You're on the ground, and I'm stuck off-site for the moment." The way he said "stuck off-site" made it seem like he was really resentful of the fact, champing at the bit to get back into the action.

"Of course," she answered, but telling him the problem was the one thing she couldn't do. Smirnov had made that much clear. Markus might be handsome and sweet, but that didn't mean he wasn't a gangster. The fact that she liked him made it all the more likely. Gabby never liked anyone good for her.

Gabby was alone.

CHAPTER 21

Tuesday, only a few minutes late for work, eStocks Enterprises

The only saving grace was that it should be a quiet day at eStocks. Make coffee, smile, and order appetizers for that damn party. She could autopilot her way through that as much as possible while looking for the codes. This couldn't be any worse than a party for ten-year-old boys or, even worse, preteen girls. For Kyle's birthday party last year, Gabby had thought the kids were going to watch all three *Pitch Perfect*s and eat pizza. Instead, they'd divided into factions, some drama over a boy. There had been a lot of crying. She'd spent the night on the phone with various parents: "Would you mind coming to pick up your daughter?" Phil had slept through the whole thing. Mobsters couldn't be any worse than that.

When she pulled into the office parking lot, Gabby slipped her earpiece in and turned it on. "Hey, Markus."

"Hey, Gabs," he said. "What's on the agenda today?"

"The usual." Like she'd been working there for ages, she bustled in and got everything started. Before she could add Valentina's list of spies to the guest list, Kramer barked, "Camille, my office. Now!"

From the tone of his voice, she had done something horrible.

"Where's the invite for that party?" Kramer's gaze was burning her alive. She was one of those ants Lucas had burned with a magnifying glass last summer.

"Um…"

"That should have been done yesterday."

"I was just about to pick out the venue so I can send the Evites this afternoon."

"Are you fucking kidding me? The party is on Saturday. This should have been done the minute I told you."

A sinking feeling came over her. "Which Saturday did you mean?"

"This Saturday, as in four days from now? What Saturday did you think I meant?" he asked, sounding like he was about ready to bite off her head. And she'd only been at the job twenty-four hours.

"I thought you meant the next one." Even that was a tight squeeze. This Saturday was insanity. You'd have to be a professional to do that, which made her think…

"If I meant next Saturday, I would have said 'next.'" He growled into space like an angry bear, looked down at the floor, and then back up at her. "If it wasn't all-hands-on-deck this week, you would be walking to the parking lot with a box of your things right now."

Gabby froze. Fear slammed into her like a freight train. She couldn't lose this job. Smirnov would kill her if that happened. He would kill her kids.

In her ear, Markus said, "We can turn this around. Ask for a second chance."

It was going to be Kyle's birthday party all over again.

"I don't even know what to do with this." Kramer drummed his fingers on the desk. "I'm half thinking of canceling the party. Orlov and I can go out for drinks alone. Actually, that's what I'm going to do, in which case—" He looked at her and, with emphasis, declared, "I don't need you."

"We need that party," Markus said. "Convince him you can do this, Gabby."

She couldn't, but she knew who could.

"Mr. Kramer. I'm so sorry for the misunderstanding, but I can do this. Give me the afternoon to pull it together. I'll have the venue locked down and Evites sent out. It'll be the best party you've ever seen."

He stared at her for a minute, letting her stew in her own discomfort before sloughing the whole thing off. "Fine. Prove it to me. If you don't get it done today, the party is off, and you're fired."

The minute she got out of his office, she leaned against the wall and took a few deep breaths. Spying was too much.

For his part, Markus was in problem-solver mode. "Go somewhere we can talk. Let's figure this out."

But Gabby didn't want Markus's help on this one. If she told him her plan, he would probably try to talk her out of it. Bringing in Justin wasn't a classic EOD move. No doubt Markus would be worried about her compromising her cover. The rules had been clear: "Not one word of your role at the EOD or your undercover work to anyone in your real life. All they can know is that you're a personal assistant for a financial adviser. That is it!"

The only rule Gabby was following right now: it's better to ask for forgiveness than permission. It was a matter of national security, and she needed the best party planner in Hollywood. If he could plan a celebrity wedding in a month, he could do this.

"Markus, I got this handled. Don't you worry."

"Are you sure?"

"Yep. I just didn't understand the assignment before." With Markus still in her ear, she walked out to the parking lot to make a call. "Justin," she said stepping into the sunshine.

"Gabby, is everything okay?"

In her ear, Markus groaned. "Gabby, don't do it. We can take care of this in-house. Valentina can help."

Sorry, Markus. There was no way she was ignoring the fact that she was best friends with LA's top party planner.

"I have an emergency," she said, like she was talking to 911 dispatch.

Justin gasped. "The kids? What happened?"

"No, nothing like that." Although if she couldn't do her job, Smirnov would make it that kind of emergency.

"I have to throw a party this Saturday. If I don't pick the venue and send Evites by this afternoon, I'm fired."

With a self-satisfied laugh, he said, "Honey child, you have called the right man."

"Charge whatever you want. I'll bill my boss." She'd be long gone by the time he had time to complain. "I can't guarantee he'll be good about paying. I don't know him well enough." Easier to explain than "he might not pay his bills because he'll be in jail."

Justin immediately shifted into party-planner mode. "I want the guest list as soon as you hang up."

"Okay."

"I need to square away essential details in the next hour or two. When does he need the Evite by so that you don't lose your job?"

"By end of the day."

"You go do executive assistant things. I'll let you know if I have any questions, but it'll be easier if I can get this planning done on my own."

"Thank you, Justin. I owe you."

"Yes, you do. Don't worry, I will be calling in so many favors."

Just as she was about to hit END CALL, Justin interjected, "Before we hang up, do you have any thoughts? Anything I should consider while I'm putting this together?"

"None. As long as I don't lose my job." Her incompetency was officially getting in the way of national security. This was worse than the time she managed only one shift at Chili's.

And the hits just kept on coming. Before she could catch her breath, the school called. Lucas had forgotten his lunch.

If it were Kyle, she wouldn't worry, but Lucas had allergies. She hustled down the hall to the bathroom to discuss. "Markus, I have a problem," she reported. Her voice sounded panicked even to her.

"Another one? Already?"

"I know." This morning was coming at her full force, all after a night of almost no sleep.

"What is it?" His voice went high alert. "Do you need backup?"

She'd love some backup.

"I don't think the EOD is available for this mission. My kid forgot his lunch."

"What? Can't the school feed him?"

"If only. Lucas has an anaphylactic reaction to a bunch of different foods. Eggs, milk, *any tree nuts*." She said "tree nuts" like it was a nuclear weapon. That's how it felt. Her whole world could be destroyed by a hazelnut. And Nutella was literally everywhere. Those little single-serve packages. Lucas always wanted one so bad because she wouldn't let him have them. At the thought of all the dangers at school, she started to panic for real. Her voice started quivering, and her hands shook. How was she supposed to take care of her Lucas and do this job?

"So what you're telling me is that this is a life-or-death situation."

Finally, someone got how she felt. "Yes." She'd never said yes with such conviction. The nurse and the principal and the classroom teacher all knew that Lucas had allergies, but did they feel it deep in their souls? She wanted anyone who handed Lucas a snack to feel like they had his beating heart in their hands. Was that too much to ask?

"Can he go without lunch?" Markus asked.

"Technically, that would be fine, but I know he'll just eat something. Someone will feed him." She said it like it was a threat.

"Let's figure it out then."

"It'd take me an hour of driving to get home, get his lunch, and get to school," Gabby said.

"How about some Uber Eats?"

"The school has a strict policy about not ordering in lunch. I've tried that one before." It probably had something to do with tightening campus security in light of all the school shootings. Stopping people from ordering burritos didn't seem to be the answer.

"What about your ex?"

"He's in Sacramento." Phil embodied Sacramento.

"There's only one answer then. I'm going to have to go undercover to deliver your kid lunch." He sang the James Bond theme song. "Dum di-di dum."

With a laugh, she asked, "Really?"

"It's life or death, and we have to keep you on the job, so I have no choice. I'll be in your ear the whole time, so you won't be able to notice a difference."

Markus could not be the mole. There was no way someone who was double-crossing her would spend an hour of his day delivering an eight-year-old an allergen-free lunch.

"He eats at eleven fifteen."

"Damn, that's early. I better hustle." Sounds of Markus grabbing his keys and jacket filtered through the earpiece.

Gabby busied herself finishing the budget spreadsheet she'd started yesterday. By the time she'd finished entering the data, Markus came online. "What's your front door code?"

For a moment she froze. Just last night, Smirnov had told her that he had someone on the inside watching her, working for him. It could be Markus. Was she trading peace of mind over Lucas's lunch for everyone's safety? For years, her fear for Lucas had crowded out everything else. Here she went again. She could still call it off, say she changed her mind...but Markus had already driven all that way. And Lucas needed a safe meal.

"It's four-eight-five-three."

"'Kay. I'm in." The sound of Bubbles going crazy came through the earpiece.

The plan that had felt so perfect a minute ago had her questioning everything. What had she just done? Had she invited the enemy in? She had notoriously bad taste in men: Phil, Mr. Bubbles.

"Hey there, buddy." Markus spoke low and sweet to Bubbles. "It's okay. Wanna scratch?"

Bubbles went from loud barking to a rumble in his throat, a quick de-escalation for Bubbles. That said something. Dogs knew how to see past words and actions to intent.

"Hey, cutie, you know you want a scratch."

She wasn't sure how they were working on the dog, but Gabby

let Markus's words soothe her. There was nothing she could do now. She'd given the code over. She might as well relax. "I bet his lunch is in the kitchen still. It's in a Pikachu lunch box."

"So what's this kid eating anyway?"

She had packed a bento box with baby carrots, grapes, and a gluten-free sun butter and jelly sandwich, all topped off with a little note: "Have a great day! Love, Mom." Markus must have cracked it open, because he said, "Damn. This ain't the free lunch program."

Lucas was a little spoiled, but it was for safety.

"So where does this kid go to school?"

"Queen Palm School. I'll call and let them know to expect you."

Fifteen minutes later, Shamika, a woman who lived for gossip, buzzed Markus into the school. She could hear Markus introducing himself. He sounded like he was performing an official duty for the EOD rather than just dropping off food.

Shamika practically cooed in response, making noises like a mourning dove. Before long, she heard another voice. The principal joined to introduce herself.

"You're a little more popular in the front office than I am." Gabby cleared her throat.

"They seemed very friendly, a really engaged staff."

"Uh-huh," she said. More softly, she said, "Thank you, Markus. That really meant a lot."

"No problem. I've got your back."

She'd never wanted to believe anything more.

CHAPTER 22

Tuesday, after lunch, finally about to get some work done, well, after a cup of coffee

For Gabby, the eStocks job was more about snooping than being the best executive assistant she could be. Getting to know her co-workers was paramount to that goal, meaning she needed to network, aka gossip.

"Hey, Fran, want to grab a coffee?" There was a Starbucks down the street with her name on it. "My treat."

In her ear, Markus said, "Is that worth your time?"

Fran might be a stick-in-the-mud, but at least she wasn't working for Smirnov—more than she could say for the EOD agents.

"Really?" Fran narrowed her eyes.

"We haven't had a chance to talk about anything but work." She added, "At least lately." Who knows. Maybe Fran and Darcy used to talk.

Two professional women walking down a sunny LA street toward the closest Starbucks—finally, something Gabby could get into. A row of palm trees marked the way, each probably a hundred feet tall, and leaning the same direction, naked except for one silly bunch of leaves at the top.

Reflecting on the trees, Gabby said, "The palm tree really only had one idea: get tall."

Fran frowned back.

"They have a real last-minute, I-threw-this-outfit-together vibe. Don't you think?"

Fran frowned harder. "What are you trying to tell me?"

"Just goes to show you really only need one idea, but you need to commit to it." It was the lack of sleep talking—it always turned her into a pothead philosopher.

"Are you…suggesting something? I know I come across as single-minded sometimes."

"You are being cryptic," Markus agreed in her ear. "Are you accusing Fran of something?"

If anyone was limited by one idea, it was her. Her identity started and stopped at "mom."

Fran was in the zone, though. "You're right. I've been working too hard." She shook her head. "I really thought I was getting ahead, about to make some real money, move up the ladder. And then, wham, someone else is hired from outside the organization and given the good work. Happens every time."

Gabby's jaw dropped at the prospect of juicy gossip. "Who was hired above you?"

"You, Camille."

"Me? I'm just an executive assis—" She cut herself off. Maybe it seemed like a dumb job to her, but if it was Fran's dream, she didn't want to knock it. "I had no clue this was your dream job?" Gabby hadn't even been aware of an office hierarchy. Was she above Fran?

"I need money. LA isn't cheap."

Gabby felt that deep. That seek work order from the court was what started this whole mess. She was just trying to keep the kids and the house and stay out of court.

Fran opened the door for Gabby, and a blast of air-conditioning hit, drying the sheen of sweat she'd worked up on the short walk. "It's for my kid's tuition. Public schools haven't been the best fit. He has some sensory issues…" She shook her head. "I don't know what to do, but I might as well be sending him to Harvard."

Gabby's heart squeezed. Of course Fran was killing herself at work, making a pest of herself trying to look valuable. "Good job, Mama. I totally get where you're coming from."

A lightbulb went off. "You're sending him to a Waldorf School, aren't you?"

Fran's eyes went wide. "How'd you know?"

In her ear, Markus said, "Wow, nice detective work."

"There's a rumor going around that you're living out of the Waldorf Astoria." Gabby laughed at the absurdity. What kind of assistant could afford that? "I saw Waldorf on your caller ID yesterday. Do you have a partner or are you doing this on your own?"

"I got the job at eStocks right after the divorce."

With feeling, Gabby said, "Girl, let me get your coffee."

Fran looked at her skeptically. "You don't need to do that."

Gabby smiled. "We women have to have each other's backs. It's not like Kramer's going to understand. That man's phone background is a picture of his car."

Fran unzipped her purse, a cross-body brown leather bag that looked like it had seen better days. Poor thing was spending all her money trying to give her kid a better life.

Gabby won the quick-draw competition and slid a card with the name Camille Walker into the machine. "That's what friends are for."

When Fran said, "Thanks, Camille," Gabby smiled back, the fake name ringing in her ears. She couldn't keep any of the friends she made on this job. It was summer camp without pen pals.

At 4:59 p.m. the Evite arrived. She was saved! Thank you, Justin!

First Annual eStocks Investor Soiree
Calling all Mob bosses and capos for the party of the year!
Where: Velvet Underground Speakeasy,
behind Velvet's Drag Bar
Password: Capone
When: Saturday 5 p.m.
Theme: The Mob!

Gabby's jaw dropped. Justin had sent the actual Mafia invitations to a mob-themed party with the suggestion to "take a break from racketeering. Channel your inner Capone! Wear a hat. Fake guns only."

Fake guns only—this was insanity.

When she dialed Justin in a frenzy, he picked up immediately. "You're welcome!" he trilled.

"Justin..." She didn't know where to start.

"After I picked the venue, it all came together organically."

When she didn't respond because she was trying not to have a panic attack, he said, "What, is it too on the nose for financial people?"

He had no clue how on the nose this theme was.

"Gabby, I don't think you're grasping just how amazing this

is for three hours of planning. I went for simple and easy. And I picked up your kids!"

Simple and easy would have been an overpriced caterer and a rented conference room at the Marriott.

"Trust me, it's going to be a hit."

Wrong choice of words. A hit was exactly what she was worried about.

At least she had provided an invitation. Gabby poked her head into Kramer's office and waved an overly cheerful goodbye while he was distracted so she could slip out before any discussion of the invitation or her job status. Better to give him a minute to process that one. "See you tomorrow, Mr. Kramer. The invitation should be in your inbox."

CHAPTER 23

Tuesday, finally the end of the workday, driving home on the 405

It had been a long day. One of those days that was so long that she couldn't even vaguely remember where she'd parked. Disoriented, she scanned the parking lot for her minivan before remembering that's not who she was anymore. She hit the button on the key fob, and Darcy's car beeped a quick hello.

In the driver's seat, the automatic preferences went to Darcy's settings, a quick reminder that she was driving a dead woman's car, stepping into a dead woman's life. Even more than that, she was filling in for a woman who liked to drive with the seat way back. Had she driven with one hand on top of the steering wheel, relaxed dad–style? In Gabby's mind, Darcy was a 1980s action hero, casually saving the world, probably uttering one-liners. She might not have met her, but she could feel Darcy's "yipee-ki-yea, motherfucker; hasta la vista, baby" energy. It struck Gabby that all those taglines were meant to be uttered as the bad guy took his last breath, a final goodbye. Instead, Darcy was the one who was gone.

Gabby moved the seat as close to the steering wheel as possible, as if that would give her control of the road, and gripped the wheel tightly at ten and two, her knuckles whitening at the thought of

Darcy. At this time of day, it would take her at least forty-five minutes to get home, enough time to come up with a plan. As much as she wanted to bury her head in the sand and watch *Nailed It!* until she passed out on the couch, she couldn't.

Smirnov had told her not to move the kids, but not moving them was just leaving them like sitting ducks, waiting to be taken hostage.

And Markus. She had given him the code to her house. Was he as trustworthy as she believed, or was he just handsome?

Emotionally unavailable alpha types were always her undoing. It would be so much easier if she could just sit with everyone, have a conversation, and figure out who the mole was. Trying to make decisions without all the stakeholders in one room was almost impossible.

She needed to move the kids.

Option one: send the kids with Phil. Smirnov didn't even know she was divorced, so he definitely didn't know Phil was in a hotel. Sure, she wanted the kids to live somewhere with warm beds and a kitchen, but at least Phil's hotel didn't have the Russian Mafia.

Option two: send the kids with her mom. This would be better in some ways. Time with grandma, who happened to live in another town. But what if Smirnov found out? Would she just be roping her mom into the danger too?

Option one was up first. "Siri, call Phil."

"Gaaaaabby," he answered, dragging out her name. She could just see him leaning back in his office chair and putting up his feet, getting ready to kick around her agenda like a hacky sack.

Keep control of the conversation. "Are you back from Sacramento?"

"Yeah, that was a day trip. I hate that town."

"I was wondering if you were around this weekend. I thought you might take the kids."

"Um, what? I don't really know what we'd do in a tiny hotel room for a whole weekend. I mean, I thought you didn't want them living out of suitcases." After a pause, he said, "Maybe if I could have the house. You could have the hotel."

She sighed. That wouldn't solve anything. The only one out of harm's way would be her.

"No thanks, Phil."

"You know, that's a new thing divorced parents are doing."

She noticed her speedometer clicking up. She'd gone from sixty-five to eighty. Further proof that she did not make good decisions around Phil. If she gave him ground on the house, pretty soon she'd be living with him again.

"It's just that we have a bit of a ... pest problem." Sticking with the same lie was the one way she was simplifying her life this week.

"What, are you doing a bug bomb this weekend?"

"I was thinking about it. Maybe I can call one of those humane exterminators. I'll figure it out." She wanted to get rid of the Mafia, but she didn't want to see her reluctant kidnapper dead. He still had a chance to turn things around.

Phil's voice was at maximum smugness when he said, "Gabby, if you want to stay in the house, this is the kind of thing you have to be able to handle. What is it, roaches?"

"Something like that." Smirnov was definitely a roach.

"Just go to the hardware store. Get some of that roach spray that's safe for pets."

"I'll figure it out, Phil. Have a good weekend."

"Good luck. If you need any help with the house, you know who to call."

Not Phil—that was for sure.

After she ended the call, her exit popped up. What had she been thinking calling Phil as option number one? The less entanglement with Phil, the better. If marriage had taught her anything, it was that. Plus, don't ever let him have the remote, and be responsible for your own orgasm. Anyway, she'd just load up the kids and take them to her mom's. It would be better for the kids, and Smirnov probably wasn't going to follow her kids to Bakersfield.

She pulled up to a four-way stop a few blocks from her house, where she turned from Lemon Lane to Avocado Avenue. She hit the blinker and waited for the other cars to go.

The slow click, click, click of the blinker contrasted with her racing heartbeat, her fingers drumming on the steering wheel in a nervous tap dance. She ran through the packing list in her head: enough clothes for a week, toothbrushes—she couldn't forget swimsuits. The kids loved her mom's pool. Life jackets because her mom was going to be loosey-goosey about safety. She'd just run into the health food store on the way out of town so her mom didn't have to work so hard on feeding Lucas. She'd get five of the frozen pizzas he could eat and a bunch of gluten-free chicken strips. And macarons for her mom, the really pretty box with all of the flavors.

She took a right and pulled up behind a white SUV. It was a veteran's license plate with an American flag frame, personalized to read DOG MOM. Gabby's heart sank. It was her mom.

No problem. This was a problem she could deal with. She'd convince her mom to have a quick dinner, and then she'd load the kids up and send them all off to safety.

"Hi, sweetie!" Her mom popped out of the driver's seat, her freshly dyed hair glinting copper in the sun. "Where's my Bubbles?"

On cue, Mr. Bubbles ran out, tail wagging and tongue hanging. "What a good boy," she cooed. "Gabby, you look incredible!" Her mom stood back and took her daughter in. "Maybe divorce was a good idea." Her mom had been a lukewarm supporter of her split from Phil: *Are you doing enough for him? Remember, he's your third child. That's what a husband is. You're supposed to hate them—that's just how it goes. Even Michelle Obama said she couldn't stand Barack. But you need to try harder. Go on a date, stop worrying so much about Lucas's allergies and go to a hotel for a weekend.* The Michelle Obama quote got to her. Phil was the one who left, though.

Before Gabby could say something righteous and offend her mom, Justin came out of the house in drag. Betty Danger was full volume and looking fine.

Betty stage-whispered, "Drag happy hour tonight. Did you forget?"

Shit. She had meant to go. If she wasn't so busy balancing the Russian Mafia, the EOD, and kids, she would have snuck down for a drink and cheered on her bestie. The fucking Mafia was really getting in the way. "I'm sorry. I totally forgot."

Her mom, goggle-eyed at Justin, said, "And who is this? Did you hire a Hollywood star to watch the kids?"

Betty waved her off with a dramatic "Oh, stop!"

Gabby did not have the energy to tell her mom she was talking to Justin whom she'd known for ten years. Plus Justin was clearly getting a thrill out of it.

"I'm watching the kids after school for Gabby." Justin looked like the perfect 1950s housewife with an apron on over what looked like a cocktail dress. "And I whipped up some dinner for you all."

He was making her look so bad. Gourmet food, glamour. It was like watching men's figure skating after the women's— everyone landing their jumps.

"Where did you get that dress?" her mom gushed.

"Macy's, just last week."

"If I wasn't rushing out, I'd have to go look, not that it would look good on me. You must work out—"

"What? Rushing out?" Gabby's casual annoyance with this conversation screeched to a halt. She needed her mom gone and with the kids. "I was going to ask you to take the kids with you. You know how I'm starting that new job. It's just gotten to be more demanding than I'd expected. And I have that roach problem."

"Gabby, you need to set boundaries so this job doesn't turn into a permanent disaster." Betty nodded in agreement, having given the same advice this morning.

Gabby let out a tight, anxious laugh. Little did they know.

The passenger door swung open, and Granny popped out. "I must have fallen asleep. Where're my babies?!"

"Ohmygod." Gabby could feel the heat rise. Avocado Avenue was tilting beneath her feet. "You brought Granny?!" She mouthed, "I told you—"

"I couldn't change my plans, sweetie."

Gabby stared in horror as her eighty-year-old grandma came out in a shiny pink tracksuit and a pair of Yeezys. "Gabby! I've missed you, sweetie. And look, your hair is finally the right color!"

She, her mom, and her grandma all had the same shade of red hair. None of them natural redheads. "It runs in the family!" Granny said.

More like shopping at Walgreens for L'Oréal intense red copper ran in the family, but c'est la vie.

"Choice is more important than genetics," said Granny. "You've finally chosen to be one of us." Granny put her hands on her hips and looked around the neighborhood, the sky tinged pink over Avocado Avenue. She yelled, "Burt, we're home."

"Burt?"

Her mom smiled slyly. "You'll love him, Gabs."

"You don't mean...?"

Her mom kept smiling as the horror of the situation rose like a black sun. Granny opened up the door to reveal an old man in a fedora and a Hawaiian shirt sleeping with his chin on his chest. Granny hollered, "Burt, we're here. Wake up."

Her grandma wrapped Gabby in a bony hug. "Gabs, so good to see you. Meet your new grandpa."

Burt let out a big snore, and Granny held out her left hand. "He proposed."

Grandma had on a rock that would make JLo jealous. "He got it off QVC." She whispered as if not to brag. "It's from the Jane Seymour collection."

When Gabby didn't respond, she added, "You know, *Dr. Quinn, Medicine Woman*?"

Gabby nodded.

"Burtie, wake up!" she shouted. With a snort, he jarred himself awake. Then he shook off the sleep and looked at Gabby and the quiet street. "The new digs. What's for dinner?"

What's for dinner? Gabby's blood started to boil. Did this old asshole think he was moving in, uninvited, and she was going to make him dinner?

"Actually, Mom, can I talk to you?"

"Gabby, it's all settled. You need the help, and they need somewhere to stay. Betty, can you help me get the bags?"

Gabby stood in the driveway paralyzed as she watched her plan go to hell. She wasn't loading up the kids to safety. Betty Danger was moving Granny and Burt into the house. With Betty, her mom, and the kids, it looked like a house party with entertainment. When they opened the door to walk in, music filtered out.

Grandpa yelled, "Which bedroom is mine. Is it soundproof?"

CHAPTER 24

Wednesday morning before work and school, Greene household

It was Granny's first day watching the kids. On her way out the door, Gabby called, "Remember, no gluten!" Also fingers crossed that Granny was safe behind the wheel. LA traffic for an eighty-year-old woman who hadn't gone anywhere for years—that was no joke.

"Gluten?" Granny said the word like she'd never heard of it. "What is that anyway?"

"It's in bread."

"What? Who can't eat bread?" Granny was incredulous. "Gabby, how do you expect that boy to grow?"

"Lucas has allergies. He can't eat eggs, dairy, nuts, or gluten."

Granny squinted at her. "What *can* he eat?"

That was a fair question.

Before she left, Gabby looked at Lucas and said, "Granny is in charge this morning, so you listen to her." With a deep breath, she said, "I need you to be a big boy. You know what you can and can't eat, right?"

He nodded.

"It's your job to be careful and take care of yourself."

"Huh?" He looked confused.

Was this the first time she'd ever mentioned this to him, the first time she'd asked him to take personal responsibility? He could build a world in *Minecraft* and knew everything about sharks. She could probably ask him to do a little more.

"Lucas, I can't always be there, so you need to pay attention. You copy?"

Another realization smacked her upside the head. This was probably how someone became a Phil, man babies who couldn't do anything for themselves except make money. Phils weren't born. They were made. In doing everything for these kids, she was shirking her responsibility to make them into decent humans.

She looked at Kyle and said, "I love you. Make sure Granny doesn't kill anyone."

Kyle laughed—a real laugh. "Okay, Mom. It's fine."

What was going on? Everything was going to hell in a handbasket, she wasn't doing any of the mom things she normally did while she messed around with the EOD and the Mafia, but something in Kyle had loosened. An error screen flashed in her mind. The inputs did not compute. Had she been holding on too tight?

Granny thrust a coffee into Gabby's hand and handed her her purse. "Relax, Gabriella. No one is going to die."

Gabby clicked her seat belt and pushed PLAY on her audiobook. It had been a week since she'd spent any time with her personal divorce/life coach, Sloane Ellis. Markus—damn him—had mentioned that the chapter on coping mechanisms helped his work-life balance. Markus giving her any advice was suspect. First off, probably a mole. Second, a guy without kids talking to her about work-life balance issues—talk about a joke.

But she needed help figuring out how to deal with him, and Sloane was her best bet. As usual, the freeway was jam-packed. The EOD probably didn't have to give anyone from LA tactical driving lessons, because that's what it took to get to work. She swerved around a random shopping cart someone had left in the right lane, and sped up to join the mass movement toward downtown. A world of concrete subdivided into eight lanes of cars spread before her.

She'd always trusted people based on instinct—were they nice to her? Did they seem genuine? What kind of energy did they put out into the world? Markus passed all of her tests with flying colors, but even he had said, "There are no friends in espionage."

"Hello again, this is Sloane Ellis, your favorite life coach." Sloane's voice filled the car with calm authority, the kind Gabby would like to project. "Today we're going to talk about managing your daily life. After divorce, you might have more tasks, more responsibilities. Do you feel stressed all the time?"

An unhinged laugh escaped Gabby's lips.

"Often the stress of divorce comes from managing life alone. You no longer have a partner to do the dishes, pay bills, take kids to school, or bring in half the income."

That was true. At least Phil had taken care of the bills before.

"I can help." Sloane's promise rang through the car like a siren song.

Gabby turned up the volume.

"Number one: Say no to the tasks that don't need to be done. Set strong boundaries. There is no balance without the word no."

Justin had already told her this.

"For stressors that can't be avoided, I recommend compartmentalization. Divide up the tasks. Put 'bills' in one virtual box and 'making dinner' in another. Do one thing at a time."

Gabby laughed. Like she hadn't tried.

"The world might be loud and filled with demands. You can't change that, but you can make your own calm. Note, that I didn't say 'find.' I said 'make.' Create a room in your mind. Make it beautiful, peaceful, empty. When you need to complete a task—pay the bills, do the laundry, make dinner, book a vacation—go in the room you created for yourself and don't let anything in."

Is this where all the men were when you needed them?

At work, she marched into Kramer's office before she had even made his coffee. Better to rip off the Band-Aid and see if she still had a job straightaway. "Did you get the Evite?"

"Ah, the Evite. I better RSVP, huh?" Markus said, completely unaware of what he was walking into.

This was as good as she could hope for. At least she could get everyone's response over with at the same time.

Kramer sat up and put his elbows on his desk as if she'd just reminded him to yell at her about that. "I did get the Evite. Are you out of your mind? This isn't a fucking Halloween party! This is an investment business. Do you think you work for a frat?"

In the earpiece, Markus gasped. "Did Justin do this? What the hell? Why?"

Gabby took a deep breath. At least she didn't have to go through this explanation twice. "Themed work parties are a trend," she explained. "The goofier the better. They help people loosen up. It gives them something to talk about. I read an article in the *Wall Street Journal* about it." She hadn't, and she doubted Justin had either. "Fran agrees." Also a lie.

"It's going to be a huge hit. Mafia-themed parties are very in. Not to mention, it goes with the venue." Parroting Justin's words, she said, "It came together organically."

Kramer said "but" a few times, but it's not like he could explain the real reason it was a problem. In a serious voice, Markus said, "You've placed the whole mission in jeopardy over this stupid invitation. What were you thinking?"

"The response has been overwhelmingly positive," she said, ignoring the overwhelmingly negative reception. "Orlov already RSVP'd yes with the comment 'Very funny.'" He'd probably meant that to be sarcastic, but on its face, he just wrote, "Very funny."

Kramer chewed on that for a minute. Orlov was the whole point of the party. Really, as long as he was showing, nothing had gone too wrong. Still not looking happy, but his anger defused, Kramer dismissed her. "I've got enough to worry about. Just go get my coffee and don't do anything else dumb."

Her job at eStocks was almost one hundred percent making sure that that man never had to lift a finger. That's how Kramer compartmentalized. He outsourced everything but the financial analysis and client contact. Pretty much the same as Phil had done.

Markus wasn't moving on quite as easily. "Gabby, you invited the Mafia to a mob-themed party." She could hear him trying to keep his voice out of the red zone. "Do you think this is a joke?"

She walked to the bathroom. The man needed some talking down. "Markus, I know it was bad, but Justin had no clue. And there was no harm done. I didn't lose the job, and the party is happening." It might just be a little awkward. Would the mob be offended when Justin got mob culture all wrong, like cheap cultural appropriation, wearing a Pocahontas costume to a traditional powwow? Or maybe it was open season because of the whole criminal element.

"I'm compartmentalizing," she said, like she knew what she was doing. "You should too."

"What is this?" He laughed at her advice. "*You* are giving *me* spy lessons now?"

Tension broken, she leaned into the joke of her being in charge. "Markus," she said in a faux serious voice, "I might not be able to achieve the deep focus necessary for compartmentalization with another human in my ear all day. If I put two sugars in that man's coffee, I might lose my job."

"I have faith, Gabby. And it's different, we're focusing on the same job together, isolating ourselves in the same virtual room."

"Sounds romantic now," she said. He made it sound like they were on a road trip and there was only one queen bed left.

With a laugh, he said, "You wish."

After grabbing coffee and a donut for Kramer, Gabby knocked on his door out of courtesy. As usual, he didn't even look up but just kept talking. Money, money, money—she could practically see the dollar signs in his eyes. Wealth management made sense. People needed money to exist in the world, but Kramer didn't make it look good.

"Are you sure you are ready to close out the accounts?" Kramer scrolled through a screen. "The investment still has potential." He was scrolling too quickly, almost frantically. "Whatever you want, though. You're in charge."

The person on the other end of the line must have said they wanted out, because Kramer said, "Okay. That's no problem. I can wire the money now. I just need the account number."

Wiring money.

Account numbers.

Ding ding ding!

Gabby held her breath at the buzzwords. Markus's voice came through the earpiece in a whisper. "This is it, Gabby. Hang out as long as you can. See if you can get any more info. Anything. This is the break we've been waiting for."

Gabby made a split-second decision to spill Kramer's coffee all over the white rug. Drawing on a lifetime of clumsy mistakes, she made a show of tripping on the edge of the carpet, which really was a hazard. She lurched forward and let the coffee fly.

"Ohmygod. I'm so sorry, Mr. Kramer." She looked up, horrified for real at the coffee stain on the white rug. "I can fix this. I pro—"

He glared hard and made a "be quiet!" gesture with his hands. His whole demeanor screamed, "Shut the fuck up. I'm busy."

Gabby mouthed, "I'll just clean this up."

Kramer spun his chair in the other direction to hide her from view while she grabbed a napkin and made a show of dabbing at the spilled coffee. Luckily, Kramer wasn't watching her at all, because the napkin was rapidly disintegrating on the rug. She was making a bigger mess. It was Lucas and the blue paint episode all over again.

Kramer hit the button to fog the transparent glass to his office, which she hadn't noticed until now. Just like in the movies, he opened the painting on the wall behind his desk to expose a safe.

"That's offshore, right?"

Gabby, still crouched on the carpet behind his desk, didn't

move a muscle. Markus wasn't even breathing into the earpiece, silently waiting for Kramer to hang himself. This had to be big—Gabby didn't know much about money laundering, but he was hitting all the buzzwords.

Kramer punched the keycode into the safe and pulled out a locked laptop while Gabby peered around the corner of the desk, making sure Markus had a view through her brooch.

Markus barely whispered, "That's it. That's gotta be where he makes all of his transfers."

Gabby stopped scrubbing the carpet and watched him boot up the computer and punch in some numbers.

"Okay, can you confirm the transfer?" After a brief pause, he said, "Excellent."

Just when the conversation turned to golf, Gabby took a breath. She scooped up all of the napkin crumbs and was about to stand, when she lost her balance and dropped back on her butt, right onto the donut, with a squish of crème filling and the muffled crack of the plate.

"Damn it!"

Kramer looked her way. "What are you still doing in here?" he said, as if she hadn't been in there for the last five minutes pouring a coffee on the ground and grinding a napkin into the carpet. When he saw her scraping a donut off the ass of her cute jeans, he laughed it off. "Jesus Christ, Camille."

"I know. I'm such a klutz," she said, shaking her head, playing up the whole "I can't be a spy because I'm such a bumbling idiot!" angle, easy to sell because she believed it herself.

"Just get me a new coffee," he said as he slid the computer back in its safe and shut the painting over it.

"I did what I could with the carpet for now. I'll finish cleaning later." She'd actually massacred it, but that would give her something else to do in his office later.

Before getting Kramer a fresh coffee and donut, she went to the bathroom to scrape the donut off her pants.

"Nice one," Markus ribbed her.

"Doing a squat in heels isn't in my wheelhouse at the moment." If she was going to continue in this job, which she obviously wasn't, she would need to get a handle on her fitness.

"Well, you're not a stripper. Actually, you shouldn't be wearing heels at all. Spies only wear heels in movies. You need something you can maneuver in."

"Valentina wears heels every day." She good and damn well wasn't going to be wearing orthopedic shoes while Valentina dressed like a TV spy. "I'm not even forty." Granny could probably do this better than her.

"I'm sure you can get back in twerking shape, if that's what you want," Markus said dryly. "That laptop, though. That could be our big break."

"Oh, that's good news," Gabby said as she finished cleaning glaze off her pants.

"A laptop like that is too impenetrable to access remotely. All of his transfers must be on there, maybe even a stored password."

"Uh-huh," she murmured, letting him mansplain money laundering to her. This part seemed pretty simple. Gabby showed her ass to the mirror and craned her neck around to make sure she got all the donut flakes off.

"You know I can see you, Gabby."

"Oh, sorry. But you know I can't walk around with cream filling all over my—"

"Just stop talking and turn around. I refuse to say any more on this topic." He took a cleansing breath. "Anyway, as I was saying, that laptop has got to have all of the Russians' best tech on it."

"Russian tech?" That didn't sound too impressive. Gabby leaned over and brushed crumbs out of her cleavage.

"That's enough with the mirror," he said, exasperated. "Button up your shirt, give that man his coffee, and stop messing with me."

"You're kidding, right?" He wasn't really affected by her wardrobe adjustments. He couldn't be. Phil had been treating her like the lunch lady for literally years. She might as well be wearing a hairnet and ladling up cafeteria spaghetti.

"Why would I be kidding?"

"Well, okay," she said, not quite believing him. Maybe because he was the mole and he was trying to butter her up. He wasn't too good-looking to be a spy. He was exactly good-looking enough, a honey trap seducing her into spilling her secrets. A cocktail of confusion, power, and elation surged through her veins.

She dropped the topic and headed back to Kramer's office. Mid donut delivery, Kramer had another request. "Camille, get me some curry from that Thai place."

She was about to order it through Uber Eats, when he said, "Pick it up yourself. Last time the delivery guy got my order wrong. I want red curry, spicy, no bamboo shoots."

Her afternoon was going to go sideways because Kramer had too many bamboo shoots in his curry last time. That man. As she left on another dumb errand, all she could say was thank god Justin was doing the party.

In the car on the way to pick up curry, her thoughts drifted back to that laptop. Kramer had definitely done a transfer on it. It only made sense that the codes Smirnov wanted were stored there too. She knew they weren't on a Post-it note somewhere. And it's not like Kramer would use one of those password-keeping apps for transferring millions of dollars.

When the car came to life and Gabby's phone connected, Sloane Ellis's voice filled the car. "Give yourself enough time to complete tasks. Focusing on one task at a time instead of letting your mind race through twelve activities is always more efficient."

With men it was always "I can't, I'm fixing the car" or "I'm mowing the lawn" or "I'll be at the office." Meanwhile, they left the thousands of other household tasks to women. And it was always a laundry list: The kids need dinner, but you forget to get the gluten-free noodles, so you have to figure out how to make a zucchini lasagna. Oh, and his mother needs a present because it's her birthday (he forgot), the laundry and dishes need to be done, and the kids have to do their homework. To top it off, someone needs to check in and talk to the kids about how they are doing because if no one does the emotional labor, you're just raising well-fed sociopaths. Or maybe it was psychopaths? Whichever one was just an asshole but not a serial killer. Knock on wood. Oh, and nobody brushed their teeth.

She said, "You know, focusing on one task at a time seems like a male privilege to me."

Markus said, "I don't get what you mean."

"Women multitask. Men compartmentalize. Men are from Mars, women are from Venus."

"I get what you're saying, but you're not at home. And your feelings are some of the things you should be compartmentalizing. Literally, save them for later because they're making it harder for you to focus on the task at hand."

Her voice Ginsu sharp, Gabby said, "What are you talking

about, Markus? If I'd wanted to compartmentalize things, I would have started selling Tupperware with Shelly."

"Huh?"

That's right. It's not like he knew who Shelly was.

Markus let out a breath. "Just breathe, Gabby, and turn off Sloane. I don't know what's going on, but you seem on edge today. Is there something bothering you?"

"Take your pick, Markus. There are about twelve major problems today alone."

"You need to figure out how to handle the stress. Compartmentalizing isn't a joke. We're counting on you."

"I'm fine." Her voice sounded angry, even to her own ears. She was angry.

"I need you to get that laptop."

"How, Markus? You saw where it is. It's behind Kramer's desk, and he never leaves. He doesn't have to because he makes me run all of his errands. I'm driving across town to get his favorite curry right now." Speak of the devil, a text came through on Camille Walker's phone. Kramer probably needed her to pick up his dry cleaning too.

"Gabby, you are the one in the office. You see his patterns. Watch him a little more closely. Does he take a long poop at the same time every day? Is he late some days of the week? What are his weaknesses? Does he like pretty girls and we could send in someone to flirt with him while you break into the safe? Think."

"I'm doing this job with less than a week of training while single parenting." Just to complicate things, the Mafia was threatening her family, but she couldn't say that part aloud. She'd been holding it together, keeping all of her frustrations in, rolling with each new punch. With each comment from Markus, she could feel the dam start to break.

"I know, but you can do better." He expelled a frustrated breath. "You aren't even listening. Yesterday, you hired an outside person, which could compromise the mission. You almost got fired."

"You think I don't know that? I am doing my best. Back off, Markus." This was a warning for his own good.

"Your best isn't good enough. Do better."

Gabby gasped. "Compartmentalize this, Markus!" And she yanked her earpiece out and threw it on the passenger seat next to Camille Walker's phone.

CHAPTER 25

Wednesday afternoon, Lacha Somtum Thai Restaurant,
East Hollywood

Ten minutes later, Gabby pulled the car into a space in front of Kramer's favorite Thai place and stepped out without putting the car in park. It rolled into the vehicle in front of it, luckily not causing any damage. Gabby was unfocused, fuck-compartmentalizing, not-safe-behind-the-wheel mad. Goddamn Markus. *"Your best isn't good enough"* rang in her ears, echoing all of her insecurities. After Markus had been so sweet to her, the words were a betrayal.

It wasn't as much of a stretch to imagine Markus as the bad guy now. Watching *Novaya Bitva Ekstrasensov*, breaking into her house, and telling her she wasn't good enough—there was a lot about Markus she didn't know. It's not like Valentina divorced him because he was too handsome and patient.

The Thai place was cute. Not too fancy, and neat and tidy with colorful Thai art all over the walls and a whole herd of lucky cats in various colors and sizes sitting next to the cash register. Actually, not a herd, a "clowder." Just last week Kyle had informed her that was the name for a group of cats. Kramer was spiritually at odds with everything in this restaurant, including the clowder of lucky cats, but the man knew his curries.

Compartmentalization might not be her thing, but Gabby knew about retail therapy and eating her feelings. Stupid Sloane Ellis had skipped those chapters.

"How much?" she asked about a small lucky cat. Retail therapy always helped.

"Twenty bucks," said the woman.

A little luck was worth twenty. And a girl needed to eat her feelings sometimes. Plus it was lunchtime. Gabby got her own curry, a lucky cat, and a bag of tamarind candies for the kids. Her three different bosses could all suck it. The curry was made with fresh coconut milk, fragrant with lemongrass, and healing in a way that only good food could be.

When her phone buzzed with a text, she got ready for the next issue in her life. The school nurse or Kramer, but no—the lucky cat paid off. It was Valentina. Meet at HQ after work. Lessons, as promised.

Halfway through her bowl of restorative curry, Markus stepped through the door. She glared and set down her chopsticks. With a quiet, "I will stab you with this chopstick if you come any closer" energy, she said, "I need a lunch break, Markus. Do you know I haven't sat down for lunch once this week? And it's only Wednesday." Ten minutes alone with a bowl of curry—was that really too much to ask?

He settled into the chair across from her. "Do you mind if I sit?" He waited for her to nod her assent.

"I do actually."

When the waitress came by, he said, "I'll have one of what

she's having," pointing at Gabby's meal without even asking what it was.

"I said I want to eat alone," Gabby reiterated. She didn't need to have lunch with a guy who very well might be reporting her activities to Smirnov. "Isn't this dangerous anyway? What if someone sees us together?"

Markus shrugged. "No one followed us. I've been watching. And this place is way out of the way. Not to mention, empty." It was them and one waitress. With the waitress out of earshot, he leaned in closer. "I'm sorry. I shouldn't have pushed you like that."

She didn't respond, so he went on. "You're doing really well, and I don't know, it feels like we've been working together forever. I forgot for a minute that you aren't a seasoned agent like Darcy."

That seemed like a line of BS to her. "Half an hour ago, I fell on my ass onto a crème-filled donut while I was trying to be sneaky. I think my limitations are pretty in-your-face."

He shook his head in the negative. "It was *after* you tried to be sneaky. And you know it just made you look like you didn't know what you were doing, like any old ditzy office assistant."

She looked inept because she was. "I'm not going to forgive you that easily. Do you know how stressful this is? I am worried constantly about my kids. I have arranged for someone different to pick them up from school every day. Kyle has missed all the lessons I've paid for, and no one else seems to be worried enough about Lucas's allergies." She looked at him. "I am pinch-hitting here. This isn't even my job."

"I know. I don't need to be putting any more pressure on you than you already have." He opened a pair of chopsticks and started clicking them together nervously, not normal for Markus. "Me snapping was more about me than you."

Every word tempered the anger she was trying to hang on to. If she could just feel more indifferent toward him, it would be easier when it turned out he was the mole. Those butterflies she felt when he walked into a room, the rush of adrenaline when he texted her good night, that was what she didn't need. Staying mad was the key.

He blew out a breath. "I didn't tell you before, but Darcy and I were close."

She looked up, softening against her better judgment. "I'm sorry."

He looked down at the table, rearranging the little bowls of hot sauce, probably just for something to do with his hands. Markus never fidgeted. "We were partners for a couple of years." His voice breaking up, he said, "She was my best friend. She was there for me through the divorce with Val, sort of like your friend Justin." He shook his head.

She reached across the table but stopped short of putting her hand on his. She picked up an errant straw wrapper like she had meant to. "I didn't know."

"We were in the field together for years. When you are facing life-or-death situations, you get close fast. My therapist said it's called trauma bonding."

She knew what he meant. The closeness developing between the two of them—was it just trauma or was it something more?

His eyes flicked up, a flash of warm honey brown. "It's not like that bond happens with everyone, but when you click with someone, it puts your relationship into overdrive."

Warmth flashed through her. He was talking about Darcy but also them.

"I want to be in the field. I want to take out her killer myself."

"Why didn't they just plant you as a security guard or something? *You* could break into the safe."

He huffed out a sad laugh. "I would, but Alice knew how torn up I was. She took me off field duty until psych clears me."

"Oh," she said with just a hint of surprise, not because she was shocked but because Markus seemed so together, so stable. "Are you okay?"

He nodded. "I'm fine."

Nothing said "not fine" like "I'm fine."

After their curry was gone, Markus said, "All I want is to bring Darcy's killer to justice."

She gave a single nod. "I'll do my best."

The waitress interrupted. "One check or two?" She lingered on "one" while looking directly at Markus. He said, "Sure."

Gabby raised an eyebrow. "Work's paying, right?"

"Nah, it's on me."

As he signed the receipt, a secret smiled played across his features. "Compartmentalize this—that might be your tagline."

On the way back to the office, Gabby dialed Justin, who had no clue that he'd created such an uproar. "How's everything going?" she asked.

"You are going to love this party. All my queens are coming through. These bankers are going to be en-ter-tained!"

Gabby could see it now, Justin sashaying into the party and giving the actual mob tips on how to be more mob-like. As long as they survived the night.

"Thanks, Justin. You are the best best friend that ever existed in the history of best friends."

"Maybe we should get BFF necklaces?" he suggested.

She was definitely getting necklaces.

Back at the office, Gabby had a clear objective: figure out how to get into the damn safe. Markus was right. Her best wasn't good enough. She needed to do better if she was going to save her family.

"Mr. Kramer, I'm going to work on getting the stain out of this rug."

"Fine. Just stay out of the way."

On her hands and knees, she started in on the carpet. After twenty minutes of scrubbing and surreptitiously glancing at Kramer, he was still on the phone, showing no signs of leaving the office. So far this week, he hadn't left his seat for longer than the time it took to pee.

"Mr. Kramer, have you thought about having a lunch meeting with your clients? That would be nice, wouldn't it?"

He glared, but she went on. "There is a great Italian place just down the street."

"Camille, I don't need any suggestions."

Frustrated, she went back to her desk for a breather. She sat in the chair for just a second and rubbed her temples.

"You doing okay?" Fran looked up from her computer.

"Ugh. Just having one of those days." She shut her eyes before diving into another hour of pretending to clean the carpet in case Kramer actually left the room. "Do you ever get sick of this, Fran?"

Fran looked right at Gabby. "Yes. I've been trying so hard for so many years, working late, anticipating his every need." She shook her head. "The things I have done for that man."

"How long have you worked here?"

Fran sighed. "Oh, it's been a while. It's a boys' club."

"So you want to be a financial analyst?" Fran seemed happy to serve Kramer's every need, but she hadn't talked about actual finances at all.

"I want to be at the top. I want to make real money."

"I'm feeling pretty *9 to 5* about him today."

"What?" Fran flashed a blank look.

"Oh, you have to see that movie. It's a classic." She got fired up just thinking of Dolly Parton, Jane Fonda, and Lily Tomlin taking out their sexist boss with rat poison in his coffee. Fifty years later and Kramer was pretty much a Franklin Hart Jr. Maybe Gabby wasn't going to murder him with rat poison, but she was going to take this guy out for her and Fran and all the women out there who were underutilized and underpaid, coming home to sinks full of dishes.

She raised her coffee mug. "Here's to us, Fran!" After a fortifying gulp of lukewarm coffee, she dove back into the carpet cleaning. Sometime later—god knows how long, because her brain had shut down—Kramer stood up. The jerk was finally going to leave the room.

Instead of leaving, he stood over her and glared at her dumb project. "What in the hell are you doing over here?"

She pointed to the stain. "This is a tricky one. I was thinking of renting a carpet shampooer. I could run down to the hardware store right now, if you don't mind me staying a little late."

"Camille, I'm not going to pay you overtime for something the cleaning crew will do anyway."

"Okay, I can do it tomorrow during the day. It'll be easy." Anything to give her extra time in the office.

"I have a full schedule tomorrow and I don't need you underfoot.

And Friday, the security team is coming in to upgrade things around here. Finally."

"But—"

"It's five thirty. Go home."

With a backwards glance at the Bugatti portrait she hadn't even managed to inspect, she left the office.

At least she'd found out about the security upgrade, not that it was going to make her life any easier. If Kramer was going to booby-trap the office on Friday, that only left tomorrow for spy shenanigans. She had one day to figure out how to get Kramer out of his office and steal his computer.

CHAPTER 26

Wednesday after work, EOD headquarters

After work, Gabby walked into HQ to meet Valentina for shooting lessons with the same feeling she had going for a Pap smear. Gabby had never wanted a gun. Once, she'd found one in the park. Too scared to touch it, she'd poked it with a stick and then called the authorities. A very polite officer had informed her that it was a cap gun. Better safe than sorry, though.

"Better safe than sorry" meant something new this week. She still didn't want a gun, even a little—but she needed a gun. She sure as hell wasn't going to count on the EOD to save her ass.

She found Valentina in the clean room, talking quietly with Alice about some important work things. What wasn't important at the EOD, though? Everything involved national security. Working at the EOD was like being part of a dysfunctional family with a ramped-up drama level.

Gabby said, "Nice to see you, Alice. How's your week going?"

"Agent Greene." Alice gave her a nod in greeting and cut to the chase. "I heard about the laptop in Kramer's office. We need a plan to get our hands on it ASAP."

Gabby brightened at the sound of the word "we." Were they going to help her?

"He keeps the computer behind a painting of a Bugatti," she reported. Kramer was an overgrown little boy. "All we have to do is break in. I assume one of you is going to crack the safe?" She glanced at Valentina. "Do you know how to do that?" In the movies it was always a beautiful girl in a black catsuit listening to the pins in the safe like a lover's heartbeat. Valentina fit the bill.

"No, Agent Greene," Valentina said. "That's your job."

"Umm…are you kidding me?" She hadn't even been able to get in to her high school locker with a code. All those "turn right" and "two spins to the left" directions were too much for her.

"You might not have to open the safe. Just distract him while he has the computer out. Much simpler, don't you think?"

"You all told me that I was just going to be making coffee," she said, her voice strident with frustration. "You said this was a low-stakes mission."

Valentina sidestepped the criticism. "We're not sending you on any night ops or asking you to leave the office. This can happen during business hours while everyone is in the office with you."

Bad things happening during the light of day were even scarier. "It's not low stakes. Do I need to remind you that Darcy died on this mission? Now you want me to steal files from a guy who is working with the Mafia, maybe is Mafia himself. What if he catches me?" She looked around the room. "What is the matter with you two?"

Valentina repeated herself. "It's a low-risk operation. We're not putting you in the same position Darcy was in. You just need to get Kramer out of his office and get into the safe."

"Easier said than done. That man never leaves his office. If he needs something, he calls me. If I'm not available, it's Fran's job. In three days, he hasn't moved. He has an attached bathroom so he barely even leaves to pee. I tried to stay late tonight, and he kicked me out."

Valentina shrugged. "There must be something that will get him out of his chair."

Gabby shook her head. "You've got me." She blew out a frustrated breath and glanced at the clock. "I don't mean to be pushy, but can we do the shooting lesson? I would like to see my kids before bed tonight. It's been a long week."

Alice made a quasi growl noise in the back of her throat. "I don't like the idea of you with a gun."

Neither did Gabby, but how else was she going to protect herself? "I don't feel safe," Gabby said loud and slow, trying to communicate her real fear with intonation. She sure as hell couldn't explain the Smirnov issue. For all she knew, Alice was the mole.

"Let's see how the lesson goes, and then we'll talk," said Alice.

Why was the EOD so eager to throw her to the wolves with no protection? She set her jaw, determined to come up with some way to defend herself. She didn't want to be the only one bringing a leaky bag of trash to a gun fight—again.

Ten minutes later, they were in the EOD gun range. Four stories belowground, it was colder than anywhere else in the building, all concrete, all business. Before they entered the range itself, Valentina handed her ear protection and adjusted the volume knob on the side. Somehow, the gun shots were muffled but the voices were amplified.

Another agent was practicing.

Boom.

Boom

Boom.

Even with the ear protection, every shot reverberated through Gabby's body, the danger and power of the weapon shaking her all the way to her core. Gunpowder burned her nose and strengthened her resolve. She didn't have a choice.

Last time she'd been down here, it was different. She had been nervous, but not scared for her children's lives. This time, it wasn't theoretical—it was life or death.

While Gabby was on edge, Valentina moved smoothly, seemingly at ease with all-or-nothing stakes. "How are you so casual?" Gabby commented more than asked. All she could think of was the implications of this practice: death. Either the threat of death or causing death.

Valentina gave her a look that said, "Chill out."

Together, they crowded into a single lane, Valentina's musky floral perfume competing with the gunpowder for dominance. Valentina set the gun down in front of her with intent. "Do you know how to load the magazine and insert the clip?"

Markus had done that for her last time, so she shook her head no.

Valentina muttered, "Men. You can't ask them to do anything," and demonstrated how to put one bullet in the clip before ordering Gabby to do the rest. Gabby fumbled the bullet and it clattered onto the countertop. Her mind clouded with dark thoughts.

"Get out of your head, Agent Greene," Valentina barked. "You are an agent for the Elite Operatives Department, and this weapon is nothing but a tool." In a quiet but powerful tone, she said, "Load the damn gun."

Gabby took a breath. Valentina was right. She focused and shoved the clip in with a metallic clunk. At the same time, something inside of her shifted. The gun was ready, and so was she.

"You're right-handed, correct?" Valentina asked. When Gabby nodded, she said, "Pick up the gun with your right hand. Keep the finger off the trigger. Point the gun downrange." She demonstrated with her own gun how to hold it.

Less emotionally than before, Gabby picked up the gun. Valentina showed her how to adjust her grip so the slide didn't hit her thumb when the gun ejected the bullet casing.

"What happened last time? Was that the first time you had ever shot a gun?"

Gabby nodded. Guns were a ubiquitous part of life—squirt guns, Nerf guns, guns in the movies, guns on the news, but before the lesson with Markus, she had never held an actual gun, one that could take someone's life. Heavy in her hand, cold and unfeeling metal, the harsh recoil, it had served to freak her out. Too much power. That's why dudes wanted to be strapped—the power to take away life itself—and it was exactly why she had never wanted one.

Valentina nodded. "Markus should have had you try again right away."

That was probably true.

"Your gun isn't ready to fire until you chamber a bullet. Do you remember how to do that?"

Gabby pulled back on the slide. In the movies, guys were ka-chunking their guns all the time, pulling back the slides like they were toys. In reality, the slide was difficult to pull back, like getting a tough lid off a pickle jar, and the metal of the slide bit into her tender palm. Just chambering the bullet, she was slow and clumsy. In the field, she would probably already be dead.

"The more you practice, the easier it will be. When you're ready, aim and pull the trigger gently."

Just a week ago, she'd been in this exact spot, aiming at an identical paper target of a man with a bull's-eye over his sternum. Last week had been one thing—she had been scared, but unfocused. Her kids hadn't been in danger.

Gabby had been frustrated by life plenty of times—her marriage that fizzled, lack of respect at home and in the office, lack of respect for herself. With all her feelings of disappointment and frustration, she had never burned with an anger so hot that she could take a man's life. It wasn't in her nature, but she grabbed onto her anger and stoked it.

Smirnov had threatened her kids. She held the gun firmly, took a deep breath, and released it as she slowly squeezed the trigger.

In the chaos—it was just all noise and recoil—she couldn't tell if she'd hit the target. All she knew was that there wasn't steam coming from the pipes. "Did I hit it?" she asked, squinting at the target.

Valentina gave her a slow nod. "Almost a bull's-eye. Good work."

Gabby whooped as Valentina yelled, "Finger off the trigger. Aim it downrange."

An hour of practice later, the range was filled with the smoke from her shots, and there was a sickly-sweet taste in the back of her mouth.

"What is that taste, or am I imagining it?"

"Violence has an aftertaste, doesn't it?" said Valentina dramatically.

"No really, what is that? Is it in my head?"

"It's lead."

Gabby blanched. That couldn't be good for them. "How do I pack this thing up? Is this a self-checkout situation or do I sign out?"

"You sign out."

"Gotcha." So it was basically like checking out a library book.

Valentina looked her dead in the eye. "You're doing much better, but you haven't had any practice in the field. Shooting in a real situation at a real person is different."

"You're not backing out, are you?" Fear gripped Gabby, the kind of visceral, alone-in-a-parking-garage-with-no-one-but-a-guy-in-a-van fear. Valentina was abandoning her, leaving her helpless against Smirnov's goons.

Valentina shook her head. "Gabby—"

"I can do it." She said it in the eager way of someone who wants something desperately but clearly cannot do it. "I am a different person than I was last week," she pleaded.

"Well, that's good news," Valentina said dryly. "Still, I am not ready to send you with a gun. Yet."

Hands in the air, Gabby groaned. "You're kidding me."

"You did well tonight, but you've had one lesson. I'm not counting that disaster with Markus. I don't want you bringing a gun into your home. I've seen that circus."

It was her circus. She had to take care of it.

"Val, I...I need protection."

"Why? Why do you need protection so badly? Is there something you're not telling me?" Valentina scrutinized Gabby's expression, leaving her desperate to tell the truth, to ask for help.

Gabby bit her lip. "This is a dangerous job. Darcy died."

"Nope, not giving it to you."

Valentina set a small package on the table between them. "But I have something for you. This is a dart gun. The darts can be fired out of the gun like you see on animal shows. Or if you're in a close-range situation, you can just stab someone. You want to hit them in a big muscle group—ass, thigh, upper arm—to paralyze them for an hour or so."

A *dart* gun. What was she, a zookeeper? With a laugh, she realized Valentina had already told her—she was a circus ringmaster. Maybe not even the ringmaster. She was just in the circus.

Valentina continued explaining even though Gabby had shut down. "They're a paralytic, good for immobilizing someone, and they'll knock them out for about fifteen minutes. The paralytic effect lasts longer."

Gabby couldn't bring herself to care. The EOD wasn't taking her seriously, wasn't taking her safety or her children's safety seriously. And why was Valentina so intent on keeping her from having decent protection? She was starting to seem like the mole.

"You can use them on your ex if you want." Valentina wagged a tranquilizer dart in the air. "I won't tell."

Gabby didn't crack a smile. Valentina was not going to paper over this disrespect with one comment. "I need protection. For real."

Valentina held up the dart gun. "This is protection."

Gabby huffed.

Unimpressed with Gabby's attitude, Valentina went on. "You're going to want a holster. If you want this to be useful, you need to have access to it. You can't be searching around in a closet when a bad guy is coming at you."

Gabby nodded. "Fine."

Valentina gave Gabby's figure a cursory glance. "You're too hippy for a standard holster that dudes use."

"What?" Was that an insult?

"So am I. I'm just saying that the gun print will be visible, and staying hidden is the number one priority. A gun would blow your cover." Valentina pulled out a shoulder holster and helped Gabby slide into it. The dart gun fit along the side of her breast, completely invisible.

"Try drawing it a few times."

Gabby did as requested. Valentina might be the mole, and she wasn't going to be chill about being denied the same protection the other EOD agents had, but the dart gun wasn't bad.

Her mind drifting to tomorrow's mission, Gabby asked, "What's Kramer's family like?"

"You were supposed to read the file," Valentina said, all of her jokes dried up and back to her normal accusatory self.

"I did read the file." Gabby flashed an annoyed look. "It says he has a wife and two kids, but the guy is in the office before me every day and he's always the last to leave. Most of the time when his wife calls, he has me tell her he's in a meeting. He could be clipping his toenails and he makes an excuse not to talk to her." Gabby shrugged. "Like how are they still married?"

Valentina nodded. "That tracks."

"You know what he does love, though?" Gabby raised her eyebrows. "His cars."

"Your point?"

"Well, he won't leave the office for his wife. He doesn't seem interested in his kids. He has a bathroom ten feet from the safe. His cars, though…"

Valentina raised an eyebrow. "I like the direction you're headed here."

"I think I have a plan to get the codes," Gabby said. "But it'll have to be tomorrow afternoon."

An hour later, Operation Gabby's Idea was on the books.

CHAPTER 27

Wednesday, Lucas's bedtime, Greene household

What do you want to read tonight?" Gabby asked Lucas. "We've got *Diary of a Worm*, *Benjamin Bunny*, some Walter the Farting Dog…" She scanned the titles on his bookshelf.

Lucas's eyes were at half-mast, and a teddy bear was tucked in his arm. "I'm not tired," he said, yawning.

Gabby smiled. "Which book, though?"

"*Megalodon Versus Great White*!" He broadcast the title like a sports announcer.

So much for a peaceful fifteen minutes with a bunny.

She tucked in under the quilt next to Lucas. Now that Granny and Burt had taken over the master suite, Lucas had a better setup than her, starting with an actual mattress.

"Which one do you think is going to win?" she asked.

"Megalodons. They're bigger."

"The bigger things don't always win," she said, more to herself than Lucas.

"The things with more teeth maybe then," he added with another big yawn.

"It's also about intelligence, commitment, preparation."

"Preparation, Granny said that today. Preparation H. Is that for fighting?"

Her brain screeched to a halt. "What?"

"Granny stopped and got some for Burt. He said it was because his—can I say a bad word?"

She shook her head and held up her hand for him to stop. "I think I know why she bought it."

At the sound of muffled giggling, Gabby looked up to see Kyle in the door frame. Present, accounted for, and wearing a pair of previously unworn unicorn pajamas that Gabby bought for her as a present. Gabby didn't say anything. Don't scare away the teenager.

"Mom, Mom." Lucas bid for her attention. "It was for his—" And he pointed dramatically to his butt.

Gabby shook her head, and a look of understanding passed between her and Kyle, a "how are we gonna make it?" look. Everything wasn't perfect, but at least they were in it together, on the same side. Victims of Burt.

"Megalodons can fit a car in their mouths," Lucas said, thankfully onto another topic.

"Nice science brain, kid." She laughed and rumpled his hair. "Cool."

"Mom," Kyle said in a judgy voice, "that's not science. You are participating in the 'everyone gets a trophy' culture. Give us something to aim for."

Gabby gave her daughter a nod. Maybe she should raise her standards.

Kyle sat down on the other side of her, and Gabby's heart filled to the brim. She read *Megalodon Versus Great White* to both her babies. After they officially found out that megalodons would beat great whites in a fight, Gabby said, "I miss picking you guys up and seeing you after school."

Kyle didn't say anything, but she dropped her head to Gabby's shoulder. Gabby practically held her breath. "Did you have fun with Granny and Burt?"

"Um…" Kyle looked like she was processing something.

"I liked bingo," said Lucas enthusiastically. "Granny got me a 7Up."

"Bingo?"

Kyle caught her mom's eye and clarified. "They took us out for bingo and chicken wings after school."

"What?" Gabby's brain flashed an error message. "What about horseback riding, and did you get that essay done for English?"

Kyle shook her head. "No, but I won fifty bucks."

Gabby's jaw dropped. She was going to kick those old farts out on their asses. Her kids needed to participate in extracurriculars, things they could put on scholarship applications, not bingo.

Oblivious, Kyle went on. "The bingo person said I had to be twenty-one to gamble, so they wouldn't give me the money at first, but Granny lied and said she had been playing two cards." She fiddled with the ties on her pajamas. "Until I'm old enough, Granny is going to play for me, but take a cut. Can I go to the mall this weekend?"

Gabby blinked back dumbly at her daughter for a second. Granny sounded like she was in the Mafia. A Russian immigrant who played by her own rules. She and Grandpa had run a butcher shop for years. For all she knew, they could have been tied to the mob. Finally, she managed, "Who else was at bingo?"

"Just a bunch of old people. It was pretty gross, but…I don't know, kind of fun."

Gabby didn't respond. On the one hand, they didn't go to their after-school activities. On the other, they were spending time with family.

"So anyways, will you take me to the mall?"

With a sigh, Gabby relented. "Sure. Want some more purple in your hair?"

"Actually, I kind of want a tattoo."

Gabby stared in shock.

"Just kidding."

"Thank god."

"Plus Granny would help me with the tattoo anyway." Kyle laughed at her joke, but it was real. Granny was not the responsible caregiver she needed.

Downstairs, *Family Feud* was playing at top volume in the living room. The sound of dishes clanking and running water carried up the stairs from the kitchen. Was this her new normal?

From the sink, Granny yelled, "Gabby, where's that cocktail shaker?"

Gabby ignored the request and poured herself a glass of wine. "You took my kids to a bingo hall?" she said in an accusatory voice.

"What's the matter with that? How much do horse lessons cost? Kyle can make some money instead. She's good."

"How can you be good at bingo?"

"For one, she can hear all the numbers."

Gabby almost spit her wine out.

"But it's also an energy thing. The winning cards choose you sometimes. She's just a lucky kid. So is Lucas."

Gabby added more wine to her glass.

"Pour me one, Gabs."

"What about your blood pressure medication?" Gabby asked. "Isn't that supposed to be bad?"

"Gabby." Her granny sat up straight and looked over her gold-rimmed glasses. "I am an eighty-year-old woman, not a child, and I can manage my own risks. You can't mother me. It'll drive me insane."

"But—" Someone had to worry about Granny's blood pressure.

They were interrupted by a knock, followed by the noise of the door opening and footsteps through the living room. Instead of Justin with a martini shaker and a bag of limes, it was the only drop-by that shouldn't surprise Gabby. Phil meandered in with a CVS bag and a lukewarm smile.

"Phil." His name came out like an accusation. "You can't just wander in unannounced. You don't live here anymore." He was the one who left.

"You need me, Gabby," he announced as if saying it out loud made it true. "I brought some necessary items." Like he was Santa Claus, he reached into the bag and held a spray bottle up high.

Gabby squinted at the orange and black bottle. Why was he bringing cleaning spray over at ten at night?

"It's roach spray. I can't have my family living with cockroaches."

"Oh…" Her lie about needing his help because of an infestation of "roaches." She sighed. Roach spray probably wasn't going to work on Smirnov or his goons. If only.

A little too loud, Granny said, "You didn't mention any cock-roaches."

Gabby sighed. "It's okay. I haven't seen any roaches today." That was true.

Granny scanned the countertops. "Well, that doesn't mean they're not here."

Also true. Smirnov could be anywhere. One of his goons had been taking pictures only two nights ago.

Phil set the can on the counter looking pleased with himself. "Well, at least you have something to defend yourself with now."

And a dart gun. That would only work on the larger-sized roaches, though.

"Thanks, Phil." She cut herself off before saying anything else nice. Phil reeked of regret and second-guessing. The roach killer was basically a text message at 3:00 a.m., Phil's version of "Hey, u up?"

But she would not let this man, who saw her as no more than his personal support staff and not a valuable partner, weasel his way back into her life with one bottle of roach spray. Not that second-guessing wasn't happening for her. She might not have had red hair and potential last week, but she also wasn't scared for her life. She and the kids used to be safe.

Scratch that, Gabby had always been scared to death about everything, but the threats needed WebMD research before. Nothing like an actual threat to put a suspicious rash into perspective.

"When I was over the other night, I noticed a few bulbs were out." He pulled a pack of bulbs out of the bag and flashed a high-wattage smile. "I know you're not tall enough for the bulbs in the hallway." He swaggered in that direction and started unscrewing the glass dome.

Dear god. She was never going to be rid of him. "Phil, we were just about to go to bed."

"I know you need help, Gabs." He smiled over his shoulder.

That light had been out for approximately three years. This was the definition of too little, too late.

Before she could usher him out the front, someone knocked on the back door. Mr. Bubbles sounded the alarm and ran, ready to eviscerate whoever dared to knock. For once, that seemed like a good idea. Gabby's dart gun was under her bed, and the only person who had threatened to stop by was Smirnov. Not that the Mafia knocked.

"Wow, I didn't know you had a social life, Gabby." Granny was sitting back and, from the look on her face, enjoying the show.

Phil paused unscrewing the dome and stared at the door like the visitor was interrupting his evening. "What kind of asshole is dropping by this time of night?" Phil, of all people, asked.

"Probably Justin." She prayed.

"It's late. Let me answer it." On the way to the door, he said, "We should talk. I mean, how much are you relying on your grandmother?"

"Later, Phil." Sure, she could question her Granny, but Phil had lost that privilege.

For a second, he dropped the annoying shtick. "I'm serious, Gabs. I know I've screwed up in the past, a lot. But we have kids. I'm here. I still...well..."

Gabby sighed. Phil was lonely. He missed them, but this was too much. "Okay, I hear you. I could use some more help. Can we talk about it next week, though?"

She answered the door, and all six feet plus of Markus's lanky self stepped from the shadows. Dressed in a low-slung pair of sweats and a tank that showcased a pair of arms any girl, no, anyone would dream of—Markus didn't look like he belonged in her mushy suburban life.

Phil bristled. "Who the hell are you?"

"Phil, this is Mar—" As soon as she started saying his real name, it hit her that she should hide his identity. "This is...Mar-shall."

Markus held out his hand, unfazed by his dumb, new name.

"This is Phil, my ex-husband." She gave Phil a meaningful glance. "Phil was just leaving."

Suddenly resolved to finish changing the bulb, Phil said, "Don't mind me."

He had to be kidding.

Markus rolled with it. "You want me to hand you that Phillips head?"

Phil shrugged and took the screwdriver, looking way too intent on his job.

Granny, clearly amused, called, "Do you boys want beer?"

"Would love one, Granny," Phil said, because of course he did. Gabby could kill him.

"So what is this?" Phil asked. "A Tinder date?"

"Phil." She said his name sharply. "It doesn't matter. Not to mention, aren't you on Tinder?" She recalled the profile photo of him swinging a golf club and staring off into the distance, the kind of picture that falsely advertised a lot of deep thoughts.

When Granny returned from the kitchen with a beer, Gabby grabbed it and flashed a warning look. Granny was no help. The woman was taking way too much pleasure in this.

"Phil, it's late. I need to talk to...Marshall and get to bed. I have work in the morning."

Phil looked like he wanted to smack "Marshall" in the face. Instead, he stood and just stared him down for a minute, like all he wanted to do was kick this guy out of the house that used to be his.

"Phil." Gabby said his name in a cautioning tone.

"What? I'm just changing a lightbulb." He passed Markus the dome and screwed in the bulb. "It's important to have a well-lit entryway, for security."

Markus said, "If you're busy, I can take off. I just wanted to go over a few things, and, well, apologize for earlier."

Gabby couldn't help but smile at him. He was even being nice to Phil.

After another five minutes of screwing the dome back to the ceiling, Phil was finally done. Gabby took his beer and started walking to the door.

"Who the fuck is that guy?" Phil asked.

"None of your business, Phil. You left."

"Are the kids safe with him? Have you run a background check?" He shook his head. "If he's really just some guy you met on Tinder, you can't have him over to the house with the kids and your grandma. That's messed up, Gabs."

Gabby started to laugh because Phil was so off the mark. Funny he should ask about the kids' safety, though. It's not like she'd forgotten her suspicion, but she couldn't bring that up with her doofy ex-husband hanging around making a spectacle of himself over a lightbulb.

Phil must have felt his own anger outpacing reason, because he took a breath and said, "Well, I don't like it."

"That's fine." She shut the door on him and hurried back to Markus, stopping to smooth her hair and put on lip gloss. At the last minute, she undid one of the buttons on her blouse and repositioned the girls. Just in case he wasn't the mole. God, she hoped he wasn't.

"Markus," she said with a big smile that belied the fact that she'd just kicked her ex out the front door, "what are you doing here?"

He glanced toward the front door where Phil had just left. "He seems...nice."

"I know, right?"

"Does he stop by all the time?"

"I asked for his help because of work this week, and he's taken it as an invitation to come back whenever. Working outside the house has added some...complications I didn't foresee."

"Gabby!" Granny came around the corner, her eyes only for Markus. "You didn't tell me you were having *a man* over."

Markus held out his hand. "I'm Markus," he said. "Sorry to interrupt your evening." When Gabby gasped, he said. "My real name is fine, especially with your granny."

"Oh, I was just about to tuck in for the night." Granny smiled and yelled, "BURT!" at top volume. "It's time for bed."

Burt startled and let out a loud snort. "What?"

"We're going to bed."

Markus hid a laugh.

After Burt managed to haul himself out of the La-Z-Boy—it took a couple of tries—he headed to the kitchen despite Granny's efforts to steer him to the bedroom. He gave Markus a man-to-man look. "You here for Gabby?"

Markus nodded.

Burt took a pill and said, "Take your vitamins. These girls are redheads, if you know what I mean."

Granny fluffed her glossy head of freshly dyed curls. On closer inspection, it might even be a wig. But being a redhead was more about identity than genetics. What wasn't these days?

"Markus and I work together," Gabby said, stressing the word "work."

Granny nodded. "Uh-huh. I'm so proud of you, Gabs. A new job." She stage-whispered, "And *two* men!" Just in case Gabby hadn't heard her, she held up two fingers.

Markus cleared his throat. "Um. She's doing a great job at work," he said in a diplomatic tone of voice.

"She got it from her grandma."

Gabby topped off her wine and slid a glass across the counter toward Markus.

"Burt, get to the bedroom. Let's leave these two to…" She winked dramatically. "Have fun, kids. Don't do anything I wouldn't do."

Gabby covered her face and groaned. It was all too much.

As Granny tottered off, she said, "I need to catch up on *Novaya Bitva Ekstrasensov.*"

Markus came to attention at the sound of Russian. "I watch that too!" Markus said, "What do you think of Natalya?"

Granny gave him a sly look. "Ty govorish' po-russki?"

"Ne ochen' khorosho," he answered smoothly.

Granny harrumphed and looked between the two of them.

"What did you two say?" Gabby asked.

"Not much. She just asked if I could speak Russian." He looked at her more closely. "You didn't tell me your grandmother was Russian. Do you speak?"

Gabby shrugged. "I wish I had learned something. This is probably the most time I've ever spent with her."

"Why now?"

"That's sort of your fault. She's here to 'help out.' Also, she was evicted from her nursing home."

Overhearing, Granny corrected, "I defected from that old folks' home, just like I defected from the USSR."

He raised an eyebrow. "Why doesn't that surprise me?"

"I'm going to bed," she announced. "Good night."

Markus watched her walk toward the bedroom and asked, "Is she helping?"

"Uh...she did pick the kids up from school, but she brought them to bingo. I mean, is that gambling?"

Markus threw back his head and laughed. "Um, I think it depends on how much money exchanges hands. And it's racketeering if it's run by a criminal enterprise."

"Well, if Orlov happens to run a bingo hall, my grandma can be part of the sting operation." Granny would love that.

"Are you sure she's not involved already?" he commented. He took a sip of his wine. "So I was actually dropping by to go over tomorrow's operation."

Gabby took a deep breath. In the chaos, she had briefly forgotten about tomorrow. Maybe all she needed to successfully compartmentalize was too much to do. If your life is a three-ring circus, you can only worry about one ring at a time.

"I have a few tips."

She plopped on one of the high stools and grabbed a slice of American cheese from the fridge. Justin would be horrified. Last time she put out American cheese, he looked at her like she was dead to him. "I feel like I don't even know you anymore."

Markus reached for a slice. "You have any crackers?"

"If you're hungry, we had meat loaf for dinner."

"Actually, I'm starving. I went straight from work to the gym. I've only had a protein smoothie."

Her gaze flicked to his biceps as she plated him up a hefty slice of meat loaf.

He shut his eyes and savored. "Mmm. Gabby Greene..." She could tell when the taste, and—if she was honest with herself—the texture hit him, because he opened his eyes and struggled to swallow. "You can't cook for shit, can you?"

She started laughing. She couldn't.

"It was nothing but God that we recruited you. Someone had to save your family from this."

"You are so right. I hate cooking." She plopped a bottle of ketchup down for him. "This should help."

He slathered the slice in ketchup. "So my advice for tomorrow..." He swallowed a gulp of wine to wash down the meat loaf. "Number one, no heels. I want you mobile. All of your clothes should be tactical, nothing that restricts your movement."

She flashed back to falling on the donut earlier.

"Like those black pants you were wearing on Monday." He gave a nod of approval. "Those would be perfect."

Maybe he just thought they looked like track pants, but she blushed anyway.

"Second, you want to keep other people out of the way as much as possible. Fran is gonna be all over you, getting in the way and messing things up. Distract her."

Good advice.

"But mostly, relax. Let your crazy grandma take care of the kids in the morning so that you aren't too stressed when you get to the office. You've got this."

"Thanks, Markus." She didn't know what to say to him. So many thoughts and feelings were bubbling to the surface where he was concerned. She didn't know whether to trust him or if she could trust herself. Mostly she needed some sleep.

"Do you want to take some home?" She gestured to the meat loaf. "I made it for everyone to eat for dinner, but Granny fed them chicken wings at the bingo hall."

"Actually, yes."

"Man, how hard up are you?" she teased, depositing a heaping portion into a Tupperware, locking in the freshness as her own anxiety spiraled.

"You have no idea," he said, making it sound like it had been a really long time since he'd gotten some.

"Oh, I bet I do." If anyone knew about being hard up for some loving, it was her. The algorithm wasn't wrong with all those vibrator ads.

He raised his eyebrows, and he looked almost about to say something.

At the door, she handed him his leftovers.

"Don't worry, Gabby. You are doing so good. I've got you."

All of her insecurities must have played across her face, because Markus said, "Do you need a hug?"

She nodded yes, and he wrapped her in the most comforting, warm, manly hug she'd ever had. All of her suspicions dissolved with his arms wrapped around her. She leaned in and shut her eyes. When she looked up, her lips brushed the skin on his neck. They stood like that for a few seconds too long, both probably considering what to do next. Markus looked at her, his eyes heavy-lidded. He leaned down as if to kiss her. After letting his lips just lightly brush hers, he backed away.

"I'm sorry, Gabby. I shouldn't have done that."

Shyly, she admitted, "I wanted it."

A smile like he'd won the lottery lit up his face. He let his hand trail down her arm. As he was squeezing her hand, he slipped a flash drive into her palm. "Copy the files onto this." A little huskier, he said, "Maybe we can revisit this after the mission is done?"

"Yes, please."

Finally alone, Gabby collapsed on the couch with Mr. Bubbles. *Family Feud* was still playing, muted with the closed captioning on. She didn't even have the energy to change the channel. Exhausted, Gabby wolfed down emotional chocolate and finished Granny's wine.

CHAPTER 28

Thursday morning, Greene household

The next morning, on the day of Operation Secret Laptop, an inconvenient fact smacked into Gabby's consciousness like a surprise asteroid headed for earth. She needed two flash drives.

She was a double agent, not a single agent. She needed one copy of the contents of the laptop for the good guys and another for the bad guys, using the term "good guys" pretty loosely. How had she not thought of this earlier? Sort of almost kissing her handler last night had made her forget everything, which is why you aren't supposed to do things like that. If she weren't running late, she could swing into OfficeMax, but when was she not running late? Never.

"Kyle, do you have a flash drive?" she yelled as she looked for her keys and shoved her feet in some shoes. Shame washed over her. The EOD and the Mafia had tapped her to do a mission, and here she was putting it together last minute using her fourteen-year-old daughter for tech support.

"Uh, I don't know," Kyle said, with her usual level of helpfulness. When her daughter looked up, she must have sensed Gabby's panic. "I can look, though."

Sure enough, there was a flash drive in the front pocket of Kyle's backpack, jammed in there with a partially eaten Nutri-Grain bar. Kyle peeled the jammy sections off the drive and brushed the remaining crumbs on the floor. "I don't think there's anything on it but that report on Oobleck."

Aah, the Oobleck report. Oobleck: the only substance, besides toothpaste and Silly Putty and, let's be honest, K-Y, that defied the laws of physics. For every action, there should be an equal and opposite reaction, except for Oobleck and toothpaste. She glanced at Lucas's hair, still jagged from where all the Oobleck Kyle had made for her report had gotten stuck.

Kyle grumbled. "I can't believe I got a C on that report."

Gabby couldn't either. Between helping Kyle with essay writing and driving to the grocery store at 11:00 p.m. to get ingredients to make Oobleck for a demonstration, that report had been as much work as double agenting. At the science fair, it had been obvious that the other parents had done a much better job on their kids' assignments than Gabby had, though.

Gabby looked at the flash drive, another item she didn't use regularly. "You don't happen to know how to transfer files from one USB to another, do you?"

Kyle shrugged. "Just put them in a laptop at the same time, open them up, and drag and drop."

Gabby ran over the directions twice in her mind, threw a laptop into her purse, and hit the road. It was go time.

An hour later, she was at her desk waiting for Kramer to make his transfer. During her endless hours of carpet scrubbing, good for something at least, she'd overheard a client demand a wire transfer. Kramer had scheduled a call at ten, the transfer to take place during the call. As soon as she saw Kramer on the phone, she needed to set the plan into motion. Everything hinged on her. She needed to be alert and quick to react—basically the opposite of who she was.

Even with the whole world resting on her shoulders, she went all schoolgirl when Markus talked. Was it just her or when he said, "Hey," was it a little softer and sweeter than yesterday? He couldn't be the mole. The universe couldn't be that cruel. She had a kiss to revisit.

"So this morning," Markus said, "a few of the other agents are going to be looped in on our conversation. Valentina and Fredo. Let us know when you're in position, guys."

Valentina came on. "Locked, loaded, and waiting for your signal, Gabby."

"Same here," Fredo said. "The whole team is ready to go. Emergency services are on standby."

Butterflies erupted in her stomach. An entire team of agents was waiting for her, waiting to execute her plan, a plan she thought of last night. What if she hadn't anticipated something? This could go very wrong.

While inadvisably drowning the stomach butterflies in coffee, she stared intently into Kramer's office. For his part, he was doing nothing, checking his email and scrolling through his phone like he didn't have a care in the world. Meanwhile, a SWAT team dressed in black with helmets and goggles and body armor was waiting at her beck and call. At least that's what she imagined.

Like he was just messing with her, Kramer spun in his office chair and drummed on his desk with his fingers like he was in a metal band. Of all the days for him to be loose and fun! He hit the intercom and said, "Run to the liquor store and get extra bottles of that Beluga Gold Line vodka. I want some in the freezer here. And plenty at the party. And you're picking up caviar, right?"

"Of course, Mr. Kramer. I'll get right on that," she lied. Right now, she had bigger things to worry about than snacks for Orlov.

"Oh, and don't forget those little crackers."

She was a big-time secret agent, and it was still about food, the lady with the fanny pack filled with Band-Aids and Goldfish crackers.

"Boo!"

Gabby squealed and about jumped out of her chair.

Carmen started laughing. "A little edgy today, huh?"

Gabby giggled like it was a great joke, as if "boo" was ever a great joke. Carmen was right, though. She was jumpy in the way you get when you're running on nothing but caffeine and adrenaline. Just a bundle of raw nerves in an office chair, liable to overreact to anything.

Fran clomped over in her orthopedic shoes next. Talk about a woman who could not sneak up on anyone. "Camille, can you help me in the file room?"

Gabby was about ready to explode. Managing her office job and a spy mission at the same time—this was next-level multitasking. Worse than Christmas, almost.

Markus piped up. "Get rid of her. Don't worry about being polite this morning."

Fran had the worst timing. "Um, can I do it in an hour? I'm really focused...on this...party planning. Kramer wants so many last-minute things."

Fran gave her a funny look, probably because it was obvious

that Gabby was doing absolutely nothing but sweating in her chair. That wasn't a crime, though. Half the employees at eStocks were texting or scrolling the internet for someone to DM.

She glanced back at Kramer, who was still fucking with her. He drew back one of the balls in the Newton's cradle in his office, six smooth heavy metal balls suspended on strings. The ball he had pulled back smacked the row of balls with a satisfying thwack.

Thwack. A ball hopped.

Thwack. Another balled hopped.

Thwack. And so on.

In her ear, Markus said, "Don't worry. Valentina is one of the best in the business. I'm sure everything is fine on her end. All you have to do is sit tight and wait for the call." He must have been able to feel her crawling out of her skin with anxiety.

She wasn't worried about Valentina. Valentina was competent and probably hadn't slept on a futon on the other side of a thin wall listening to bouts of chainsaw-like snoring. Burt needed a CPAP machine. She might not be a sleep doctor, but she knew sleep apnea when she heard it.

Her part of the plan was the simplest. All she had to do was stay on her toes and pay attention. Valentina had the arson to commit.

But if she screwed this up…Gabby's breathing picked up, and she started to sweat. At the feel and smell of her own sweat, she sweated more. How was she going to protect her family? If this mission failed, she had to get them out of town. She could just imagine telling them all to hurry, Burt in his La-Z-Boy with *Family Feud* droning on endlessly, Kyle whining about her iPads and AirPods, Lucas hiding because he thought it was a game, and Granny wanting an explanation for the hasty departure. There was no choice but to leave Burt and tell everyone else they were going out for ice cream. She'd take them to In-N-Out and then keep driving.

Just then Kramer stood up and fogged the glass. It was happening.

"Gabby, just breathe. Focus on this and only this. Compartmentalize," Markus said.

She visualized pulling a big Snapware out of the pantry and shoving all of her worries inside. Because it was a vision, she found the lid without searching and snapped the latches two at a time. Snap. Snap. Smile. She smoothed her hair and tightened her apron.

Fran yelled, "Gabby, it's your lunch break."

What the—?

"In a minute, Fran."

"It's just that the microwave is available right now. If you don't get your lunch in now, you'll miss your window."

"Fran, not now." The microwave availability window was not her major concern.

"But the microwave needs cleaning. This is last call!"

Gabby looked between Fran and her phone. She took off for the break room at a near sprint because Fran wouldn't leave her alone if she didn't put something in the microwave. In a big fucking hurry, she threw in a chunk of meat loaf she didn't even want and punched some buttons. On the way back to her desk, she gave Fran a glare. "I'm a little busy. Just take it out if it beeps. Okay?"

"I'm sorry. I didn't mean to hurry you."

She flashed a tight smile. Just as she sat down, the phone rang, and Gabby's nerves jangled louder than the ringtone. She took a deep breath and prepared herself for action.

Fran, who could just not mind her own fucking business, appeared out of nowhere. "Go get your lunch. I'll answer the phone."

What was Fran's problem today?

"I got it." She practically threw herself on top of the desk to block Fran. "eStocks Enterprises," she said. "Good morn—"

"Camille!" Laura Kramer yelled her name into the phone.

"Mrs. Kramer?"

"It's Laura Kramer. Is George there? It's an emergency. Ohmygod. I don't know what to do." Laura Kramer was clearly distraught, her voice high and frantic. "There's smoke coming from the garage, and ohmygod, I see flames. Flames!"

"Let me get him." Gabby practically ran across the hall to Kramer's office. She barged into the room without knocking. "Mr. Kramer," she yelled.

"Camille! Knock, would you? I'm busy."

"But—"

"Get out, Camille."

"It's your wife," Gabby rebutted, shoving the phone into his hands.

He shook his head and glared at her until he heard his wife screaming. "A fire? Did you call nine-one-one? I'm not the fire department, Laura."

Gabby's heart went out to Laura.

Then his tone changed. "The garage!" He leaped to his feet. "Fuck. You can't be serious. Don't tell me . . . the cars?"

"Geez, this guy," Markus muttered in her ear.

Gabby heard Laura scream.

"Not the Bentley!" He groaned like someone had physically hurt him.

Gabby laser-eyed him from across the room. He hadn't even asked about Laura or the kids, just his stupid cars.

"The Lambo." He cried out. "No. No. No!"

They were going up in flames one by one, just like Valentina had promised.

"Where the hell is the fire department? Where are my fucking taxes going anyway?" Kramer couldn't sound more Republican if he tried.

The fire department was on standby. The EOD had no intention of harming Laura or the kids, just getting George Kramer to get out of his office.

He hung up the phone and reached to shove a few papers in his briefcase. "Cancel all of my meetings for the rest of the day," he barked. "Call Ted and tell him the rates are too high. He needs to sit tight." He glanced back at the computer. "And call Jeremy to verify that the wire went through on his end." As he mentioned the wire transfer, he glanced back at the computer and the safe, its door swung wide open. "Fucking A." He threw his briefcase down and started to head in that direction.

"Mr. Kramer, I've got it. You have to hurry."

When he hesitated, she said, "Your cars. Maybe you can still save some."

This was true. The sooner she copied his files, the sooner the fire department would get the go-ahead to put out the flames.

With a nod, he said, "Put that away. Lock up."

As soon as Kramer ran, the fire alarm in the eStocks office also went off. What the hell?

Smoke was billowing from the break room, and the smell of burnt meat loaf filled the whole office. No one was paying attention to the alarm but rather running toward the burning leftovers.

Gabby slammed the door shut and pulled the flash drive from her pocket. She jammed it into the port on the side of Kramer's secret laptop and started copying every file on the laptop.

Copy.

Copy.

Copy.

Copppppyyyyyyy…

Just like every spy movie, a little bar tracked what percentage of the material had downloaded. Halfway through, the fire alarm shut down. Three-quarters of the way through, she heard Fran yell, "Camille, how long did you put your lunch in for?"

Gabby had practically sweated through her shirt because of nerves. All she needed was one more minute, and she'd have everything she needed. The EOD. Smirnov. She could go back to her normal life and get out of this ridiculous job. Making lunches, picking up kids, tucking them in at night. She needed everyone to be safe. And she needed to put the laptop back in the safe.

It was almost done.

Just as the whole office started calming down and wandering back to their desks, the meat loaf debacle over, the download finished.

Gabby collected the flash drive, slid it back in her pocket, fat with secrets. More satisfied than that time when she had lost ten pounds and zipped up her skinny jeans, she slid the computer back in the safe, shut the door, and replaced the painting on the wall.

Markus said, "You did it, Gabs. I knew you could."

"Gabby, where have you been?" Fran said, exasperated.

After she mumbled some sort of excuse, Fran said, "Well, you're going to have to buy lunch today."

Gabby nodded. "Oh-kay."

"Oh, and have you started on goody bags for the party on Saturday?"

Gabby stared. Goody bags—was Fran being serious? "I've got it covered. I think I'll step out and grab some lunch."

She slung her purse over her shoulder and strode out of the office like an eighties action hero, the whole place up in smoke behind her, or at least her meat loaf. A smile spread across her face as she stepped out onto the street.

She had done it. Almost.

"Markus," she lied, "my nerves really upset my stomach. I'm going to run back inside and use the bathroom. I'll be back in a minute."

She didn't need a bathroom. What she needed was time alone to copy the files for Smirnov.

He laughed. "Click me back in as soon as you're done. I don't like the idea of losing contact when you're holding codes that are worth millions of dollars to the Mafia and Kramer."

"Markus, just let me go to the bathroom."

She took out the earpiece and the brooch with the camera. After a quick air-kiss to Markus, she turned off the camera and ran.

CHAPTER 29

Thursday, after lunch, eStocks Enterprises

Gabby might have stolen the files, but she had three things left to do: 1) transfer the stolen goods to a second flash drive, 2) deliver one flash drive to EOD, and 3) bring the second flash drive to Smirnov. Only then would she be home free. On and off throughout these activities, she was going to have to pretend to be in the bathroom. Markus wasn't going to like that...

Gabby drove Darcy's car a few blocks away, out of view of nosy eStocks employees, aka Fran. On the passenger seat, she set up Kyle's laptop and inserted the flash drive. Then she pulled the cartoon bunny head off Kyle's flash drive and shoved it into the remaining USB port. Eat your heart out, James Bond.

Not surprisingly, whatever was supposed to happen when she put in the flash drive didn't, and because she didn't have anything but a surface understanding of anything technical, she couldn't troubleshoot. Damn her for letting Phil do all of the finances and tech stuff for the last fifteen years. Damn her for always taking the easy path. It was not fucking paying off.

She drummed her keys on the steering wheel. Markus texted. U ok?

IBS. A sexier lie would have been nice, but that was all she had.

"Siri, call Queen Palm Elementary and Middle School." There was nothing to do but to get tech support on the line.

"Hi, Shamika. This is Gabby, Kyle and Lucas's mom."

"Oooh, hi, Gabby." Shamika sounded amused. "Who was that who dropped off Lucas's lunch the other day, because whoo-eeeee."

Gabby was breathing too fast. She didn't have time at the moment to gossip about the hot EOD agent who had inexplicably dropped off her kid's allergy-friendly lunch. "He's cute, isn't he? Can you get Kyle on the phone for me? It's sort of an emergency."

"Okay." She paused for a second and said, "It looks like she's in PE." To someone else, she called, "Wayne, can you run and grab Kyle from the gym?"

Gabby wanted to knock her head into the steering wheel. Wayne was the kid who was always at the principal's office because he could not follow directions. Her family's safety and a delicate national security mission now rested on Wayne's shoulders. The child had pulled the fire alarm twice in the last year, and Kyle reported that Wayne was the one who had plugged the boy's toilets with Orbeez in the epic plumbing fiasco of 2021. The school had been shut down for a week.

Shamika said, "So about that fine-ass man..."

Before Gabby was forced to answer any more questions, she heard Kyle's voice, and Shamika, sounding disappointed, said, "Kyle, it's your mom on the phone."

She was going to buy Wayne a pizza.

"Mom?" Kyle said her name as a question.

"Sweetie. I need your help. It's sort of an emergency."

"Okay," Kyle said, her voice tinged with confusion.

"Nothing to worry about. I'm just trying to impress my boss, and I can't get that flash drive to work. Can you walk me through it?"

"Okay. They were making us do a sit-up challenge, so this is great."

Kyle proceeded to walk her through transferring the files. "Insert both flash drives."

"At the same time?"

"Yes, Mom."

Kyle made it sound easy, but Gabby had never had a computer issue go smoothly.

"Is there supposed to be a box that pops up?"

"Yes. And then you drag and drop the files where you want them."

"Ohmygod, I only see one."

"Seriously, Mom?" Kyle groaned. "Just take it out and put it back in. See if it pops up this time."

"Child, give that phone here," Shamika said loudly in the background.

"Bye, Mom."

"Gabby—" Shamika sounded impatient, as if she were actually involved in the mission rather than just bored at work and getting involved in everyone's business. "Are you on a Mac?" Shamika asked. Before Gabby could answer, she got sassy. "Why did I ask? Of course it is."

"What's that supposed to mean?"

"Come on, your shed-free, allergy-friendly dog probably has a Mac too."

Gabby laughed. Fair enough.

"Go to the Finder. Do you know what the flash drive is called, Kyle?"

"BunBot," Kyle called from the background.

While Gabby looked, Shamika said, "After all this, you should definitely bring that man by. At least slip him my number."

"Uh—"

"Don't tell me. You're already after him. Of course you are." Shamika paused her narration to sigh. "I don't blame you, but..."

When Gabby finally copied everything, she ejected and pocketed the flash drives and yelled thanks to Kyle and Shamika, who was still conjecturing about her relationship with Markus.

First mission accomplished, she flipped on her earpiece and camera. "Hi, Markus. I'm here."

"Feeling better?"

"Much," she said, still a little breathless, not from intestinal distress but from tech anxiety.

At the end of the day, Gabby shut her computer down, neatened her desk, and grabbed her lunch box from the fridge. The Tupperware with the flaming meat loaf was in the dumpster out back, probably where it belonged in the first place. It was too bad about the Tupperware, though. It had been a really nice, medium-sized container that fit in her lunch box. Tupperware with a lid that hadn't disappeared into the back of the cabinet never to be found again—that was as hard to come by as a pair of matching socks.

Now, off to the EOD to hand off the flash drive. Compared to Smirnov, the EOD was nothing. She might as well be heading to the petting zoo. And to think she'd been in a near panic over them just a week ago.

In the car, she called Granny. "Want me to pick up dinner on the way back? I have two errands that will hopefully be quick. I was thinking sushi."

"No. Prepare yourself. I cooked."

"Mmm. Really?" Granny was a notoriously bad cook. It was a proud family tradition, along with red hair and, apparently, gambling.

"Yep. I'm still trying to impress Burt. We're in the beginning of this relationship. He doesn't know I don't do housework yet."

Gabby rolled her eyes. She was eighty and acting like a teenager. And who in the hell needed to impress Burt. BURT!

"He used to be a doctor, you know."

"You're kidding me."

"No, he did a lot of side work at the home."

"So what'd you make?"

"A frozen lasagna, but he won't know the difference. Your taste buds start to go at a certain age. He probably only has a few years left."

"Lucas can't eat lasagna."

Granny groaned. "Gabby, that boy is not allergic to everything you think he is. I think you should get him retested or just let him try a few things."

Gabby released a breath. Granny was half-right. Lucas might have grown out of some of these allergies. It was probably time to reintroduce a few things before he was thirty-five. If she could take down the Mafia, she could face Lucas eating a baked good made with eggs. Maybe. The doctor had mentioned a few times she could let him try it in the ER parking lot to alleviate her anxiety. She'd always responded, "If he has to eat it at the ER, he doesn't need it at all!"

"Let's get through Saturday before we change anything, okay?"

"Okay, honey."

Like it was nothing, Gabby went through the biometric screening and wandered in as casually as if it had still been International Rug. Actually, more casually. International Rug used to have some really good sales.

Inside the EOD, everyone was waiting. Valentina and Alice were in the conference room when she arrived. She planned to hand the flash drive over, say thanks, and keep it cool.

A guy she didn't know clapped. She smiled awkwardly.

Valentina begrudgingly nodded her head. "Good work, Agent Greene."

Markus appeared from out of nowhere with a bottle of champagne. "You ready for a toast?"

Alice said, "Markus, we're on duty. Put that away," to which he held up the tiniest glasses imaginable.

"There's more alcohol in that kombucha than one of these cups."

Under her breath, Valentina said, "I think we can wait until we make the arrests for that," but Markus ignored her.

As he poured the glasses, Alice said, "It was a great day. Everything went like clockwork. No one was hurt except for a couple of cars. Everyone here did their job. Good work, especially to Agent Greene. Your first mission is a success."

Gabby felt herself blush furiously as everyone raised a glass to her. The Elite Operatives Department singing her praises, incidentally in the former throw pillow section of International Rug. Someone needed to get her a cervical collar, because she was getting whiplash.

"Thank you," she managed to say through her absolute swell of feelings. She, Gabby Greene, mediocre housewife with a failed marriage, had managed an EOD mission.

But it wasn't completely untarnished. Among the faces smiling back at her, one of them was working for Smirnov, a person who would have ratted her out if she talked. A person who cared more about money than her or her family. Did that person know Smirnov had threatened her kids?

Whoever it was, she'd really made their day. They were probably going home with a fat wad of cash, and they hadn't even had to strong-arm her.

After all of those congratulations, Gabby reached into her pocket for the flash drive and accidentally handed Alice the wrong drive. The plastic bunny with its bucktoothed smile looked up.

"What's this?"

"Oops. I lost the one that Markus gave me, so I grabbed one of my own. Don't worry, it's goofy, but was really highly rated on Amazon."

Valentina poured herself another miniature glass of champagne.

Alice frowned. "As long as you have the information on here."

"I do."

Alice plugged the flash drive in and nodded as the files appeared. "The bunny did its job."

She might have only worked for the EOD for a short time, but it was intense—life-changing even. This would be the last time she was here. Saturday at the party, they would arrest Orlov and Kramer, and she would go home, back to her regular life. As she looked around at the people who had trusted her to run a mission, tears burned the back of her eyes.

Markus put a hand on her shoulder and made eye contact so direct, she almost wilted. He said, "Hey, Gabs, you did good." The way he was looking at her she couldn't help but recall how he wanted to "revisit" their kiss.

"Only because you were with me every step of the way."

With a laugh, he said, "Well, most of the way."

She'd talked more to Markus than she had to Phil in the last few years. Sure, she talked to her kids, but she was their mom. Besides Justin, no one knew her better.

The Starbucks gift card she bought for him was burning a hole in her pocket. It was her go-to, end-of-the-year teacher gift. He was technically her teacher. It had seemed like a good idea at the time, but now she was so uncertain, especially after last night. They'd embraced, and his lips had brushed hers. That wasn't the kind of moment you followed up with a Starbucks gift card. Was it too much, not enough, or, most likely, completely off-key?

Abruptly, she reached into her purse and pulled it out, thrusting it into his hands too forcefully. "This is for you."

"Really?" he raised his eyebrows, clearly expecting something meaningful. "You didn't have to?"

A smile quirked his lips, and she said, "I mean, if it's weird, you can just give it back."

He held it out of reach. "No, I want it."

Valentina, smelling blood in the water, stepped closer as Markus opened the card. "What, I didn't get one?"

"Ohmygod. I'm so sorry. It's just that Markus was in my ear all day. I should have gotten one for everyone." This was the same problem she had at the end of the year. There was a classroom teacher, a teacher's aide, music teachers. It was almost easier not to buy anything so she didn't offend everyone.

"Well, anyway," Gabby said in a too-perky voice, "I know you need a lot of caffeine for all of your missions, so…" Her sentence dissolved into thin air. She looked down at her feet, her hair falling into her eyes.

Tenderly, Markus brushed her hair out of her face. "Maybe we can get a coffee together and debrief after it's over."

In the corner, Valentina choked on her champagne, probably at the word "debrief." Gabby almost choked on that one too.

As perfect as he was, she couldn't get rid of one nagging thought. Now that the mission was over, Gabby might never know if Markus had been the mole or if he would have followed through on Smirnov's threats. She could maybe trust him, but she wasn't sure if she should. Nothing expired faster than trust, except for dairy.

Alice thankfully interrupted Gabby's anxiety with more business. "Okay, everyone, while I have you all here, let's talk about Saturday. Are we ready to go?" she asked, looking at Gabby.

Gabby said, "Yep. It's going to be a great party." Justin had spent the last forty-eight hours doing nothing but preparing. All she could hope was that there wouldn't be fireworks and a live band. The only thing holding him back was the time limit.

Alice nodded. "Good. We have six agents posing as guests, including the three of us. Hopefully, you won't need us before the arrest, but we will be there if anything goes down."

Gabby nodded.

"Gabby, just act natural and focus on keeping the party running smoothly," said Markus. "We don't need any logistical problems throwing us off."

Alice adjourned the meeting with a "That's it. Everyone get some rest before Saturday. I'll need you all on your toes."

As Gabby was walking out, she heard Alice say, "The Oobleck report…what is that? Someone get me a dossier on Oobleck. I think we have another Mafia boss on our hands."

Gabby snuck out before they started reading about the unpredictable behavior of slime. Kyle might have gotten a C, but she did some A plus work today.

Gabby had given out the end-of-the-year coffee gift card and toasted success with the crew, but it wasn't over yet. She still needed to hand the other flash drive over to Smirnov. There would not be champagne and a promised coffee date after that one. He had given her a burner phone with only one number programmed in. Thank god she hadn't lost it.

She texted the code 8675309 to the anonymous contact. Why was it so easy to remember? Then it hit her, the song—"Jenny, don't change your number." Like every other fifty-some-year-old guy, Smirnov loved eighties music.

He texted her the meeting location: 3501 Montlake. North Gate Hollywood Reservoir. Above the dam.

Were they going to throw her in? Why couldn't they have just met at Starbucks like civilized people? At this time of day, it was going to take forever to get there. Damn rush hour. At least Granny was making dinner.

After an hour in traffic, she pulled onto Montlake and found her way to the designated location. It wasn't the kind of place Gabby would ever stop. Barbed wire fence. Tow-away zone with no stopping at any time. Based on the map, she was above the upper reservoir and dam, but she could see only an abandoned building and scrubby trees. It might be scenic if she weren't scared for her life. A sign on the fence read 3501 MONTLAKE, RESTRICTED AREA. Was this where he'd taken her when he kidnapped her?

Gabby gripped the steering wheel and kept her eye on the rearview mirror. A few minutes later, the same van that had abducted her pulled up, her BFF in the driver's seat and Smirnov riding shotgun.

Smirnov stepped out while his goon scrolled through TikTok. "You got it?" he asked.

With a nod, she slipped him the sleek black flash drive that Markus had given her.

When she made a move to leave, he said, "Where do you think you're going? I have to make sure this works." He opened up his laptop on the hood of her car and slid in the flash drive. A songbird trilled from a bush nearby, ignorant of the mob business going down in his territory.

"It's all there," Gabby said, impatient to get home.

"The codes?"

"Everything Kramer has is on there." Markus had been one hundred percent sure.

"Dasividaniya, Agent Greene. Spasibo." He slipped her an envelope.

Gabby opened it up, just to see what it was, and Smirnov said, "It's all there."

"Pozhaluysta," she said, pulling out one of the six Russian words she knew. Please, thank you, whore, bitch, and shithead. Thank you, Granny, for the Russian language crash course.

"I keep liking you more, Gabby Greene. So many tricks up your sleeve."

She returned a smile, unsure what to make of being complimented by a mob boss, but sure she was going to hang on to the moment forever. That time she had spent in the Russian Mafia—no one would ever believe her.

Smirnov's van left in a plume of dust, leaving Gabby standing on an empty road in the middle of Hollywood. She watched the van get smaller and smaller until it disappeared. She had done what she needed to do, and they were out of her life forever.

Out of curiosity, she opened the envelope, and gasped aloud at the fat wad of cash.

She was standing next to a NO TRESPASSING sign and a barbed wire fence, nothing but trees, a reservoir below her and mountains behind. Everything was just fine, though. She'd done her job.

As soon as Gabby got through the party, she was walking away from spying forever. Double agenting was over. Hell, agenting was just about over. Like her favorite robe said, Gabby Greene was just a mom.

CHAPTER 30

Thursday, middle of the damn night, Greene household

At the sound of a thunk, Gabby rolled over and crammed the foam earplugs deeper down her ear canals and pulled her eye mask down farther. Could her granny possibly take one night off midnight sex? The woman was eighty freaking years old—didn't she need some rest? Not to mention maybe Burt "Used to Be a Doctor" Jones would be more alert if he tried sleeping through the night.

"Go to slee—" she started to yell out of sheer frustration, when an arm reached out, yanked her out of bed, and covered her mouth.

"Shh!" a masculine voice hissed. "Shut up, suka."

Gabby stifled the scream building in her chest. The better-than-nothing dart gun was out of reach under her bed, in a locked case to boot. This was bad, real bad, but it could get worse. The kidnapper was right about one thing, she did need to be quiet. The spare room she was sleeping in was tucked right between Granny and Burt and the kids, whom she didn't want to wake. Instead of screaming, she bit the hand clasped over her mouth.

"Pizdets!" The kidnapper let go and shook his hand. He grabbed her upper arm and dragged her out of the room, down the stairs, and into the kitchen.

Smirnov was sitting on one of the high stools. Mr. Bubbles was at his feet, duct tape wrapped around his muzzle. Silenced and shamed, he belly-crawled to Gabby in apology with a whimper. Gabby reached down to scratch poor Bubbles, but the goon pulled her to her feet and shoved her on a stool across from Smirnov.

"Did you hurt my dog?" she said, prepared to exact vengeance, if necessary.

"No, do I look like an asshole to you? I shut him up so that I wouldn't have to." He reached down and scratched Bubbles. "He's a good boy."

Well, that was something. But why was he here?

Smirnov picked up a piece of Lucas's leftover pizza. "Are you feeding your children this shit?"

"It's a cauliflower crust and Daiya cheese. Why are you here, Smirnov? I gave you the codes."

He glared at the pizza and took another bite. "I never would have hired you if I knew about this."

"Allergies. My boy has allergies, and he's dairy- and gluten-free. It's really a challenge." She stopped before she gave her usual allergy mom speech, and gathered her breath. "But I gave you the codes."

The grizzled mobster, too big to fit in her kitchen, looked back at her. "Where is the father, Phil, I think?" Smirnov shook his head. "Girls can eat cauliflower, but boys." He gestured to Lucas's school picture. "Look at that boy. He needs some meat and potatoes."

Gabby shook her head. "What is it with men and meat?"

Smirnov looked at her like she didn't understand anything, and then held the pizza slice high and dropped it on the counter like it had personally offended him. "Enough with the pizza." Staring directly at her, he announced, "You fucked up, Gabby Greene."

Chin high, she said, "I copied all the files on Kramer's secret computer, the computer where he makes his transfers. The codes should have been on there."

"They weren't."

She looked around the kitchen for anything she could use to defend herself. The roach spray Phil had brought over was almost within reach. This man was going to kill her and her family if she didn't do something. She lunged for the spray, aimed at Smirnov's face, and pulled the trigger, but nothing came out.

The goon who had brought her downstairs wrenched her arm behind her back and took the weapon away. He held the roach spray up and announced, "You can't shoot with the safety on." He twisted the nozzle to the ON position to demonstrate. He shoved her back in the chair.

Smirnov tsk-tsked her. "What can I do with you now? Did you give the EOD the codes?"

She shook her head no. "They got the same thing you did."

"How can I trust you?" With resignation, he said, "It's over. Mischa, bring the family down." He pulled out a gun and set it on the counter in front of him. "We'll see if she's lying or not."

Gabby's heart rate went through the roof.

"How many kids do you have?" With a glance at a family picture he said, "Two, the one with the purple hair and the one who can't eat real food."

Gabby's breathing tightened. The walls were closing in and her vision was starting to blur. She shut her eyes and focused. If she didn't get them out of this, no one would.

"Please don't hurt my family."

"Oh, I'm hurting your family, one by one until you tell me where the codes are. And if you don't tell me anything I believe, you are all going to die. You last. That's what happens when you fuck with the Mafia."

Her stomach heaved, and she vomited on the floor in front of her.

"Pizdets," he swore. "I thought you were a professional, Greene."

Gabby wiped her mouth on her sleeve. "I will do anything," she pleaded.

"What do you think, I will trade a blow job for your life?" He laughed. "You're more naïve than I thought. I need those codes. That is all that you can do for me. If you can't do that, then you're done."

"You don't understand. I'm not even a spy. I don't work for the fucking EOD." She blurted out the truth in an impassioned frenzy. "I never even heard of the EOD until last week."

He laughed. "Whatever. You've been working for them for months."

"No, that was Darcy. We just happened to look alike, and when she was murdered, the EOD found me and asked me to take her place. I'm just a housewife who happens to look exactly like a double agent!" The words came out in a rush.

Smirnov stared at her with a flat expression, like he was trying to think of how to respond. Then he started laughing, first quietly, then louder. Thank god she had those white noise machines for the kids. They could sleep through anything.

"I have to hand it to you, Gabby Greene, you're funny." He gave her an amused look. "You might want to try writing, because that's a pretty good story."

"It's true!" she yelled.

He snorted. "Go get the kids," he told the goon who could definitely do more with his life.

"Mischa," she pleaded, "we had a moment in the driveway the other day. I know we did. I know you are a good person. Please leave my kids out of this." Then she turned to Smirnov. "Just give me until after the party. Kramer is meeting with Sergei Orlov there. They have to be exchanging the codes then. Give me one more chance."

Smirnov held up a hand. "One more chance, but if you don't deliver, I will kill your family one by one while you watch."

Burt chose that moment to wander into the kitchen right while Smirnov was making a motion to slit someone's throat. Oblivious, Burt pushed past the Mafia boss, who was taking up some of the space in the aisle, and grumbled about no one pushing in their chairs. "Damn kids."

"Excuse me," Smirnov said in a loud voice.

Burt grunted and pulled a wedgie from between his butt cheeks while he checked out the food options. The fridge light cast an eerie glow on his old, wrinkled face in the otherwise dark room.

"Who the fuck are you?" Smirnov asked Burt.

Burt rearranged a few bottles until he found the prune juice, because apparently constipation was his only concern at the moment, not the Russian Mafia literally wagging a gun at his backside.

"Hey, you!" Smirnov tried again while Burt poured himself a glass like no one was in the room with him. Did he ever notice anyone?

Smirnov repeated himself. In a loud voice, he said, "Hey, who are you?"

Burt looked around for the first time and blinked in Smirnov's face. He threw back the prune juice like it was a shot of tequila and shook his head in disapproval. "How many boyfriends do you have, Gabby?" he asked, more judgmental than impressed, and kept moving until he got to the bottom of the stairs.

To Smirnov he said, "Make sure and use protection. This girl gets around. Just like her grandma." Then he did finger guns with a clicky noise.

Unbelievable. Gabby stared after him with her mouth hanging open. Thanks a lot, Burt. She really needed to talk to Granny about this guy. A hot sex life at eighty—aspirational. Burt—no thank you.

"Who the fuck was that?" Smirnov asked, staring after Burt like he wasn't sure whether to kill him. "I'm trying to threaten you, and he's pouring a fucking glass of juice?"

"My grandmother's new boyfriend. He's an idiot."

"Do you want me to take care of him? We might have beef, but I would do you this favor." He clenched his fist and growled. "If someone was threatening my granddaughter."

Gabby smiled. "Thanks, but I think I'll do it myself."

"Attagirl." He nodded his head.

"No, I mean, I'll just evict him."

"That's up to you, but I don't think it'll work. If you want to end something, you end it."

He stood up and brushed the wrinkles out of his pants. "Get me the codes by Saturday. I don't want to repeat this."

She took a shaky breath, crisis averted, at least for the moment.

"And don't try anything. I'm going to have people watching the house until I get those codes. No sneaking the kids out. No getting a new security system. No nothing."

Gabby nodded.

He stood. "I'll see myself out. Good to see you again, Gabby."

An hour later, Gabby finished cutting the last of the duct tape off of Bubbles. Thankfully, she hadn't taken him to the groomer's for a while, so she didn't have to cut close to the skin. As she finished, Granny wandered out in the satin robe Gabby had bought thinking she might be able to glam up SAHM life. It still had the tags on it.

Granny went straight to the liquor cabinet and poured two fingers of whiskey in a tumbler and slid it to Gabby. She poured another for herself.

Plopping down on the stool Smirnov had vacated, Granny said, "Okay, tell me what's going on."

With a dumb stare, Gabby just managed an "umm." There was nothing she could say. Also why burden her grandma?

"Is it man trouble?" Granny asked with a knowing look.

Bingo. That was safe. "Yes. You met Markus last night." Last night felt like a week ago so much had happened.

"Mm-hmm. Easy on the eyes, that one."

"It's just that we work together, and..."

"Gabby, you're an assistant. If you find true love, or even just some really hot—"

"Yes, good point, Granny." Gabby cut her off. "Also, I'm not sure if I can trust him."

"Listen to your gut, but remember you don't have to trust him to enjoy him, if you know what I mean."

Gabby shook her head. "We only have a few days left working together." Laughing at herself, she said, "I gave him a thank-you gift."

Granny burst into laughter. "A what? Isn't the man supposed to be giving you the gifts? Gabby, play hard to get, why don't you?"

"It's 2024, Granny."

"Things haven't changed that much."

"Anyway, it was a little awkward."

Granny shook her head. "Okay. Here's my advice—no more gifts. You wait for him to make the move. And if he wasn't sweet enough when you gave him that present, tomorrow, go in salty. That's what works for me. Keep 'em on their toes." She nodded, satisfied with her own wisdom.

"Good advice, Granny."

"You can invite him over to watch that Russian psychic show we both like." She popped an ice cube out of her whiskey and crunched it. "I want to get to know this boy you don't trust a little more."

Gabby harrumphed. That wasn't a bad idea. Let Granny vet him. They each finished off their whiskeys, and Gabby crawled back onto her futon. What were the odds the Mafia would haul her out of bed twice in one night?

CHAPTER 31

Friday morning, Greene household

The good news about Friday morning was that Gabby awoke to an alarm clock instead of 1) the rhythmic thumping of her grandma's headboard against the wall, or 2) an abduction by Russian mobsters.

Gabby was adding another of her own chapters to *Divorce: A New Beginning* along with retail therapy and eating your feelings. This one would be called "Low Expectations: If You Don't Expect Anything, You Can't Be Disappointed." Sloane Ellis hadn't covered this topic.

Actually, Gabby's expectations couldn't get low enough. A glance out the bedroom window showed that Smirnov had made good on his threat. Mischa was parked in a gray sedan right at the end of her driveway. She had a great view of him recklessly sucking down a Big Gulp like he had access to a bathroom. He clearly hadn't given birth twice. The remnants of last weekend's sidewalk chalk art were right in front of his car. Lucas had spelled "POOPING!!" at the end of the driveway next to a picture of a guy pooping. Yesterday, she would have shaken her head in consternation. Today, she was ready to fiercely defend her child's right to draw all the crappy artwork without a fucking mobster watching over him. Mischa needed to get out of her sight.

Filled with righteous fury, Gabby slipped on her Crocs and marched down her driveway, ready to read that mobster the riot act. Fuck Smirnov for threatening her children, for putting her in this position. How was she supposed to focus on ransacking Kramer's office today with a murderer parked at the end of her driveway?

On impulse, she dragged the sprinkler toward the street. The least she could do was make him uncomfortable. How dare he drink a blue raz slushie like threatening her family was no big deal? After some effort, because the hose was stuck on something, she made it to the car, panting. She threw the sprinkler down. "You need to move!" she shouted. "I have children—" The hose was twisted, and she couldn't get the damn thing to point toward the car.

"Gabby, what are you yelling at Mischa for?"

"Granny?" Gabby blinked at the scene before her. Her grandmother was standing at the driver's side, leaning casually into the window. She appeared to be chatting up the mob security.

"Have you met Mischa?" Granny asked, as if Mischa were some long-lost cousin. "He's just here…What did you say you're doing again, Mischa?" she asked.

"Um, the city hired me to…uh…review traffic." Mischa's accent was thick. A person might assume that his dumb job description was a misstatement.

Gabby raised an eyebrow. "What the fuck is a review of traffic? This is Avocado Avenue."

"Mischa is from the old country." Granny patted his forearm fondly and rattled off a few sentences in Russian.

Mischa threw back his head and laughed. Gabby was ninety-nine percent sure it was a joke about her. Whatever it was must have been hysterical, because it launched a rapid-fire conversation entirely in Russian, leaving her standing and staring at the two of them.

"This is not polite," she insisted. For all she knew, Granny was giving out the code to the house, not that she hadn't been a little loose with that herself this week.

"Mischa was just saying that he is not having much luck with American girls. What's the problem with them?"

Mischa rattled off some Russian, and Granny laughed. "They talk too much, eh." Granny nodded in sympathy, as if she had the same problem. "What's your favorite food, Mischa?" Granny asked.

"Pelmeni," he answered. "You can't get a good dumpling in Los Angeles."

This was unbelievable. Maybe it would help, though. It might be harder for him to kill them after Granny spent all day talking him up. Or easier.

"I have to head into the office in a few minutes," Gabby said.

Granny looked at Mischa. "Let me know if you need anything else."

Gabby fought the urge to shake her grandmother as they walked back to the house.

No matter what, she'd be done tomorrow. If she handed over the material to Smirnov and the EOD arrested Orlov, it would be over. No more Mischa. No more EOD. Failing—she tried not to think about that. Before she went in the house, she turned the water to the sprinkler on and was rewarded by a gratifying string of Russian profanity.

Twenty minutes later, as she was leaving the house, Gabby paused and looked her grandmother right in the eye. "Granny, you know the guy parked outside . . . he's not really here for a traffic study."

Granny raised an eyebrow. "Gabriella, I know that. I wasn't born yesterday." With a nod, she said, "He's a nice boy, though."

"What do you think he's here for?"

Granny chuckled. "I don't know, Gabby. You tell me."

Gabby fought the impulse to confess everything to her grandma. It would be the right thing to do, to let her grandma understand the risks. But Smirnov told her to keep quiet. What if Granny called the police? Gabby had made this mess, and she would get them out of it. Granny could just take the kids to bingo and act sort of normal.

Granny, clearly not understanding the stakes, killed the moment of almost honesty with a stern look. She shook her head in disappointment. "I said to be salty with that young man, not scare him. You look like roadkill."

After not sleeping all week and not bothering to Spanx in her muffin top, Gabby looked worse than roadkill. The roadkill in her closet went for $500.

As she pulled out of the driveway, Gabby locked eyes with Mischa. He gave a businesslike nod, and a grim understanding passed between them. He didn't look eager to kill her, but if Smirnov ordered five hits, he'd deliver.

On the way to work, she popped into an overpriced hipster coffee shop, the kind that served coffee without sugar or syrup and fifteen-dollar avocado toast. On impulse, she bought a quad-shot latte and a couple of five-dollar scones, one for her and one for Fran. Doing something nice for someone else was always a good idea. Now that she knew Fran was killing herself trying to become Kramer's partner or whatever, Gabby couldn't help but feel bad for the woman. "That Jan" couldn't even get his coffee right—Kramer couldn't care less about her.

As she thought of Kramer, he texted, Plz reschedule security team. Not going to be in today.

Finally, a break. At least she could look for the codes in peace.

At eStocks, she pulled into the lot for the last time. Four short days had somehow flown by, but also felt like an eternity. It was sort of like raising kids—the days are long, but the years are short. The same principle applied to spy work. With a sigh, she turned on her earpiece. "Markus, you there?" she said, more abruptly than usual.

"Hey, superspy!" he said. "Smooth sailing today, huh?"

She answered with a half-hearted "Yep, it's gonna be great."

"I thought you'd be more excited now that the hard work is over. You did it, Gabby."

If only. "I'm just tired. It's been a big week, and I haven't slept much." Understatement of the year.

In the office, there was plenty to do. Justin had the party taken care of, but she still needed to prepare advertising pamphlets, print off business cards, and dumbest of all, finalize an investment PowerPoint. It would essentially be a Wikipedia-level report on what an investment was.

But first ransacking. She needed to find the codes. Kramer's office was empty, the chair neatly tucked under the desk and the computer shut down. Before she searched, she needed to do some research. What the hell did a code even look like and where would someone keep it? Yesterday, Markus had said they were on the laptop, so she'd copied the whole thing, but she didn't really know what a code was.

She googled "wire transfer codes" on her phone. After scrolling through several pages of information, she decided she was looking for a SWIFT code, which was a common part of international banking. Nine digits were used to identify the bank.

A nonbanking related search result captured her attention: "Scientists Prove That Women Really Prefer Larger Penises." With a laugh, she switched to that. It contained a quote from the scientist who "discovered the G-spot." Also funny. The takeaway was that if vaginal orgasms were real, big penises were better, so maybe men should be insecure, if women weren't just imagining things. Gabby hoped to live long enough to find out.

Oh fuck, the bank codes. Where would a person keep a wire transfer code? The banks Kramer was using probably weren't in Orange County.

Abandoning the search for the moment, Gabby popped back to her desk. "Is Kramer coming in today?" she asked Fran. Better safe than sorry.

"I don't think so." She shrugged. "I'm sure he's dealing with cleanup or insurance claims after the garage fire."

Mourning his Bentley, no doubt.

The only problem was how to justify spending the whole morning ransacking Kramer's office like the DEA on a drug raid. Fran would probably have something to say about that.

"This friend of yours is not going to be at the party, is he?" Markus interrupted her train of thought.

This wasn't going to be an easy conversation, so she walked down to the bathroom and locked herself in. "Of course Justin is going to be at the party. He's a perfectionist."

"You can't have a civilian who could potentially blow your cover at the party. Tell him he can't come."

"I need his help."

"You have to," he said. "For national security. And for your safety."

"No," she said. Who was he to talk about her safety when either he or one of his EOD buddies was working for Smirnov. Justin was the only one at the party whom she could trust implicitly.

"Why do you need help with a party? What else are you doing today anyway?"

His statement was an echo of so many others, Phil, her mother-in-law, her own mother, Shelly: "Aren't you just sitting at home? Can't you...help with the bake sale; walk my dog; pick up so-and-so from the airport; watch the class pet (Maribel, the corn snake) over winter break, oh, and Maribel eats live mice; be a shoulder to lean on for anyone having a bad day, aka do every damn thing that no one else had time for. Oh, and don't forget Thanksgiving." Here she was, at work full-time, moonlighting as a double agent, and someone was still asking her to plan a goddamn party. Fuck him.

"It might be a party, but there are serious consequences here," Markus reiterated. "Justin can plan it, but he shouldn't be there."

"I am doing my best, and if that isn't good enough, you can find some other woman to do the job."

She yanked the earpiece out with a guttural noise of frustration and slammed the bathroom door on her way back to her desk. How much could one woman take? Two new jobs, inadequate childcare, almost zero sleep, multiple death threats for her *and* her kids and her ex-husband, whom she didn't like that much but didn't want dead. If Markus mentioned the damn party one more time, she would throw whatever kind of party she wanted, and the EOD better be happy with it. Like she told the kids, "You get what you get, and you don't throw a fit."

She wasn't Darcy. She wasn't a superspy. Hell, she wasn't even that great a mom or housekeeper. If there were a stay-at-home-mom Olympics, she would come in near the back of the pack. She let the tears run down, partially to just let it out but also so Fran could see it.

It was always a party that was her breaking point. Life was hard enough, and then you had to bake a cake, put on a smile, and act like you wanted the neighbors to come over. Shelly was bad enough. Kramer—untenable. She rubbed her eyes, ensuring that her mascara went everywhere.

All she needed was to find the codes and stay alive, and she sure as hell wasn't counting on Markus. If she said she needed privacy . . . yelling on the phone and crying was her best option at the moment. Her plan: Operation Pick a Fight with Phil.

Phil picked up the phone on the first ring. "Gaaaabs." He drew out her name like a car salesman trying to slide into a deal. "What's on your mind? You need something?"

"Phil, we need to talk." Her voice was loud and strident, very un-Gabby-like.

"Whoa. We already got divorced or I'd be worried about the tone of your voice."

"It's about the pig," she announced loudly, anger tinging her voice.

Fran must have heard things escalating quickly, and clogged over with her perfect posture. "Can you keep it down?"

Gabby covered up the mouthpiece. "Sorry. Fight with an ex." She frowned. "I really need to take this. I'll just go in Kramer's office for a minute. Oh, and I forgot—" She pointed to the bag on her desk. "I got you a cinnamon scone."

After turning off the brooch camera for privacy, she hustled from her desk to Kramer's office, not waiting for Fran's reaction. Just to really sell it, she said in an impassioned voice, way too loud for the office, "I want the pig back." Carmen poked her head around the corner, wide-eyed, and mouthed, "The pig?" to Fran.

Yep. She was putting on a fairly decent show.

"Jesus, Gabby. What's your problem?" Phil said. "We're talking about a guinea pig. You never even liked the thing." That was true, but it wasn't about her. This was about Kyle and about getting into Kramer's office.

"It's Kyle's pet, and she misses it."

"You have the dog and the house. I think I should get the guinea pig." Phil was being so petty it was unbelievable. A grown man living in a hotel did not need a guinea pig.

"No, Phil. It's not for you or me to split. Kyle should get the guinea pig. It's hers."

With the windows fogged for privacy, she commenced ransacking. Phil, completely invested in the debate, gave a bunch of dumb reasons he should keep the guinea pig. He named it (he did not), he was better at guinea pig care (um...for real?), and he was all alone in the hotel.

That last one stopped her in her tracks. Phil was lonely, and he had just admitted it. For once, he'd been vulnerable and honest. For a second, she wanted to fix it, to rescue him from his loneliness, but she couldn't. Not right now.

Focus on fighting about the guinea pig, Gabby. He started blathering again, at which point she went back to searching drawers. There wasn't a lot of paper in the sleek office. Glass walls, glass desk, no knickknacks. In the digital age, physical transparency didn't mean anything, because there was nothing to see, no piles of cash or diamonds sitting around. Everything worth hiding was already in the cloud. She'd searched everywhere just as he finished talking. Ransacking was pointless.

"Phil, you left. You chose to leave. It's one thing to make that choice, to take your things, but to take Kyle's pet? It's more like you're holding it hostage so that she comes to see you. Dr. Piggie belongs with Kyle. Not to mention, are you even allowed to have a guinea pig in that hotel?"

He made a growly noise, probably because she was right.

"Just be a good dad. Maybe find somewhere to live where the kids can be a part of your life." With a furtive glance out the door—no one was looking for once—she sat down at the computer and booted the sucker up. It's not like she knew what the codes looked like or what the file name would be. She didn't know what she was doing, but it was the only place in the office left to look.

To her shock, Phil relented. "I'll drop the pig by later."

"Thank you."

Instead of hanging up, he hung on the line for another beat. "You're right. I should look for an apartment."

"That's a great idea." She thought about saying more, about how she wanted to do better co-parenting, to remain a family, but just in a different shape. Instead, she said, "See you later, Phil."

She hung up the phone, no closer to finding the codes, but on the other hand, she'd really made some progress with Phil. It only took spy training and being threatened with death to be able to stand up to her ex. If she survived the night, life was going to be better. She kicked back in Kramer's chair and savored the moment.

As usual, Fran couldn't mind her own business. She burst into the office without knocking, catching Gabby red-handed relaxing. "What are you doing, Camille?"

"I needed some privacy. Some personal stuff came up."

"There was a lot of noise in here, Camille. What was with all of the banging?" She narrowed her eyes with suspicion. "I hate to bring this up, but—"

Gabby leaned back. "Oh really?" Did Fran know she was an EOD plant? How could she?

"You're stealing office supplies. My favorite coffee cup is missing, and I don't know where any of the roller-ball pens are. And now you're going through Kramer's things? That's audacious."

Gabby started laughing. Fran was so far off base it was funny. "You're kidding me."

"If I tell Kramer you're stealing supplies, you will lose this job."

Why would Fran care if Gabby was stealing supplies? Who didn't steal supplies now and then? Pens? Come on, Fran!

Gabby stood up to her full height. "Fran, I could give a damn about your stupid mug." She shook her head in disgust. "I was trying to be your friend."

Fran frowned at her. "Just because Kramer isn't here, doesn't mean it's a free-for-all."

Gabby flashed an insolent look and shrugged. "I'm going to sit in here and work. Feel free to report me to Kramer." Might as well work on the PowerPoint for the party in comfort. She did just that, but like she told her kids, "Not everything worth doing is worth doing well." Done was going to be good on this one. She found a stock photo of a graph going up and titled the slide "Profits are rising!" It was pure stock photo bullshit, pretty much the same as the office décor, come to think of it.

With one slide to go, LISTSERV sent her a notification. "There's a guy parked outside the Greene house." In the comments section, Shelly said, "What's with all the guys this week, Gabby? Are you doing a reno?"

Gabby laughed. If only.

"Getting some quotes," she answered. It was always better to give them an answer of some type or they'd keep asking. Shelly was relentless. Sure, there was nothing but suspicious activity this week, but that was just incidental. No one could do anything without Shelly having an opinion about it.

After Gabby had spent a few hours in Kramer's office, her smartwatch announced it was time to go home in half an hour. At this point, who cared? She might as well be Phil looking for his wallet. It was hopeless. There was nothing to do but leave early.

She brushed past Fran on her way out, leaving the woman shell-shocked. "What about the party?" Fran called.

"Cross your fingers and hope for the best."

CHAPTER 32

Friday, 5:00 p.m., Greene household

A reminder alert sounded on her phone. The party was at five o'clock tomorrow, twenty-four hours from now. How could someone kill children over some bank codes? Fucking codes. Smirnov was going to kill her, the kids, and probably Granny and Burt over—she didn't even know how much money. It had better be a lot.

But this wasn't a horror movie where she could peer between her fingers or step out and make popcorn until the scary part was over. It was her life.

She passed Justin's. A new Botticelli-style statue was in his garden. The TWENTY IS PLENTY sign in Shelly's yard missed the actual danger lurking outside entirely. As she turned in to her driveway, Mischa gave her a big wave, almost like he was glad to see her. She didn't return the greeting because what the hell, Mischa.

A flash of light caught her eye as the setting sun glinted off Shelly's front door slamming shut. Gabby slunk low in the driver's seat, but it was no good. In the rearview mirror, she saw Shelly's angled bob making a beeline right for her like she'd been waiting for Gabby to pull in. Gabby shut her eyes and gathered herself. What was it going to be? Was she supposed to volunteer for something or host a neighborhood party or . . . it could be literally anything. There was no bigger busybody than Shelly, except Fran. There was one in every neighborhood or office.

Gabby could do it. Compartmentalize. Talk to Shelly. Box the feelings up to process later or discard when they'd expired. Make dinner. Save her family. Save the world.

With a deep breath and the calmest expression she could muster, Gabby stepped out of the car to find Shelly standing at the end of her driveway, tears streaming down her face, holding Tarragon, who was supposed to be in Gabby's closet, not causing any trouble. How the hell had Shelly gotten it?

Mischa sat up and took note.

"GABBY FUCKING GREENE," Shelly hollered slowly and loudly.

This was not supposed to be happening. She did not deserve this anger. She hadn't killed the cat. She hadn't stuffed him, or even bought him at the Pacific Palisades Farmers Market. Tarragon had been in her closet, safe and sound, until she was ready to deal with this problem, which is when she remembered—it wasn't her closet anymore.

"Your grandfather brought me this cat and had the audacity to ask for the reward money."

Jesus, Burt.

"Like I would give him a thousand dollars for returning him in this state." Shelly was trembling with rage. "How did this even happen? What kind of monster are you?" she cried, her voice quavering.

Justin, the vegan taxidermist, and Burt—they were all going down.

"No no no. I'm so sorry. This is a big misunderstanding." An epic misunderstanding. The mob surveillance was now leaning his head out the window watching. It was undoubtedly the best show he'd seen all day.

"How? You had my dead cat in your closet. That's not a misunderstanding. That's depraved."

Gabby took a deep breath and shut her eyes. She did not have time for this. In the even tones of a hostage negotiator, or Sloane Ellis for that matter, she said, "Tarragon was hit by a car. Justin found him for sale at a taxidermy booth at the Pacific Palisades Farmers Market."

Shelly cocked her head to the side. "What?"

Mischa blurted out a laugh, and Gabby glared at him.

Shelly yelled, "See, it doesn't make sense to—" She gave him a confused look and finished, "Whoever the hell that guy is." In a too-loud voice, she yelled, "You've been putting up flyers for a cat you were keeping dead in your closet. What kind of person does that?"

Mischa flinched and shook his head. Shelly was clearly winning him over.

"Sorry. I was just trying not to upset you. I didn't know how to break it to you."

"Grow a pair, Gabby. I'm an adult. I know bad things happen. What I don't get is you."

Shelly thrust the cat into Gabby's arms. "I can't display my dead cat like some kind of psycho." She stormed off in a cloud of righteous energy, leaving Gabby holding Tarragon at the end of her driveway, a Russian Mafia goon staring her down like *she* was the bad one.

"Killing animals..." He shook his head at her. "That's cold."

Her eyes practically bugged out of her head. "You—" She couldn't even finish her sentence. "You're going to kill my whole family if I don't do what your boss says."

"That's just business." He gestured with his head toward the cat. "That's some serial killer shit."

Just then Granny walked out and saw the cat in Gabby's arms. "Did you get the reward?"

"No, I didn't get the reward! I'll be lucky if she doesn't call the cops."

"Why?" Granny looked confused. "Didn't she want it back?"

"Alive! She wanted it back alive!"

"Sorry to interrupt," the mob goon said, "but do you mind if I use the bathroom?"

Gabby blew her top. She was "the ref made a bad call, and I'm from Philadelphia" mad. "Are you kidding me? What, do you want a snack too?"

"It's number two," he said, unfazed by her yelling.

"Figure it out, jerk-off." In a huff, she stalked back toward the house.

Granny caught up to her in the front entryway. "Did you need to talk to him like that? He's very nice."

"He's not our friend, Granny!" Gabby said too sharply.

Granny raised an eyebrow and let Gabby have her fit. "His mother is from Sviyazhsk, right on the Volga. Such a pretty town."

Gabby plonked Tarragon onto the table by the door with the mail she hadn't read in the last couple of weeks. If she didn't figure her shit out by tomorrow, Tarragon wouldn't be the only dead animal. Granny was bringing snacks to their executioner.

When she clicked the door shut, someone yelled, "MOM! I'm trying to use the bathroom, and Lucas won't leave me alone."

"Lucas, get in here."

Lucas crab-walked into the room like Stephen King had written him into her life and he needed an exorcism.

"How much sugar have you had?" she asked, knowing the answer. Telltale Starburst wrappers littered the floor.

Lucas, clearly high on a gallon of Mountain Dew and at least one bag of Starbursts, squealed in delight and scuttled out of the room. The minute he went around the corner, he set Kyle off. Gabby's nerves sparked like frayed electrical wires. Her eye was twitching almost nonstop.

She took a calming breath. If she could just find the codes and keep her kids alive, she could turn them into decent human beings tomorrow. If they could just let her think...

"LUCAS! STOP IT! MOM!"

Gabby rubbed her temples as she walked into the kitchen. She only had twenty-four hours left.

"Gabs, boil some water for the dumplings, would you? I can't get the TV to work for Burt's show."

Gabby shut her eyes. "I thought you were cooking." The kitchen was fragrant with fried onions and ground beef cooking on the stove.

"I made the pelmeni, but we have to boil them."

"Yum!" Granny almost never made the little Russian dumplings, only on special occasions. The last time Gabby had had pelmeni was her eighteenth birthday. Granny had made dumplings and given her a necklace from the old country. "I wore this the day I defected," she had said. "It'll keep you safe too, pupsik."

"I'm making them for those poor boys outside." She shook her head. "Mischa is from Moscow. Poor thing hasn't been home for years. And he has a friend with him today. Ivan is a sweet boy too."

Gabby's jaw dropped. "You're cooking for *them*?"

"Don't worry. There's enough for all of us. Actually, I'm making our batch now. They can have theirs whenever I get to it."

Gabby stared at her grandmother in shock.

"Close your mouth. You're going to catch flies." Apparently done defending herself, Granny said, "Do you know the password for Hulu?"

"I don't know any of the passwords," she said, except the ones written on the whiteboard. Come to think of it, Phil had signed up for Hulu, and she'd never thought twice about it. She started to text Phil, but then she stopped herself. The Hulu password would probably be as hard to find as Kramer's transfer codes. This was more than a password-lookup issue; this was a division-of-the-assets issue. She should probably get her own subscriptions, but on the other hand, she was more worried about living through tomorrow.

Granny yelled down the hall, "Is *Family Feud* on Hulu, Burt?"

"Only the celebrity one," he yelled from the bathroom. "It's not as good as the regular."

Gabby's eye twitched harder. They were all about to die, and he was worried about which season of *Family Feud* to watch. If he wanted to see a family feud, she was about to show him one.

"But I've got another problem, Vera. Would you come here?" Burt asked.

Gabby could have a glass of wine, boil dumplings, and gather her thoughts. At the end, she would feed everyone, and they'd stop screaming for as long as it took to eat dinner.

Trying to channel the calm she wanted to feel in the house, Gabby set a pot of water to boil. The steam on her face and the prospect of carbs did some work to calm her.

A few minutes later, she pulled the doughy balls of goodness from the pot and plopped them on a tray with sour cream for dipping. For just a second, a sense of well-being and purpose filled her. Just like Shelly said, not to mention every queen on *RuPaul's Drag Race*—she was Gabby motherfucking Greene. One foot in front of the other. Put food on a plate, get the kids to bed, try to figure out how to steal the codes. She had this handled.

"Um, Gabby." Granny's voice quavered uncharacteristically.

"Is there something wrong?"

Granny took a deep, troubled breath, like she didn't know how to say what she needed to say, which was concerning, given that the mob didn't even raise her blood pressure.

Gabby raised her eyebrows. "What?"

"Burt took too many Viagra."

You could have bounced a Ping-Pong ball off Gabby's face. She was dead. Smirnov couldn't even kill her now.

"Kids, it's time to eat," she called while robotically dialing the nurses' line at the clinic. When the nurse asked her to describe the problem, she said, "Eighty-three-year-old man who took too much Viagra. He's had a..."

Granny spoke into the phone.

"A painful erection that won't go away."

The nurse took it in stride and put her on hold.

"Yuck," Lucas complained. "What are these? Can I have something else?"

And that was it.

"No. This is what Granny made. Say thank you and eat it."

Kyle breezed by her and got out the third glass in the last hour because she didn't care about dishes. "Geez, Mom. Lighten up."

Gabby's eye twitched violently.

"No, Kyle, I will not lighten up." She slammed a plate of dumplings onto the counter for dramatic effect. "Damn it, everyone," she said in a not-quite-yelling voice. Suddenly the room was quiet, except for the clinic's hold music and Bubbles' toenails on the hardwood as he ran to her side, probably confused by her tone of voice. Gabby never yelled at anyone. Seething with anger and still twitching, she started listing her complaints. "I am not your maid. Your chauffer. Your nurse. I am not tech support. I started a new job this week, and I am stressed. I need you all to get it together. Kyle and Lucas, you aren't babies. I need your help. Granny." She looked at her. "You can live here, but...I don't even know where to start. I can't deal with your dumb boyfriend. I do not exist purely to serve all of your needs."

She looked back at Burt, who was peering from around the corner. "Particularly Burt's needs."

At that moment, the nurse came back on. "Ma'am."

She'd set the phone on the counter on speaker. The nurse continued. "How long has he had the erection?"

Kyle's eyes about popped out of her head.

Completely unselfconscious, Granny said, "Just an hour. Is that right, Burt?"

"Is your grandfather on any heart medication or have a history of heart or blood pressure issues?"

"No, he's as healthy as a horse," Granny said in the same tone she had announced that he used to be a doctor.

"After four hours, go to the ER. In the meantime, see if he can resolve the issue with sexual intercourse or masturbation. He should also rest and drink plenty of water. You need to bring him in if it takes any longer. He could suffer permanent erectile dysfunction and it will begin to stress his heart."

That sounded like a good solution to Gabby.

"I heard that it might explode after four hours," said Kyle.

Why had Kyle heard anything about Viagra boners?

Breathing too heavy, tears burning at the backs of her eyes, Gabby rushed out of the kitchen to her room, which wasn't even her room. She sat on the stupid futon and let the floodgates open. The tears streamed down her face. What had happened to her life? What had she done?

Everyone was in danger, and it was all her fault. She knew the risks. Darcy was murdered, and she had taken over her job. No matter how safe the EOD made it seem, she should have known better. She was the person who hugged the wall when walking up a stairwell. A person who couldn't enjoy balconies. Peanut butter was basically arsenic in her mind. The one time she'd dismissed her caution, ignored her better instincts, she'd gotten burned.

Bubbles pushed his way into the room and hopped up next to her. The little dog licked the tears from her cheeks as she sobbed. His fur was still mangy from where she'd cut the duct tape out yesterday.

There was no one she could ask for help. She had never been so alone in her life.

"How am I going to get us out of this mess, Bubbles?"

Bubbles looked back with his tongue hanging out, and she realized he was begging. No one had even fed him dinner.

CHAPTER 33

Friday night, Greene household

When she was a teenager, Gabby would cry herself to sleep in the middle of the day because she didn't have anything to do but lean into the despair and wake hours after the sun had set—disoriented and hungover from sobbing over god-knows-what. It had been twenty years since she'd done that. In the foggy twilight of her wake-up, a moment of perspective hit. Just existing as a teen was comparable angst-wise to running from the mob and CIA while caring for children, grandparents, and getting divorced. Being fourteen with math homework, an unreciprocated crush, and a couple of bad zits was rough.

Just like after a healthy teenage crying jag, Gabby walked downstairs to find the TV on and everyone doing stuff like the world had only fallen apart for her. It was falling apart for them too, not that they knew it.

The kitchen was clean, and everything had been picked up. Kyle was sitting at the kitchen table with a notebook and pen. It looked like she was actually doing her homework.

It was as good now as it had been bad before. No one was screaming or fighting. Bubbles was in his dog bed chewing on a bone. Granny was packing lunches for tomorrow with Lucas. Guilt about her freak-out warred with total satisfaction. She was Mother of the Year. Sort of. Not really. Either way, it was peaceful for now, and Gabby knew enough not to tap the glass. Plus she needed to seek the advice of counsel. It was time to call on Justin.

She slipped on a sweater and her Crocs and stepped outside. The neighborhood was quiet, the sound of distant nighttime traffic as comforting and monotonous as ocean waves. While she had slept, it had rained, almost like she and Mother Nature had had the same idea. She breathed in deeply. There was nothing like the smell of wet asphalt. Wet dirt was probably okay too, but Gabby was a city girl. Smirnov's goon gave her a nod and watched her walk next door. A single car passed by, splashing through a shallow puddle.

Justin's house was an oasis of light, music filtering onto the street. When he opened the door, he took one look at her face, and he ushered her in. "Oh no. Who did it?"

At his loyalty, tears pricked at her eyes again. "It's all my fault. I screwed up, Justin. Big-time."

"Honey, you don't know anything about screwing up until you try to do the splits in front of a crowd of a hundred people, sprain a groin muscle, and have to be carried off the stage on a stretcher *after* the paramedics cut you out of your Spanx in front of the still-rapt crowd." They sat down in some comfy chairs. He flipped on a fireplace and yelled, "Hugh, it's an emergency. Gabby is experiencing... some sort of disaster. Can you make cocktails?"

Hugh, who was the steady one in the relationship, slid his glasses up his nose and set his book down. He was a history professor at UCLA and fulfilled the stereotype. No one looked more like a history professor than Hugh.

"I can't get drunk," Gabby said. "A little something to loosen up would be fine, though."

"Okay, spill. What happened? Is it Phil?"

"It's everything." She bit her lip. Where did she even start without discussing the EOD or the Russian Mafia?

She gave him a rundown on the things she could explain:

- Granny and Burt
- Sleeping on the futon
- Child gambling
- Getting Dr. Piggie back from Phil
- Shelly's cat

As she was talking, a timer went off on her phone.

"Are you burning something?" Justin asked.

She shook her head and exhaled dramatically. "No, that's the erection timer."

He spit out his water.

"I know. This is my life. Burt took a handful of Viagra *before* dinner. The nurse said he should go in if the boner lasted more than four hours."

Justin raised his glass. "To Burt."

Hugh joined in. "To Burt."

"That nursing home kicked him out for a reason. He's barely housebroken."

"Your granny likes him though, right? Have you tried to get to know him?"

"I bet she was just bored." Gabby had read an article about high-achieving women choosing to be with dumb idiots. That was Granny.

"Maybe she thinks she can change him," Justin said, which made Gabby laugh.

"Change him at the age of eighty-three." An image of Burt's wrinkled gray ass came to mind.

In an overly serious voice, he said, "She's doing God's work. Don't be getting in that woman's way."

"But anyway," Gabby said, "that's just the background noise. Work is the real problem. It's so much pressure. They want me there all day. And I've been getting...texts and calls at all hours of the night." Being kidnapped was part of her job these days. Bad guys didn't keep their schedules nine to five, so neither could she.

Justin gasped. "For an executive assistant job?"

"My boss had a family emergency yesterday..." She didn't mention that it was because she had the bright idea to light his garage on fire. "I've ended up with more stuff to do than normal."

"That's a lot on top of Burt's erection," Justin said dryly.

"Especially depending on how well-endowed Burt is," Hugh added as he passed them each a Grand Marnier. "Just a little digestif."

"Thanks again for handling the party, Justin. I don't know what I would have done without you this week." The worry started to creep back in. "And I'm worried about the kids." She didn't specify that she was worried the guy parked outside was going to shoot them.

"Why?" Justin said flippantly. "They're great kids...for the most part."

"Their safety. With Burt and Granny in charge," she clarified, as if that justified her anxiety level.

He raised an eyebrow. "It sounds like Burt and Granny have lots of energy. They might as well watch your kids. And wasn't your grandma an Olympic gymnast? That woman is in better shape than either of us."

"Justin, I'm being serious."

"Look, Gabby, it's going to be fine. To me, it sounds like you're worried about a lot of things you can't control. You can't be with the kids every minute of every day. You have to trust someone else. You have to trust me with the party. If Burt loses sexual function because he can't read directions on his pill bottle, that's not on you." As her breathing got faster and shallower, he said, "Take a deep breath, relax."

She nodded. "It's just—"

"Nope." He shook his head. "No excuses. I don't care what's on your plate. You can only do what you can do. Everybody has stuff to worry about. We can all only handle one thing at a time."

Compartmentalizing—was that all anyone could talk about this week? But she nodded. It was a fair point, and she couldn't risk telling Justin any more than she already had. Plus he was right. They might be bad, but they were just potential problems.

"Gabby, I gotta be honest with you. This is a personal assistant job with a jerk boss. And you are in a childcare transition. That's stressful, but none of that is unusual. You can handle it."

He was sort of right.

"Gabby, I love you, but I've watched you start and quit almost everything you've tried. You sold Avon for a day."

And she had the closetful of makeup to prove it.

"Scrapbooking."

She had ordered all the books and fancy papers. Except for the first page, they were almost entirely empty.

"Knitting. SoulCycle."

It's too bad SoulCycle hadn't stuck.

"Bird-watching. Bird feeding. Gardening."

Maybe those binoculars would come in handy...

"Don't quit. You can do this."

"You're right. I should stick something out, but it's more than that this time." At least she thought so. "This job is scary."

"Gabby, don't be dramatic. That's my role in this relationship."

She laughed and he continued. "I don't really understand why you're scared, but if you focus on what you're scared of, that's all you'll see. Focus on tasks you can accomplish, one at a time. How do you think I got through my last celebrity wedding?"

Gabby shut her eyes and tried to calm down, but he must have felt the small-dog energy radiating off her, pink skin peeking through curly white fur and trembling. She was more of a small dog than Bubbles was.

"Do you know how I judge a good queen?" he asked.

"Lip-synching and makeup?" she guessed.

"Well, that," he said, "but there is more. There are four qualities that a queen should have: one, charisma; two, uniqueness; three, nerve; and four, style." Just in case she didn't take him seriously, he said, "That is straight from RuPaul."

He waited for her to show she was listening.

"If you've watched *Drag Race*, you'll see there isn't one standard to shoot for. Not one body type, not one style, not one anything. Success comes from embracing your own unique talents and maximizing." After a drink, he said, "It's like they say in the Army, 'Be the best queen you can be.'"

She stared back flatly.

"Walk the runway, make a dress, check your email, whatever. Do them one at a time, and Gabby Greene the shit out of them."

That was a truth punch she couldn't ignore. She couldn't be

sexy like Valentina. She couldn't martial arts her way out of situations like Markus. She couldn't be anyone but her.

Justin continued. "You are a mama bear who will do anything for her kids. You are a MILF, especially now that you got that makeover last week. Honey! And you are sort of good at almost everything."

She laughed.

"That's just a fact, and you might as well use it. You can half-ass the shit out of almost anything. That's called makin' it work. Same as MacGyver."

Loud as fuck he said, "You, my dear, are Gabby motherfucking Greene."

He was right. She could half-ass things as good as anyone— make a recipe with half the ingredients, get the kids to school every day sort of on time, plan half a trip to an Irish castle and sell it to a guy from Pasadena. Maybe she couldn't find the codes, but that didn't mean she couldn't keep her family alive. She needed to stop trying to be a superspy and solve the problem Gabby Greene–style. An idea started to take shape in her mind. It was probably a bad idea, but it was a start—a little bit reckless, a little bit half-assed, and all her.

"Thank you, Justin." She squeezed his hand. He might have just saved her ass.

"I'm going to give you something for good luck tomorrow." After rifling around in the bathroom, he returned with a tube of red lipstick. "Tomorrow, I want you to be as bold as your lip color. Now go home, because Hugh took a Viagra an hour ago."

Hugh looked up from his book with a "What?"

When she blurted out a laugh, he said, "Just kidding. But we both need beauty sleep before tomorrow's party."

As she was leaving, Justin gave her some final instructions. "Make sure to use lip liner, fully line your lips, and then lightly powder your whole face to set the color."

"I love you, Justin."

"I love you too, babe."

Earlier that week, she'd told Markus that no one had ever believed in her before, but that was straight wrong. Justin always had.

It was time to stop whining, and half-ass her way out of this situation.

CHAPTER 34

Saturday morning, Greene household

The day of the party dawned bright and cheerful, California's unrelenting sunshine a false backdrop for the day. Dread pooled in Gabby's stomach like battery acid. She took a shower, Spanxed in her muffin top, and slid on her shoulder holster over a plain black tee. Extra cartridges, she strapped to her ankle. Compared to the hardware everyone else carried, the dart gun was a training bra.

Downstairs, Granny was the only one up, brewing coffee and doing her stretches. "Can you even touch your toes, Gabby? You need some exercise, sweetie."

"Spanx is more efficient." Just strap in the fat and go.

Granny shook her head. "You know I was in the Olympics. Not one of you took after me." She shook her head in disappointment. "I'm working on the kids, though."

Unfortunately, that was true. Out of everyone in the house, Granny was the only one who could perform a cartwheel. If she ever recorded herself, she could be famous on TikTok.

Gabby changed her tone, stopping short of taking Granny's hand and looking into her eyes. "I'm worried about today. I have that party and—" She exhaled a shaky breath. "I'm worried it might not go well."

"It's a party, Gabriella. Aren't those supposed to be fun?" One of her drawn-on eyebrows raised an inch as she said, "Is that hunk who came over still giving you trouble?"

"Eh, it's worse than that." She wanted to tell Granny everything, but the truth caught in her throat. If Granny approached Mischa or called the cops, the whole thing might blow up. Still, in the silence between them, Gabby was pretty sure her grandma understood, maybe not the details, but the seriousness of the situation.

Like it was gospel, Granny said, "Just serve more liquor. That always works." She placed her hand on Gabby's, and in a firm voice that contrasted with her paper-thin skin and blue veins, stated, "Don't worry, I've got the house covered. I defected from the USSR and Shady Acres Nursing Home. Whatever it is, I've got it."

When Gabby asked, "Is that why you're with Burt?" Granny just laughed.

Before Gabby left, she made one last stop in the bathroom. The minute she did, she shouted, "Lucas Daniel Taylor, get your butt in here," before mentally slapping herself for saying the word "butt," which would only encourage him.

Lucas had drawn stick figures with big round butt cheeks all over the wall by the toilet. The artwork was subpar, and Lucas was clearly immature, even for his age.

Lucas walked into the room unrepentant, until he saw the wall. His eyes went big, and he started laughing hysterically.

"Lucas, this is not funny."

"It was supposed to be invisible," he said. "I did it with my spy pen."

He also wasn't good at reading directions. "Lucas, give me the pen. It's mine now. And I want this clean before I get home." She choked up a little at the threat. Hopefully, she would be coming home.

After she pocketed the pen, she gave him a hug and kissed the top of his head. "Love you, Lukie."

Before she left the house, she slipped on her granny's necklace, not for luck, but to remind her that she came from a line of women who could do anything. Gabby squared her shoulders and lifted her chin. It was half-assed plan or bust.

The Velvet Underground Speakeasy was as fabulous as it sounded—booths tucked into corners, dim lighting, and an ornate bar with a mirror surrounded by carved figures of Bacchus. It looked like a place where secrets would be kept. Kramer wasn't there yet, still moving slowly after his garage fire. Carmen was bellied up to the bar flirting with a bartender, and Fran was bustling around doing things Gabby didn't even realize needed doing. Justin, coming as Betty Danger for the evening, was on his way.

"Thanks for the help, Fran. I really appreciate it."

"My pleasure." Fran laughed at herself. "You know I like to get involved in everything. Some have even said 'over-involved.'"

Was that an apology? At the very least, the self-awareness was endearing.

Fran looked around at the club. "I was worried—I mean the theme seemed a touch off—but I have to hand it to you, Camille. This is going to be a night to remember."

Gabby had almost forgotten that Fran had accused her of

stealing office supplies just yesterday. In retrospect, that seemed almost silly, and the least scary thing that had happened to her this week. And really, she had been trying to steal something, so Fran wasn't wrong.

"I'm sorry I snapped at you yesterday," Gabby said.

Fran set down the projector and really looked at Gabby. "And I'm sorry I jumped to conclusions about office supplies. I'm pretty sure it was Carmen." She shook her head in Carmen's direction.

"Nah, Carmen couldn't care less about office supplies."

"Maybe I should drop it," Fran said, in one of those gratifying moments of unexpected growth. Gabby almost teared up.

Fran might be a pain, but there was no one more competent and reliable. In a different world, Gabby could have been her friend, following a lot of needless rules about office etiquette and helping to police expired yogurts in the break room fridge. Every friendship came with its own oddities. Instead, tonight would be the last time she'd see Fran, just when they'd overcome their first disagreement.

"What made you decide on the mob theme?" Fran squinted at the speakeasy.

"That was the party planner, Betty Danger. I have to admit I wasn't supervising very closely." Understatement of the year. She'd just said "you decide" to every question. She'd fallen into a mob theme the same way she'd fallen into a lukewarm marriage and an undercover job. Really, this was a moment she needed to learn from. Take action. Make decisions.

Just then, Betty Danger walked in. Betty was dressed to the nines as the mob boss's best girl, Judy Garland meets Susan Lucci.

Before Betty had a chance to yell, "Gabby motherfucking Greene," at top volume and expose her true identity in the most sensational way possible, she ushered Betty into a private booth.

In a hushed voice, Gabby said, "I need to tell you something. And look at your legs! It's not even fair."

Betty Danger's legs went all the way up.

"Don't make me blush, darling." Betty wiggled all the way into the booth and whispered, "Tell me what's going on," she said conspiratorially. "I knew something was up this week. Besides Burt's penis."

Gabby grabbed Betty's hand and leaned forward. "This isn't going to make any sense, but I really need you to call me Camille tonight. I can't explain why."

Betty leaned back to get a good look at her friend. Whatever she saw must have satisfied her. "Okay… *Camille.* That's nice. What's your last name?"

"Walker. Camille Walker."

"*Walker?*" Betty narrowed her eyes and then just threw up her hands. "I think you could have done better than that, but okay." She gave Gabby a "this isn't the end of this conversation" look and said, "I'll roll, but you better dish over cocktails this weekend."

Gabby smiled ear to ear. "You're the best. Thank you." Her best friend's only enemy was boredom—the mob wouldn't even faze her.

"*Camille*, before the guests arrive, you should change."

"Change?" She had planned to wear yoga pants and a black turtleneck and just blend into the background.

"You're the host, Gabs. You have a part to play." She pulled a garment bag off the back of a chair. "Plus, I brought you something."

"You know I need to be comfortable tonight." She needed to wear something she could run away in.

"Don't worry. This will be perfect." Betty unzipped the bag to reveal a pair of high-waisted, pin-striped black slacks with a pair of suspenders and a white collared shirt.

"I change my mind. That's cute."

"Of course it is. Don't forget your lipstick." Betty waved her off. "Go get changed."

With her bold red lip and girl gangster costume, Gabby looked like the star of a black-and-white film.

When she tried to weasel away without any eye makeup, Betty put her hands on her hips. "*Camille*, I don't know what you're up to, but what I do know is that you need to fully inhabit the role you're playing. If you don't believe it, no one will. Wear the costume, walk the walk, talk the talk. This eyeliner"—she held up the tube of liquid liner—"isn't about enhancing your natural beauty. It's about becoming."

Gabby sighed. So much drama.

"Have you read Michelle Obama's book?"

She hadn't. Justin had loaned it to her like a year ago.

Betty waved her hands as if to keep from crying. "In the words of the most righteous bitch of the twenty-first century, 'If you don't get out there and define yourself, you'll be quickly and inaccurately defined by others.'"

Gabby didn't point out that Betty was literally dressing her up like a doll.

"Stop smiling. I'm trying to give you a bold, smoky eye."

When Betty finished, she stood back and nodded in approval. "Go get 'em, tiger."

Being a wife and mother had taught her a lesson that being a double agent had really hammered home. Gabby Greene needed to rescue her own damn self. It had only taken her until thirty-eight to learn that lesson.

Betty Danger sashayed into the center of the room and snapped her fingers in the air. "Okay, everyone. Let's get to work. We have one hour to be party ready. I want it to look like an episode of *The Sopranos* in thirty minutes, but a classy one. This ain't the Bada Bing, baby."

"Who is the entertainment tonight?"

"Me and some of the other queens. We're going to tone it down and channel Nina Simone. You'll love it."

"Perfect." Gabby had to admit that having Betty's crew, all six-foot-something badasses in heels, was comforting.

"You over there," Betty said loudly in the direction of . . . Gabby did a double take. It was Markus. She hadn't even noticed him arriving.

Markus smiled at Gabby and held out his hand. "Marshall Townsend. Nice to meet you." Marshall, the name she'd given him the other night.

"Nice name," she said, her voice sweet but with a tinge of "I see what you're doing here."

He glanced over her shoulder at Betty Danger and shook his head almost imperceptibly, his frustration palpable.

Gabby smiled and held out her hand like she hadn't heard him. "Camille Walker. I'm Mr. Kramer's personal assistant. And this is—"

Flirty to the max, Betty introduced herself. "Danger, Betty Danger."

Gabby rolled her eyes. "Stop flirting. You're married."

Betty held out her hand dramatically to be kissed and dismissed Gabby's reprimand. "I'm in charge here tonight."

Markus practically choked on his own spit. "You're in charge?"

"Yes, of the whole operation. I'm LA's premier party planner," Betty announced with no shortage of confidence.

If only she knew how much she'd pissed off everyone with this particular plan.

Markus flashed an "is she for real?" look at Gabby, who confirmed, "Betty is number one."

"Marshall," Betty said, angling for something by the tone of her voice, "can I bother you for some...assistance?" She gave him an up-and-down. "I see you have plenty of muscles."

So did Betty for that matter.

Markus looked like he was biting down on his tongue, hard. Gabby tried not to laugh. After all of Markus's whining that Betty couldn't be at the party for national security reasons, here he was stuck doing her bidding. Gabby could watch this all night.

"What do you need?" Markus asked, sounding like he was ready to get this over with.

"Could you be a dear...there are some heavy boxes in my car. Could you carry them in?"

"Fine."

"Oh, and first, can you hand me this vase? I can't quite reach it."

It was Markus's turn to give Betty an up-and-down. Betty was taller than Markus, especially in her heels.

Markus handed her the vase unceremoniously and barked at Gabby, "Camille, why don't you come help me with the boxes?"

Outside, Markus took a deep breath and slowed down. "I need a minute to catch my breath."

"Sorry Betty was bossing you around."

He laughed. "She would not make it as a government employee." After a pause, he said, "It's not her. This is my first field op since losing Darcy." His voice almost powered down at the end. He could barely get the words out.

"That wasn't your fault, Markus." Gabby couldn't explain why, but it really wasn't his fault. Darcy had been a double agent, doing double agent things. There was no way Markus could have protected her from something he didn't know was happening. Assuming he wasn't also a double.

"She was my partner, my best friend." He looked at her. "Now it's you. You're only here because of me. I argued for you. I trained you."

"Markus." Gabby looked at him. "I appreciate all of your support more than I can say, but I am my own woman. I chose to accept the job. I chose not to quit. I am responsible for my own decisions and the risks that I have taken. I don't need you to take that on for me."

Funny, but she might as well be talking to herself regarding the kids. They were their own people. She needed to let go just a little. How many times had Granny told her that roots-and-wings proverb? It took this for her to finally get it. "There is a saying about parenting. You need to give your kids roots and wings. I think you are in the same position. You taught me hand-to-hand combat skills, and you have to trust that I can use them."

He gave a light chuckle. Admittedly, it was a bad example. They both knew Gabby was not the one to bet on in a fight.

With a confidence she only started feeling after Betty helped her with a costume change, she said, "And you did a damn fine job. Look at me."

Markus gave her a glance that made her feel like a morsel he would be more than happy to gobble up. "That's part of why I don't want you in a dangerous position." In a voice like butter, he said, "I like you, Gabby Greene."

"I like you too, Markus. That's why I gave you a coffee card and not Valentina."

He laughed and said, "I knew that. I liked your little excuse about me being your main teacher, though."

"And I thought I got away with that one," she said.

"You look...nice, by the way." He might have said "nice," but from the look on his face, he meant more.

Gabby took a deep breath and stepped into the darkness of the speakeasy like she was diving into the deep. She greeted guests while Lady Eleganza Le Tuck crooned along with the piano, ice cubes clinked in glasses, and the hushed murmurs of conversation filled the room. Justin had knocked it out of the park, and he'd been right. Everyone loved the cheeky theme. The password and secret back room—the guests were relaxed and enjoying themselves.

Sergei Orlov, a man with a narrow frame and slicked-back hair, made a beeline for Kramer the minute he arrived. Innocuous and talking about financial things she'd always ignored, Sergei and Kramer could be Phil and any of his partners. Just like tonight, her life had hinged on what Phil had been doing too, and she hadn't paid attention. She wouldn't make the same mistake this time.

It was time to enact her half-baked plan.

With the party just starting to simmer, Gabby stepped outside to make a call on the burner phone Smirnov had given to her.

"Smirnov, I have the codes. I'll text you my location."

CHAPTER 35

Saturday evening, Velvet Underground Speakeasy

Waiting to enact the most high-stakes, last-ditch, Hail Mary plan of her life, everything hinged on Smirnov. He said that he'd be there in half an hour, and Gabby couldn't tear her eyes from the door.

"Waiting for a hot date?" Betty whispered in her ear.

Gabby laughed nervously.

Everyone else was worried about where the ice cubes were. This was the bad part of being undercover. Guaranteed the guys who dropped out of a plane to kill Osama Bin Laden weren't being harassed about cocktail napkins and ice cube dimensions, but here she was hostessing at T-minus the end of her world.

"Camille, should Kramer do his presentation before or after the dessert rolls out?"

Who the fuck cares. I'm about to die.

"Camille, where do we put our coats?"

Light them on fire if you want.

"Camille, where are the tiny drink straws?"

Another state. Plastic straws are illegal, bitch.

"Camille, can you tell the performer she's too loud?"

There was no way she was going to tell Betty Danger she was too loud. One, it was Betty, and she could do what she wanted. Two, she needed the distraction for the plan that hinged on Smirnov's arrival. Nothing was safe from traffic in LA. He was probably stuck on the 405.

Because Fran loved managing details and she had better things to worry about, Gabby directed everyone her way. Merry Christmas, Fran.

Valentina tapped her on the shoulder, and she almost jumped out of her skin.

She narrowed her eyes at Gabby. "You're acting like you're the one with the hard job tonight, Agent Greene."

Gabby laughed nervously.

"You have a problem. One of your kids is out front, something about her iPad."

"What?"

Just like Valentina said, Kyle was standing around wide-eyed in front of the drag club. "Why are you at Uncle Justin's club?" she asked. "And whose pants are those?"

"Why are *you* here?" Gabby asked, incredulous.

"I used Find My iPhone to find you. You have my iPad."

"What?" Gabby couldn't even with this development.

"I need it for my homework."

Gabby looked down her nose, not believing the homework line for one second. Kyle needed it for TikTok. She grabbed Kyle's hand and escorted her out to the street, where Granny was parked. She shut the car door firmly and said, in her most serious voice, "I will be home in a few hours. Go home!"

"Just bring out my iPad, will you? It's in your bag."

"NO!"

From the back of the car, Lucas said, "Can I have my pen back?"

"NO!"

Inside the speakeasy, she looked at Valentina and shook her head. "What in the hell? Why would my grandmother drive them here?"

Valentina laughed, for once looking really amused. "Did you give her the iPad?"

"No!"

Valentina laughed. "Good work holding the line. I don't know how you do it."

Over Valentina's shoulder, Gabby spied her quarry. Smirnov strode into the party in evening attire. He was at least six feet, probably more, broad, with a dad bod. Truth be told, he was kind of hot.

Gabby caught his eye from across the room, and he stalked her way, grabbing a martini off a waiter's tray without breaking stride. Everyone in this operation had James Bond training but her.

Valentina looked between her and Smirnov. "Who is that?"

Gabby laughed it off. "Another family member. I can't get rid of them tonight." As she headed toward Smirnov, she added, "Be right back. I need to get rid of this one too."

"Did you bring it?" he asked, skipping even the barest of preambles. "I like parties, but I'd prefer one without the government." A little smile quirked his lips, and he added, "Although it's not bad to get my heart rate up now and then."

"Well, thanks for coming," she said, like he was an invited guest.

"I am not here to chitchat. Hand me the codes, and we're done."

"Be patient."

Smirnov leaned in like he was telling her a secret, his breath caressing her neck as he said, "You realize that I have a man stationed outside your home. At my signal, he will kill your family."

Gabby tried to still her trembling. She was scared, but she wasn't as scared as she looked. Men never took her seriously, and now was not the moment to change that. She had spent her whole life doing as told, listening to dudes who sounded like they knew what they were doing. Phil—she'd tried to make him happy for fifteen years, and look where that had gotten her.

Kramer—that asshole couldn't even tell the difference between her and Darcy. To him, women were literally interchangeable, Swatch watch bands, only good for serving his immediate needs. Half the guys at this party were the same, only interested in her if there wasn't a prettier woman in sight. Smirnov was the worst—literally threatening to kill her children. Who the fuck did he think he was?

Gabby was done with being bossed around by average men. Why had she tolerated it all these years? To fit in with other moms in the pickup line? There were no good options for a regular woman with kids. Career-woman mode came with inadequate time off, six weeks of maternity leave, insane childcare costs, and limited time with their children—stresses that she couldn't name because she hadn't chosen that path. Until this week.

The soccer mom path came with low self-esteem and plenty of time with people who didn't necessarily respect you or want that much time with you.

Most of the women she knew thought they were selfish for thinking they deserved more. Well, fuck that.

She did deserve more, and she definitely didn't deserve to be threatened. Hell, she'd walked into this job because of some fucking divorce paperwork. Fuck Phil for the seek work order, and fuck Smirnov for thinking he could threaten to kill her family.

"I know you're scared, rybka. All I need are the codes."

She let his pandering stoke her rage, even while she whimpered. Let him think he had her where he wanted her.

Time to pull out her best Meryl Streep. She harnessed her real fear and let her breath come fast and shallow. Like she wasn't going to make it, she rubbed her temples.

Softly and menacingly, he repeated, "Where are the codes?"

"In the back. I'll show you."

As she gestured to the swinging door to the kitchen, she palmed one of the darts Valentina had given her. There was an hors d'oeuvres trolley directly in front of Smirnov, but the attendant was nowhere to be found. It was her chance. As he looked toward the kitchen, Gabby jabbed him in the ass with the dart.

Smirnov gasped, and Gabby braced herself for the whole plan to go sideways. Every reason for failure raced through her brain at once: Maybe he'd been too big to dart. Did he need a double dose? What if he screamed or he fell on the floor instead of the cart? Then his eyes drooped, and he slumped onto the cart as planned. In the background, Betty yelled, "Yaaas, Queen!" almost like it was for her. Hopefully, it was for one of the bankers.

A second later, Betty appeared. "Um, Camille…"

Gabby smiled brightly. "He had one too many. Will you help me wheel him into the back?"

Without question, Betty stepped in to help, but she looked up through her lashes with a particularly sassy look. "Girl, this explanation better be good."

"It is," Gabby said, as they heaved the cart toward the back. It would have been her luck to get the trolley with a bad wheel that pulled to the left. "This is better than a Target cart," she exclaimed.

Betty shouldered in and took the handle. "Let me push. He's

cute." When she bumped him into the wall, she apologized, "So sorry, Daddy."

"Betty!"

"You know he's a daddy. Look at him!"

As Betty pushed Smirnov through the door to the service area, she glanced at the party. No one had noticed a thing. Everyone's eyes were on Kramer and Orlov.

Betty said, "Where would you like your groceries, ma'am?"

Gabby repeated her usual line. "In the back is fine."

While Gabby held the door open, Betty wheeled him into a storage room behind the kitchen, just some boxes and dim lighting. Perfect.

"What should we do with him?" Betty asked.

"I'll take it from here."

Betty held up her hands and said, "He's all yours. I'm married anyway."

Gabby laughed. "It's not what you think, but if you can handle the party for a while, I'd appreciate it."

Betty raised her perfectly penciled-in eyebrows. "You've got some 'splaining to do, *Camille Walker*."

When Gabby walked back into the party, Valentina strode toward her with purpose. "It took me a minute to remember his face, but now that I did, I'm really confused. Why were you talking to Eduard Smirnov?"

At that moment, Gabby knew that Valentina wasn't the mole, but she couldn't risk her wrecking her plan. They were standing right next to a quiet booth, not a bad place to ride out the party… "Sit down, and I'll tell you."

CHAPTER 36

Saturday night, storage closet, way back of the Velvet Underground Speakeasy

An hour and a half later, Gabby was dripping with sweat, and her muscles were Jell-O from manhandling people larger than herself into the storage room. She'd essentially done an hour of CrossFit and was no closer to being sold on the concept. Like every mom, Gabby always carried a water bottle, but this was the first time she could remember being actually thirsty in a long while. She chugged a bottle of Perrier from the bar and surveyed her handiwork.

In the little storage room, she had assembled all the players: the EOD, all the relevant Mafia, her money-laundering boss, and anyone who might be the mole, aka, Smirnov, Alice, Sergei, Kramer, and Markus. Everyone but Valentina, who was safely slumped over in a corner booth. Gabby had dosed her again just a second ago.

As Alice started to blink awake—thank god, because there was only so long she could keep everyone locked in the back room—Gabby asked, "Is everyone comfortable?" As soon as it slipped out of her mouth, she wanted to take it back. Of course they weren't comfortable. She had zip-tied their hands and propped them against the wall on a bare concrete floor in party clothes. And to boot, the air-conditioning didn't seem to be working in this particular area of the restaurant. Spirit Airlines would be a step up.

In response to the glares, Gabby said, "I apologize for—" She gestured to the room. "All of this. It was the best I could do under the circumstances." It's not like they would have met her at a coffee shop. "And I don't mean to eat in front of you, but I'm a little shaky after all of that." She could actually feel her blood sugar dropping. "Mmm, is this fig jam? The appetizers at this party really turned out great."

A roomful of seasoned spies and criminals stared back.

After she finished a couple of bites, she said, "Thanks for your patience. Luckily, it seems like no one had an adverse reaction to the tranquilizer."

In a heavy Russian accent, Orlov asked, "Why don't you just pass out some juice boxes while you're at it."

He could laugh, but the joke was on him at the moment. Every single one of them had underestimated her. For the first time in her life, Gabby hadn't underestimated herself. And just look what she'd done.

With only a week of training, Gabby had to go on instincts, using the skills she already had, and that was sitting everyone down and letting them know what she thought of them. It had worked on Kyle, Lucas, and Granny yesterday. A good productive conversation would solve a lot of the problems. Not that everything was perfect. She hazarded a furtive glance at Markus. She'd tranquilized and tied up the first guy who had asked her out on a date post-divorce, but there was no helping this. She was doing the best she could to save her family.

The only person who looked worse than her was Kramer. If the

EOD didn't arrest him after this, the Russian Mafia would do worse. "That suka is your secretary?" Orlov said to Kramer in a flat, "murder is my business" tone of voice.

"Executive assistant," she answered for him.

Orlov made a low rumbling noise that didn't bode well for Kramer. He might not even be safe in prison.

"I brought you all here for a couple of reasons," Gabby announced from the front of the room. "Before we get to those, I'm going to give you all a little context." She paused to make sure they were listening. "I believe the story starts with Mr. Kramer laundering money for Mr. Orlov here." Gabby didn't know exactly how Orlov made his money, but Wikipedia suggested human trafficking, racketeering, drug trafficking, extortion, murder, robbery, smuggling, arms trafficking, gambling, fencing, prostitution, pornography, money laundering, fraud, and financial crimes.

Kramer didn't deny it. There was no point.

"Why? For those cars?" Gabby accused. "What about your family?"

Orlov groaned, clearly pissed that he had managed to align himself with so many incompetent assholes.

"Next, we have Mr. Smirnov. Would you like to introduce yourself?" She said it like she was introducing another kid to the kindergarten class.

"Go ahead. You seem to be enjoying this," Smirnov growled.

She was.

"Okay, just correct me if I get anything wrong. Mr. Smirnov is also in the Russian Mafia." She said it like she was identifying a hobby he and Orlov shared. "So you two have something in common, but I'm guessing you know that, not that I know how the Mafia works."

Now Alice groaned.

"Mr. Orlov, you will probably be upset to find out that Mr. Smirnov hired me to steal the wire transfer codes from Kramer. This is why we're here. I don't have the transfer codes that Mr. Smirnov wants, and I don't know how to get them. There is at least one guy stationed at my house who is ready to kill my whole family if I don't provide them tonight." She looked at Alice when she said this.

Alice sat up straighter. "Why didn't you come to me with this?"

"Because Smirnov told me one of you was a plant assigned to watch me. How was I supposed to know who? That's why you all are tied up too. One of you is Mafia."

Markus shook his head. "This doesn't make sense. If you're working for..."

"I know you trusted her, Markus, but Darcy was a double agent, working for the EOD and Smirnov."

Markus's expression turned to stone. "There's no way. Darcy was the best of us."

"I'm not saying she wasn't a good friend. She probably just needed the money. I don't know why she did it, but I have had the week from hell dealing with you." She leveled her gaze at Smirnov.

Smirnov cleared his throat. "I'm not following."

"I told you the other night. I just happen to look like Darcy Dagger. Until last week, I had nothing to do with any of this, which is why I don't have the information you want."

She looked at the group and said, "So this is where I need you all to start filling in some facts."

She looked at Smirnov. "My first question is for you. Who is the mole? Does anyone think it might be Valentina?"

Markus flashed an annoyed look at her. "Come on, Gabby. You know it's not Val. You should have just come to me a week ago." He looked around the room. "You didn't need to do all this."

"Oh, I did, Markus. I wanted to trust you, but how could I?" She looked right at him. "No matter how I feel about you, I couldn't risk my family's safety."

He shook his head like he couldn't believe her.

"Don't pout. I still want to get a coffee with you."

He laughed. "For real? You just tied me up, and not in a good way!"

"I'm sorry, Markus," she said, keeping it professional. "We just have a few things to clear up first." She gestured to the room.

At this point, a voice from the kitchen called, "Camille, where are you?" Then more sharply, "Camille."

Gabby groaned in defeat. She only needed a couple more minutes. After all this effort, she hadn't found out anything yet. This is why she should have gagged everyone.

The door handle turned.

The door swung wide open. Fluorescent kitchen lighting streamed in. When Gabby's eyes adjusted to the brightness, she saw Fran. The nosiest co-worker ever pushed her way into the room and looked around with surprise.

Gabby retracted all her thoughts about being sad not to see Fran anymore. The woman had cornered the market on wrong place/wrong time.

In a voice as flat as her love life and career prospects after today, Gabby said, "Hi, Fran."

Instead of screaming in shock at the sight of six people zip-tied in a back room, a sinister smile spread across Fran's face. "What's this? The VIP room?"

CHAPTER 37

Saturday night, still in the storage closet

Fran stood in the open doorway, fluorescent kitchen lights silhouetting her like a woman in the opening sequence of a Bond movie, but in a pair of pleated khaki pants that would give even the skinniest supermodel a front butt.

Fran raised a gun. "Hello, Camille. Or should I say…Gabby?"

For a moment, it didn't compute. Why did Fran have a gun and know her name? The answer was obvious, but it didn't make sense. Fran was annoying and frumpy and approaching middle age before her time. Could someone so worried about making sure no one ate her yogurt be the bad guy?

"Jan!" Kramer called out. "So glad you found us."

"It's Fran!" she said. "You idiot."

Fran was the mole.

Fucking A. After the initial shock passed, a wave of relief hit. It wasn't Markus. She hazarded a glance his way, and her heart squeezed. Just an innocent heartthrob, tied up for no good reason.

Confirming it, Fran smiled at Smirnov and said, "Eduard, I'm sorry this happened. Give me a minute, and I'll get you out." Her tone of voice was sweet, almost tender. Gabby recalled Darcy's notes about Fran being hung up on an ex. She was willing to bet it was Smirnov and that Smirnov could give a shit about Fran.

Smirnov grunted. "Hurry up, would you?"

"Eduard, you wouldn't be here if you had just trusted me instead of hiring this incompetent bimbo." She turned to Gabby. "Take your gun out of its holster, set it on the ground, and slide it to me, slowly," Fran commanded in a used-to-guns, been-a-spy-for-a-while kind of way.

Gabby laughed. "You know they wouldn't trust me with a gun."

"I wasn't born yesterday."

"No, I really don't have a gun."

"What's that then?" Fran pointed to the dart gun. "I'm not blind."

"Oh, this?" She didn't say "old thing," but her tone strongly implied it. Gabby held up her dart gun. "It's not lethal." When Fran gave her a hard look, Gabby gave up and slid the gun across the floor. For all the complaining she'd done about it, she'd never been so sad to see something go. Goodbye, only hope.

"Are you people serious?" Fran looked at Alice and Markus. In an accusatory tone, she said, "She's not even armed. Didn't you think she could handle a gun?" She shook her head slowly and looked meaningfully between them, zip-tied on the floor, and at Gabby, the one who'd restrained them.

Maybe Fran was the bad guy, but Gabby appreciated the vote of confidence.

"So what is the endgame here?" Fran said looking around the room, obviously confused. "Were you going to tie them all up and...what...have an open, honest conversation? A little restorative circle."

Restorative circle—that sounded like some Waldorf School lingo. Fran and her kid's tuition. Was this the reason that Fran was doing all of this? The LA schools weren't good, but were they *that* bad?

"Or is this *Scooby-Doo*?" Fran smiled. "You gathered everyone and are about to unmask the owner of the fairground who has been disguised as a monster..." Fran arched an eyebrow. "Which I guess makes me the monster."

Whoever decided to bring back mom jeans was the real monster. But Fran was right about *Scooby-Doo*. Fran had her there.

"It didn't even occur to you that I was the mole, did it?"

Gabby shook her head slowly while Fran gave her a disappointed look that burned to her core.

"I'm sorry." Gabby was the same as the rest of society, dismissing a woman in unflattering pants as a credible threat.

"You're not the only frumpy mom flying under the radar in the spy world," Fran said.

Frumpy? Fran could speak for herself. But she was guilty. "I'm sorry for underestimating you," Gabby said.

"Gabby, you're apologizing to a woman threatening you with a gun," Markus said sounding exasperated, stating what should be obvious.

That was a good point. Fran deserved to be taken seriously as a bad guy instead of called Jan and forgotten. But there was more to it than gender. The person walking through the whole office with a take-out container demanding, "Is this yours?" could not be a spy. That was a deep embed, someone who'd been there for years, not only blending but defining the office culture.

Softer, Gabby said, "You killed Darcy, didn't you?"

Fran shrugged. "You can imagine my surprise when you showed up a week later and didn't try to kill me."

"Why didn't you rat me out to Smirnov?" Gabby asked.

Smirnov answered that one. "Because she couldn't tell me she killed Darcy. They both worked for me."

"Can I just clear something up?" Gabby said. "I thought you had to be Russian to join the Russian Mafia."

Fran rolled her eyes, and Smirnov made a palms-up gesture. "There's some gray area."

Gabby was still struggling to put it together. Fran had seemed like such a committed eStocks employee, such a brownnoser. "I thought you wanted to be Kramer's assistant," Gabby said. She had been one hundred percent convinced.

"I said I wanted your job. I didn't say which one. You have several."

Gabby flashed back to the conversation at Starbucks:

"And then, wham, someone else is hired from outside the organization and given the good work. Happens every time."

"Who was hired above you?"

"You, Camille."

Fran had never wanted to be a personal assistant. She didn't give a damn about eStocks Enterprises. She wanted Darcy's job, to get a cut for selling the codes.

"How long have you been working for Smirnov, Fran?" Gabby asked.

"How long has it been, Eduard, four years? And I've been waiting for a real assignment."

Gabby winced. Fran wasn't getting love from any of her bosses. "That must have been a slap in the face when Darcy walked in off the street and was about to make some real money stealing codes."

Fran smiled tightly. "You think?"

Gabby said, "Okay, Fran. You have the gun. You're in charge. What do you want?"

She shook her head. "It's your call, Eduard."

"Do you have the codes? For all this talk, you are no better than her." He pointed to Gabby. "Also, un-fucking-tie me, right now."

Fran walked over to Kramer. "Let me get the codes first." With a smile, she said, "Mr. Kramer has them memorized."

Gabby flashed back to her code research. She'd learned two things: 1) a code was just a bank's address, and 2) men were still struggling to accept that women preferred larger penises. She said, "I'm just thinking of this now, but if Mr. Kramer hasn't laundered Mr. Orlov's money yet, then the codes are no good, right? There's no way he'll move it to a location you know about."

Smirnov said, "He already moved it, right?"

Fran nodded yes.

"Okay, so if you steal it while Kramer and Orlov are still tied up, you're good to go." When everyone else seemed to already know that, she held her hands up defensively. "Just catching up." This was her first money-laundering party.

Gabby looked around the room. It was only a matter of time before Fran untied Smirnov, and they took off. When they left, they would probably kill the rest of them, either here or at a secondary location. Probably the latter. She, Markus, Alice, and Orlov were some very big loose ends. After spending a week working with Smirnov, she suspected he wouldn't be leaving any of those around. As the only person who wasn't tied up, she had to do something.

While her wheels were spinning, Fran had approached Kramer. "Don't be coy, George. I've been at this company for five years, and I know it better than you. Those codes aren't in that safe that everyone and his brother knows about."

Ouch.

"They're not on a Post-it note. They're in your head. This can go one of two ways. I can make you tell me. Or—this would be the less painful option—you could just tell me."

"Yes. Yes," he relented. "I memorized the codes."

"Thank you," she said, all ladylike.

Guaranteed he wouldn't be calling her Jan anymore.

It was just Gabby and a woman who was trying to get in deeper with the Russian Mafia, all the actual trained operatives inconveniently zip-tied and drugged thanks to her. Why had she ever thought Markus could be the mole? He was an absolute heartthrob of a man, in evening wear no less—and what had she done? She'd tied him up. He'd been in her ear all week with nothing but the best intentions. He'd asked her out. This proved it—Gabby Greene was an idiot.

She caught his eye and softly mouthed, "I'm sorry."

He gave her an almost imperceptible nod, a "you can do this, Gabs" nod of approval. He trusted her. For whatever incomprehensible reason, he made her feel it.

"Does anyone have a pen and paper?" Fran asked, apparently to write down the codes.

And that is when she knew the answer. "I do." Gabby smiled and reached into her back pocket. She handed Fran Lucas's spy decoder pen that she'd confiscated earlier.

Except for a discreet "Spy Kidz!" label, the pen looked completely normal. It wrote normally at first, but within an hour the ink fully disappeared, only to reappear some days later and be harder than hell to wash. If Gabby had to repaint her bathroom to cover up decoder ink butts, she might as well get something out of it.

Fran shifted her gun to her left hand to accept the kiddie decoder pen and said, "I'm waiting, Kramer."

He blew out a defeated breath and looked around the room. Gabby almost felt bad for him. If he shared the codes, Orlov would probably kill him. If he didn't, Fran would. Effectively reminding him that she was the more immediate threat, Fran trained her gun on him.

His voice too high and cracking like a preteen boy's, Kramer croaked, "How is a guy supposed to get ahead in this world? All I wanted was a nice house for my family and a couple of cars?"

Fran kicked him with one of her clogs.

Kramer winced. "Fine. You can have them." Looking defeated, he started listing the numbers in a shaky voice, "Nine-five-two-three-four—"

Orlov shot Kramer a look and said his name in a menacing tone.

Kramer stopped talking for a second, probably weighing his options again until Fran reminded him who had the gun.

"One-six-seven-four-zero-one-two," he finished.

"That wasn't so hard, was it?" Fran said, like she was talking to a child. After the ink disappeared, it would look like every other page in the book. If she didn't transfer the money in the next fifteen minutes or so, she would be out of luck. Gabby couldn't be sure of the exact timing. It's not like she knew when Lucas drew the butts.

Fran smiled at everyone and said, "Well, that's all I needed. I'll be going." She looked at Gabby and sighed. "Although I guess I can't just leave you here. What'll it be? I could tie you up or shoot you?"

Gabby didn't wait for Fran to decide. She charged.

CHAPTER 38

Saturday night, still in the storage closet

Fran slammed against the wall with a thud. Gabby went for her gun arm, pinning it against the wall for just a second.

But Fran wriggled free. "Ha! Nice try, rookie."

For a split second, Gabby thought it was all over. She'd started it, and Fran was about to finish it. About to die, she had nothing to lose. Even if Fran didn't make good on Smirnov's threat to kill the kids, Kyle and Lucas would be raised by Phil alone, or Phil and his latest bimbo. Fuck no.

Gabby leaned away from Fran, called deep within herself, and pulled out her inner Billy Blanks from when she did his work-out video for two months straight in 2010. Her foot smacked into Fran's midsection with an "ooof" of expelled air. While Fran was out of breath, Gabby kicked her again, and the gun dropped and skittered across the floor well out of reach.

While the gun fidget-spun its way to a stop, Fran took her chance. Middle school bathroom–style, Fran grabbed Gabby's hair and whispered in a low, sinister voice, "I'm going to kill your family very, very slowly."

Through the pain, Gabby said, "I spent my last five dollars on a scone for you."

Fran laughed. "I don't even like scones."

Gabby gasped. What an ungrateful bitch. "It came with clotted crea—!"

A kick to the gut cut off Gabby's outrage, and she doubled over in pain. It wasn't like in the movies where she spit some blood and then kept going. As a girl who had never even played sports, she'd never taken a hit before or tested her physical limits. How much pain was tolerable? What kind of discomfort could she fight through? Was this normal?

"Hurts, doesn't it?" Fran said, a little too happy about it.

"I think I might have broken something." If she survived this, she was going to google WebMD for broken ribs immediately. Couldn't they puncture a lung?

Fran laughed as Gabby was still clutching her stomach.

Markus yelled, "You got her, Gabby."

At that, Fran swept her foot under Gabby, causing her to drop to the floor and land on her ass with a massive thud.

"I was trying to be your friend," Gabby said.

Fran kicked her in the ribs again.

"What would your kid think of this?"

"Tuition is expensive, Gabby. You know that. And my ex doesn't pay child support."

"Did you think about hiring a lawyer?"

Fran laughed in her face. "Didn't I tell you? I'm broke."

If Gabby walked out of here, Kyle and Lucas were going to some summer camps that promised enhanced learning in natural environments with gentle encouragement. If Fran won, her kid was going to Waldorf School. These kids were going to fulfill their potential, but at what cost to the mothers?

"Mother to mother," Gabby said, "maybe we're trying too hard."

"You can never try too hard. Kids are fucking expensive," Fran said, standing on Gabby's hand until she squealed.

"What is the matter with you, Fran?" Gabby said. "You're not really killing me for your kid's sake. Come off it."

"And you're not here for your kids' sake?"

Gabby was one hundred percent here for her kids, to keep custody, to satisfy that stupid seek work order. Gabby was breathing hard. Each and every breath hurt.

"What is the matter with you, Gabby?" Fran taunted. "I didn't think you'd give up so fast. This is pathetic."

She didn't want to give up, but she was broken. On the floor with what she believed to be several cracked ribs, a messed-up hand, and a bruised ass. Stay-at-home-mom life had been for the kids, but it was also safe. She didn't have to test her limits; she didn't have to change or push herself. Gabby wasn't qualified for this.

She heard Markus's voice. "Gabby, remember what I taught you. You can do this. You are strong."

Tears must have been shining in her eyes, because Markus said, "Toughen up, Agent Greene. Put your feelings in a box and get out there."

He was right. Gabby took a breath and gathered her strength. She staggered to her feet like the boxer who looked like he was almost finished off and could barely see through a swollen eye.

Fran laughed.

Gabby centered herself. It might not be much, but she did two days' worth of training, and it was now or never. Just like Markus had taught her, she stomped on Fran's foot and jammed her elbow up into her nose. Something snapped, and blood gushed. This time it was Fran's turn to stagger. She didn't hit the floor, but Gabby had one last move. Markus's advice, "Kick 'em in the balls," sounded in her mind. Gabby pushed down on Fran's shoulders and jammed her knee into Fran's crotch as hard as she could.

At this moment, Valentina burst into the room, Fran collapsed on the floor with Gabby battered but still standing. Her eyes flicked from Gabby and Fran to the restrained agents. In between ragged breaths, Gabby explained, "Fran was working for the Mafia. I'll explain the rest later."

Alice nodded her head. "Give her a hand, Val."

Valentina unholstered her gun. Instead of pointing it at Fran or any of the bad guys, she handed it to Gabby. "It looks like you already have it covered, but here you go."

Tears pricked at the back of Gabby's eyes. "Thank you."

"You earned it." Concern in her voice, Valentina said, "You're not going to shoot anyone, right?"

Gabby looked at the gun in her hands. Now that she had it, she realized that she really didn't want it. She didn't want to shoot Fran. She'd prefer Fran in jail. "No, but I really appreciate the gesture."

"I mean, a gun isn't really a gesture," said Valentina. "It's a tool. Now, go ahead and wrap this up. I'll block the door."

Gabby kept the gun aimed at Fran while she walked across the room to collect the nonlethal version. Valentina had been right earlier—a dart gun was all she needed. Like a nineties action hero, she trained the dart gun on Fran.

Markus interrupted. "Don't forget your tagline, Agent Greene."

"Compartmentalize this," Gabby said, committing fully.

"What?" Fran looked confused.

"What I mean is that, in the future, you will have to put the feelings from this trauma in a box and try to move past them." That was probably too much explanation for a tagline. It was no "Hasta la vista, baby."

From the sideline, the EOD agents were cheering. "You got her, Gabs."

When she looked uncertain, Markus said, "It's a little cerebral, but I like it. It made me really uncomfortable the other day. That's the point, right?"

"Thanks, Markus." She smiled big at him.

"Sorry about this, Fran, but you've been a real pain in the ass." She aimed the dart at Fran's ass and fired.

CHAPTER 39

Saturday night, still in the storage closet

Finally, the scene in the storage room was wrapping up. Valentina had come back from the kitchen with a pair of poultry shears to slice through the zip ties while Gabby restrained Fran, who was still unconscious. The Mafia dons and Kramer were demanding lawyers but, overall, not saying much. These were the kinds of guys who knew not to blab to the authorities.

"Val, where the hell have you been all night?" Alice didn't quite shout but almost. "Were you getting a manicure?"

"Calm down or I won't cut you free," Valentina said.

Before Gabby cleared anything else up, she had a bigger problem to solve. For the entire party, she'd managed to focus on what needed to be done, and now all she could think of was that asshole parked at the end of her driveway. How she'd managed to carry the crushing fear and keep going was beyond her. Finally, she could set it down, or at least hot potato it to someone else for the last leg of the journey.

She knelt next to Markus while cutting him free. "I still have a problem."

"What is it?" He didn't look mad at her, only concerned.

As calmly as she could manage, Gabby explained, "There's still a car of Smirnov's men at the end of my driveway." She paused to get control of her breathing she could talk. "They're going to kill my family if Smirnov doesn't call them off."

Valentina, who had overheard, looked at Smirnov. "Is that true?"

He shrugged but didn't say a word, clearly not wanting to incriminate himself any further.

Gabby wanted to punch his smug face. Instead, she refocused on Markus, and then Alice, talking to both of them now.

"There's been a guy, sometimes two, in a gray sedan at the end of the driveway for a couple of days. Can you send someone to make an arrest?"

"Are they out there right now?"

Gabby nodded. "I'm sure of it."

The railroad tracks between Valentina's eyebrows deepened as she made a phone call to HQ. "This is Agent 442 Monroe. I'm currently at Velvet's Drag Bar on Hollywood Boulevard. I need a team of agents at 113 Avocado Ave. stat. There is at least one known hit man in a gray sedan parked outside the house with a contract on people in the home, some of whom are children."

When Valentina hung up, she announced, "Agents on their way."

For the first time that week, Gabby took a breath and felt the air fill all of her lungs. She hadn't even realized how tight she'd been before, how she'd been panic-breathing for over a week.

Gabby looked at Smirnov and narrowed her eyes. She'd been willing to fight Fran, but she hadn't wanted to. Every cell in her body wanted to reach out and smack the shit out of Smirnov. "Kids and an old lady—what is the matter with you?!"

Markus reached out and placed his hand on her back. "We're going to get them, Gabby. And Smirnov is going to jail."

Smirnov leaned back and said, "You two are cute. A little office romance, huh?"

Markus didn't move his hand. Gabby realized that he wasn't going to be scared away by some asshole. He wasn't going to leave.

"Mischa, the young man who is probably parked outside—" She shook her head. "He just seemed troubled." It was hard to see young people making choices like that. Yesterday, she would have thought that more committed parenting would help, but Fran had almost killed her fifteen minutes ago for school tuition. There were a couple of hard truths: 1) no one lies to you more than yourself, and 2) there are an infinite number of paths to joining the Russian Mafia. Hell, she had briefly been a member.

"Mischa can probably get a lesser sentence after he turns on Smirnov," Valentina said. "We've been working on Smirnov for a while."

Markus wasn't so easily placated. "I can't believe you didn't say anything to me. I could have helped. That's my entire job."

"I couldn't. He threatened my kids, my grandma, even my ex." While they were talking, a couple of other agents came in to arrest Kramer, Fran, Orlov, and Smirnov.

Valentina interjected. "You did fine, Gabby. We have two Russian mob bosses in custody, not to mention Kramer. This is worth celebrating."

A moment later, Valentina took another call. She looked perplexed, but in an official voice, she announced, "Gabby, your family is safe, and Smirnov's men are in custody." It sounded like she was holding something back.

"Did something else happen?"

"When they arrived, they found two men passed out in a car at the end of your driveway with a half-eaten plate of food between them. They appear to have been drugged." She shook her head. "Our agents say it looks like Rohypnol."

Granny. Gabby couldn't hold the smile in. Granny wasn't feeding them home-cooked meals from the motherland; she was drugging them. Gabby rubbed the necklace Granny had given her to remind her where she came from, and pride swelled in her chest. How had she forgotten what a badass her grandmother was?

Valentina still looked troubled.

"Is there more?"

"Yes." Valentina shook her head. "It sounds like they had to take in one of your neighbors along with Smirnov's men for getting in the way of the arrest."

"Shelly?"

"I can't say," Valentina answered.

But of course, it was Shelly. How did Shelly manage to get in the way of everything? Really, that's why she didn't suspect Fran of more than being nosy. There were so many Frans and Shellys. Every neighborhood, every workplace, every family had one— getting in the way, messing everything up, micromanaging.

"Apparently, she was mad at the agents for not responding sooner." Valentina looked confused. "She claims to have been calling the cops all week complaining about their illegal parking to no effect."

Gabby nodded. That lined up with all of the posts on the LISTSERV.

"Long story short, during the altercation, one of Smirnov's guys came to and accused her of harassment, which was apparently reasonable. They had grounds for a restraining order, according to the cops."

Gabby laughed. "Ohmygod."

"Anyway, she didn't take that very well. They tried their best to work around her and send her back into her house, but she wouldn't listen, kept getting more agitated. They didn't want to deal with her, so they let her cool off in handcuffs."

"Any chance she'll stay in jail for a while?" Gabby could use the vacation.

"No, but it sounds like the action at your house was as wild as here."

In the corner, one of the agents started reading Smirnov his Miranda rights in a booming voice. "You have the right to remain silent. Everything you say can and will be used against you..."

As the agent perp walked Smirnov past her, Gabby stared him down. Before she second-guessed herself, she slapped him across the face as hard as she could. That fucker had threatened her babies.

Valentina laughed. "Get him, Gabs."

Gabby sighed. The violence wasn't even satisfying. It had been worth a try, though. Really, she didn't care about him as long as he was gone. "What's going to happen to them?" Gabby asked.

"They'll be arrested and booked under various RICO violations."

There was a flurry of activity outside the door, and someone called, "Help!" frantically. "Someone help me! Camille, where are you? Camille!"

All of the agents straightened up. Several hands hovered over sidearms, braced for the worst.

Valentina spoke into her comm. "This is Agent 442. There is a man calling for help and proceeding toward the back room. Anyone in the front, please head toward the kitchen to provide backup."

Betty Danger burst into the room, sequins flashing in the EOD flashlights and her blond wig filling the entire doorway. "People, we have an emergency!" she yelled, ignoring the agent response. Once in the room, she stopped what she was doing and took in the scene, which included three guys in handcuffs, the signs of a fight, and Gabby's black eye.

Valentina approached Betty with her weapon drawn. "Ma'am, what is the nature of the emergency?"

"We're out of champagne," Betty announced.

Valentina's expression said, "This bitch," as loud as words. Into her earpiece she said, "This is Agent 442 again. Stand down. There is no emergency."

Gabby threw her arms around Betty Danger. "I'll help."

Betty glanced at Gabby's battered form. "What in the hell happened to you?"

"It's worse than it looks." And so much better than it could have been. A little stiffer than usual, she walked out of the room arm-in-arm with her best friend.

Alice stopped her before she got too far. With a quick nod of approval, she said, "Good job tonight, Agent Greene."

"Thank you, Agent Strong."

Alice shook her head. "If only we'd gotten those codes." She grumbled and added, "I must have been groggy from the drugs. Normally my memory is perfect."

"Oh, we have the codes. I handed Fran my son's spy pen. The message will reappear tomorrow. I didn't read the directions, but I think it has something to do with sunlight."

"Excellent!" Alice exclaimed. "Even better work."

CHAPTER 40

Saturday night, Velvet Underground Speakeasy

The mob boss takedown in the back had certainly broken up the party but not completely. While the bartender played the piano, Lady Eleganza Le Tuck was slow dancing with a wrinkled, sloppy drunk, his face pressed into her bosom.

Gabby pulled up the ride-sharing app on her phone, but stopped herself before she finished ordering the car. Not that he'd want to give her a ride after she tied him up, but she couldn't help but scan the bar for Markus. When there was no sign of him, she went back to her phone.

Betty sidled up to the booth. "You need a ride, girlfriend?"

"Yes, please."

"Give me five minutes, and we can go home together."

While Betty wrapped up a few things, Gabby googled "did I break a rib?" As she took some deep breaths to see if it caused pain, a queen who was about six inches taller than anyone else in the room took the mic from the drunken banker and called out, "Any of y'all men in uniform looking for a date tonight?"

After what seemed like an hour but was probably five minutes, Betty strode across the bar with several bags and a sense of purpose. "Get your stuff, babe. Let's get out of here. I gotta get home to Hugh."

"Thanks so much for your help tonight." It was going to go down as an epic event that finance guys would talk about for years to come.

As Gabby slid out of the booth, she scanned the room, but there was still no sign of Markus. It was just as well. She was a grown-ass woman with kids, with no business acting like a teenager.

"So I take it you weren't doing a regular executive assistant job this week?" Betty angled for more information.

"Yeah." There was no point denying the EOD job given that Betty had seen several arrests. "It was more of a...CIA thing."

She fanned her face. "Dear lord. This is just too good. Don't tell me all at once because I want to savor it."

Gabby winced as she tried to walk down the stairs.

"Are you going to need something to sleep tonight? I think I have some Vicodin from when Hugh had that root canal."

"I might not even need it." She hadn't slept all week.

As they schlepped out to the parking lot, Markus caught up to them. "Gabby, hold up."

Gabby's breath caught in her throat. "I thought you'd already left," she said, relief swamping her at the sight of him. It wasn't like he'd run through the airport to stop her from leaving forever, but here she was feeling it, just a little.

"I saw you perform," Markus said to Betty, "you have a gorgeous voice."

Betty blushed and pressed her hand to her heart. "Aren't you sweet," she said, suddenly sounding like a Southern belle.

"I thought you were lip-synching?" Gabby said.

"Of course I was lip-synching, but don't act like that's not a thing. I still can't believe Ashlee Simpson was canceled for it. I do 'Pieces of Me' in her honor sometimes."

"That's . . . thoughtful." Markus turned his focus to Gabby. "Anyway, I was thinking you might need a ride. I know you came with Fran."

"Actually—"

Betty bodychecked her toward Markus. "That's a great idea, Markus. Gabby's house is really out of the way for me."

Before she knew it, Gabby was headed for Markus's car, her nerves on fire with awareness of him, her brain screaming that this was going to be awkward.

Markus made a show of opening the passenger-side door for her and waited until she had buckled before carefully shutting it. The feeling of being treated like a lady, especially by a man as handsome as Markus, was unsettling. She was a double agent one minute, a princess the next, and about to go home to be a Croc-wearing, lunch-making mom. It was enough to give a girl whiplash.

He started up the car and changed the playlist from what must have been his pump-up music to Sade, and he cut his eyes her direction. What was happening?

It's not like she'd ever been relaxed around Markus, but the last few times she'd seen him had been . . . less than perfect. Yesterday, she had ripped out her earpiece and given him the silent treatment. Today, she'd drugged and zip-tied him. But before that, there was the kiss. Gabby stared forward at the road. "So . . . uh."

"Yeah, I know," said Markus with a chuckle.

"Sorry again for tying you up," said Gabby.

"No problem. It was nice to see you break someone else's nose this time."

"Hey!" She elbowed him. "I didn't fully break yours . . . did I?"

At a stoplight, Markus touched her hand and squeezed lightly, and shivers ran from her fingers all the way up her arm. "Nah. I was fine. You did an amazing job, Gabs. You tied up three senior EOD agents, two Mafia bosses, and Kramer. I mean..." He scratched his head. "How the hell did you do that?"

The light turned green, and he focused on the road again, giving Gabby enough clear headspace to answer a question. "I guess no one was expecting it."

"I certainly wasn't."

It was dark in the car, nothing but oncoming headlights cutting across his face, making it hard to read his expression. Pride, amusement, sadness? She was just guessing based on her own feelings.

Was this going to be it for her and Markus?

"Before I drugged you and tied you up—" She flashed a hopeful smile. "I had a really nice time." God, she just described a national security mission as "a nice time." She could smack herself in the forehead. Parts of it had been, though.

Instead of teasing, Markus said, "Me too. I haven't had so much fun on an op in forever." His brown eyes soft, he said, "I've never looked forward to putting in my earpiece so much."

"It was really nice talking to you every day. I'll miss that." She sighed. "I guess it's back to doing laundry alone listening to Sloane Ellis's divorce tips."

Speaking of laundry, she hadn't touched a load since starting at the EOD. It was going to be bad.

Worse than that, the ride was over. He pulled into her driveway at Avocado Avenue.

"So I guess this is it," she said with an actual sigh.

"You're going to miss me," he said, teasing.

"Um, yes." There was no denying it.

"Let me walk you in. Make sure all the bad guys are gone."

That sounded nice.

"There aren't many guys you can trust with your life," Gabby said. It was true.

"Oh, I seem to remember being tied up in a back room earlier today," he said as Gabby opened the door.

"I wasn't sure I was thinking one hundred percent straight where you were concerned."

Inside, all the lights were on. Burt was in the La-Z-Boy watching local news with Mr. Bubbles on his lap. Bubbles looked up and wagged his tail but didn't move.

"I don't even get a greeting, Bubbles!" she scolded with a laugh.

Gabby never thought she'd be so glad to see Burt or his stupid TV. A near-death experience will make you grateful for the strangest things. If she didn't keep her mouth shut, she would invite Burt to stay permanently.

"Where is everyone?" she asked, looking around at an otherwise empty house.

"Vera took them out for pizza and bingo," Burt said without even glancing her way.

Gabby glanced at her smartwatch. It was ten o'clock, a solid hour past Lucas's bedtime, and he was probably playing an arcade game while drinking a gallon of soda. Before she let frustration boil over, she reminded herself that it was not a school night, and they were probably having a blast with Granny. Everyone was fine. Granny could be good cop and she'd be bad cop. After tonight, she knew she was up to it.

Markus checked the rooms one by one. There was no evidence of any danger, but an unholy mess had piled up during the last two weeks. "Do you feel safe?" he asked.

"I do." Smirnov and his men were in jail, along with Fran. Everything was in its rightful place, except for the laundry. Everyone was safe, and that was all that mattered.

"Thanks again, Markus. I really appreciate you."

"I know. I was the only one who got a coffee card the other day."

Gabby felt her cheeks flush.

"I was kind of hoping I'd get another one tonight."

"A coffee card?" She shook her head at her own foolishness. "I didn't have time or I probably would have. Or maybe something even sillier, like a potted plant or a Tupperware container of homemade cookies." She shook her head. "Activate mom-mode at your own risk, Markus."

"Cookies? You're speaking my language." Markus looked serious.

"Don't joke with me, Markus, or you're in for it. I'll end up making you ants on a log, and you'll be embarrassed to eat lunch in front of all the other spies."

He threw back his head and laughed. "You do that. I could use more celery in my life."

Before she could overthink it, she stood on her toes and pressed her lips against his. Like Betty said, she was "Gabby motherfucking Greene." If she could be a spy, she could make the first move, which wasn't even really the first move, because he'd kissed her once already.

For a blissful moment, her brain shut down. Markus placed a hand on the small of her back and pressed her flush against him. Her world was nothing but the feel of his skin against hers. "Markus?"

"Mm-hmm." His voice was soft, and his lids heavy.

When she didn't finish her thought, he feathered kisses along her jawline.

With a groan, she broke the kiss and leaned into his chest, the heat of his body melting into hers. "How do you still smell good after tonight?" she asked.

He chuckled.

"No, really. I held you hostage, and you still smell like aftershave."

At that moment, Betty Danger drove by, tapped her horn, and yelled, "Get it, gurl!" out her window.

Markus squinted. "I thought she said your house was out of the way."

With a shake of her head, Gabby said, "No, she lives like two houses down. She's my best friend."

With the spell broken, Markus smiled slyly. "So now that the mission is over, how about dinner? Next Friday, I'll make reservations somewhere nice."

The invitation sent a spike of joy through her being. She wanted to scream, "Yes!" and text everyone she knew, aka Justin, that she was going on a date with Markus, then spend all week selecting the perfect outfit that would make it look like she wasn't trying too hard. She hadn't had it this bad for a guy since, well, she'd never been this head over heels. A smaller part of her whispered, "Slow down, Gabby. You're not ready."

She wanted to tell that little voice to shut up, and hug Markus tighter. Instead, she looked into his eyes. "I really like you, Markus. Like a lot." She overemphasized "a lot" to the degree she felt it. "But...let's not do dinner, not yet."

He raised his eyebrows. "What?"

"If you haven't had a chance to use that coffee card yet, how about we grab a coffee?"

Looking a little unsettled, he said, "Um, sure, if you want to take it slow, that's fine. How about after work next Monday?"

Relieved she was going to see him outside of work, even if she wasn't ready for candlelight, she said, "It's a date."

Flirtatiously, he said, "You mean 'a date' or a *daaaaaate*?"

She laughed.

"See you after work on Monday." It wouldn't hurt to keep him guessing.

After seeing Markus off, Gabby walked back into the house in a mild panic. Had she just said no to Prince Charming? Well, maybe not Prince Charming, but the hottest man she knew in real life. No, she tried de-escalating her inner monologue—she'd declined a romantic date and counter-offered with a Monday afternoon coffee. Still, her ribs hurt more at the thought.

Stop it, Gabby. If she leaped into a relationship with Markus, she'd probably just start washing his shirts and packing lunches without ever getting her own life together. And Markus was fine, more than fine. Wondering whether he was going on a *daaaate* wouldn't do him any harm. When the time came, she'd let him know what was up. She had value and was worth waiting for.

Either way, Granny was still out with the kids, and she should take the time to wash her face and collect herself. Thank you, Granny. For the first time in her life, she had an involved co-parent. But when she flicked on the lights in the bathroom, she stared into the frightened eyes of a woman who had just risked spending eternity alone, not to dramatize the situation. Better not to think, she did a full-on skincare routine and slipped into some sweats.

She turned on the last chapter of Sloane Ellis's *Divorce: A New Beginning*. As she used the little rose quartz face roller to iron out the wrinkles, or whatever it was that the face roller was supposed to do, she let Sloane's dubious wisdom wash over her.

"Change can be difficult to accept. Even if things aren't perfect, it might feel safer to stay the same. The same routine, the same people—oftentimes, the same disappointments, the same stagnation, the same feeling that something is missing. Change means risk, but also unknown rewards and pleasures. There is no telling what life will bring when you take a different path."

In the other room, Burt snored so loud in the La-Z-Boy that he woke himself up and shouted, "Vera!" before settling down again.

Burt—now there was a risk she hadn't seen coming.

She turned up Sloane, who, for once, made sense. "But change is also inevitable. You can be dragged into new things kicking and screaming or you can embrace change with creativity and open-heartedness. The kicking-and-screaming way—that way is going to hurt, and you probably won't notice the new positives over the sound of your own complaining. Be open, and it'll go much better."

There had been so much change in the last two weeks. Before Alice and Valentina had walked into her life, she'd been frozen. The marriage might have been over, but she was still acting like Phil was about to come home from work.

Who would have thought she would do so well at spying?

And Granny...Gabby could probably be a little more open and trusting of her than she had been.

For one, bingo wasn't the devil.

For two, Granny was another driver and loved her grandkids.

For three, the kids were having an adventure with a grandma. Even though it was hard for Gabby to watch sometimes, everyone should have some adventure. It was certainly doing her some good.

It was time to hand over her old bedroom for good to Granny and Burt. She needed a new bed and new decorations that didn't reflect compromises at the furniture store with Phil. Trying to agree on a bedspread had been like trying to achieve peace in the Middle East, a sign of larger problems in retrospect.

At the thought of another night on the futon, she googled "mattress" and one-click ordered a "mattress in a box" that promised the best night's rest of her life. Sure, not everyone had given it five stars and it wasn't cheap, but she was entering a new era of calculated risks. That futon had beaten her up almost as much as Fran had when all she had to do was stop fighting for the status quo. The master bedroom was all for Granny.

She texted Justin. Will u help redecorate my bedroom?

He texted right back. Does this have anything to do with Agent Beefcake?

NO. It's not like Markus would be spending the night with her kids down the hall and Granny and Burt on the other side of the wall. Her life was a lot to walk into, another good reason to take it slow. And who knew if he was even interested in that. Or if she was ready. Working together, or even having dinner, was a little different than a real relationship with a grown-ass woman with children and responsibilities. But…she could hope, and her futon was no field of dreams. If she didn't build it, he wouldn't come. Not that he was coming, especially now that she'd downgraded the date to coffee. She needed to stop thinking about coming at all. *Stop getting ahead of yourself, Gabby Greene!*

In an impassioned voice, Sloane said, "Repeat after me: change, I am yours!"

Gabby took a deep breath and did as told. In a passionate voice that rang through the house, she yelled, "Change, I am yours!"

In the wake of silence following her passionate exaltation, she heard a crowd of people in the kitchen noticeably not talking. Granny stage-whispered, "Kids, stay where you are. It sounds like your mom—" She cleared her throat. "Has a gentleman over."

This prompted barfing noises, probably from Kyle.

"Stop it, Kyle. Your mother is a young woman, not even in her sexual prime yet."

"Granny," Gabby yelled before the kids were any more traumatized. "It's just me!" And she rushed into the kitchen to wrap Granny and the kids in the biggest hugs of their lives.

"Don't squeeze so hard," Granny complained. "You're going to crack a rib."

"I'm just so glad to see you," she said, her own ribs aching.

Kyle flipped her faded hair and said, "Mom, you're acting really weird."

Gabby put her arm around Kyle and squeezed. Illegal, low-stakes gambling was fine. Not what she would have picked, but hey.

His words rushing out in a jumble of excitement, Lucas said, "Mom, you should have seen it. The cops were here tonight. They arrested Shelly and those weird guys who were parked outside. It was so cool."

"Mischa seemed so nice. He looked just like my cousin Ilia back in the day," Granny added with a shake of her head. "I can't imagine he did anything bad."

Gabby squeezed them tighter. Maybe the week had been nothing but staying up late and pizza for them, but she had almost lost everyone she loved.

"Mom, what is the matter with you? Why are you crying?"

"I love you guys. More than you'll ever know." Gabby kissed the tops of her kids' heads and shut her eyes, just savoring her happy ending.

"Oh-kay. Love you too," Kyle said flippantly, but it was the first time she'd said it in a very long time.

"Are we going to the mall tomorrow?" Gabby asked, and wiped the tears from her eyes and tried to act normal. "Purple hair or bust?"

Kyle pulled a faded purple strand out and inspected it. "Actually, I was thinking I might go red. Maybe with one purple streak."

Gabby's heart almost stopped. "Really?" Blinking back tears, she said, "L'Oréal intense red copper does run in our family."

Kyle backed away slowly. "I'm going to bed now. You're acting really weird, Mom."

"Brush your teeth!" she shouted, in a desperate attempt to flee emotion, as the kids ran up the stairs.

It might be a new landscape—co-parenting with her grandma, fake red hair all around, a coffee date with Markus—but everyone was safe. Sloane was right; change was a good thing.

For the first time in a long time, all was right with the world.

CHAPTER 41

Sunday morning, Greene household

The next morning, Gabby awoke on her futon with sore ribs, a sore back, and the greatest feeling of contentment she'd ever known. Her children were not only safe but seemed almost happy. A hit man wasn't parked outside her house. Not a single high-stakes, life-or-death mission was on the calendar. Except for a coffee might-or-might-not-be-a-date with Markus, she was done with the EOD forever.

With no need to hop out of bed, she breathed deeply and let her eyes drift shut again. The dappled light of morning played across the room, almost like she was in a country meadow. It was you-own-a-pony-and-have-enough-money-to-keep-it-on-your-own-property lighting. Today was heaven.

Her phone cut through the sleepy peace. She didn't want to look. Hell, she wouldn't look. Everyone she loved was tucked in safe and sound. Whoever was tainting her Sunday morning could leave a voicemail.

But who was she kidding? She wasn't the kind of person who could not answer her phone. What if it was an emergency?

The name Valentina Monroe stared back at her.

Exactly who she didn't want to see. She ran through a list of reasons for Valentina to call: 1) Smirnov out on bail and hot for revenge; 2) Sergei out on bail and hot for revenge; 3) Kramer out on bail and hot for revenge; and most believable, 4) Fran out on bail and hot for revenge, or 5) some sort of "keep your hands off my man" conversation. None of the options were good.

Fully awake, she sat up and braced herself. "Hello..."

"Wake up, Gabby," Valentina said. "Debriefing at oh-nine-hundred."

"Oh-nine-hundred?" She still hadn't gotten used to military time.

"In an hour," Valentina clarified in an exasperated tone. "Meet at the office."

Just a debriefing, no imminent threat. The knot of dread in her stomach loosened. "Can this wait till Monday? It's Sunday morning, and I've barely seen my kids this week."

"It'll be short."

"Okay." One more meeting and then she'd be free to relax.

Besides Bubbles, who padded over expectantly, no one else was up. Gabby filled his bowl with kibble and gingerly slipped into her favorite athleisure wear. While heading through the Starbucks drive-through and easing onto the freeway, she found that she wasn't as annoyed as she thought she'd be. On the one hand, all she wanted was to be drinking her coffee in peace and quiet. On the other hand, she had the world to herself on a Sunday morning, and how cool was it that she was needed at an EOD meeting?

Gabby parked her soccer mom–mobile. Maybe she wasn't a spy anymore, but it might be time to pass the minivan on. Granny

could have this one, and she could get herself something sexier, basically any other car. Hell, she could get herself a midlife
crisis–mobile like Sienna's mom had done.

It was trippy walking into EOD headquarters for the last time.
She'd said goodbye to this building once already. At the International Rug "Everything Must Go!" sale, she'd bought $200 in
candles and throw pillows and a hammock she still hadn't hung
up. This was a different kind of goodbye, her last time going
through a biometric screening and retinal scan, her last finger-
print entry. Who would have thought Gabby Greene, burner of
meat loaf and all around half-assed housewife, would be a secret
agent?

And who knew she would feel so uncertain and, to be honest,
a little sad about giving it up. Her sadness had a weight to it. She
walked a little slower than normal, delaying the end of her big
adventure. Being an actual executive assistant would be a come-
down after this.

Gabby found Valentina sitting in the ops room, alone with her
laptop. Markus and Alice were nowhere to be found. There was
almost no noise in the building, none of the usual boisterous chat-
ter. Just one TV tuned to world news playing from down the hall.

"Am I the first one here?" Gabby looked around.

"No, I want to talk to you alone."

Uh-oh. "Is this about Markus? We have a little date planned
but it's not serious. I mean, I just got divorced."

Valentina looked bored with the Markus comments. "All I can
say about that is good luck, girlfriend. However, what I'm about to
say might affect your relationship."

Gabby settled into a chair and took a nervous sip of latte. If it
wasn't about Markus, then what could it be? "What happened?

Am I in trouble?" She had drugged and tied up three EOD agents yesterday. Everyone had seemed cool with it at the time...

"No." Valentina didn't elaborate. Instead she turned to her computer and finished sending an email. The woman could give a master class in compartmentalization.

If Gabby wasn't in trouble, it was probably a standard outtake thing. They probably had to revoke her security clearance and threaten her with a trip to Guantánamo again. Or maybe it was a survey. Everywhere had HR.

To distract herself, she picked up her phone and started scrolling through all the notifications that she missed yesterday. The neighborhood LISTSERV had been popping.

> 9:00 am: "That guy is still parked outside the Greene house. Does anyone know who he is?"

Someone commented, "Gabby's grandmother said he's nice. Idk."

Shelly responded. "Gabby can't have her relatives parked on the street all day. Calling cops. Again."

> 2:00 pm: "Does anyone have a favorite Korean takeout place?"

By 8:00 p.m., it was a flurry of comments. There were photos of the entire altercation, including Shelly in handcuffs and all of the neighbors in their yards watching.

"Congratulations again," Valentina interrupted.

Gabby looked up to find Valentina staring at her and ready to talk. She smiled hesitantly. "Um, thanks. How did everything go last night?"

"Our agents took everyone to interrogation after their arrest. Kramer cracked almost immediately, implicating Sergei Orlov and killing anyone's chance of pleading out with a lesser charge. They will all be going away for some time, thanks to you."

"What about Fran and Smirnov?" Those were the two who actually scared her.

"Between Fran's confession in front of three agents and a mountain of evidence in Smirnov's office, they're done."

Gabby relaxed into her chair. If she wasn't in trouble and the bad guys were locked up, why was she here?

"Thank you again." Valentina paused and swept her hair up in a ponytail. "You did far more than we asked or expected of you." Valentina made uncomfortably direct eye contact. "I know I've given you a hard time. It really did take me a minute to warm up, but you're top-tier agent material, Greene."

She heard Valentina say the words, but she didn't process them. It was like she was watching a movie of her life. This couldn't be happening. Just two weeks ago, Valentina had been sitting at her kitchen table in front of a plate of leftover pancakes and a pile of homework, looking highly suspicious of Gabby.

Today, Gabby was at EOD headquarters in a sleek op center being treated not only like she belonged but as if she were "top tier." This must be what an LSD trip felt like.

"You need more training, of course, but the raw talent you displayed on this mission shows that you will make a damn fine agent. That spy decoder pen was just—" Valentina paused to laugh. "That was the chef's kiss on this operation."

Raw talent? Gabby blinked. The pen was in her pocket because she'd confiscated it from Lucas. Nothing she did was planned, ever. She was muddling through a sea of people who needed things from her all the time—if anything happened, it was a product of circumstance. Didn't Valentina see she was a walking comedy of errors?

"Val, I'm really not good at this. A few things just happened to go my way."

"No, it's talent. Accept the compliment, Gabby. You earned it."

The weight of sadness she'd felt on the way into the building faded. In its place was something new. Instead of feeling weighed down, Valentina was lifting her up.

All Gabby had wanted an hour ago was to enjoy her morning coffee in peace and quiet and to recover from the last two weeks of insanity. The EOD was all wrong for her for the same reasons as when Valentina and Alice had first approached her: 1) she hated danger, and 2) she was a mom.

Although if she hadn't been kidnapped on Monday and tied up in her kitchen on Wednesday, the work-life balance would have been better. Double agenting was a lot more than single agenting, especially when you didn't sign up for it.

"I'd like to offer you a permanent position with the EOD," Valentina said with an assuredness Gabby could barely comprehend.

Even though she'd felt Valentina working up to this, the offer hit her like an unexpected Oscar win. It was preposterous. A secret agent for real? Not just a fill-in because she happened to look like someone.

"What about Alice? Is she on board?"

"Yes, but this is my decision. I'm in charge of field operations. She's been promoted."

The idea of getting back to normal, coming back to an empty house after the kids went to school and a day of housework and chores and chauffeuring kids from one thing to the next, that had been fine for a while, but she hated laundry.

"Would I still be filling in for Darcy Dagger?" she asked.

Valentina shook her head no. "You completed that assignment. From here on out, you would be yourself, Agent Gabby Greene."

There was a nice ring to that. A swell of pride surged through her chest, hitting her harder than the caffeine. Pride—that was the rush she'd been seeking, the one that had always evaded her. No cup of coffee, no tub of Ben & Jerry's, no random purchase from TikTok could give her the feeling surging through her body right now. This was the person she wanted to be for Kyle and Lucas, a woman with purpose, direction, and pride.

When she thought of Kyle's decision to dye her hair mostly red, she knew—secret agenting was the right move. Either that or Kyle was seeking her approval because she wasn't getting enough attention. They'd figure that out, though.

"Your second assignment should be easy for you."

"Really?" What assignment could possibly be easy? Also, she'd heard that one before. *All you need to do is make coffee and smile.* Ha!

"You will need to go undercover as a housewife."

Gabby guffawed. "Really?" Couldn't she be a vineyard owner or an art collector?

Valentina said, "What, do you think I should have Markus do that one?"

She wanted to say, "Why not?" but she kept it to herself. "I guess I can do laundry, if it's for national security purposes." That would be a hell of a lot more satisfying than scrubbing ketchup stains out of Phil's work shirts.

"So are you in?" Alice asked.

"I am," Gabby said. "I accept the position."

Valentina almost smiled and slid a badge across the desk. "Welcome to the Elite Operatives Department, Agent Greene."

ACKNOWLEDGMENTS

As usual, I have a lot of people to thank, which is great. How lucky am I that I got to write a spy novel and have people in my life who encouraged and supported me?

First of all, thank you, Alex Logan! You gave this book a home at Forever and have been an absolute delight to work with. I love you and your costumed cats. Thank you to the entire team at Forever. I know a lot goes on behind the scenes, so thank you to everyone who worked to turn my pile of words into a book.

Thanks to David Purse for giving me the idea and the opportunity. I look forward to every Zoom call with you, and not only because of your delightful Scottish accent.

Thank you to my agent Pam Gruber for being the smartest editor and never letting me out the door with my ass showing. Thank you to Barbara Poelle, who hooked me up with this situation in the first place.

Thanks to Larissa Zageris for your keen eye and for writing my favorite book about Keanu Reeves. I couldn't have asked for a better first reader. Thank you to Erica Holland for the sensitivity read. I appreciate your honesty, your perspective, and your verification of Markus's hotness. Same to Liam Mooney. I much appreciate the sensitivity read, especially from the most dashing squire at the Ren Faire. As usual, I would like to thank all the people whom I regularly whine to via text and sometimes phone: Cristina Pippa, Carly Bloom, Nikki Payne, Roselle Lim, and all of the writers at Smut University.

Also, thank you to the people at Wayfarer Studios and Meralta Films for your enthusiasm and support. Can't wait to work with you all.

Now for the people who have to live with me. Terrell, this book wouldn't be nearly as good without you. Thanks for helping me through all of the tactical scenes and for driving me around while I typed away in the passenger seat. I think I wrote ten thousand words in LA traffic. But mostly, thanks for keeping life fun. Let's keep doing that.

Joy, thanks for ordering too much sushi and putting Terrell and me up in your Honolulu apartment while I wrote, not to mention letting us drive around in your fancy car, which I just remembered makes an appearance in this book. Writing on a balcony in Hawaii—what a dream!

Kids, being your mom is the best thing to ever happen to me. Lila, thanks for the amazing honey cinnamon coffees every morning. I'm drinking one right now while I write these acknowledgments. Daphne, thanks for all the delicious meals and always keeping it real. Silas, thanks for being my sweetheart. And finally, Junior, how could I have revised this novel without someone making me origami fidgets throughout? All of you, thanks for watching me write most of a book in the kitchen and for listening to me read it aloud even when you preferred to listen to *The Outlaws*

Scarlett and Browne, which, to be fair, is a more appropriate novel for children.

Thanks, Mom and Dad, for bearing with me while I choose creativity over financial stability over and over again (notice my use of present tense). That has to be hard to watch, and I know it isn't always pretty. Just this morning Daphne told me I look like a disaster, which she then softened to "well, pretty good from here to here." In my defense, those pants were on sale. At any rate, thank you to all of the forces in the universe that aligned to allow me to write a book looking pretty okay from the waist up.

Once again, I would like to conclude with an apology to Camille Pavliska, who I suspect is still holding a grudge for that time when I accidentally thanked her insufferably perfect older sister in my acknowledgments instead of her. Thanks again, Camille.

ABOUT THE AUTHOR

When not writing rom-com/mystery mash-ups, author **Sam Tschida** (pronounced cheetah) is probably flipping channels between *Dateline* and the latest reality dating show. She braves the Minnesota winter with her four resigned children, two snuggly dogs, and one sizzling-hot husband. She doesn't drink alcohol, never touches caffeine, and is always on time. Just kidding—did you read how many kids she has?